AZTEC RAGE

Forge Books by Gary Jennings

Aztec
Aztec Autumn
Aztec Blood
Aztec Rage
Spangle

Visit Gary Jennings at www.garyjennings.net.

· GARY JENNINGS' ·

AZTEC

RAGE

ROBERT GLEASON
AND
JUNIUS PODRUG

FORGE®

A TOM DOHERTY ASSOCIATES BOOK   NEW YORK

AZTEC RAGE

This book is printed on acid-free paper.

A Forge Book
Published by Tom Doherty Associates, LLC
175 Fifth Avenue
New York, NY 10010

www.tor.com

Forge® is a registered trademark of Tom Doherty Associates, LLC.

Library of Congress Cataloging-in-Publication Data

Jennings, Gary.
    Aztec rage / Gary Jennings, Robert Gleason, and Junius Podrug.—1st ed.
        p.   cm.
    "A Tom Doherty Associates book."
    ISBN-13: 978-0-765-31014-9
    ISBN-10: 0-765-31014-7
    1. Aztecs—Fiction.   2. Mexico—History—Spanish colony, 1540–1810—Fiction.
I. Title.

PS3560.E518 A997   2006
813'.54—dc22

                                                        2006040187

First Edition: May 2006

Printed in the United States of America

0 9 8 7 6 5 4 3 2 1

For Joyce Servis

ACKNOWLEDGMENTS

Many people helped bring this book to fruition. We particularly want to thank Maribel Baltazar-Gutierrez, Eric Raab, Brenda Goldberg, Elizabeth Winick, and Hildegarde Krische.

Information about historical places and events was generously provided by curators in museums and sites of antiquity in Guanajuato, San Miguel de Allende, Dolores Hidalgo, Teotihuacán, Chichen Itza, and other places in Mexico.

We are also grateful for the assistance of José Luis Rodriguez, Dr. Arturo Barrera, Charles and Susan Easter, and Julio Hernandez.

The most memorable aspect of any battle—and, having now experienced many of them, I can say this with authority—is its dizzying commotion and confusion. But of this one, my first major engagement with the enemy, I do retain a few memories more distinct.

—From the War Narrative of Tenamáxti,
    leader of the Aztec rebellion in 1541
    (as related in *Aztec Autumn* by Gary Jennings)

AZTEC RAGE

Mountains Where the Cougars Lurk, 1541

IWATCHED MYSELF *die.*

My nightmare took life as invaders emerged from the fog like *fantasmas,* ghosts in the mist, dark figures on great beasts, menacing as shadow gods risen from Mictlán, the Dark Place. I lay in the brush and trembled, my heart pounding, my throat aching for water, the ground shaking under me as powerful hooves pounded in advance of a thousand human feet. My spear was tipped with an obsidian point, but it would fare poorly against the charge of a warhorse wearing the thick leather guard called a Cortés shield.

We set up the ambush in the rocky, mountainous terrain of Nochistian, waiting for the Spaniards and their traitorous *indio* allies to fall into the trap. As the fog settled, the enemy had come forth. Now I had a choice: to stay hidden and let my *compañeros* fight and die without me or to gather my courage and rise and fight an armored Spaniard riding a powerful warhorse.

As I pondered the decision, the dark vision came to me again: *fight and die.* I saw a violent clash, my life blood escaping, my sin-blackened soul being pulled down to hell by clawed hands.

The warhorses frightened me the most. It is said that it was not the small army Cortés brought with him twenty-odd years ago that defeated the mighty Aztec Empire, nor even the tens of thousands of indio allies he enlisted, but the sixteen great warhorses that carried him and his best fighting men into battle.

There were no beasts like these in the One World before the invaders came. The great warhorses had terrified the Emperor Montezuma and his Eagle and Jaguar Knights, the finest warriors in all the One World. The warriors believed the tall, powerful, four-legged creatures were gods; what else could these denizens from Another World be but spirits of the Earth and Sky? They ran like the wind, crushed any before them under their heavy hooves, and made the warriors on their backs a hundredfold more deadly than those on foot.

As a rider came closer, I realized that it was an indio on horseback.

¡Ayya! I had never seen an indio on horseflesh before. Horses were powerful weapons in war, jealously guarded by the Spanish, who forbade indios from owning or riding them. Tenamaxti, our leader, told us that the Spanish had mounted the caciques, the chiefs, of their indio allies on horseback so their foot soldiers could better follow them in battle. "The traitors who fight for the invaders call the horses big dogs," Tenamaxti told

us. "They rub the sweat of the horse onto themselves to get some of the beast's magic."

Tenamaxti knows the invaders well, having lived in the Aztec capital the invaders now call Méjico City. He is known to the Spanish by the name they gave him, Juan Británico.

Horses were not the only thing forbidden to indios by our new masters. When our leaders and gods failed us, the invaders captured more than the gold of our kings; they enslaved us with a terrible servitude: the *encomienda*, vast grants of power and privilege, fiefdoms given to Spaniards. We called these white men on their grand horses *gachupines*, wearers of spurs, sharp spurs they used to rowel our backs bloody as they stole the food from our mouths.

Their mighty king, the one they call the Catholic Majesty, presses his seal on a piece of paper, and thousands of indios in a region are enslaved to a Spaniard who comes to the One World with one purpose: to grow rich on our labor. To this wearer of spurs we must give as tribute a share of all that we grow on our land or produce with our hands. When he wants a noble palace built for his comfort, we stop tilling our land and carry the stones and cut the timbers needed. We must tend his cattle and his horses but not touch the meat of the farm animals or mount the horses. *¡Ayya!* When he demands, we must lend him our wives and our daughters.

Is it any wonder that when Tenamaxti gave the call, we gathered as in the days of the great Aztec kings, bringing spears to kill these invaders who enslave us?

As I watched the dark figures in the fog, one who rode taller in the saddle than any other appeared. *¡Yya ayya!* It could be no other than the Red Giant himself, Pedro de Alvarado, the butcher of Tenochtitlán, a fiend with hair and beard the color of fire. Known for his rashness and cruelty, Alvarado was infamous second only to the Conqueror himself for his brutal atrocities.

He first earned fame—and evil reputation—when Cortés was forced to leave Tenochtitlán, the Aztec capital, and rush to Veracruz to defeat a Spaniard who had landed with a force of men, intending to deprive Cortés of his command. He left Alvarado behind in Tenochtitlán with eighty Spanish conquistadors and four hundred indio allies to hold the great city. Alvarado also held Montezuma captive. Paralyzed by his belief that Cortés had fulfilled the prophecy that the god Quetzalcóatl would return to claim the empire, Montezuma was easy prey.

While awaiting Cortés's return, Alvarado heard a rumor that the leaders of the city planned to take the remaining Spanish captive during a festival. A man of unlimited expediency and utter cruelty, Alvarado attacked first: As the festival began, his men opened fire on the people celebrating in the marketplace. But it was not Aztec warriors he blasted with cannons and had put to death with swords, spears, and harquebuses . . . a few notables and warriors were killed, but a thousand women and children were slaughtered in the orgy of bloodletting.

Cortés defeated the Spanish commander who intended to usurp his authority and returned to the capital to find Alvarado and his men holed up in Montezuma's palace and besieged by Aztecs angered by the massacre of innocents. Not able to defend their position, Cortés led his men out of the city, and it was in the retreat that Alvarado, the Red Giant, gained his greatest fame.

On the evening that came to be called La Noche Triste, the Night of Sorrows, Alvarado achieved an immortal feat. The Spanish had retreated onto the causeways that led over the lake to the city. During heavy fighting, faced with a break in the causeway too wide for any man to leap, Alvarado, weighed down with heavy armor, turned his back on the Aztec warriors attacking him, ran to the edge of the causeway, stabbed his spear into the back of a drowning man who had already fallen into the water, and *vaulted over to the other side.*

Many times I had heard his amazing tale, and now I realized he was the powerful foe in the dark vision of my own death that had haunted me.

I could no longer lie upon the ground and tremble like a frightened child. I had to face the Red Giant. I rose, clutching my spear. In the tradition of a Jaguar Knight, I gave the cry of that fierce jungle beast to add the strength of the jaguar's god to my own.

Even through the din of battle that had erupted around us, Alvarado heard my cry. He swung in the saddle and turned to look at me. He spurred his great stallion, raised his sword and gave the cry of his war saint. *"For Santiago!"*

I watched myself die.

The vision of my own bloodied, lifeless body that had long haunted my sleep flashed as the warhorse charged, carrying on its back the most famous warrior in the One World. My wooden spear, even with its razor-sharp obsidian point, would not penetrate either the horse's thick padded shield or the armor of the Spaniard. The only way to defeat the invader was to bring him down by making his horse fall.

I threw my body at the horse's knees, using my spear against the ground much as Alvarado had used a spear in his famous leap.

My body broke the stride of the warhorse as if the beast had run into a huge rock. It began to topple onto me. I saw it, slowly falling . . . like a big tree, gathering speed as it came down on me. I saw Alvarado's frantic, startled look as he, too, came down, toppled from his mount, flying headfirst to the rocky ground. I felt my bones breaking, my chest caving, no breath coming, as the huge warhorse crushed me—

 **TWO**

AY DE MÍ! I erupted from the nightmare, trembling and soaked in sweat. I rolled off the cot and stood on the stone floor of the dungeon cell, unsteady at first, my knees weak, my heart still pounding.

The dark dream of an Aztec warrior had come to me in sleep as far back as I could remember. A dream that was a vision of my own death. Why this nightmare had haunted me since I was a child, was a puzzle. It is said that I was born for the gallows, a gruesome fate I had narrowly escaped more than once. That I would die violently was not the stuff of dreams but the reality of the life I had led.

The boom of the muskets of the firing squad came from the courtyard on the other side of the wall. I staggered over to the cell door. *"¡Cabrones!"* I shouted through the judas window. I gave the thick wood door a good kick. "Bring my breakfast, you cabrones."

This was my favorite taunt. A cabrón was a "he-goat," a man who allowed other men to fornicate with his wife. Such an insult is a stake in the heart of any man, no?

I gave the door another kick.

Eh, I wasn't really hungry. In truth, hearing a firing squad perform in the prison yard just outside my cell wall had quickened my blood. It was a reminder that I would soon dance a chilena de muerte, a courtship dance of death, except my rapid steps and twirling handkerchiefs would be for my executioners rather than a lovely señorita.

A guard's face appeared in the judas window. "Keep shouting and you'll have mierda for breakfast."

"Señor He-Goat, bring me a plate of carne and a jug of wine, or your wife will taste the power of a real man before I burn your casa and steal your horse."

He fled, and I returned to my bed of straw. The musty smell of old wine hung in the cell, as if the monks who occupied it when the prison was a monastery had swilled too many jugs.

Like the colony's capital city, Méjico, "May-he-kô," as the Spanish say it, Chihuahua was on a flat plain, almost surrounded by mountains. Several weeks' journey to the south of the capital, its official name was San Felipe de Real de Chihuahua, but it was known simply as the Lady of the Desert.

Nearly a mile higher than the distant sea, the region was not wet and green like the Valley of Méjico but brown and parched, with stingy grasslands, even though soaring peaks of the Sierra Madre Range were snow-capped. In Nahuatl, the language of the Aztecs, Chihuahua meant "dry, sandy place." Dry, sandy snake pit, for one sentenced to die there.

Sobbing, the sounds of a man's anguish, came from the courtyard through the barred window above me. I covered my ears with my hands; I hated to hear a man's tears.

Shots boomed from the courtyard again. I flinched from the concussion of musket balls as they struck the rock wall at my back. The biting stench of black powder came through the window above me. Leaping up, I grabbed the window bars and shouted, "¡*Cabrones!*"

Those he-goats would never hear Don Juan de Zavala whimper. I will not shame my Aztec blood with an act of cowardice when it is my turn to face the muskets. I will die as a Jaguar Knight facing the Flowery Death: No whimper, no plea for mercy would pass my lips.

I sat back down and wiped sweat from my face with the dirty sleeve of my shirt. Sweltering August heat barged its way into my cell through the same window that allowed in death and pathos from the courtyard.

I wondered who had just died on the other side of the wall. Was it a brave compañero I'd ridden with? They had come from every part of the land, by the hundreds, the thousands, and finally the tens of thousands, indios once again marching and fighting as Aztec warriors . . .

We had set the world on fire.

Closing my eyes, I put my head in my arms and listened to the cadence of another firing squad marching to its post.

I had seen war on two continents, witnessed common people with uncommon passions bare their chests to the murderous blaze of musket volleys, felt the earth tremble beneath my feet from cannons roaring death, saw the sun blackened by roiling clouds of black-powder smoke . . . and lay in fields of crimson death . . .

So much pain. So much death.

Again, the muskets cracked, and I returned to the window. "Aim true when I stand before you, bastardos! I spit on death!"

Eh, no man of good sense wishes to die, but I will depart this life knowing my name and deeds will not die with me but will thunder through the ages. Men will write songs about my final hours. Women will weep at the injustices heaped on me and at my indomitable courage as I fought mano a mano with Death, spitting in the Reaper's eye a thousand times and never knowing fear.

"Don Juan de Zavala was mucho hombre," they will shout as tears blind their eyes.

Perhaps no songs will be written or tears will flow, but a man can dream of such things in his last moments, no? And I *am* mucho hombre. No man in New Spain sits taller in a saddle, drops a hawk on the wing with a single pistol ball, parries a blade, or satisfies a woman's secret desires better than I. Nor has any man, the viceroy has proclaimed, committed more crimes against God, King, and Church.

Soon they will send a priest in to take my confession, to cleanse my soul. That will take much time, no? I have seen many things, have left my mark on many places, fought wars on two continents, and loved many women.

For certain, confessing all my transgressions will take countless hours. And it wouldn't be the first time a priest granted my sin-blackened soul forgiveness while an executioner readied his tools. But they made an error in assuming that I have a soul to save or to lose; I'm a gallows bird, born with a hangman's noose around my neck, my feet on a trapdoor ready to drop.

But the darkest stain on my soul has been to rot in this godforsaken cell of a dead, drunken monk while my captors tried to pry a secret from me. Neither the tedious interrogation of constables, the angry decrees of judges, nor the inquisitor's bone-cracking instruments of torture loosened my tongue. But prison walls have also prevented me from taking vengeance on one of the devil's own. And it is this unfinished business that arouses my passions, not the bullets that will be racing for my heart.

Regardless of my crimes, I am a man of honor: I've never stolen from the poor, taken a woman against her will, or killed an unarmed man. I had been a *gachupine*, what the common people call a "wearer of spurs," but unlike others of that ilk, I had not used my spurs on those weaker than me. I've lived by the code of the caballero, a path of machismo and knightly honor. And I have been a Knight of the Aztec Nation, a discipline that carries with it the same duty of honor and courage as that of a caballero. Those codes demand that I not face my grave until I avenge the stain on my honor.

Know this to be true: Before I die, someone else will give up the ghost, one who betrayed me and the amigos I fought beside. When that deed is done, I will happily face the muskets of the firing squad, perhaps even catching the bullets in my teeth and spitting them out.

How did it come to be that Don Juan de Zavala—gentleman and caballero, a man as skilled on the dueling fields as in a woman's boudoir—was caged like a beast in a dank cell to await the drumbeat and lockstep of a firing squad? How a man with worldly lusts and passions, a notorious rogue of infamous deeds, came to march shoulder to shoulder with a priest who had a dream to make all people free? How my bloodied sword came to fight side by side with his sacred cross? How did a caballero become an Aztec knight?

If the truth be told—and some would say that I have often been a stranger to truth—while the good padre mourns the loss of a nation, my regrets are of a more carnal nature. I will miss lying in bed and watching a woman's naked bosom gently rise and fall while she sleeps, smoking a fine Havana cigarro, sipping good Jerez wine, feeling the wind in my face and the power of a great stallion between my legs . . . *Ay*, I'll miss so many things.

But enough . . . regrets are for old women, and one thing I will not regret leaving behind is the strange nightmare vision of my own death that has taunted me so often in my sleep—To die once is enough; to die a thousand nights is punishment from the devil himself.

Would you like to know how the village priest became a fiery revolutionary and an outlaw-rogue a visionary idealist? Like a priest in the confessional booth, do you wish to hear my sins? About the men I have killed, the women I have loved, the fortunes I have made . . . and stolen?

Mine is a long tale, one that will take us from this colony called New Spain in the Americas to the ancient cities and battlefields of the mighty Aztecs, to the wars of Napoleon in Europe and back again. And it can only be told by one who has been there.

Come then, be my confessor. Lend me your ear as I take you to golden places you have never heard of, introduce you to women and treasures you have never dreamed of, as I lay bare my soul and reveal secrets not known outside the grave.

This then, is the true confession of the Jaguar Knight, caballero, and rogue, Don Juan de Zavala.

SON OF A WHORE

 **THREE**

AT TWENTY-FIVE YEARS of age, blooded horses, bloodier blades, perfumed petticoats, and fine brandy were my life's sole passions. An earlier quarrel with my uncle, who managed my affairs, had left me oddly uneasy, even wary. But as I prepared for bed, I had no reason to believe that La Fortuna, the shadowy goddess who spins Fate's Wheel and holds the rudder that directs our lives, had any plans for me other than the life I had been leading.

Caballos and mujeres, pistolas and espadas—horses and women, pistols and swords—were all that mattered to a young caballero such as myself. I prided myself not on the knowledge found on the pages of a book—in the manner of priests and scholars—but on my ability to stay in the saddle and wear out my mount, whether it be an outlaw stallion or a passionate woman.

In ages past, knights-errant jousted for dominance over other knights and for lady love. Armor and lances yielded to muskets and cannons, but a tradition of machismo to win the respect of men and the admiration of women by a display of fighting and horsemanship endured. A man who could shoot hawks on the wing from the saddle of a charging stallion or brave El Toro's horns at the moment of truth was El Hombrón—a man capable of defending a woman's honor as well as watering the sweet garden between her legs.

Although raised in New Spain since I was a babe, I was not born in the colony. My first cry for attention came in Barcelona, that jewel of Catalonia on the eternal Mediterranean, not far from the magnificent Pyrénées and the border of France.

My heritage runs deep in Spain. My father had roots in both Catalonia and Aragón in the north, while my mother was born of ancient lineage in Ronda, an Andalusian town of the south. Known as Acinipo in Roman times, Ronda was a Moorish stronghold until our Most Catholic Majesties Ferdinand and Isabella conquered it in 1485.

My birth in Spain made me a gachupine, a grandee, even though I was raised in the colony. Pure-blooded Spaniards born in the colony were criollos. Even if criollos could trace their bloodlines to the noblest of Spain, they were socially inferior to gachupines. The poorest muleteer from Madrid or Seville, who came to the colony a mewling, puling babe, considered himself socially superior to a rich criollo mine owner with a coat of arms blazoned on his carriage doors.

No caballero rode taller in the saddle than I, not only because my

blood wasn't tainted by birth in the colony but also because my skill with
horses, my daring with women, my deadliness with gun and sword blazed
throughout the Bajío, that rich land of cattle haciendas and silver mines
northwest of the capital.

My contempt for books and poems, for sages, scholars, and priests only
enhanced my fame. I never put pen to paper except to send a message to
the majordomo at my hacienda—a day's ride from Guanajuato—
concerning the condition of my mounts.

With no head for business—neither hacienda finance nor the merchant's trade—I left my fortune in the hands of Uncle Bruto. I never
thought about money except to send my bills—for saddles and boots, pistols and blades, brandy and brothel whores—to my miserly uncle, who had
over the years derided me as a spendthrift.

My father's younger brother, Bruto had managed my affairs since I was
a babe orphaned by the death of my parents. Still there was no love lost between Bruto and me. I called him "family" only because he was my uncle.
A taciturn man whose passion was pesos—*my* pesos because he had no fortune of his own—he loathed my extravagance as much as I despised his
parsimony.

My father had come to the colony after purchasing a royal monopoly
on the sale of mercury, the liquid mineral also known as quicksilver. Crucial to the refining of silver and gold, it separated the precious ore from the
dirt and the dross. Almost as lucrative as the mining itself, its sale was far
less risky than mining claims, which often played out or never showed
color.

After establishing the business in Guanajuato, my father returned to
Spain for my mother and myself. In the traveling party was Uncle Bruto.
After landing in Veracruz, we journeyed across the hot, coastal swamps
where yellow fever, the vomito negro, festered. Both my parents succumbed to the contagion.

My uncle bundled me up, hired an india teat nurse, and brought me to
Guanajuato. At one year of age, I fell heir to my father's business. Bruto
has been running the enterprise for me now for over twenty years. The
quicksilver license has made me a very rich young caballero.

But how rich? That question roiled my sleep. Yesterday I questioned
Bruto about the extent of my fortune, and he upbraided me, as if I did not
have the right to ask.

"Why do you want to know?" he shouted. "You want to buy another
saddle? Another prized stallion?"

My interest was in fact noble: the desire for a *noble title*. I want to hear
the words in my ear, "Buenos días, Señor Count," or "Buenos tardes, Señor
Marqués."

Not for my ego but for my *lust*. I needed the title to capture the heart
of the most beautiful woman in all of Guanajuato, or as I believed, in all

the world. Like me, Isabella Serrano was a gachupine, born in Spain and transported here before she reached her fifth birthday. She was more dear to me than the sun and the moon, more precious than all the pesos in Christendom. She loved me more than life itself, of that I was certain. But her family demanded that she marry a titled grandee. Her beauty, they believed, could win her the title Lady of the Realm.

The injustice of it—that I should not have the coat of arms that Isabella desired—was beyond bearing. Titles were not simply a matter of birthright; not all persons bearing noble titles were swathed in a coat of arms at birth. New Spain has many "silver nobles," former mule drivers and shovel merchants who hit pay dirt in the silver mines or financed some other lucky fool who struck the mother lode. I, the finest caballero in all of the Bajío, deserved a title more than they.

Here in Guanajuato, the first Count de la Valenciana, Señor Antonio Obregón—the discoverer of the world's richest silver vein and founder of the city's largest family fortune—purchased his title from the king with his vast wealth. The Count Valenciana, the Marqués de Vivanco, the Count de Regla, and the Marqués de Guadiana were but a few of the many who purchased a title by contributing to the king's coffers. Pedro de Terreros, a former muleteer, told the king that if His Most Catholic Majesty came to New Spain, his horse would never touch dirt during the long journey from Veracruz to Méjico City but would prance upon silver ingots Terreros would lay along the entire path. He then backed his boast up, buying the title of count by contributing two warships, one with 120 guns, along with a 500,000-peso "loan" to the royal person.

Still I believed I had a chance.

I was well informed by the viceroy's gachupine deputy that forty men in New Spain had purchased titles. Even men with indio blood rose to nobility, though they often claimed lineal descent from the coupling of conquistadors and Aztec royalty. The Count del Valle de Orizaba claimed blood-lineage to Montezuma himself.

I did not know how much a title would cost, but I knew they were still available because European wars had bled the royal purse white. The wars started by that Corsican upstart Napoleon had racked Spain like the Grand Inquisition. Our navy had not recovered from a British victory over the joint Spanish and French fleets near Trafalgar that sent most of Spain's fleet to the bottom, but Spain was at war again, this time united with France. The king needed bullets and bread for his soldiers, both of which required dinero, and a jackass could see that the royal treasury was bare.

"Is this not the time to buy me a title?" I asked my uncle. "When the king is eager to sell? Do you not want to see me well married? Isabella was born in Spain."

"Her father trades in corn," Bruto said, through gritted teeth. "In Spain he was a clerk for a grain merchant."

I held my tongue and didn't remind Bruto that in Spain he had kept accounts for a toolmaker before my father brought him to the New World.

"Isabella is the most beautiful woman in the city, a prize for a duke."

"She's an empty-headed flirt. If you weren't so—"

He stopped when he saw the fury in my eyes. Another insult to my beloved and I would have drawn my blade, opened his chest like the Aztec priests of old, and ripped out his penny-pinching heart. He took a step back, his eyes widening in shock at the look on my face. I kept a rein on my rage, but I shook my fist at him.

"I'm taking control of my own fortune. I'm going to buy a title."

He retreated down the hallway, and I stormed out of the house. I went to an inn where I gathered with friends most nights to drink, play cards, and, when drunk enough, mount the tavern putas.

I drank much and thundered my murderous rage at my uncle's refusal to let me spend my money as I desired. After I returned home, José, Bruto's personal servant, brought me a goblet of the brandy my uncle kept for his private use. Bruto had never shared his private stock of fine Jerez spirits, so I believed he sincerely sought peace.

"Your uncle asks that you accept this brandy as a symbol of his affection for you," José said.

I was not in a forgiving mood. José left, and I stared at the goblet. Even drunk, however, I knew I should make amends with Bruto. I knew nothing about the quicksilver trade and less about managing finances. After I had purchased a title and married Isabella, I had planned to return management to him.

I called José back. "Thank my uncle for the brandy. And take this one to him," I handed him back the same goblet, pretending it had come from my own stock. "Tell him I ask that he also join me in a drink to seal the family love and blood loyalty I bear him."

I went to bed, still much disturbed by the earlier disagreement. Bruto and I had few quarrels. Our views of life differed, but we rarely clashed. His interests were in ledgers and pesos, mine were swords and guns, horses and whores. Our preoccupations kept us from colliding. Other than to complain about my spending, he seldom even spoke to me.

True, I was a loner, and perhaps that affected my relationship with Bruto. But it didn't explain the lack of familial warmth between us, the subtle undercurrent of ill will that I sometimes sensed. But only once did true animosity toward me slip out.

As a boy, bleeding from a cut, I had run into the house. Sleeping in a chair, Bruto snapped awake.

"Get away from me, you puta's bastardo," he shouted.

To call me a whore's son was not just an insult to me and my mother but also a grave offense to my father, who, were he alive, would have avenged the slight with a blade. It wasn't just Bruto's words that were hurtful; I also felt hatred in his heart. I never understood the source of his animosity. Withdrawing into myself, I never sought his help again.

The only other time we had a serious disagreement was when, at age fourteen, he sent me to study for the priesthood. ¡Ay! Don Juan de Zavala a *priest*?

Besides those who heard God's call, the priesthood was a refuge for the younger sons of the affluent. In the church they would have income and position when the family property was transferred to the eldest son. To send the firstborn—and in my case, the only born—to a seminary to study for a life in the church would have left the Zavala family fortune heirless. Only those called upon by God were driven to such a radical act, not that I fear serving God; with horse reins in my teeth, a red-hot smoking pistol in one hand, and a Toledo blade in the other, I would happily dispatch God's enemies to everlasting hellfire.

But serving Him with prayers, alms, and abstinence was not in the cards. The seminary prefect cashiered me after unfortunate incidents: I horsewhipped a fellow seminarian who branded me a sodomite after I described my lurid deflowering of a servant girl. Turning white as a winding sheet, the youth raced straight to the prefect to inform on me. When the prelate attempted to whip me, I brandished a Toledo dagger, offering to castrate him like a steer if he bloodied my back.

I went to confession after each transgression, repented for my sins, made a good act of contrition, deposited a few pesetas in the church poor box—along with a pouch of gold for the priest—and then recited a dozen or so Hail Marys. My soul was cleansed, and I felt redeemed—and privileged to transgress again. Finally, I was sent home. Bruto showed his disappointment but made no further attempt to geld me.

All I acquired from my short-lived preparation for the priesthood was an unusual ability to learn languages: I mastered Latin, the tongue of priests, and French, the language of culture, quickly, by ear, simply from hearing them. I already spoke the Aztec dialect of the vaqueros on my hacienda.

I had just dozed off when I heard a disturbance in the house. I got out of bed and went into the hallway, as my uncle's servant, José, came out of my uncle's room with a chamber pot.

"What is it?" I asked.

"Your uncle has stomach problems. He's been vomiting."

"Should we call a doctor?"

"He insists that none be called."

If he was not sick enough for a doctor, it was no concern of mine. I still smarted from his wicked utterances about my beloved Isabella. I wondered whether God was torturing him for his foul words.

That night I suffered one of the nightmares that had plagued me since childhood. In every violent dream, I found myself not a Spanish grandee but an Aztec warrior, fighting—and dying—in bloody battle. Years ago, while drinking too much with the vaqueros at my hacienda, I had in jest consulted an india witch who told me that my nightmares were not dream-sleep but nighttime visitations from the ghosts of Aztec warriors who had died while fighting the Spanish. Fool that I was, I believed the old woman at the time, but as the dreams became less frequent and finally stopped, I realized the dreams were created by the many stories I had heard about the wars between the Spanish and the Aztecs.

But of late the nightmares had come back, more violent than ever. On this night I had seen myself in Mictlan, the Aztec underworld, where the dead must endure the trials of nine hells before their souls are extinguished.

¡Ay! I erupted from sleep drenched in sweat and with a heavy sense of dread. Packs of hellhounds had snarled at my heels, murderous beasts my priest had warned me would drive my sin-blackened soul to Fire Everlasting. I'd even felt the flames sear my flesh. Trying to return to sleep, I tossed and turned, my thoughts crowded with those baying hellhounds snapping at my heels.

In the morn I got out of bed, leaving those hellhounds under the covers, I hoped. But irritation dogged me. My manservant, Francisco, had not yet brought my morning cup of cocoa, invigorated with chili, herbs, and spices, nor had he emptied my chamber pot. I found him in the kitchen kneeling on the floor next to Pablo, my vaquero, engaged in casting copper coins at a clay plate across the room.

The indio groveled. "My apologies, patrón. I didn't know you had awakened."

He was lazy and had corn mush for brains, though the men of his Aztec race were known for being hard workers.

As I left the kitchen I stopped and studied the new india kitchen maid. I agreed with my fellow gachupines that indias were dutiful and delightfully concupiscent.

I have been told that these Aztec women do not favor the male of their own species, because the men make them work in the fields all day, even while heavy with child. Later, while her man relaxes with his amigos and putas in the evening, the india must prepare dinner and work into the night to prepare the tortillas and other food for the next day's breakfast.

Life is so harsh for indias, my priest claims that many indias kill their own girl babies at birth to spare the girl the terrible burdens that she will carry through her lifetime as a woman.

She looked shyly at me. I found her pleasing. I knew she was not married, so I marked her fine figure in my head for later. Now I had to meet Isabella on the paseo.

My head swarmed with plans to capture a title and Isabella. But no man can fight his destiny, eh? We can't stand before the galloping horse of

Fate and make her stop. She's a fickle nag, no? We can shout and struggle, conquer and kill, but Señora Fortuna rules the mast and controls the rudder directing our lives as we brave her storm-tossed sea of chance.

Still, I had not counted on that foul puta to tip the scales and send that blood-crazed pack of baying hounds on my trail, howling for my hide.

 **FOUR**

IN MY ROOM, after I sponged off, Francisco helped me dress in my finest riding clothes. My hat was black, with a large brim and a very flat, low crown. The crown and brim were both laced with gold and silver worked into an elaborate mesh. My shirt was white silk, with a high collar, under a short jacket of black with silver thread and calico patterns. My breeches were covered with leather chaps emblazoned with dozens of silver stars. Boots made in the colony were among the best in the world, and I wore only the finest. Of cinnamon color, the leather was cut in relievo in an elegant pattern by indios who spent weeks on a single pair. From my shoulders, held on with a silver chain, was a cloak, raven black and laced with silver.

I thought highly of myself, but Isabella said my complexion was too dark against her alabaster skin, my brown eyes too common compared to her dazzling emerald orbs. Eh, my crooked nose came from being thrown by a horse at the age of seven; my forehead scarred from butting heads with a bull when I was playing matador at the age of eleven. My hair was black and came down as thick sideburns almost to my chin. Because of my looks, when I was small, the vaqueros called me El Azteca Chico, the Little Aztec.

"You are no beauty," she told me, when we were introduced soon after her family moved here from Guadalajara last year. "If I didn't know you were born in Spain, I would take you for a lépero!"

Her comparison of me to the street trash of the colony caused her girl-friends to squeal like piglets being tickled. Had a man jested thus, he would have tasted my blade. When Isabella so mocked, I melted like a timid boy.

I left the house and went into the courtyard, where Pablo was waiting with my horse. I checked the stirrup length and cinch. As usual, they were exact.

As my personal vaquero, Pablo was the finest cowboy at my hacienda. I kept him in the city most of the time to help train and exercise my horses. A mixed-blood mestizo, he had neither the bronze complexion of Aztecs nor the lighter shade of Europeans. I didn't care if Pablo had claws and a tail if my mounts prospered under him.

Pablo had saddled my favorite stallion, Tempest, the one I always rode when courting Isabella. Its former owner claimed that Tempest was a direct descendant of Cortés's fabled mounts, the sixteen warhorses that enabled Cortés and his men to conquer a kingdom and carve out an empire. But almost every horse trader in New Spain claimed his horses hailed from that sacred stock, most notoriously from Cortés's own warhorse.

Tempest was sloe-black, with an inky sheen that blazed like blueblack fire in the noonday sun. His tack was even more ornate than my caballero attire. An elaborately decked-out ebony saddle with expansive stirrup leathers and a broad black pommel, it was richly embellished with silver, treasure more precious than a peon saw in a lifetime. He was skirted by a "Cortés shield" of thick black leather, all of it heavily embossed. The shields dated from the age when every caballero's mount was a warhorse.

I only burdened Tempest with fancy tack when I rode him into the city to visit Isabella. When I rode him into the llano to hunt, we only wore and carried what we needed.

Before I swung into the saddle, I waited while Pablo dropped to his haunches and heeled my boots with spurs that had three-inch Chihuahua rowels of hammered silver, burnished to a mirror gloss—spurs fit for a gachupine.

Pablo had the bridle knotted across the pommel. As was the custom, my bridle was small, but the bit large and powerful so the horse could be stopped abruptly, even when racing, though that was not always easy with Tempest; he earned his name.

I saw my uncle's servant come out of the house. I yelled at him as he hurried for the gate to the street as if one of the hounds I dreamt about was snapping at his heels.

"José! How is my uncle?"

He threw me an odd look, gawking as if I were a stranger instead of one of his masters, then disappeared through the gate. The fool never answered my shouted question. He would pay for his impertinence later, though I knew how cantankerous my uncle can be. He had probably sent José on an errand and told him to move double quick or he'd get a beating. José got more beatings than any other servant in the house. But why José would ignore me was a mystery. Certainly I was not known for sparing the rod. His rudeness fueled the gloom that had already blackened my morning.

After riding through our compound's gate, I headed toward the paseo and the lovely Isabella. I hadn't gone far when I was accosted by a lépero, a disgusting gutter rat, the kind that beg and steal on the streets when they are not passed out from cheap drink. Léperos are human maggots with the social standing of lepers. These peons were addicted to pulque, a foul, stinking indio beer made from the cactuslike maguey plant.

"Señor! Charity! Charity!"

The lépero grabbed at my horse's polished silver saddle flap with a filthy hand. I struck the creature's hand with my riding crop. He staggered back against a wall. *¡Ay!* He had smeared his filth on the flap. I raised my crop to scare him away when someone shouted.

"*Stop!*"

An open carriage had pulled up behind me. The person who shouted the command—a priest—leaped out and rushed toward me, holding up the skirt of his robe so he wouldn't trip as he ran.

"Señor! Leave that man alone!"

"Man? I see no man, padre. Léperos are animals, and this one placed his filthy hand on my tack."

I let the lépero escape without striking him. The priest glared up at me. He was hatless, a man somewhere in his fifties, showing his age, with a ring of white hair circling his bald pate like the crown of a Roman emperor.

"Would you kill one of God's children for a smudge on your silver?" he asked.

I sneered down at him. "Of course not. I would have merely cut off the offending hand."

"God is listening, young caballero."

"Then tell Him not to let street trash touch my horse." I could have told the priest that I would not have inflicted serious injury on the street trash—the code I lived by did not permit me to harm someone who could not fight back—but I was in no mood to be lectured.

As I maneuvered Tempest around the priest, I noticed for the first time that a young woman was in the carriage.

"Buenos días, Don Juan."

I nudged Tempest with my spurs to hurry him along even as I replied, "Buenos días, señorita."

I trotted away as quickly as the far reaches of politeness permitted.

¡Ay! My gloomy premonitions on awakening this morning were all coming too true. She was none other than Raquel Montez, a young woman I tried my best to avoid. The priest who loved léperos probably thought I had no conscience, but in truth I rushed away from Raquel because I am a very sentimental hombre.

Well . . . not exactly sentimental, but I am not devoid of compassion, at least toward women. Perhaps because I was given a succession of wet nurses rather than my mother, I found it more difficult to deal with women than men. While I would be the first to draw my sword if an armed man insulted me, I didn't know how to treat women, except to please them with the tool only a man possesses.

In the case of Raquel, I rushed away because I cringed under her wounded-doe eyes. What sins did I commit against her? Did I despoil her? Abandon her to a cruel fate after stealing her virginity? *¡Ay!* Her griev-

ances are many and all true, but the fault was not mine, at least not entirely
so. Marriages in the colony, among people of quality—like those in Spain
herself—are financial arrangements, taking into account the bride's proffered dowry and the groom's prospects for a family inheritance. The rela-
tive social position of the bride and groom are also critical.

Raquel was once my betrothed, in fact, the only woman to whom I
have ever been set to wed. As shocking as it may sound, I was promised to
her despite the fact she was a mestiza.

Raquel's father was Spanish born, of a good family that long hailed
from Toledo, a town on the Tagus River, not far from Madrid. Toledo is an
ancient city with a worldwide reputation for producing fine swords and
daggers, a profession that had thrived there since the time of Julius Caesar.
The younger son of swordsmiths, he came to the colony to seek his fortune. He soon shocked his family by marrying an attractive young Aztec
girl.

The poor soul. He not only wed outside his bloodline, but the young
woman did not even bring a dowry to the marriage bed. One can imagine
the consternation of his family: The fool married for love when he could
have wed a gachupine or wealthy criolla widow and kept the pretty india as
his lover.

He became a merchant of daggers and swords, selling blades shipped
to him by his family. Only moderately successful at that trade, I am told he
lacked the ruthless rapacity and relentless greed to garner truly great
wealth. However, Señora Fortuna smiled upon him and rewarded him with
an interest in a small but profitable silver mine, which he had grubstaked
for the prospectors. The sudden wealth and a marriage connection made
by his family in Spain opened the door to an even more profitable venture:
the quicksilver license.

Sí, the same royal license that was the basis of my own fortune. The
king held a monopoly on the right to sell quicksilver. In turn, the right was
granted by royal license to a merchant in each mining area to supply the
mines with the substance. For over two decades, Bruto had kept control of
the license in Guanajuato. Now we were threatened with its loss.

"Just as bad," Bruto explained, "the king's quicksilver agents can pit us
against each other in a bidding war and bleed us both dry."

By "bidding war" my uncle meant paying bribes, of course, a war of
the ubiquitous mordida, "the bite" that bureaucrats expected for doing
their duty. Bruto obviated the threat by arranging a marriage between the
Montez and Zavala families. The betrothal sent a shock through the city's
highborn: a gachupine marrying a mestiza . . . only loco passion or financial
desperation could impel such a marriage arrangement!

It was a shock to me, too. Isabella had not moved to Guanajuato at this
time—she came the following year—so my love for Isabella did not play a
role in my reaction. My first response was fury. I asked my uncle how long

he expected to live once I had shoved my dagger into his throat. Not only was Raquel a mestiza, but she also wasn't a great beauty in my eyes. It was true that the men of the colony held a common belief that the mixture of Spanish and Aztec blood produced women of exceptional grace and beauty, but that did not make her acceptable as my wife.

When I started to list my objections to Uncle Bruto, he cut me off. "Do you enjoy your fine horses?" my uncle asked. "Thoroughbreds that a duke would envy? The wardrobe of a prince? Your card games, expensive wines, imported cigarros, and whores every night with your amigos? Tell me, muchacho, would you rather get a job as a muleteer? Because you will be working with your feet in manure if Raquel's father is granted the license."

¡Ay de mí! Such a fall from grace was unthinkable. I agreed to the match. And decided I would also get to know the señorita, though with an arranged marriage knowing your bride-to-be well before the wedding night was not considered prudent.

While not possessing attributes that I prized, Raquel was a woman of many talents. Educated not only in the ways of running a household and serving her husband, she had studied art, literature, science, mathematics, music, history, even philosophy—all the things I despised.

"I read and write poetry," she told me, as we walked in her family's garden during my first visit. "I've read Sor Juana, Calderón, Moratin, and Dante. I've studied Juvenal and Tacitus, play the piano, corresponded with Madame de Stael in Paris, read Mary Wollstonecraft's *A Vindication of the Rights of Women*, in which she proved that the education system deliberately trains women to be frivolous and incapable. I've—"

"*¡Ay María!*" I crossed myself.

She stared at me openmouthed. "Why did you do that?"

"What?"

"You made the sign of the cross and spoke the name of the Holy Mother."

"For certain, I always seek the protection of heaven when I am in the presence of the devil."

"Is that what you think of me? A devil?"

"Not you. The devil's servant is the person who permitted you to delve into such nonsense." I'd heard that her father was permissive toward his children. I was stunned by the damage his permissiveness had done to the poor girl's mind.

"Do you think because a woman has a brain and uses it for something besides household chores and babies that she's a demon?"

"Not a demon, señorita, but a woman who is damaging her mind." I shook my finger at her. "That is not my opinion alone; all men share the view. Music, philosophy, poetry—those are the interests of priests and scholars. Women have no business contemplating such matters."

Everyone knows that a woman's mind is not capable of dealing with matters outside the family and household. Like peons, women are of limited intellect, not estúpido, of course, but mentally incapable of comprehending politics, commerce, and fine horses—the things most important to society.

"Women should read books and study the world," she said.

"A woman's place is in the kitchen and in a man's bed."

She shot me a look of angry determination. "I'm sorry, señor, that you find I will be an unsuitable wife."

She left in a huff. I went after her and used my best charms to soothe things over, the grim specter of laboring in a stable still snapping at my heels.

We rode out the crisis, and soon I courted her in the proper way. After I presented her with a gold and pearl necklace, I stood under her balcony on Saturday nights to serenade her with love songs and a guitar.

We avoided talk of her book learning. Secretly, I feared the harm done to her tender mind by those mountains of words and ideas was already beyond repair. Could I undo the damage? Could she still perform her duties as a wife?

I discussed my fears with my drinking compañeros, and we all concluded that the problem was her father: He was a weak-willed fool, filled with too much book learning himself. His library of over a hundred volumes had clearly muddled both their minds.

Some dandies at the paseo struck another blow at my composure when they derided Raquel for sometimes riding horses. Now, mind you, women have been known to ride caballos. Revoltingly mounted on a ridiculous contraption known as a sidesaddle, some headstrong women have humiliated themselves on the paseo. One sometimes glimpsed women of the lower classes, the wives of vaqueros and rancheros, seated on a horse or mule in front of their husbands, while he holds her waist with one hand and the reins with the other. But Raquel had *ridden a horse like a man,* wearing split skirts and petticoats. *¡Dios mío!* Now the whole city was mocking me.

The dandies shut up and moved away when I spurred Tempest toward them. They knew if they did not leave they would face me on the field of honor—and I was not one of them, a soft, silken caballero. I earned my big spurs not simply through an accident of birth but in the saddle, outriding, outshooting, and outroping the best vaqueros on my hacienda. On horseback, I chased a bull out on the range until I came up behind it and sent it to the ground by grabbing its tail. These paseo peacocks knew my abilities. They disliked me for them but dared not call me out.

Raquel scandalizing herself was so serious, however, I again brought the matter up with the compañeros I drink and whore with. They concurred that she needed a strong hand to know that I was her lord and master, even before marriage.

Thinking about their advice, I decided to seduce Raquel, to learn whether her education had damaged her beyond the point of being able to perform her most important matrimonial duties. The plan, however, was not without risk. If I impregnated her, there would be scandal, and we would both lose face. But a smart caballero knew the art of coitus interruptus, the sin for which God condemned Onan. If I left my seed in a whore or a servant girl, pregnancy was of no consequence. The law ignored offspring from such casual liaisons, affording them no privileges or rights. To deflower a woman of quality, however, would bring down the wrath of God to say nothing of her male relatives: pistols at dawn and financial retribution.

While Raquel was a mestiza, her father was a gachupine, a man of wealth and substance. To such a family, virtue and virginity not only were synonymous, they also were prized because the loss could bar a woman from a financially advantageous marriage.

That a man was free to conjugate beyond the marriage bed was understood. God in his indubitable wisdom had designed, ordained, and predetermined man's peripatetic lust, thus making it divinely destined, the way of the world.

¡Ay! It was extremely imprudent to debauch one's intended esposa, but my mind and body have not always obeyed society's dictates.

One evening after dinner I persuaded her to stroll with me in her family garden. I was in a jovial mood, my stomach full with rare beef and rarer wine. The evening was mild, even a little warm, and the air was fragrant with roses. The only damper on my plan was the elderly aunt who accompanied us on our walk. A young lady required a chaperone even in her own garden. She followed behind us, a little unsteady. At last, she sat wearily on a rock bench and closed her eyes.

"Poor dear, she's old and tired," Raquel said in a loving tone.

The old woman's chest rose and fell in a steady rhythm.

"She drank too much wine."

I pulled her roughly to me and put my arms around her, ready to kiss her.

"Someone might see us."

"No one is around but your aunt, and, look, the old woman is fast asleep," I whispered. "Come with me. I want to show you something," I told her, my voice thick with desire. Grabbing her hand, I pulled her behind a row of bushes.

"Juan, what has gotten into you? The wine has made you crazy."

We tumbled to the ground together, myself on top. "I saw the way you looked at me this evening," I said.

"You are a striking figure of a man."

She didn't stop me when I kissed her on the mouth. In fact, she returned my kiss with surprising ardor, and the wine spurred me on.

"I see longing in your eyes," I told her.

"I want my husband to be pleased."

I looked at her, bewildered.

"But—" she said, almost with a pained looked on her face.

"What is wrong?"

"I have so much to learn," she said hesitantly, lowering her eyes, "about pleasing . . . you . . ."

I couldn't help but laugh. "*Ay,* I will teach you. Give me your hand."

I already felt the heat rising in my body as I guided her hand to my loins. "Now touch it."

She looked around and hesitated for a moment.

"It's getting hard . . . and big . . . and growing bigger!" she said, confused.

My pride swelled as did my garrancha from the pressure of her grip.

I spun for her the fables men have spun for women since the beginning of time: promises of love eternal, faith and fealty, inviolable discretion . . . now . . . forever . . . I promised to cherish her until the sun died blind, blackened to the heart; until man, Earth, the stars themselves were blotted out. I swore the deity Himself would bless our consummation . . . and that after all I was her husband in all things but the ring. We were to be married, were we not?

Desire rode me like a ram in rut. I pulled her cotton blouse down and sucked her breast. Discarding my boots and pants, I frantically fumbled through her mounds and mountains of petticoats. Removing her undergarments, I gingerly spread her legs apart. As I pushed my throbbing organ against her pristine loins, into her immaculate yet magically sensuous opening, she let out a soft strangled cry—half pain, half pleasure—and a sigh, another sigh, the word *yes,* faintly audible above her sighs, and again *yes.* At the same time she enveloped my hips with her legs, squeezing me, holding me, then hanging on for dear life. She had to, for I was bucking now—as if I were an outlaw llano stallion and El Diablo himself was mounting my back and roweling my ribs, as if I were possessed by wind and rain and fire, by a sword of fire. Deeper, harder, I bucked, riding us both into a whirlwind of rain and fire, but the latter, a hurricane of fire, a chaos of fire, a fire of fires, straight on through to the hell-hot core of the sun.

When I was spent and gazed down at her, not without tenderness, her eyes were closed though I felt her body shudder whenever I touched her. Her face was expressionless save for a trickle of tears. From pain or joy I did not know.

•　　•　　•

Eh, I had made a terrible mistake, one that started as a mud slide but was soon an avalanche. After I had taken her, a change took place. She began to look at me with doe eyes. *¡Ay!* She had fallen in love with me. She was six-teen years old and had had her first intimate experience with a man. All sixteen-year-old girls are idealistic about love, but I had not realized that the poetry and plays she read had so usurped her mind and comman-deered her heart. To be frank with you, I prefer my women hardened to my lust . . . like a brothel *puta*. Her affection embarrassed me, even though we were betrothed.

And then her world exploded: A rumor spread that her father was from a converso family. *Converso* was an ugly word, over three centuries old, dating from the time of Ferdinand and Isabella. It denoted the worse kind of blood taint.

After the Moors were conquered and separate Christian kingdoms united to form a country, the Spanish church and crown decreed that Jews and Moors had to convert to Christianity or face seizure of their property and expulsion from the country. Those who converted were known as con-versos. Many conversos and their descendants were prosecuted by the In-quisition, accused of pretending to convert in order to stay in the country and save their possessions, though it was sometimes whispered that accu-sations of fraudulent conversions were made so the Inquisition could en-rich itself by seizing the fortunes of people who opposed their black deeds.

Eh, all the fuss over so many things I cared nothing about. Perfumed petticoats, gambling and pistols, horses and whores—the things I cared about—were my religion at the time, and they required mucho dinero, which was my sole interest in Raquel.

When "witnesses" swore her grandfather in Spain was a converso, the accusations burned through Guanajuato society like a firestorm. Soon the crown barred her father from the New Spain quicksilver trade. The busi-ness that earned him his fortune, the importation of fine Toledo and Dam-ascus blades, suffered as well when his customers deserted him. Forged in infidel flames, Damascus blades drew special scorn. In the wake of the ac-cusations and Raquel's loss of a dowry, our betrothal unraveled. Fortu-nately, her father was a man of honor, and the engagement was canceled because he could no longer afford the dowry.

That fickle Slut of Chance continued to spin her shadowy wheel, carry-ing misfortune into her father's life. When an ill-set charge collapsed a shaft and blew out a stope, his silver mine was racked to ruin by fire and flood.

Soon after, Raquel's father came, uninvited, to our house. Trembling with rage, tears on his cheeks, he accused my uncle of spreading the con-verso slander. "You think me not so white as yourselves?" he shouted.

The dispute raged, but I said nothing. Criollos and gachupines raised the issue of "whiteness" continually, but the question was always rhetorical. People posed it only when others treated them with contempt, as if others treated them like peons. The "white" the old man referred to, of course, was the "color" of blood not skin.

Voicing other accusations, he charged my uncle with sabotaging the mine and starting the fire—a suspicion I harbored myself. As he shouted, something broke in him. Perhaps his heart burst or a brain fever consumed him. He suddenly keeled over, hitting the floor like a toppled oak. He lay there portentously inert. Taking a door off its hinges, we carefully placed him on it and had servants carry him down the street to his own house. He died a few days later without regaining consciousness.

The world changed for Raquel after her father's loss of fortune and death. No longer able to maintain a great house, she and her grieving mother moved into a smaller house, keeping but a single servant. Poor Raquel. As if blood taint and financial ruin weren't enough, leaving her without even a dowry, she was also deflowered.

When I saw those sad doe eyes staring at me, asking in quizzical silence where those vows of love had gone, I cursed that I had ever met her and wondered why her fall from grace so racked my calloused soul. Was it my fault that her world collapsed? When I took her, did I know she would lose not only her virginity but father and dowry? Should not the girl have fought me off, knowing how important her virgo intacta was?

But it was all for the best, at least for me. Isabella, my angel, soon arrived. From the moment I saw her, I knew she would be mine.

Still Raquel's sad eyes plagued me. *¡Dios es Dios!* As sure as God lives. I must have rutted a thousand lecherous wenches and legions of brothel bawds, but none with her wounded eyes.

They will haunt me to the grave.

 **FIVE**

I RODE TEMPEST through the narrow, crowded streets of the city, making my way toward the paseo, a pathway in a park beyond the city streets. As their peers did in the two famed parks in Méjico City, the Alameda and Paseo de Bucareli, wealthy señoritas in their carriages and caballeros on their fine blooded horses paraded the paseo in Guanajuato. I went in the afternoons to show off myself and my great stallion before the flirtatious women who stayed in their carriages and laughed behind Chinese silk fans at the displays of machismo by the caballeros.

Despite the size of the city, Guanajuato's central zone could not accommodate a spacious park. Unlike the capital, it was not situated on flat terrain but was a mountain mining town. Sprawling over steep hillsides at the junction of three ravines, its elevation was almost seven thousand feet.

Plagued by rainstorms and floods, the indios called the city the "place of the frogs," implying it was only fit for frogs. Its windswept cobbled streets rose narrowly into little alleys, or callejones, consisting of a few stone steps. Flattening out, the callejones yielded to more stone steps, twisting uphill, past colorful buildings of cantera stone.

Guanajuato was famed throughout New Spain for its magnificently ornate La Valenciana Church, with its elaborately hand-carved altar and pulpit. Its most prized possession, however, was in fact singularly secular: the celebrated Veta Madre, the mother lode of silver, acclaimed as the richest silver find in all New Spain, perhaps in all the world.

Second in population only to the capital, the city boasted over seventy thousand people, including its environs and surrounding mines. In wealth and importance, Guanajuato was the third city of the Americas, surpassed only by Méjico City and Havana. Not even that place called New York—in that country to the northeast that had declared its independence from Britain when I was a child—compared to the three great cities of the Spanish colonial empire in size and importance.

Guanajuato was the leading city in the Bajío. A rich region of cattle, farming, and mining northwest of the capital, it boasted many fine haciendas, picturesque villages, and elegant baroque churches. The Bajío was not in the Valley of Méjico but was still in the heart of the colony, that central expanse called the Plateau of Méjico. New Spain was a vast territory, extending from the Isthmus of Panama to regions far north of the arid deserts of New Méjico and California. The colony's population was said to be about 6 million, with the greatest portion thereof concentrated in the central plateau. I am told that the entire population of that entity known as the United States, the only independent nation in the Americas, would be almost equal to New Spain's if that northern nation had not kidnapped a million slaves from Africa.

What kind of people lived in this place called New Spain? About half—nearly 3 million—were pure-blood indios, the remnants of ten times that many who had occupied the land before Cortés landed nearly three hundred years ago.

That infelicitous mix of indio and Spanish bloods called mestizos amounted to fewer than half that many. And there was also a small number of mulattos, people of indio and africano blood, and an even smaller number of chinos, people with yellow skin from that mysterious land across the Pacific Ocean called Cathay. Another 1 million of the people in the colony were criollos, colony-born Spaniards who owned most of the haciendas, mines, and businesses.

The gachupines were the smallest yet mightiest social class of New Spain, that privileged population into which God and our fickle goddess of fate, Señora Fortuna, had so fortuitously inserted me. Though we numbered perhaps only ten thousand—a minute portion of the 6 million surrounding us—we were imperially favored by God and the crown. We controlled the government, courts, police, military, church, and commerce.

Rapacious wearers of our razor-sharp spurs, we drove our rowels into the flanks of not just the Aztecs, mestizos, and others that made up the peon class but also the proud and disdainful criollos, who dreamed of the day when their Spanish blood would make them our equals.

More than money, horsemanship, skill with weapons, or the sensuous subjugation of señoritas, the "color" of a man's blood was the sine qua non of status and honor. By any application of the limpieza de sangre—the test of blood—mine was pureza de sangre, pure Spanish blood. Without the purity of my blood, little separated me from the peons.

Blood was the God-given difference between all people, even those with the same skin color and speech. A vaquero on a hacienda may be a fine horseman in the saddle of a horse or with a woman, he might work cattle and shoot game with deadly aplomb, but he was a peon and could never be a caballero. Caballeros, the knights of New Spain and the Mother Country, had pureza de sangre, pure Spanish blood.

Purity of blood transcended wealth, nobility, and artistry, for blood alone conferred honor. The tradition arose from the centuries of wars that made the Iberian Peninsula a battleground between Christians and the infidel followers of Allah we call Moors. Like the mestizos of the colony, those with a mixture that included Moorish blood were ostracized.

Not even skin color was more important than pureza de sangre. Many Spaniards did not have pale white skin. The Iberian Peninsula, where so many cultures have existed and clashed for thousands of years, produced many hues of skin and hair.

While birth, not lineage, conferred honor, and mixing blood was the ultimate degradation, colonial birth by itself was enough to sully a bloodline.

The climate in New Spain ranges from deserts in the north to jungles in the south. It is unhealthy for birthing, rendering criollos unfit for high office, whether it be in the government, church, or military.

Eh, there is grumbling from some criollos that the real reason power was kept only in the tight fist of gachupines was to keep control of the colony in the hands of the Spain-born because they had strong ties to the king. Most of the gachupines who administered the colony came over for only a few years, made their fortune, and returned to the homeland. The church also kept real power out of the grasp of colony-born priests.

To understand why my birthplace made me what is vulgarly called a gachupine, you must know a little more about New Spain. It was nearly three centuries ago when Cortés and his band of five or six hundred adventurers conquered the mighty empire of Montezuma, emperor of the Aztecs, and found themselves masters of indio empires that stretched a thousand leagues and were populated by over 25 million people.

Though we refer to all indios as "Aztecs," twenty or more indigenous cultures resided in the central region when Cortés landed. Many more indio cultures dotted the lands farther south, among them the mysterious Mayas and the gold-rich Inca empire of Peru. Seizing the wealth of the indio royalty and nobility, conquistadors and their Spanish rulers soon rounded up another type of "treasure," *the indios themselves*, conscripting them as laborers and exacting an annual tribute for their new Spanish masters.

The Spanish carved the indios' empires into vast grants, but smallpox and other plagues—carried to the New World by Europeans—killed ninety percent of the indigenous people in a few short decades. Fortunately, for Spain, a new treasure was discovered: *silver*. Silver made the colony Spain's prize possession.

The Spanish Empire was the largest on earth, a domain so vast, the sun never set upon it. Neither Britain's colonies in Africa and Asia, nor the Czar's illimitable Russian domain, spreading across so much of the northern portion of the globe, compared in size to the far-flung empire of Spain.

History, of course, was the interest of priests and scholars. What was important about it to me was that New Spain's mountains of silver dwarfed the wealth of all other Spanish colonies, and my quicksilver business, which controlled the magic element that alchemized silver out of mining rock, would buy me the noble title necessary to win the hand of my true love.

 **SIX**

WHAT DOES A woman admire most in a man? Gentleness? Kindness? *¡Ay!* Those are the traits of priests. Wealth? A woman may desire riches, but it is not what she most admires. No, she covets most his virility: the power of his loins in the bedroom and his dominance over other men in the saddle and, when necessary, on the field of honor. Knowing this, when I entered the paseo, I sat tall in the saddle. Even Tempest flaunted his machismo, prancing and snorting at the mares.

I spoke to a few of the caballeros, merely nodded to others, ignored those whom I considered too far beneath me socially to command even a flick of my eye or head. I usually rode alone, while other caballeros went about in groups of two or three or more. In truth, I did not count many men as my friends. I was known as a loner, one who stayed mainly to himself.

Most men my age were fools, and the young caballeros I competed with at night across the gaming tables were no exceptions. While my uncle referred to them as my amigos, they were acquaintances rather than friends. They bored me less when we were playing cards, and only the gaming table and a succession of upturned brandy bottles could provoke me to socialize with them at the inn in the evenings. I preferred the company of my horse and long rides into the wilderness, hunting or just exploring. Isabella says I am like a jaguar, the great jungle cat that hunts alone.

There she was, by the grace of God, the most beautiful woman in Guanajuato! Her carriage was surrounded by criollo caballeros, all begging for attention. I had Tempest prance by her carriage, ignoring her and the mob of admirers begging for attention. She eventually waved me over, laughing. She was as lovely as a goddess, regally attired in a gown of royal purple, embroidered in gold. Her eyebrows were blackened with burnt cork, giving her a wanton air that stirred my sin-black soul.

"Ah, Don Juan, so nice to see you. How were you able to free yourself from your tedious excursions in the wilds and honor us with you presence here on the paseo with the other caballeros?"

"Having observed the ways of your caballeros," I spoke loud enough for several of them to hear, "I prefer the company of horses."

Isabella laughed, that tinkling sound that thrilled my heart. But there was no doubt she deplored my wilderness treks. She continually scolded me for the time I spent with my horses rather than socializing. She especially detested the rides I enjoyed with the vaqueros on my hacienda and the bow hunting I indulged in. Such activities callused my hands and hardened my muscles, neither of which the dandies who vied for her attention favored. Isabella's diversions were carriage rides, lavish balls, flirting, shopping, and dancing, activities I found maddeningly dull.

I rode alongside as her carriage rolled down the dirt path that circled the park. A female friend rode beside her in the open coach. Her friend flirted with another rider while I quietly conversed with Isabella. She covered her mouth with her silk fan to keep her voice from carrying.

"Did you speak to your uncle about purchasing a title?" she asked.

"Yes, everything goes well," I lied. "And your father, did you speak to him about a marriage to me?"

Her fan fluttered. "He wants me to marry a count or marqués."

"Then I will purchase a dukedom."

Her laugh again tinkled like a bell. Dukedoms were not for sale. A marqués was lower than a duke and higher than a count, but any noble title would thrill her.

"My father has his eye on a particular marqués. I would nonetheless favor you, even if I married him." She allowed me a flirtatious smile and batted her eyes coyly. "I would keep you as my lover if you promise never to marry and worship only me."

My chest swelled with macho vanity. "Señorita, you will never marry anyone but me because I will kill any man who tries to marry you."

"Then you will be very busy I'm afraid, señor, since all the men in Guanajuato desire me."

"Only the blind would not desire you."

She pointed toward an oncoming rider. "Isn't that your servant, the one who cares for your horses?" Isabella asked.

Pablo, my vaquero, hurried to us on his mule.

"Señor, your uncle is very ill."

 **SEVEN**

DID I NOT foretell this would be a bad day?

The vultures had gathered at the house by the time I returned with Pablo. A pack of demanding cousins who had come over from Spain and continually entreated us for handouts hovered about. I ignored them, as I always did. I didn't grow up with any of them and shared no family resemblance, experiences, or common interests with them.

The doctor came out of the room when my presence was announced. He blocked the door so I could not enter my uncle's room.

"You must not go in," he said. "You uncle is very ill, I would say near death."

"Then I should see him."

He avoided my eyes. "He does not wish to see you."

"What?"

"He has asked for his priest."

I did not know what to say. I left the room and went down to the stable to check my horses. My uncle was dying and did not wish to see me? True, we were not close, but other than that grasping pack of importuning cousins, I had no other family in the colony. Were there to be no last words between my uncle and me?

His sudden illness puzzled me. I had never known him to be sick. I went back upstairs after the priest arrived and waited in the anteroom outside my uncle's bedroom. After a while the priest came out. I thought for a moment he would speak. He stood in front of me, wide-eyed, his jaw moving, then fled the house. I stood at the window and watched him rushing up the street. Eh, he too had hellhounds at his heels. Where was he rushing to? Was it not the duty of the priest to be at my uncle's bedside when he gave up the ghost?

The doctor came out of the bedroom, saw me sitting in the anteroom, and ducked back into the bedroom, slamming the door.

Dios mío, what had happened to the world? Had the earth stopped revolving around the sun? Was the sky about to fall? Nothing would surprise me.

I went back down to the stable to talk to my horses, taking a jug of wine with me.

When Pablo informed me that Luis de Ville, the alcalde, had arrived, I only shrugged. That the mayor of the city had rushed to my uncle's bedside was unexpected, but then everything that had happened that day had been *muy loco*.

Minutes later, Pablo informed me that the *corregidor* had come.

The mayor and now the chief officer of justice. To my uncle's deathbed?

Yet they failed to summon me, Juan de Zavala, who was both my uncle's heir and his employer. I was the imposing, important personage, not Uncle Bruto. Nothing would happen after his death except I would bury him and find someone else to manage my affairs.

I decided to remind the offensive fools that I was both gachupine and a man of substantial means.

The entire group—doctor, priest, mayor, and officer of justice—was in the anteroom when I came in. They turned and stared at me as if I were the one who was about to give up the ghost.

"Bruto de Zavala is dead," Señor Luis de Ville, the alcalde, said. "He is in the hands of God."

Or El Diablo, I thought.

The alcalde grabbed my arm and rushed out of the room. "Come with me," he said.

I followed him into the kitchen. He turned and stared at me, at my face, intensely.

"Juan, I have known you since you were a child."

"True," I said.

"Bruto spoke to all of us before he passed. He told us something."

"Yes. Is it bad news?" I asked. "He has mismanaged my estate, is that what he told you? How bad is it? How much do I have left?"

"Juan . . ." The man looked away.

"Alcalde, what is it? What are you trying to tell me?"

"You are not Juan de Zavala."

EIGHT

LAUGHED AT the nonsensical statement. "Of course I'm not Juan de Zavala. And you're not Don Luis de Ville, the alcalde of Guanajuato."

"You don't understand." His voice rose to a shout. "You're not who you think you are."

I shook my head. "I am who I am. Have you gone loco?"

"No, no, no—you're not a Zavala. Bruto confessed his sin to the priest, then had us hear his deathbed confession."

"What confession?"

"Over twenty years ago, Antonio de Zavala and his wife—"

"My mother and father."

"The brother and sister-in-law of Bruto, landed in Veracruz with their child, Juan. Bruto was with them. Before they reached Jalapa, all three suffered yellow fever, the deadly vomito negro. They died."

"My parents died."

"Antonio de Zavala, his wife, María, and son died."

"What nonsense is this? I'm the son of Antonio and María. Are you saying there's another?"

"They had only one child. Juan de Zavala died at the age of one year, along with his parents."

"Then who am I?" I shouted.

He stared me for a long moment. When he spoke, the words punched me in the face.

"You are an hijo de puta."

Son of a whore.

NINE

WALKED THE streets of Guanajuato aimlessly, going nowhere, not even aware of where my feet took me. Night was falling. I walked in a daze, the alcalde's words playing over and over in my mind.

"A changeling," the alcalde told me.

Un niño cambiado por otro. A child changed for another.

Bruto had come across an ocean, not just accompanying the man and woman I was told were my parents, but relying upon their royal license for the wealth he himself intended to also gather.

Bruto told the alcalde that when his brother and brother's family died, the legal right to the license would die with it and revert back to the royal treasury. To keep the license in the name of his brother's family, he bought an infant about the same age as the year-old Juan and passed him off as his nephew.

The child of a whore.

I was not Juan de Zavala, Bruto told them.

I was not a gachupine—not a caballero born in Spain, a wearer of spurs—but an Aztec whore's child, lower than lépero street trash.

"Bruto didn't know what race your father was."

It made no sense. I was Juan de Zavala. That is the only name, the only identity I knew. I wasn't someone else just because a dying man claimed it.

"It's revenge," I shouted at the night.

That's what it had to be. Bruto was angry because I was dismissing him, menacing his livelihood.

How could they take the word of a dying man against my own?

"The portrait speaks the truth," the alcalde had told me.

Bruto had hidden in his quarters a portrait painted weeks before Antonio and María de Zavala boarded a ship for the New World with their child. Antonio and Bruto both had light hair and eyes. María had golden locks and green eyes, as did the child in the portrait.

Did I mention that my eyes and hair are dark brown? My skin light olive?

As I left the house, more Zavala family vultures were arriving, those beggar-bastards both Bruto and I hated. They came to squabble over their shares of *my house, my possessions, my money.*

I left with the clothes on my back. I went to the stable to have Pablo saddle Tempest, and the vultures followed me with a constable who escorted me to the front gate without the horse. When I turned to say something, the gate was slammed in my face.

"Peon!" I heard a cousin shout from the other side of the gate. A few hours earlier, I would have drawn my sword and split him down the middle, but I was too numb, too mentally paralyzed to defend my pureza de sangre, too dead inside to be horrified. It made no sense. My feet moved me away from the house, my mind reeling, my eyes filled with panic but seeing nothing.

If Bruto was right, if I wasn't Juan de Zavala, what was my name? How could a few words take away my name, my entire persona? It was stealing my soul.

"I know who I am!"

A dark chill settled over me. I found myself in front of the inn I usually came to at night to drink and gamble with other young caballeros. My feet had instinctively brought me there.

I went inside, suddenly relieved. I knew men here, a friendly innkeeper. I would be able to talk about this insanity, clear the fog and confusion that was keeping me from thinking, from reasoning out what I had to do.

They were there, three caballeros at a table, my chair empty. I went right to the table and sat down, shaking my head.

"I have a tale to tell you all," I said, "one you will not believe."

No one said anything. When I looked at Alano across from me, he turned his head. The others turned their heads as I tried to catch their eyes.

All three of them got up and moved to another table, leaving me sitting by myself. There was not a sound in the inn. I sat frozen, unable to get my mind or my legs to work.

The innkeeper came up, wiping his hands on his apron. He, too, did not meet my eye. "Perhaps you should leave, Señor. This is not the right place for you."

Not the right place.

It took a moment for his words to register, for me to understand why it was not the right place. Spaniards frequented the inn. He was telling me to go to an inn where peons gathered.

I rose in anger.

"Do you think me not so white as yourselves?"

 **TEN**

BACK ON THE street, my anger evaporated, leaving me drained. Dazed and confused, I couldn't maintain even simple rage. The fight had run out of me. I walked aimlessly, going nowhere, letting my feet guide me again. I didn't know what to do, where to turn. Where was I to sleep? Eat? I would need a change of clothes. Already I was becoming cold. I needed a warm cloak, a fireplace, food in my stomach, brandy to heat my blood.

An inn was across the street, one had I had never been in before. I crossed and entered. The smells of sweat, pulque, and greasy food—smells that would have offended me hours ago—filled the tavern. I sat down at a table, weary.

The inn keeper came over immediately.

"Señor?"

"Brandy, your best."

"We don't have brandy, señor."

"Then wine, Spanish wine, none of your vinegar. Give me good wine."

"Of course, señor, we have fine wines."

He had recognized me as a gentleman from the cut of my clothes. I glanced around. I had come to an inn that was a step or two above a common pulquería. A pulquería was the bottom of the barrel, serving pulque, the cheap, smelly Aztec "beer" peons got drunk on. This place was more respectable, a place perhaps where indios and mestizos who held actual jobs as clerks and shop assistants came. Pulque was still served but so was cheap wine, too bitter for Spain and consigned to our colony. Forbidden to grow grapes and produce wine, New Spain had to take whatever Spain sent.

As soon as he set a jug and goblet down, I poured and drank. It was not good wine, but I needed a drink too badly to complain. "Bring me a good slice of beef, none of your gristle, mind you, the best in the city. Potatoes and—"

"I'm sorry, señor, we only have beans and tortillas and peppers."

"Beans and tortillas? That's garbage for the poor."

He said nothing, but his mouth tightened.

I just shrugged, puzzled at his reaction. "If that's all you have, bring it to me."

After he walked away, I realized I had insulted him. I had never insulted a peon before, not knowingly. How can one insult a peon? my card-playing compañeros would have asked.

The goblet shook in my hand. *¡Ay!* Bruto had said I was of the lower classes.

No! It's not true.

The alcalde was wrong: I was a Spaniard. The pieces to the mystery suddenly fell into place. My cousins had schemed this fraud to steal my property, to cheat me of my rightful—

But what about Bruto? *Bastardo!* I should have put a knife to his throat, cut out his tongue before he spoke such lies.

I took a silver case from my belt and took out a cigarro. Using a piece of the bundle of straw sitting by the fireplace, I lit the tobacco and returned to my table, wishing I had put Bruto's feet to the fire and tortured the truth out of him.

The innkeeper brought me my food: a plate of corn tortillas, a bowl of beans, some peppers, and, from somewhere, he had drudged up a bone with a fatty chunk of beef on it. Garbage! I wouldn't feed the swill to pigs.

I struck the tray with my arm, sending it flying off the table. It hit the floor, breaking the clay bowls and splattering on the pants of the innkeeper.

He looked down at the mess on the floor and on his pants and stared up at me, his mouth agape.

My stomach was in knots. My mind felt as if it had been twisted and wrung out by strong hands. I started to walk out but was stopped by the innkeeper.

"You haven't paid."

I stared at him stupidly. I never paid for anything. Innkeepers sent the bills to my uncle. I felt my pockets. I had no pesos, which was not unusual, I rarely carried money. "I have no money."

He stared at me as if I had just told him I'd raped his mother.

"Send the bill—" It suddenly struck me that there was no place to send the bill.

"You must pay."

He grabbed my arm as I started around him. I hit him, and he staggered back, banging into a table and knocking its plates and goblets onto the floor. For a moment the room was silent. Then two dozen men stood and faced me. I was ready to take on every one of them.

Daggers appeared in a dozen hands. Some had machetes as long as my arm. One had a rusty ball-and-cap pistol.

I saw something in the corner of my eye. I started to duck as I realized a piece of iron pipe in the innkeeper's hand was coming at my head. My reactions were too dulled. A light exploded behind my eyes, burst into a hundred fiery fragments, which in turn detonated into smaller slivers and shards that smoked, sizzled, and faded.

IN DURANCE VILE

MY HEAD FELT as if Tempest had kicked it. I came to, lying on the inn floor, blood flowing down my face. People milled around me. I tried to rise, but a voice in the fog told me to stay down and kicked me in the ribs. I stayed down. The fog had lifted a little by the time two constables arrived. Listening to the innkeeper's story, they booted me in the belly and bound my hands behind my back.

"You're lucky they didn't kill you," a tall, uniformed constable said, as they led me to the jail. "If you had not been dressed as a caballero, they would have cut your throat and left you in the gutter. Do you think you can cheat an honest innkeeper of his due? An innkeeper works hard for his money; he's not a worthless dandy like you."

"He's no caballero," his partner said. Shorter and stockier, his uniform was dirt-smeared, rumpled, and his foul, floppy-soled boots had not been blacked in decades. He wore his beard and hair disheveled, and, like his partner, he wore a short sheathed sword strapped to his belt. He shook a heavy wooden truncheon in my face. "He's a stinking lépero who robbed and killed to get those fancy clothes, then cheated a poor, hardworking innkeeper."

I had paid the innkeeper many times over, him and whoever else had plundered my possessions while I was unconscious. The silver buttons on my jacket and pants were gone. So were my silver belt buckle and cigarro case.

Smart people, no? I should have thought of it myself: One button alone would have provided a fine meal and night's lodging without the necessity of being beaten by a mob. Now the law was marching me to jail, my hands bound behind my back, a rope lashed to one ankle, its other end to the taller constable's wrist. If I tried to run, he would jerk the rope and drop me like a vaquero toppling a tethered steer. Then his partner would club me into unconsciousness.

We passed few people on the street because it was dark. For that I was thankful. When we arrived at the jail, the constables tied my ankle-rope to an iron ring and stepped aside. I watched curiously as each pitched a copper coin at a line scratched on the floor a dozen feet away.

The winner was the short, stocky unkempt constable. Grinning at me, he sat on a bench and began pulling off one of his boots. "Take your boots off."

"Why?"

"I won them."

I stared at him like the innkeeper had stared at me when I told him I had no money. "You can't win my boots, you puta-bastardo."

He swung his truncheon at me but I was ready for him. Slipping under his swing, I rammed him with my head. But even as he toppled backward, his partner was yanking my ankle rope, causing my left leg to shoot straight up in the air and my body to flip forward. Standing on the back of my neck, the tall constable immobilized me until his companion found his own feet and clubbed me into submission.

With pain in a dozen places and sure all the bones in my body were broken, I lay still and bleeding as my boots were removed and the silver trim stripped from my breeches.

I was barefoot and coatless when they led me into the cell block. Clanging a pipe against the iron bars, they summoned a trustee from the cells below.

Shaken, bleeding, knees trembling, I asked the taller of the two constables, "All this over a plate of frijoles and tortillas?"

He shook his head. "You'll hang for the murder of Bruto de Zavala."

"Murder? You're mad."

"He poisons a man and says you're crazy!" his partner howled.

A trustee arrived. They unshackled my hands, unfastened the ankle-rope to my ankles, and opened the iron-barred gates.

"Lighten him up for the hangman," the constable wearing my boots said, shoving me through the gate. "He prefers them thin so their necks don't break with the fall."

The trustee led me down a dark, dank, stone-walled corridor. He stopped before opening a second gate. He was a mestizo with an unkempt beard and a dead eye.

"Have any dinero?"

I stared at him, mute, expressionless.

"Coppers, anything?" he asked.

"Your thieving friends took it."

"Then give me your pants."

I swelled with rage. "Touch my pants and I'll kill you."

He just stared at me for a moment, no real expression on his face. Then he nodded.

"First time in jail. You'll learn . . . You'll learn."

He let me pass peacefully, then banged me on the back of my head with his fist. I staggered forward and turned to defend myself but he had closed the gate with him on the other side.

"I know who you are," he said. "I saw you prancing down the street on your great white horse, proud like a king. I stepped into the gutter to beg the price of a cup of pulque." His voice became a hoarse whisper. "Without even glancing at me, you lashed out with your whip." He touched his face. A scar ran down his brow and onto his cheek. The whip had struck his eye, blinding him. "You'll learn," he said.

As he turned away, I gripped the bars and shouted at his back. "I don't have a white horse!"

He spoke without turning, and I barely caught his words.

"You're all the same."

I stood for a moment, gripping the bars, hanging on for support, my knees weak, my stomach volcanic with fear. Behind me was another dark stone-walled room. I pushed away from the bars and took steps down to a chamber ill lit by a single candle. I made out men, perhaps twenty of them—indios, mestizos, all poor trash and stinking léperos—some sleeping on the bare stone floor, others standing up. The place stank of sweat, piss, feces, and vomit. Some were half-naked; others wore foul and dirty rags.

A group of five or six gathered before me, vultures looking for carrion. One stepped forward, a husky indio, short but broad. I remained two steps up, the commanding heights.

"Give me your pants," he said.

I stared at him for a moment, then looked beyond him. As he glanced over his shoulder, I lashed out with my foot, my heel hammering his chin. I heard the crack of his jaw and teeth. He staggered backward and went down, banging his head on the stone floor.

I stepped down, into that pit of hell. The flocking vultures broke up and backed off. Finding a space against a wall, I sat on the floor, my back against the wall. I leaned back and watched the man I had hit. He had gotten into a sitting position, holding his face, the fight gone out of him. Another man eyed him . . . for what? A piece of food he had hidden? For his filthy, ragged pants? Or just the notion that he *might* have something?

Animals, I thought. *They're animals.* I knew I must never show fear or weakness around them.

I couldn't keep my eyes open. I was exhausted and aching, stunned by hunger and fatigue. My eyes burned, my head throbbed.

He poisoned a man . . .

How did such an insane accusation come about? How could they accuse me of poisoning Bruto? What possible—

¡Dios mío! I realized what must have happened. Bruto had sent me brandy, which I had returned, saying it was a gift from my own stock. There was poison in the brandy!

In an attempt to poison me, Bruto had poisoned himself.

It thundered at me like the charge of a bull. Bruto had raised me for a single purpose: to ensure his management of an estate that brought him money and prestige. As long as I devoted myself to horses and whores—and delegated my finances to him—his life's dream was secure. And then I threatened to take it all away from him.

Just the night before, I had told him in the heat of anger I was seizing control of my assets, dismissing him. I didn't mean those words; I had no intention of acting on them, but he didn't know that.

Bruto would lose everything he'd worked for. I owned the quicksilver license, the hacienda, and the house in town. If he had any assets of his own, I didn't know of them.

More pieces fell into place. Years ago he had had me sign a will in which he was my heir. The document had meant nothing to me, I had signed it without even reading it. But he would have lost that status when I married Isabel.

And the seminary school he sent me to in my youth . . . no wonder he tried to turn a born rogue into a man of the cloth. Had I become a priest and never married, he would have remained my sole heir and had a free rein forever over my assets.

He had tried to poison me with the gift of brandy—and ended up drinking it himself when I returned it.

Bruto had been slain by his own hand.

I started to get up from the jail floor, anxious to dispel the charge that I had poisoned my uncle. I sat back down. Who was I to tell? The snoring indio sleeping off too much pulque on my right? The lépero dog I had kicked in the face? The trustee who imagined that I had blinded his eye?

I would wait till mañana. I knew nothing about the law, but I understood that the viceroy didn't hang men until they were tried. Wasn't I entitled to an abogado, a lawyer? I wasn't sure of exactly how they did their work, but I knew lawyers advised people and spoke for them in court.

Regardless, now I knew the truth, and I would have a chance to explain it. The world was reasonable, was it not?

Once I was out of this jail I would . . . I shook the thought off like a dog shaking off water. I had no idea of what I would do, where I would go. *Isabella!* I did have her, one true unswerving friend who would help me. When she learned of my plight, she would come to my aid.

Like most women, she had no money of her own, but out of love for me, I was sure she would pawn her jewels. The loss of fortune and the accusations against me, including the foul lie that I had impure blood, would shock her at first, but her love for me would prevail.

The realization that I had someone who cared for me outside the stone walls of the prison buoyed my spirits. I was certain that Isabella would charge to my rescue with the same passion that the French girl Joan once led an army.

TWELVE

THE GRAY LIGHT of morning filtered through small, barred windows high up on the stone wall. The windows were large enough to let in night's cold, damp air but too small to air out the stench. Three latrine buckets lined against a wall. The buckets smelled no worse than the men around me.

I spent a bad night on the hard stone floor, awakening over and over, cold, miserable, in pain. In the light of dawn, I saw that it wasn't a single chamber. One end had a small, barred cell, big enough for two men to stretch out in. A young Aztec occupied it alone. He pulled a loaf of bread and a bottle of wine from a basket.

"Who's that?" I asked a nearby man.

"The son of a cacique," he said.

A cacique was the headman—in the old days literally the chief—of an indio village. With a little fast dealing, the heads of large villages could acquire significant fortunes.

"He stabbed another man. His family keeps him well. He'll leave soon."

I got the idea. His family paid the guards and trustee to make life comfortable for the man until he received the "justice" that his family could afford to pay.

The prisoners began forming a line into the corridor leading out of the cell.

"What's the line for?" I asked a mestizo.

"Food."

I got in behind him. My stomach was in knots. I wasn't hungry, but I needed to keep up my strength.

"When do we see our abogado?" I asked.

He stared stupidly at me.

"An abogado who will defend us, when do we see one?"

He shrugged. I realized he didn't know what I was talking about. He probably didn't know what a lawyer was. I would have to wait and ask the guards.

"How do you get a message out?" I asked an indio behind me. I had to let Isabella know I was being held.

"Dinero," he said.

"I have no money."

He nodded down. "You have pants."

True, not only did I have pants, and some of the men did not, but even after being stripped of silver, my pants were of high quality. But I would give up my life before my pants.

The one-eyed trustee was at a small table at the front of the line. He slopped a watery corn gruel into clay bowls. Two guards stood talking and smoking nearby.

I stepped out of line and approached them. "Señors, I need your assistance. I—"

"Get back in line!"

They grabbed their truncheons.

I backed up. "I just need to ask—"

"In line or you go to the stocks."

"Shut up," the other one said, when I started to speak again. "Prisoners speak only when spoken to."

"Madness," I muttered, back in line.

"It is not so bad, señor," someone behind me said. "They'll feed us, then we'll work cleaning the streets. After a few days, they let us go."

They would not let me go after a few days, not a man accused of murdering an important man, a gachupine. But I said nothing to the indio, who had probably been scraped off the street for public drunkenness.

When I came up to the table, I picked up a clay bowl and held it out for the half-blind trustee to fill with the gruel. The concoction looked disgusting, a thin, slimy, yellow liquid.

The trustee gave me a toothless grin. And poured the ladle of gruel on my pants. I hit him with the bowl, breaking it across the side of his head. As I came around to hit him with my fists, I knocked over the pot of gruel. I saw the guards approaching and backed up, throwing my hands in the air.

"He attacked me!" I yelled.

They clubbed me to the ground.

I was dragged back into the guard area, my hands chained behind me, to a set of triple stocks, a heavy wooden frame with holes for the head, hands, and ankles. They had me sit on a small stool behind the stocks. They opened the contraption and put my ankles in first, bolted a wood yoke over them. After locking my wrists and my neck into another yoke, I was entrapped in all three areas. Then they kicked the stool out from under me. My body weight bent my neck, almost to the breaking point.

"We'll remove the neck stock in an hour if you keep your mouth shut. Open it again, and it goes back on, and it'll stay there until your neck is stretched as long as your leg."

THIRTEEN

M*IERDA!"* I YELLED.

"Eh, how true, how true," the trustee said. "The excrement from animals, isn't that what you call us, Señor Caballero? Those of us who eat frijoles and tortillas and live in huts you wouldn't use for your horses?"

After two days in the stocks, certain that I was permanently deformed into the shape of a horseshoe, I was sent back to the cell, to the tender ministrations of the cyclops trustee. My first assignment was to empty the excrement from the three latrine buckets into a barrel, which was hauled away and dumped somewhere outside the city. After emptying their foul contents, I had to scrape the buckets clean with a spoon and rinse them with a little water.

María, Madre de Dios, have mercy on me! The stench, the filth. The closest I had ever gotten to a bucket of excrement in my life was using a chamber pot that the servants kept clean and fresh.

I had to lug three buckets at one time, two of them awkwardly with one hand. As I staggered under the weight, the two that were unbalanced slopped and spilled, splashing onto my bare feet.

Outside, by the jail's back entrance, I emptied the buckets into a waste barrel sitting in a donkey cart while a nearby guard watched. Using a wooden spoon, I scraped the sides of the buckets, poured a little water in them, splashed it around, and poured the slop into the barrel. I used dirt to wipe the splash off my feet and hands.

Two men came by, well-dressed merchants, no doubt on their way to visit a government office as my uncle frequently had done. I had seen one of them before, the manager of a mine who purchased quicksilver through my uncle, but I didn't know his name. Giving me a wide berth, they placed handkerchiefs over their noses. The man I had met before glanced at me, perplexed, as if he thought he knew me.

I said nothing because a guard stood by, musket at the ready. I'm sure if I had spoken to the two men he would have butt-stroked the back of my head.

Three days after I was released from the stocks, another unruly prisoner relieved me of bucket duty. The guards then lined me up with the other prisoners to meet an official.

The official sat behind a small, crude desk and made notes on paper with quill and ink as he spoke to each of us in turn. Finally, it was my turn.

"Name."

"Juan de Zavala. Are you my attorney?"

He looked up at me. "You have money?"

"No."

"Then you have no attorney."

"Who are you?"

He sniffed a nosegay, a scented pouch that relieved the smell of me and the other prisoners. "Your tone is offensive, but I know who you are. I've been warned about you. A murderous Aztec who once masqueraded as a gentleman. You're here because you killed a man who'd befriended you."

He had an empty look, cold and unfeeling, a piece of stone with no marks on it.

"None of that's true. Please hear my side of it. I'm innocent, but no one will listen."

"Shut up and answer my questions. I'm a notario, my job is to take your explanation of why you committed the crime. It will be presented to the judges of the audiencia. They will decide your fate."

A notary was a clerk who legalized papers, gave oaths, performed clerical duties of filing governmental papers, and took statements from those charged with crimes. They were typically criollos, which, given the dominance of gachupines in New Spain, meant they were not of great importance. However, at this moment, the man was as crucial to my survival as the musket at my shoulder when I faced a charging jaguar.

"Will I be permitted to speak to them? The judges? To tell them what happened?"

He waved away my questions with his hand. "I will report to them, and they will decide how to proceed. New Spain is a nation of laws, and the courts are just, but you'll taste the whip end of the system if you're a troublemaker. I'm informed by the jailors that you're a violent man who wreaks violence even in jail."

"More lies. I am the victim here, not the aggressor. If there's justice in this world, let God be my witness." I made the sign of the cross. "Señor Notario, I'm innocent. I didn't poison my uncle. He tried to poison me and poisoned himself by mistake."

His eyebrows went up. "Some of that shit you have waded in has gone to your brain. Do I not look white to you? Do you take me for a fool or an indio? How could he have poisoned himself?"

"Please, señor, listen to me. José, his servant, brought me brandy the night before my uncle died. We had had an argument earlier, and I had threatened to seize control of my own money. The brandy was a gift of conciliation. It was fine brandy, from a supply my uncle kept for himself."

"Bruto de Zavala was not your uncle, and you are not a gachupine. You have no money, no estate, no right or claim to any estate. You are an imposter, an Aztec or mixed blood who tricked an old man into believing you were his nephew."

"That's ridiculous. I was raised from childhood to believe I was a Zavala. I was one year old when my parents died, and I inherited their estate. Bruto made up this lie about my parentage because—"

"It was not your rightful inheritance. You were an imposter. Bruto discovered your deception, and you killed him to keep the fraud hidden. He exposed your true identity on his deathbed."

This notario had fewer brains than the intoxicated indios who had been brought here from the gutters outside pulquerías. How could a babe in arms be an imposter and trick a grown man? I wanted to shake some sense into him and beat the arrogance out of his voice, but I had already found that fists alone did not suffice in jail.

"Señor Notario, please listen, even if what you say is true—that I'm not Juan de Zavala—that still doesn't prove me a murderer. If Bruto brought me in as a changeling to claim the estate, when he thought I was going to take control of the money, he sent me the brandy—"

"His servant said *you* sent Don Bruto the brandy, that soon after he drank it, he became ill. The doctor examined the dregs of the brandy left in the goblet, he could smell the poison."

"My uncle—"

"He was not your uncle."

I took a deep breath. "Bruto de Zavala, the man who claimed to be my uncle, sent the brandy to me, I sent it back—"

"Eh, so you admit you killed him by sending him poisoned brandy."

He began to write frantically, dipping the quill in the pot of ink repeatedly as his hand flew across the paper. I stared down at the paper in complete puzzlement. The man was estúpido, an ignoramus. How could he conclude such nonsense?

When he was finished, he turned the paper around, so the bottom of the page was in my direction. "Sign here."

"What am I signing?"

"Your confession."

I shook my head. This miserable little maggot of a criollo clerk, a week ago had he brushed me on the street, I would have sent him tumbling into the gutter and stepped on his face.

I leaned forward, and he rocked back in his chair, grabbing his nosegay. "You stink worse than any of the others."

"The only thing I confess, señor, is that I have squashed barn mice with my foot that have more brains than you. What do I look like to you? A—"

"You look like a filthy creature who murdered a gachupine. One who will hang for his crimes."

I was still boiling with anger and disappointment when I was returned to the cell, angry at the fool, angry at myself. I was foolish to have threatened the notary, foolish to have lost control, a folly that has plagued me all my life. I would need more than brute aggression to escape this place alive.

When I returned to the jail chamber, a newcomer had commandeered the private cell, recently vacated by the cacique's son, whose crimes the facile touch of dinero had scrubbed clean.

I recognized the man immediately, not his name, but his status: Like the notary, he was both a criollo and some sort of clerk, scholar, or lower-level government employee. His clothing lacked a caballero's splendor. His hands were meant more for quills and paper, books and ledgers than for horses and pistols. Most important, however, was his food basket.

Did I mention that I was hungry? I had lost weight in jail because of the putrid corn gruel. The more I ate, the more it chewed on my intestines and flushed through my bowels.

I stepped into his cell and sat down beside him, grinning at his startled expression.

"Amigo, I am Don Juan de Zavala, gentleman and caballero. I will consent to share your lunch."

I grabbed a big turkey leg and clamped my teeth into it.

He jumped up. "I'm calling the guards."

With my free hand, I reached up and grabbed the crotch of his pants, getting his two little cojones in my fist.

"Sit down before you lose your manhood." I gave them a squeeze that caused his eyes to bulge.

As soon as he was seated, I nudged him with my elbow. "You hear my voice, see my mannerisms. Like you, I am a gentleman."

"You smell worse than rotting meat."

"A fallen gentleman. Look." I nodded at the prisoner chamber outside the bars of the small cell. "What do you see?"

His eyes bulged more, and his jaw went slack. Prisoners, the worse street trash, had gathered before the cell.

"They know you're not strong," I told him. "You smell the jail stink on them, and they smell fear and weakness on you. They're a pack of wild animals who will devour you whole. You can call the guards, and the guards will beat me and a few others, but the animals will come for you in the night, when it's dark and the guards are asleep."

I nudged him again. "Do you understand, señor? I can protect you. I can keep the animals from eating your liver." I took a big bite of turkey leg. I spoke as I chewed it, the savory juices running down my chin. I'd forgotten what real food tasted like. "You feed me, and I protect you."

He looked at me askance, his facial expression shouting that he did not know what was worse, me or the pack of wild men.

I grinned at him as I chewed the succulent meat. "It's not a match made in heaven, but I will be your friend." I grabbed the wine bottle from the basket, uncorked it with my teeth, and spat out the cork. "But if you prefer to battle this rabid pack of baying hounds yourself . . ."

He stared through the bars at the beasts of prey. They settled onto their haunches and stared back, transfixed by his food and drink. My new-found friend turned pale enough for a trip to the grave.

 **FOURTEEN**

MY CELLMATE'S NAME was José Joaquín Fernández de Lizardi. He was thirty-two years old, born in Méjico City. Although his parents were criollos and claimed to be closely allied with the city's most affluent families, they themselves were not wealthy. As it is said about those of modest means with connections to wealthy families, their heads are in the clouds and their feet in the mud.

His mother was the daughter of a bookseller from Puebla, his father a physician in Méjico City. Most doctors were criollos because it was a profession not highly esteemed, although those who had a reputation as healers could earn a comfortable living. Many people preferred barbers when they needed leaching or bleeding. And, of course, most surgery was performed by barbers.

I knew of his kind immediately. He was a "Don Nadie," which meant a "Señor Nobody," a criollo from a family with Spanish faces but without significant property. Not poor, certainly, but not of hacendado and caballero status either. They probably owned a small, open carriage pulled by a single horse—unlike the grand, gilt carriages that carried people of quality—and would more likely live in a modest, two-story house, walled, with a small courtyard in front, managing with but a single servant.

They would not sit at the viceroy's table and would not ascend to high rank in the Spanish royal forces or even the militia. They would never own government monopolies on government-controlled products or services, licenses that manipulate prices, markets, and the supply of those goods and services. People like his parents were New Spain's shopkeepers, teachers, small ranchers, priests, petty bureaucrats, and comprised the lower ranks of our officer corps. Their sons—at least those who failed to follow them into shopkeeping or failed at the priesthood—were sometimes letrados, learned young men, scholars like the one I sat next to in this jail cell, a man of book learning but no common sense.

When he told me what led to his arrest, I asked, "A pamphlet? You are in jail for something you wrote? How could one be arrested for something written on paper?"

Lizardi shook his head. "You are singularly ignorant. Have you not heard of the Revolution of '89, the revolt during which the French killed the king and made themselves a republic? Or the Revolution of 1776, the year of my birth, when the norteamericanos revolted against the British king and made themselves independent? Do you know nothing of politics, of the rights of people, of the wrongs perpetrated against them?"

"You confuse indifference with ignorance. I know of those things. I just don't care about politics and revolutions, which are concerns of fools and bookworms like yourself."

"Ah, señor, your disinterest only confirms your ignorance! It is because of your kind that tyrants rule and wrongs are not righted."

And so it went. Lizardi was university-educated, conversant in Latin and Greek, philosophers and kings, and yet knew nothing of life. He knew the rights of man but not the rites of man. He was a bad shot, a terrible horseman, and an even worse swordsman. He could not play the guitar, serenade a señorita, and ran from fights with his tail between his legs.

His only courage flowed from his quill onto paper, bleeding India ink instead of crimson blood. He hemorrhaged pamphlets full of poems, fables, dialogues, moral lectures, and politics. In the end, his writing landed him in jail.

"I wrote a criticism of the privileges the gachupines enjoy and the viceroy's tolerance of the situation. We criollos are blocked in our ambitions in every direction. The gachupines come here from Spain, and they are little more than provisional guests. When they leave their families at home, they remain only to sow bastards and reap riches. They usurp high office in our government, universities, army, and the church. They plunder our trades, mines, and haciendas, sneering at criollos the entire time.

"The reason for the system has nothing to do with purity of blood. The Spanish crown wants incontestable control over the colony, that's all. Why else is New Spain denied the right to raise olives for oil and grapes for wine? Why are we forbidden to fabricate the tools we use? We are forced to buy products from Spain even if we can make them cheaper here."

Eh, listening to his complaints reminded me that I, too, once wore and wielded the sharp spurs.

"I poured my thoughts into writing and published a pamphlet in Méjico," Lizardi said, referring to the capital. "I challenged the viceroy, demanding that he remedy these inequities by banning gachupine oppression and decreeing that no one be allowed to come from Spain to seek their fortune unless they plan to remain. I demanded that the colony be allowed to grow and manufacture what it needs and to compete with Spanish products, exporting them even to Spain itself.

"Of course, the viceroy spurned my ideas. When I learned officers from the audiencia sought my arrest, I fled the city. They caught me here in Guanajuato this morning. Traitors informed on me."

"You were recognized?"

"No, I still had many pamphlets left. Informants spotted me, and I was arrested distributing them."

"Ah! And you call me ignorant!" I scratched myself.

"Why do you itch so much?" he asked.

I picked a louse off my ankle. "This hombre finds me appetizing. You will feed his brothers tonight."

"What are you doing in here?" he asked. "I can see that despite your ignorance and arrogance you have the speech and manner of a caballero. What crime did you commit?"

"Murder."

"Ah, of course, an affair of the heart. Did you kill the woman or her lover?"

"I'm accused of killing my uncle."

"Your uncle? Why would you—" He stared at me. "Ay de mío! I know who you are. You're that rogue, Zavala."

"You've heard of me? Tell me, what have you heard?"

"That you're an imposter, that you pretended to be a gachupine, convincing an old man you were his nephew, then killing him for his money."

"Eh, did you hear that I also raped nuns and stole from orphans?"

"You did those crimes, too?"

"I committed no crimes, you fool. I'm the victim. You claim to have some knowledge of books and right and wrong, tell me if you have ever read anything as unjust as this." I gave him my sad tale of being accused of existing as a changeling, of being raised to believe I was a Zavala, of the horrible events of late.

Lizardi listened quietly, intently, interjecting a question only occasionally. When I was finished explaining how Bruto had managed to poison himself, he shook his head.

"I write fables, using the fantastic characters to emphasize my points, but indeed, Juan de Zavala, I don't believe that anything I have ever written is as astounding as your true life." He paused and frowned at me. "If it is true."

"I swear on the grave of the whore who, as they say, bore and sold my body that it is true."

"Actually, I believe you. You're not intelligent enough to create such a provocative tale."

A week ago I would have offered this bookish buffoon his choice of weapons and forced him onto the field of honor for a final reckoning. But with so much folly staring me in the face, I could no longer maintain the pretense of my honor. And I had become a dog, eating his scraps.

The trustee entered the chamber carrying a food basket and a mattress of straw held together with a cotton cover. He came to the small cell, set down the basket and dropped the mattress.

"I already have a mattress," Lizardi said.

He nodded at me. "It's for the *caballero*." He used the word sarcastically.

I jumped to my feet. "How am I entitled to this treasure? Has the viceroy realized the error of the Guanajuato authorities and sent me a gift?"

"The only thing the viceroy will send you is a taut noose to break your neck so the hangman doesn't have to drop the trap twice." He gestured at what he delivered. "A servant brought these and a little for the jailers but refused to divulge your benefactor's name. But Don Murderer, even a lowly mestizo like me can infer your benefactor is a woman. Only a woman would be so stupid."

¡Ay María! I knew it! Isabella sent the mattress and food basket. No one else loved me as much as she. Bruto was wrong; Isabella was not the vain, silly girl he said she was. My fall from grace would mortify her parents, but the gifts proved beyond trivialities the redemptive grace of her love. I was eternally relieved, because I, too, had doubted her, wondering if the unkind words I had heard from Bruto and others were true. Now I knew that they had played me false. My darling Isabella would free me from this hellhole, and I would again ride beside her coach on the paseo.

I lay on my new straw mattress, my stomach sated, my thirst appeased with wine, and belched. Lizardi lay nearby but turned the other way, claiming that my stench would knock a buzzard off a meat wagon.

My eyes were closed, and I was fading when Lizardi whispered: "You're wrong about the notary."

"What?"

"He wasn't ignorant."

"How could he believe that as a babe I tricked a grown man?"

"The story the notary told you—that you're a fraud and trickster—was the same story told at the inn where I stayed. People talked about nothing else. Everyone talked about how you had tricked Don Bruto into believing you were his nephew—"

"I was a baby!"

"So you keep saying, but the story I heard was word-for-word what the notary spoke."

"The story is probably the work of my cousins who covet my money. I must get out of jail and let the world know what happened."

"You still don't understand. The alcalde and the corregidor, two of the most powerful gachupines in the city, were present at your uncle's deathbed, were they not?"

"What are you saying?"

"The notary repeated a tale spread by the city officials. Who ordered them to spread the lie? The governor? The viceroy?"

I sat up. "Tell me why the governor and viceroy would spread this slander?"

"Gachupines, Spain-born Spaniards—whatever you want to call them—control the colony. If I accept your story as true, you passed as a gachupine for more than twenty years. Everyone around you, including the Zavala family itself, accepted you as one of them. If the tale is true, you are not a gachupine, or even a criollo. You're a lowly peon, yet the gachupines accepted you as one of their own.

"Don't you see the predicament you've created for the viceroy, for all the gachupines of the colony? They claim to be superior to everyone else: Mestizos and indios are little more than farm animals; even criollos—pure-blooded Spaniards—are not fit to govern. But *a peon has been accepted as a gachupine*, not just as a Spaniard but as a caballero who was admired as a gentleman-knight of the colony. Your life belies everything they stand for."

I sat up and stared at Lizardi, who was barely visible in the flickering candlelight. "I don't wish to destroy them. I am a gachupine. I only want a chance to explain."

"You thick-headed fool, don't you understand? They don't want to hear your story or have anyone else hear it. To protect their positions, keeping the people in fear of them, they can't be the subject of laughter."

"Is that what I am? A cause for amusement?"

Lizardi sighed and lay back down. "No, you're a threat."

"I've done nothing to them."

"If you are lucky, they will kill you or pay someone to cut your throat. To hide you here until you are old, gray, and your brain is soft as the rancid gruel, that fate would be worse. But either way, they can't release you. They can battle rebellion, force us to buy their crooked plows and rotten wine, throw truth-tellers like me in jail, but the one affront they cannot abide is ridicule. We Spaniards are proud, whether we are born in Madrid or Méjico City. To laugh at us is to turn our machismo lethal."

I spoke quietly, little more than a whisper, as if the walls had ears. "You're right. No one could be as dull-witted as that notary was. The confession he wrote out was concocted in advance. He will lie, say that they were my words he transcribed and that I confessed to the crimes they accuse me of. You are right, amigo. They'll kill me."

"And bury the truth."

We were silent for a moment, and then I said, "I was wrong about you, Señor Lizardi. You know little about horses and women, guns and blades, but I now see that men kill as thoroughly with paper and quill as with pistol and sword."

I listened quietly for a reply until I realized he was softly snoring.

Ay, some of the insanity made sense. My life was no longer spinning down a maelstrom of madness. No, Lizardi had spoken the truth. The notary was not a fool but had told the story *on orders*. No doubt his masters would send others like him to inns, social gatherings, and card games to spread the lie. They'll start by assassinating my character. When they've succeeded, they'll take my life.

How could I defend against them? No doubt they thought of me as soft, that I would break in this hellhole of a jail, but unlike most caballeros, I rode and worked alongside the vaqueros at my hacienda. I enjoyed a life in the saddle: breaking mounts, herding cattle, gelding bulls, branding steers, fording rivers. I spent many months each year on the open range and in mountains, hunting and fishing, living off the land. I was not the dandy that they imagined.

But the most pressing question now was how to free myself from this prison-house, find pistol and blade so I could make them pay for their crimes.

 **FIFTEEN**

TWO DAYS LATER another disaster struck.

"I gave my remaining funds to the trustee last night," Lizardi said. "We'll be evicted from our comfortable quarters and have to join—" he sniffed in the rabble's direction, "them."

I had devoured my own basket of food, and no more had come. Lizardi, who had been in jail before, explained that the person sending the food had to know who, as well as how much, to bribe or else the package would end up in the wrong hands. I suspected that Isabella still sent food baskets but did not know the proper way to get them in my hands.

"What about your family?" I asked.

"They're in the capital. I've sent a message. My father detests my politics and has disowned me."

"How many times have you been arrested?"

"Twice. You see, amigo, we're both in the same quandary. They'll bury me alive in their dungeons or slit my gullet. They may try me first, but my fate is assured. Your case, on the other hand, will never see daylight."

As if he had heard our whispers, the trustee suddenly materialized.

"Out of here, you peso-less léperos. The best room at this fine inn has been reserved by another guest."

The new prisoner was a big burly mestizo shopkeeper who was in trouble for cheating on his taxes. He didn't appear to be someone I could bully as easily as Lizardi, so I joined Lizardi in our new home, a space big enough for our rear ends on the floor with the wall against our backs.

Lizardi moaned and buried his head in his arms. "The pity of it, I—a university-educated pure-blood Spaniard—forced to live in filthy conditions among you lowly léperos."

I batted him across the side of the head. "Insult me again, and I'll stick your head in a shit bucket."

But I felt no malice toward the man. I had discovered that he had great courage when it came to speaking ideas, though he was more cowardly than the commonest cur when it came to physical duress. I found his verbal valor and physical timidity a curious combination. I, on the other hand, was brave as a bull but devoid of ideas, philosophies, and burning beliefs. I functioned solely in the here and now, living day by day, taking what I wanted, discarding what I tired of. I had no interest in religion or politics, about colonial governance, divine rights of kings, or whether the pope was the Chosen Hand of God, though I was forced to listen to Lizardi expound for hours on end on these matters. But the pamphleteer had not instilled his ideals in me; I still believed in nothing. And at least now I knew it.

Lizardi was dozing when the trustee came in and ordered all of us to line up. "Road work," he said.

"What's that?" Lizardi asked me, after the trustee left.

"Labor for work animals. The warden rents prisoners out to businesses. We're to work for the contractor who repairs the roads."

"How often do we do this?"

I shrugged. "This is the first time I've been selected."

"I'm a criollo. This is an outrage. I will speak to the jail warden."

"Do that. The more they think about you, the quicker they'll hang you. You'll get a clean rope, of course, because your blood's so white."

A guard shackled my right and left ankles together with a two-foot chain, then fitted Lizardi with leg irons as well. Only Lizardi and I were so restrained. The constabulary had hauled the rest of the prisoners out of the gutter after a night of drinking. They wouldn't run farther than the nearest pulquería.

We were marched single file out of the jail. We stepped into blinding sunlight, and I took in a deep lungful of the fresh air, the first breath I'd tasted in ages that the prison's effluvium hadn't befouled.

I stared at my hands and bare feet: My skin was filthy. ¡Ay de mí! What I must have smelled like. The streets seemed strange to me, though I'd been down them hundreds of times. Now I saw them differently, picking up details I'd never noticed before: the colors brighter, sharper, gaudier than before; the smells more pronounced, more pungent, more distinctive; the people more vivid, more animated, more vibrant.

In the past, I had always been so focused on myself and on my position in life, almost always riding above the crowd on a fine horse, that I hadn't studied the world around—and beneath—me. Now I stared at the people on the street as they moved out of our path and away from our smell. I wondered if they had heard about me, if they had been told the big lie about Juan de Zavala.

I had little respect for the common people, even the respectable ones who were shopkeepers and clerks. Now they would repay me at my execution. Hangings were public spectacles, and they would battle the rabble to watch the trap drop and my neck snap . . . close up.

We were marched to the road that led up to the paseo. A rainstorm had flooded it out, and we were to pave it with cobblestones. Eh, how many times I had come down this road, riding tall on Tempest, saluting the señoritas along the way.

Now I came filthy, barefoot, and in leg irons, my feet raw and sore by the time we reached the street. I tried to ignore the pain and remember those days when I rode as a caballero with a powerful ebony mount beneath me, when I terrified servants, and titillated señoritas who giggled and hid behind Chinese silk fans when I promised to slay Englishmen and dragons for them.

My reverie was interrupted by a shout from the contractor's foreman. He stood before a line of carts loaded with stones. "I'm paying these devils to work, and work they shall. The first time any of them loaf or malinger, they will taste my boots. If I catch them again, they will taste my whip."

Loading the cart's cobblestones into sacks, we lugged them to the worksite at the end of the barricaded street. There, prisoners dug narrow holes and inserted the cobblestones lengthwise into the predug slots. Soon my feet were raw. Lizardi's feet were protected by boots, but his hands, like my feet, were blistered and bloody.

"The hands that held the pen of truth are red with the blood of bondage," he said, wincing.

"Save it for your pamphlets," I muttered.

As I worked, young caballeros on horseback and wealthy señoritas in carriages passed by. I recognized many of them; none, God be praised, recognized the filthy, stinking creature with blistered hands and bleeding feet, staggering under loads of rock, though for a time I stood rooted in shame and shock.

Gawking at my former acquaintances in their fine clothes, riding their handsome horses, I wished I ate as well as their horses . . . until, that is, the foreman kicked me in the shin hard enough to break the skin and bruise the bone. "Get to work, swine!"

Returning to work, my leg bled from where the foreman kicked me. A couple of weeks ago if a man had kicked me, I would have . . . Ay, that had been a different life, a different world.

One night, eons ago, sleeping under the stars with my hacienda's vaqueros, one of them described the Aztec hell, an underworld where people suffered one ordeal after another: swimming raging rivers, crawling among deadly snakes, fighting wars, jungle jaguars, and other brutal tests. He called that hell Mictlán, and I wondered if by some twist of heaven or hell the Aztec gods had plunged me into it.

Mictlán's nine regions of horror and torment must be overcome, the vaquero had said, before a person cast there can find peace. Only after years of transcending torments and enduring ordeals would the person reach the place of oblivion, where a dark god of a nether region would destroy his soul, not so the soul might ascend to heaven but so that it might suffer no more.

Perhaps my fate was to have Mictlán test my resolve with one hideous torment after another, only to find in the end not paradise but eternal night.

 **SIXTEEN**

AS I LUGGED another rock load toward the worksite, a paseo carriage caught my eye, stopping me in my tracks. One of the most expensive open carriages in the city, it conveyed the most beautiful woman on whom I have ever gazed upon.

"Isabella!"

I ran . . . No, I hobbled in leg irons toward the oncoming carriage, shouting her name again and again.

Isabella half-stood in the coach, gaping as I ran toward her. She screamed and fell back down as her driver whipped the horse. The carriage surged forward, toward me, bouncing up the rough unpaved road, throwing Isabella and a señorita sitting across from her about the carriage.

Dodging the horses and carriage, I grabbed hold of the side of the carriage door, stumbling alongside it as it took off. "It's me, Isabella!"

She screamed in horror and hit me with her parasol. A caballero, coming behind the carriage, charged me on horseback. I saw the horse and man coming and let go of the coach. Dodging the horse, my hobbled legs did not move me fast enough to avoid a blow. The rider hit me across the top of my head with the shot-loaded buttstock of his whip as he swept by. I stumbled and fell, almost passing out, hitting the ground hard and rolling, bleeding from the head.

Before I could get up a guard was on me, hitting me with the butt of his musket. I took the beating, in stoic silence, knowing resistance would only exacerbate my punishment. Only when the foreman grabbed the man's musket did the guard desist.

"I'm paying for that man's work. If you cripple him, you must pay me for his lost labor."

With that, I was able to get dizzily to my feet and stagger along with work. And work I did, keeping my head low, ashamed of what I had become, ashamed of what I had done to poor Isabella. No wonder she panicked, fool that I was for charging her carriage like a wild animal. She hadn't recognized me, of that I was certain, for had she known it was me, she would have ordered the driver to stop. After all, had she not sent me rations and a mattress?

Lizardi nudged me. "You're woolgathering. Keep working or you will get another beating."

I knelt on painful bleeding knees and placed rocks in position. As we worked, he spoke to me.

"The señorita, she's your love?"

"Yes, she has captured my heart."

"Captured it and chopped it into little pieces, from what I can see. Along with most of your brains."

I glared at him. "Watch your tongue, señor, or it'll get cut out."

He raised his eyebrows. "I only wonder if your heart's desire is as desirous of you as you are of her. You called out her name, she must have recognized your voice . . . but didn't seem pleased to see you."

"She didn't recognize me." I punched my chest over my heart. "I know this woman; our hearts beat as one. If I asked her, she would fling herself into a den of lions." I sneered at him. "You don't understand, you worthless worm of a scholar. No woman would want you because your cojones are the size of peas."

We trudged back toward the jail, wearily dragging our feet, one step and then the next. Lizardi clutched the back of my pants to keep up. His sedentary scholar's life had not prepared him for hard labor, and while my life had been active, I had been active on a horse. I was not used to hauling and lifting on shank's mare. I left bloody footsteps in my wake.

Lizardi muttered behind me, sometimes praying, sometimes lamenting how la Fortuna, the puta of chance, had weighted the dice against him.

If I had had the energy, I would have mocked his mournful utterances. Eh, if Señora Fortuna had rigged the game of life against anyone, it was Juan de Zavala, no?

Later that afternoon we stopped for a rest, sitting in the gutter, while the guards smoked, drank from wine bodas, and talked to a pair of putas, probably discussing price. I had had one of them a few months ago.

One of the guards broke off negotiations. Unrolling a piece of paper, he read off a dozen names. When he called a prisoner's name, the inmate wandered off down the street. Over half the work crew was released.

"Drunks," I told Lizardi, "serve only three days and are released."

An indio in white cotton pants, a white collarless shirt, and the leather sandals of his class approached me.

"For you, señor."

He dropped a pair of boots in front of me.

"What—?" I stared at the boots in surprise.

"From the señorita," he said, pointing up the street, where a woman wearing a black dress, her head covered by the traditional long scarf, disappeared around a corner.

I asked her name, but the Aztec walked away without answering. I quickly shoved my feet into the boots. The boots were worn but sturdy and finely crafted. Indio tradesmen had hand-worked the deep cinnamon-color leather until it was as soft as a glove, the boots of a caballero, similar to the ones stolen from me at the jail.

The dozing Lizardi woke as I pulled on my boots.

"Where did you get those?"

"You cucaracha of a man, you woman in pants," I said, jovially, no insult intended, for I was in high spirits, "did I not tell you that my Isabella wouldn't forsake me?"

"She brought you boots?"

"A messenger, but I am sure they came from her." I nudged him with my elbow. "My luck is changing; Señora Fortuna has thrown the dice again, and this time I am the winner. Soon I will be out of this jail, a full caballero, all rights restored."

"You are deranged."

I ignored his cynicism. The boots had redeemed my faith in Isabella. In all honesty, the worm of doubt had gnawed at my brain when she failed to recognize me—ay, she hit me with her parasol and screamed—but no, she was my true love, faithful and resolute, ready to throw herself to the lions for me. Although I hadn't seen enough of the woman in black to identify her, no one else in the city would have helped me except my sainted Isabella.

The world suddenly was bright again. I felt stronger and more capable of facing my next hellish ordeal. But I had not considered that the viceroy also spoke in New Spain, in words that the deaf could hear and the blind could see.

 **SEVENTEEN**

YOU'RE BEING SENT to Manila," the notary told me.

It was the next day, and I once again had an audience with him. I stared at him, wondering what he was talking about.

"Manila?"

"Certainly you've had enough education to know where Manila is. It's the capital of our colony called the Philippines."

"I am well aware of where Manila is," I snapped. Actually, all I knew was that the Philippines were somewhere across the vast Pacific Ocean, near Cathay, the land of the chinos. I recalled hearing other things about that colony—all of them bad—but at the moment, my mind had gone blank. The call to appear before the notary had caught me by surprise. To be told I was going to be shipped to another city in a distant land rather than being hanged had stunned me. Perhaps they had discerned my innocence.

"They found out I'm not lying, haven't they?"

He put his nosegay to his face distastefully. "You have caused your betters trouble and consternation. Some wish to try you in court, then hang you. Others wish to turn you over to the Inquisition to be tortured hard and burned at the stake."

"The Inquisition? What have I done against God and the church?"

"You *exist*." He struggled to maintain his composure. "You may thank God that the viceroy is not hanging you and the Inquisitors are not burning you alive . . . after breaking you on the rack."

"I have done nothing wrong," I said stubbornly.

"Get out of here, you swine, before I order you racked, flogged, castrated, and quartered myself."

Lizardi was waiting in line to see the notary.

I whispered to him as I came by, "They're sending me to Manila."

His jaw dropped, and he made the sign of the cross on his chest.

What's wrong with him? I wondered. I got good news, and he acted like I had been sentenced to the holy fires of an Inquisitional auto-da-fé.

I went back to the cell and lay on my straw mattress. Lizardi and I were both back in the small, private cell. Someone—my Isabella, for certain—was again paying for me to have decent food and treatment. I was just as certain that she had arranged my voyage to Manila and that she would meet me there.

When Lizardi came back, he was ghostly white, his face haggard and drawn.

"What's the matter?"

Full of gloom, he crossed himself again. "I've been sentenced to Manila, too."

"So? We were facing the hangman, and we have been saved. Now we can—"

"Are you so stupid?" He collapsed next to me, rubbing his face with his hands.

"What's wrong with Manila?" I demanded.

"It's a death sentence."

I shook my head. "*¡Mierda del toro!* Manila is a Spanish colony like New Spain—"

"No, not like New Spain. A jungle, nine or ten thousand miles from here, a journey that many prisoners never survive. Chained in the ship's sewage-filled hold, the prisoners spend half their time wallowing in bilge, the other half fighting off rats. The survivors are sold into slavery on jungle plantations where fevers, snakes, and spiders kill more men than the Veracruz corridor when the vomito negro lies in wait." He laid back on his straw pad and closed his eyes. "Then there are the wild savages who eat human flesh."

"Something will turn up."

"Our bodies. They will cross the galleon captain's palm with silver, and as soon as the ship leaves port, our throats will be slit and our bodies thrown overboard." He stared at me, terrified. *"We're not meant to survive the voyage."*

I guffawed. "I see you are no longer just a bookworm and pamphleteer of ideas but a tomorrow-teller, like Europe's gypsies."

An india servant who once tended to me when I was small, told me that her people believed the most intelligent creatures in the world were the worms that burrowed in books. I had never seen a bookworm, but this was how I viewed Lizardi, as a worm of knowledge.

"Juan, you don't understand guile because you were raised in a silk cocoon here in Guanajuato, cosseted by money and consumed solely by your desires. You've never dealt with the politics of the capital, where the viceroy and the archbishop have dissenters strangled in their cells at night."

He sat up and locked eyes with me. "They have to get rid of us, can't you see that? They don't want either of us to have a public trial, to give me a forum to criticize their corrupt regime, to suffer the embarrassment of your acceptance as a gachupine. What better way to get rid of us than a sentence to Manila? Everyone knows no one returns from the exile. And if we die en route to those distant islands . . . not an eyebrow would be raised."

My instincts were screaming that he was right. They would cut our throats and feed us to the fishes before we were a league out to sea.

It was a death sentence, not a reprieve.

"Señor," I said, "we are doomed."

He nodded. "You are finally beginning to understand life in New Spain."

EIGHTEEN

SEVEN MORE DAYS passed, each one an agony of hard labor. My mysterious benefactor, whom I knew in my heart was Isabella, financed my private cell and sustenance. Lizardi still had not heard from his family, and I shared the bounty with him, telling him that I considered him the brother I never had, that I was repaying him for having shared his with me. These statements were not exactly true; he had only shared with me out of fear that I would harm him, and had the worm been my brother, I would have arranged a mortal accident for him. I shared with him because I knew in time he would be up again and I would be down. Eh, Don Juan the Caballero was learning to scheme like prison scum.

I could not truly love Lizardi as a brother because he carried a sense of racial superiority about him: He was a Spaniard and I was a peon. I still did not think of myself as of the lower classes—I was certain that I was indeed the real Juan de Zavala and that my uncle, in his final illness, had contrived the changeling story in revenge for the poisoning. As he lay dying, no doubt he assumed I had deliberately poisoned him.

Lizardi's attitude rankled me. He was especially contemptuous of my intelligence, conveying at every turn that I was intellectually inferior. Sometimes he treated me as if I were a naughty child, too immature for serious thought. It wasn't lost on me that I had treated my servants in the same way.

As the days went by, my hands, feet, and muscles hardened from the work. Thick shoulder and thigh muscles, and hard hands that evinced hard labor were unfashionable among caballeros. A slim silhouette on horseback was the fashion.

We had returned from a day's work and were finishing off my food and wine basket, when the trustee called Lizardi out. The trustee spoke to him privately. As Lizardi returned to our cell, I could see in the distance he was grinning, but when he approached the cell, he wiped the grin off his face and frowned.

"What news did you get?" I asked the worm.

"My family has forsaken me. We are doomed to the Manila galleon."

I patted his arm. "As long as we go together, it is all right with me. I have come to think of you as the brother I never had. To share death with my brother would be fitting."

He was a rotten liar. His news had been good, but he didn't want to share it with me. The only good news I could think of was that he had arranged some way to avoid the Manila death sentence, perhaps by betraying me in some manner. He was a puzzlement to me: a man with the courage to offend the viceroy and church with fiery words but a physical coward.

I waited until late at night, when the only sounds were the snores and mutterings of other prisoners, before I made my move. I held him down and gagged him to keep him from shouting. I pinched his nose shut so he couldn't breathe. When he started turning purple, I released his nose.

"If you make a noise, I'll smother you. ¿Comprénde?"

Still holding him pressed down, I whispered, "Mi amigo, you hurt my feelings when you lie to me. You received good news and yet you deceived me. Now I must hurt you." Holding him down with an elbow, I took an insect out of a jar that a fruit spread had come in. I dropped it in his ear. He began to wiggle and squirm. I let him turn over and slapped the side of his head to dislodge the insect. It fell out and scrambled away.

"Do you know what that was, worm? The kind of vermin that burrows into your ear and into your brain. I have a jar full of them. Now tell me what the trustee said, or I will pour them into your ears and let them eat your brains."

I was certain I saw the whites of his eyes even in the darkness. I almost broke out laughing. I loosened the gag and let him catch his breath.

"What good news do you have? Your father has agreed to help you?"

"Sí, but—"

"*Shhh*, not too loudly. What's being done?"

"Another will take my place."

"Who?"

"It doesn't matter. One of these disgusting creatures will be José Lizardi for a day. He will be paid, I will replace him."

I nodded. "Ah, you will exchange places. He will be put on a wagon for Acapulco and the Manila galleon, you will be sent to work in the streets. At the end of the day, you will be released as an ordinary drunk who has fulfilled three days of work. That is it, no?"

"Sí."

I released him.

"You are a disgusting animal," he groaned, digging at his ear. "You are violent and dangerous. I truly believe you murdered the man who thought he was your uncle."

"Believe this, señor—I will murder you if you betray me again."

"How have I betrayed you?"

"Have I not protected you? Shared my bounty with you? Thought of you as my own blood and brother?"

"I'm not your brother. I'm a criollo, not a peon."

"Keep slandering my blood and you'll be a dead criollo. We'll see what color your blood is as it gushes out your throat."

"I can bring the trustee down on you with one shout."

"That's all you would be able to do. And it would be your last shout be-cause I'll rip out your tongue." I leaned closer. "And gouge out your eyes with my thumbs."

"Animal," he muttered.

"Have you thought about what you will do on the street? You can bribe your way out of a jail, but where will you go once you have your freedom? Fool that you are, you wouldn't make it out of the city."

"I'll make it."

I could tell from his voice that he had doubts. "You will be freed at dusk. Do you think you can stay in an inn for the night and leave the city the next day? You're a stranger in town, you'll be easily spotted by the constables. You can't escape without a horse. And you don't know the city well enough to escape even if you had a horse. I have horses here in the city, ready and waiting."

He was quiet for a long time. Then he asked, "What do you want?"

"Fund both of our escapes. I will see you well mounted and put you on the road to Méjico."

"And if I refuse?"

"I kill you."

My tone surprised me and chilled Lizardi. It left no doubt I would go through with the threat.

In the shadow of the gallows, life seemed less sacred.

"José de Lizardi! Juan de Zavala!"

Two léperos stood in front of me, and I jabbed them each in the back, whispering "That's you two."

They had been lifted out of the gutter three days ago. We chose them because the guards would release them today, and even sober, their wits were dim, their vision blurred, their brains befuddled by decades of drink.

In exchange for a few pesos and the promise of much more, including a trip to Méjico City and a tour of its pulquerías they agreed to our take our places. The capital was a fabled place to these two, léperos who had never ventured far from Guanajuato's gutters.

That I was a changeling again did not escape my notice.

I grinned at Lizardi as the men were led out, chained in a tumbrel for the trip to Méjico and from there on to Acapulco and the Manila-bound galleon.

"I hope they like fresh ocean breezes," I said, "and can swim well."

"The jailers at the capital will know they've been duped."

"We'll be on our horses and on our way by then."

A few minutes later, we lined up with the nearly hundred other prison-ers. Since we were assumed to be common drunks, no one slapped leg irons on us.

This time we were dispatched to a pasture outside of town, where the mule trains transporting goods encamped. Mules transported almost all goods, whether imported or exported, throughout the colony. The only other transport system was the backs of indios.

At the pasture, we were to shovel manure into the back of wagons. The manure was hauled to local farmers and rancheros to use as fertilizers. In times past, the stench would have bowled both of us over, but in truth we smelled worse than manure and the fact that this was our last day in hell compensated for the stink.

An hour before darkness, the guards lined us up for the trek back to the city.

"We should return here tonight and steal the mules for our escape," Lizardi whispered to me as we walked.

"I told you, we'll leave on my horses."

"I don't understand how you could still have horses if you—"

"Horses are my specialty. You just think about the next pamphlet you'll write when you return to the capital."

Dusk had fallen by the time we reached the heart of the city. When the guards stopped for a smoke break, Lizardi and I were released with the other drunks.

"Where are we going?" Lizardi asked.

"To a pulquería with this trash. You have pesos the trustee passed you from your family?"

"Yes, but I'm not going to buy that poisonous Aztec drink."

"If an alarm is sounded, a pulquería will be the last place they would look for two Spaniards."

He glanced at me for including myself as a Spaniard but wisely did not correct me. "What about our horses? When do we—"

"After dark, so we won't be spotted on the streets." I slapped him on the back. "Stop asking questions, worm. We are free. Enjoy it. Tomorrow they may catch us and hang us."

We left the pulquería well after nightfall and walked down the deserted streets of the city. Lizardi had been antsy, but I insisted we not leave sooner. The streets where the rich lived were guarded at night by watchmen who walked along carrying a candle in a lantern. While the lantern offered little light, it identified the watchmen as the homeowners who could call for help in case of trouble. The watchmen did not come on duty until ten o'clock. We still had an hour to get to my horses before that time.

"Where are we going?" he whispered. "I still don't understand how you could have horses if everything was taken away from you."

"We're taking them back."

Lizardi stopped cold. "What are you saying?"

"We're going to steal two of my horses."

"Steal? I thought perhaps your woman had arranged horses. I'm not going to steal a horse, that's against the law."

That was a laugh. "I see you would rather be hanged for being a book-worm than a thief."

"I'm not stealing a horse."

"Then adiós, amigo, go your own way."

"You can't abandon me; you said you thought of me as your brother."

"I lied."

"We have pesos. Why not buy two mules?"

"We need good horses, ones that will outrun constables if we're chased. Have you thought about the roads out of town? Unless you travel in a large group, you're easy prey for bandidos. Our horses must outrun them, too. Before I was jailed, I had the finest horses in the city. We are go-ing to my house to get them."

"But they won't let us just walk in and take them. You said your cousins had taken over your house and they hate you."

"They're at the table supping now, attended by servants. Only one man tends to the stable. When night falls, he leaves the house and goes to a pul-quería where more of his kind congregate. The horses will be ours to sad-dle and lead out."

He mumbled a prayer as we continued down the street.

"Have courage, worm. Don Juan de Zavala, gentleman and caballero, will protect and defend you."

 **NINETEEN**

THE LIGHT SHONE from the house's second-floor windows, but, as I pre-dicted, the downstairs was dark. The servants were upstairs attending the swine who stole my property.

I led Lizardi through the back gate to the stable doors as if I owned the property, which in my own mind, I still did. Four horses were inside. Two, which I didn't recognize, probably belonged to my cousins. The other two I knew intimately: Tempest and a smaller gelding I named Brass, after his color.

We saddled my two mounts. At first Tempest shied away from me, stamping from the strange smell I brought with me, but I soon calmed him down with the purr of my voice and a caress of my hand.

I grabbed two machetes from the tack room and a long knife for myself. Pistols and muskets I had kept upstairs in the house, but I kept a bag of black powder hanging in the tack room. I hooked it onto my saddle horn. The only spurs available were vaqueros' iron rowels, which we put on.

I had Lizardi mount first. "I'll lead my horse to open the street gate and close the gate after we get through. Keep your horse at a slow walk on the street. We don't want to attract attention."

I led Tempest to the stable doors and opened them. And stopped in my tracks. A big black mongrel faced me. The beast growled, barked, and came at me with snapping, slavering teeth. Tempest reared up. I couldn't reach my knives to dispatch the cur. The dog backed away from the stallion, but howled loud enough to wake the damned. As I mounted Tempest, the dog continued his barking fang-bared attack. My recurring nightmare about the hounds of hell had reached back and bit me.

I gave Tempest the spurs, and he leaped forward. As we shot out the stable doors, a man came running down the stairs to the house, carrying a musket.

"Stop! Thief!"

He leveled the musket at me, and I jerked the reins, sending Tempest at him. He got out of the way, the musket going off, the ball flying skyward. I turned Tempest and took him to the gate, with the hellhound now snapping at Lizardi. I kicked the street gate open and flew out, struggling to keep control of the stallion. Lizardi suddenly shot out of the gate, the dog barking at the rear hooves of his horse and biting his flanks. Wheeling around, I returned to the cur. Unlimbering a machete, I sent his soul back to hell, where I'm convinced I will meet him again.

Tempest flew down the street, passing Lizardi's horse.

Street dogs by the score began a chorus, like all the banshees in Hades howling to get out. People flocked to doors, porches, and windows. As our horses galloped on the cobblestones, their horseshoes struck sparks, and they barely maintained their footing. I had to pull Tempest in, to keep him from slipping and going down.

Now a second dog, a densely spotted monster big as a mastiff, was giving chase. Leaping up beside me, he missed my leg but bit through the bag of black power. Ripping it open, its contents covered the canine's face, causing the cur to drop back.

I spurred Tempest north out of the city, and Lizardi followed. Behind me I heard him yell, "You son of a whore, this is not the way to Méjico City! You lied to me again. You have no honor! You're a lépero devil!"

Ay, I could see that this was to be my fate in life: to have a hound of hell constantly howling at my heels and to lie my way through life. While the circumstances of my departure from the city had not been entirely to my satisfaction, I had no intention of heading toward the capital. The most heavily traveled road in New Spain, it would also be the most watched. Instead, I headed in the opposite direction.

Besides, our uproarious departure would rouse legions of constables— the human equivalent of hellish hounds—and I was starting to suspect that the worm, like myself, was born under an unlucky star.

.   .   .

We rode a league north by the light of the moon until we were stopped by
the gates of a mining hacienda. I turned us east, and we rode another
league. When the terrain became too dark and rough to risk a fall by a
horse, I told the grumbling Lizardi to halt and bed on the ground with his
horse blanket.

"This ground is harder than the stones we slept on in jail," he whined.
"It's cold, and we have nothing to eat."

"You would complain to St. Pedro about the comforts of heaven." I got
down on my hands and knees and kissed the ground. "This is free
ground—no stocks, chains, floggings, or lice."

"We will be poisoned by snakes and mauled by jaguars."

I shut my ears, lay on my back, and stared up at the night sky, my head
on Tempest's saddle. Unlike Lizardi, I was used to sleeping on hard
ground, having done so on my hunting trips, though I'd always had food in
my stomach and a fire to warm my feet.

As I stared up at the night sky, I said, "Tomorrow is a new day."

"What kind of mindless remark is that? Every day is a new day."

"I have spent the first twenty-five years of my life as Juan de Zavala,
gachupine caballero in the Bajío. Tomorrow I will be someone else, and
who knows where my feet will take me?"

"You will go back to Guanajuato feet first if the king's constables catch
up with us."

DOLORES

OUR DEPARTURE IN the morning put us on the road to the town of Dolores, more than a day's ride northeast of Guanajuato. Dolores lay outside the mining country, but Guanajuato's mountains made the going slow and tedious, oftentimes little more than a narrow path fit for a donkey hugging a sheer drop of hundreds of feet.

Dolores was a slow-paced community of haciendas and rancheros. Its most attractive feature, besides the difficult path out of the Guanajuato mountains making it undesirable for a posse, was that I had no connection to the town.

We stopped at a village of Aztecs where we ate a simple breakfast of beef rolled in corn tortillas.

"This village is part of the Espinoza hacienda," I told Lizardi. "I know Espinoza. He lives in Guanajuato. Two weeks ago, I would have stopped at his hacienda, and his servants would have prepared a feast and a fiesta."

After we descended down the mountains to a wider road, four men came out of the tree line near a hillcrest two hundred meters from us.

"Vaqueros from a hacienda?" Lizardi asked. "Your friend Espinoza?"

"They're not vaqueros. Look at their mounts."

They had an odd assortment of mounts: Two were on mules, the other two rode donkeys. Vaqueros mostly rode horses, though a mule would not be unusual. The donkeys stood out—being small, donkeys were primarily used by indios to haul their crops, not by men who herded cattle—and these donkeys were even smaller than most.

The clothes of the men were also jarringly mismatched, ranging from the rags of a lépero to the clothes of a gentleman. Even at that distance, I knew the man wearing the best clothing was a lowlife, not a gentleman.

"They're bandidos," Lizardi said.

"True."

"We have good horses; we can outrun them."

"You're not a good enough rider. A hard chase over broken ground and steep mountain trails would unhorse you. Besides, I'm not running back in the direction we came, into the arms of pursuing posses."

The men on the hillside urged their mounts toward us. Only one appeared to have a pistol; the others wielded machetes.

"There's four of them," Lizardi yelled. "We can't fight!"

"Like hell we can't!" I drew the machete from its sheath and slapped Tempest's rear with the flat of the blade, yelling "¡Vamos caballo! ¡Ándale! ¡Ándale!"

Tempest shot forward. The stallion was my best weapon. He was a head taller than the mules, and the small donkeys only came up to his shoulder. But what the mules lacked in height they had in girth.

I drove at a donkey rider first, spurring Tempest into the mount. The donkey went down as I slashed the bandido across his shoulder.

The mule rider before me leveled his pistol at me. I had less fear of the pistol than I did of the men with machetes. The flintlock weapons were notorious for misfiring even in the hands of an experienced shooter. When the hammer-flint struck the steel plate, its spark was supposed to ignite the powder charge and blow the lead ball out the barrel, but any one of a dozen things could happen, eleven of them bad. A well-placed machete blow, on the other hand, had catastrophic consequences.

Since the bandido had only one shot in his pistol, I was unperturbed.

"*¡Andale!*" I shouted, driving Tempest at the shooter's mule. The mule stumbled and spooked getting out of the way. The pistol went off, but the shot went wild as the rider was unhorsed.

I wheeled about. The other mule rider came into machete range. Swinging the big broad blade like an axe, I caught him in the side of the neck, nearly decapitating him. As he dropped from the saddle, his head flopped and the mule bolted.

Reining Tempest in, I wheeled him around. Their love of combat rapidly fading, the shooter had gotten back on his mule and had joined the other donkey rider, who had simply ridden by me and kept going in the direction of Guanajuato without offering a fight.

As I anticipated, Lizardi's horse had thrown him, but as he pulled himself to his feet, I saw that he had miraculously maintained a grip on the reins.

But the battle wasn't over yet. The bandido with the shoulder wound had remounted his donkey and was urging it toward Lizardi, knowing he would not get far on that small slow-footed burro with his life's blood pouring from his shoulder. His machete in his good hand, his last chance at a fast escape was Lizardi's horse.

I slapped Tempest with the flat of the machete again and went for the donkey rider. Smarter than its rider, the burro heard the big horse's hooves and veered off, heading back up the hill. I came up from the rear, laying open the bandido's back with the machete. He screamed and dropped from his mount.

I was surveying the battlefield when Lizardi came beside me on his horse. "You've killed two of them."

I saluted him with the bloody machete. "Have I thanked you for your courageous assistance, señor?"

His mount still spooked by the violence and the blood, Lizardi had to fight the reins. "Fighting is for animals."

"True, but dying knows no bloodlines . . . as you almost found out."

I went through the pockets of the dead bandidos. In the pocket of one, I found only a few centavos and some coca beans, which among indios were negotiable currency. But the other had a neck pouch with pesos, silver and gold crucifixes, and expensive rosaries, the ones favored by wealthy old women and venal priests.

Blood was on the two gold-chained crosses. It wasn't blood I had spilled; the crosses had been in the pouch.

"Bandido blood?" Lizardi asked.

"No . . . and not Blood of the Lamb, either."

We dragged the two bodies into nearby bushes and brushed away the drag marks. When we were through, I stared up at the hill where we'd first spotted the bandidos.

"Why do you keep staring up at that hill? We have to get out of here. There may be passersby, maybe even constables."

"They might be up there."

"Who?"

"Whomever those trash killed. They must have killed them shortly before we came along. They didn't have a chance to divide up their booty before they spotted us and thought they could increase their wealth."

We found them on top of the hill, tied sitting down with their backs to trees, their throats cut.

"Priests," I said. "They killed two priests." I crossed myself.

"They're not priests. They're Bethlehemite monks, a lay brotherhood known for its healing arts. But I suppose in the eyes of God they are the same as priests."

Lizardi and I both knelt. He offered a prayer, and I mumbled along with him as best I could. I admit that I was not suited for the church, but I was raised, as all in the colony were, to consider priests to be proof against life's sins and temptations. To kill a priest was a great offense against God.

An idea seized me as we got onto our feet.

"Are there many of these—What did you call them?"

"Bethlehemites. No, you don't see many," Lizardi shrugged. "Certainly not as often as you see other monks and brothers. They come over from Spain to do missionary work among the Aztecs, staying for a few years until they are replaced by others of the brotherhood. Skilled healers, they lack the evil reputation that doctors in general have, and I say that as the son of a medical man."

I rubbed my beard. "Señor Worm, the only thing that distinguishes us from these two bearded monks—other than their severed throats—are the robes they wear."

"What are you getting at? You think you can make yourself a monk by putting on a robe?"

" 'Veni, vidi, vici,' as Caesar would say." I wasn't sure I had the Caesar quote accurate, but it captured my mood. "Were we not both seminary students? Besides, you say these two are not really priests, that they only look like priests. We, too, will only look like priests."

I slapped him on the back. "Brother José, let's get these robes off these two and wash them in the river below before the blood dries. On our way to Dolores, you can instruct me on the tricks and alchemy your father uses in his treatments. Who knows, someone may need our healing services."

 **TWENTY-ONE**

BECAUSE WE HAD interrupted the bandits' pillaging, the thieves had barely touched the monks' baggage. We found food, wine, fresh linen, Bibles, medical supplies, and, most welcome of all, soap. We scrubbed clean at the river, washed the blood off the robes, and lit a fire to dry the clothes and cook a meal.

We camped on a hillock off the road that night, watching it for a posse. The next morning, feeling human again with fresh clothes and our bellies full, we continued on the road to Dolores. As we set out, Lizardi correctly noted the flaws in my disguise.

"Your horse is a pure-bred stallion, not at all what a monk would ride. Mine is much smaller and would be acceptable, but mules are more priestly. The two mules the bandidos had probably belonged to the monks. We need to trade the horses for mules."

He was right, but I wouldn't give up Tempest even if the Lord High Constable himself were on my tail, not if the devil were to offer me a fine woman instead . . . Eh, perhaps that wasn't true, but I was not about to trade Tempest for a mule.

"If we get chased by constables, I will need Tempest." I grinned at Lizardi. "To draw them away so you can make your escape."

"You refuse to wear the sandals we took off the monks and insist upon those caballero boots."

"You can't control a stallion like Tempest with sandals. He obeys boots, quirts, and spurs, not the gentle touch of sandals."

Among the monks' possessions were two saddlebags containing medical supplies. Lizardi went through the bags as we rode. He had assisted his physician father for several years and knew the purpose of the medicines and implements. He took a vial out of the monk's medicine pack. "Monks use this elixir to clean wounds. Known as aqua feu, it can discolor hair and turn black hair lighter. We can mottle your stallion so he's not such an obvious sloeberry thoroughbred."

I gave Tempest a brown forehead star and markings on his shoulders and rump so that he did appear more of a mixed breed.

"This glass tube has mercury in it, the quicksilver you once sold to the mines to separate out silver." He showed me a round glass tube about as thick as a finger and as long as a man's foot. "It's called a Celsius thermometer. You stick it in a patient's mouth and wait ten or fifteen minutes. If he goes above this mark, thirty-seven degrees, he has a fever. You have to leave it in the mouth to get an accurate reading, so you must use a candle and bend down by the person's chest to read it."

"So what does it mean if the person has a fever?"

"It means . . ." he shrugged, "he's sick."

"Any fool could tell when someone is sick. The person tells you that."

Shaking his head, he held up other items from the bags. "This is a small bone cutter," he held up a two-handled instrument that looked like it would be best employed snapping twigs off tree limbs, "and this is a bone saw."

"The monks were barbers?"

"No, many physicians now do surgery. My father is that kind of doctor."

I didn't say anything, but the reason most surgery was done by barbers is because the practice is so dangerous and disreputable. As many people died from the surgery as from the injury. I had no intention of butchering patients like dressed-out deer.

"The scalpels incise flesh, and a tourniquet chokes off bleeding." He held up a contraption with a large screw holding two metal plates that in turn held leather straps that went around an arm or leg.

"Here are medications, salves, oils of violets. A metal rod you heat red-hot for cauterizing, and, ah, amigo, this is especially for you." He showed me a very thin, foot-long rod. "To extricate musket balls, you slip it into the wound and probe for the lead ball. Once you locate it, you use these forceps to extract it." He held up an instrument that had scissor handles, but had two long narrow rods with "cups" on the end. "You clamp the lead ball between the cups and pull it out. Clever, eh?"

"I'd just as soon leave the ball in me than dig into my flesh with that thing."

"Not if the wound became infected, you wouldn't." He pulled another instrument out of the bag. "This one you use on your worst enemy."

It was a silver tube, long, thin, and curved.

"What is it?"

"A catheter."

"A what?"

"A catheter. This one is for a man. You stick it into the opening at the end of his penis and push it in."

"*¡María Madre de Dios!*" I shuddered and crossed myself. "Is this one of the Inquisition's torture devices?"

"No, it relieves blockage in a man's urinary tract. The tube is hollow and permits the liquid to escape through it. The technique is ancient. Even the Greeks and Romans used it."

"It's an instrument of the devil. Throw it away."

He put it back into a saddlebag. "You must know these things if you are called upon to treat a patient."

"If I am called upon to treat someone, I will cut his throat and say that it was God's will."

 **TWENTY-TWO**

WHEN WE REACHED Dolores, we veered off the main road and circled partly around the town to enter from a different direction than one from Guanajuato. The town was under the jurisdiction of the Intendency of Guanajuato, as was much of the Bajío region.

As we approached the town, we rode past a large vineyard. Row after row of grape vines twisted like snakes around acres of trellises, horizontal rope strands strung from stakes. The law forbade cultivating grapes, at least in quantity, but the constables often looked the other way when grapes were grown for personal use.

Lizardi knew much more about the prohibition. "The king outlaws cultivation of the vine to insure that only wines produced in Spain are sold in the colony. This is obviously a commercial vineyard. Look at those wine cisterns. They're for pressing. The fermentation barrels must be inside that building."

A young Aztec woman about my own age came across the road in front of us. She carried pruning shears.

I saluted her, forgetting that I was wearing a monk's cowl instead of a caballero's hat. "Buenos días, señorita. We were wondering who owns this fine vineyard."

"It belongs to our church, Nuestra Señora de Dolores, padre."

Our Lady of Sorrow. The town had taken its name, Dolores, which suggested sorrow, sadness, or pain, from the church. Many towns adopted the name of their church as their own.

A remarkably beautiful india with tanned skin, large brown eyes, long dark eyelashes, and waist-length ebony hair, she was tall for the women of her race, with shapely legs and graceful arms.

Dismounting, I grinned at her. "I'm not a padre, señorita, but a lay brother, nor am I bound by priestly vows of chastity."

Her eyes widened, and I heard Lizardi groan. Perhaps lay brethren were not meant to be so frank with women?

A priest came out of a building and was hurrying toward us.

"Who is that, señorita?"

"Padre Hidalgo, the curate of our church."

Hidalgo was a little shorter than I. Large limbed and round shouldered, he was of somewhat stout proportions, with a casual but distinguished air about him. He was bald on top, with a ruff of white hair. His eyebrows were prominent and nose straight. As with most secular priests, he was clean shaven.

He wore short black trousers, with black stockings made of a material similar to that of his trousers, a loose raglan also of black cloth, leather shoes with large buckles, and a long gown with a cape.

The padre gave us a wide enthusiastic smile. "It is always good to see members of your fine brotherhood. Few orders are as dedicated as you Bethlehemites in treating the sick."

Lizardi introduced us: I was Juan García, and he Alano Gómez. Lizardi had insisted after we assumed the roles as lay brothers that I keep my first name the same. "Yours is the most common man's name in the colony," he had said, "and you're not bright enough to remember a new name."

We were still at each other's throats, at least with insults, but I'd decided we made a good team. Lizardi supplied book knowledge; I was wise in certain ways of men. We needed both sources of strength now that we had to act like priests but were not and had to know something about healing but didn't.

The priest had a scholarly stoop, created no doubt from hunching over books. His eyes were bright and clear, full of intelligence and curiosity. He appeared inquisitive, as if he analyzed everything that fell within his sight.

"You must join us for dinner," he said, "and, of course, you will lay your head on our pillows tonight. Marina, make sure to let the housekeeper know we will have special guests."

Lizardi and I mumbled our eternal thanks. Like the priest, I also had an exploratory mind—of sorts. I wanted very much to explore Marina in my bed that night.

"Come, my brothers, let me show you what my indios have achieved."

Tethering our horses to a hitch rack, we followed Hidalgo. The young woman looked over my horse before we followed behind Lizardi and Hidalgo.

"Do you know horses?" I asked her, to make conversation, knowing, of course, that horses were beyond the comprehension of women. I never believed for a second that she would see through Tempest's "disguise."

"A bit, yes. My husband and I owned a caballo rancho. After he was killed, I raised the horses myself, from birthing the mares to saddlebreaking the colts, from working the pony herds to breeding the studs."

"Muy bueno," I said. But it was not good. What a terrible hand Señora Fortuna had dealt me again—a woman with knowledge of horses when I was trying to hide Tempest's pedigree.

Marina tenderly stroked the side of Tempest's face. He let out a snort that indicated he liked it when she caressed him.

"I see your stallion has fine lines, champion lines. Other than the . . . *unusual* markings, he is a finer caballo than any in Dolores."

I could have told Marina that no horse outside of a few in Méjico City could match Tempest. I quickly changed the subject.

"What happened to your husband? An accident training horses?"

"An accident with his pants. He let them drop once too often, and a jealous husband shot him."

I mumbled my regrets and dutifully crossed myself.

"It's all right," Marina said, "the wronged husband saved me from the gallows. I would have killed him myself. I'm sure you know, Brother Juan, a man can kill a woman he finds in flagrante delicto, but a woman who slays her husband for the same reason will share the scaffold with killers and thieves."

Marina gave me a look when she spoke of killers and thieves. Did I have bandido written on my face? I found it strange that a woman would use a Latin expression. I knew the Latin phrase for a bedroom indiscretion, having been accused of committing it more than once myself.

"But, of course, Brother Juan, that is just one of the unjust laws we must change."

I was shocked to hear her speak this way. Raquel had spoken of ideas and philosophy, but at least she was part Spanish. Now I was hearing an india speak of politics and justice . . . and horses. Perhaps my recent ordeal had befuddled my brain more than I realized.

"I have disturbed you with my blunt remarks," Marina said.

"No, my child. You are just mourning the loss of your husband."

Throwing her head back, she laughed with derision. "I mourn the loss of my horses. A good horse is hard to find, but men . . . they are easily replaced."

I looked Marina up and down. Although she lacked Isabella's striking beauty, her voluptuous body was more shapely and sensuous than Isabella's. Moreover, I was genuinely interested in what she said. This was disconcerting. In truth, I had never viewed indias as anything more than serving wenches or repositories for my lascivious lust. Now I found myself conversing with one.

My male physical needs were undeniably urgent, and I suspected she knew it. In fact, when she looked me in the eye, her smile seemed to search the darkest dankest depths of my sin-stained soul, as if she discerned every dirty deed I had ever done.

It had been a long time since I lay my head upon a woman's bare breasts, kissed her soft lips, and caressed the hidden treasure between her legs. I wanted this Aztec woman of wit and bearing more than I had ever wanted any woman in my life.

"Why did you give up your horses?" I asked.

"Men refused to buy horses raised and trained by a woman. More than one suggested the only business fit for a woman was to raise babies, make tortillas, and break her back in bed. I soon tired of their ignorance and came to work for the padre. He is the most enlightened man in the colony."

"Brother Alano and I will sup at the padre's table tonight. Perhaps, señorita, afterward we could take a walk together? I have some questions about the area that you may be able to answer."

"I will also be at the dinner. We can discuss the matters then."

I wanted to tell her that it would be difficult for me to have a discussion with a servant when she was attending to the dinner guests, but I held my tongue. After dinner and her cleaning chores were done, I might be able to arrange an assignation.

As I followed "Brother Alano" and Padre Hidalgo around, I learned more about Dolores. Not only was the padre growing grapes and making wine, he also had started a number of industries, all employing indios.

The priest bubbled with enthusiasm, telling us about his work with the Aztecs. I listened but could not stop staring at the padre. He reminded me of someone I could not place.

"When we came to the New World," Hidalgo said, "we Spaniards did not conquer savages but great and proud empires. These indios we call Aztecs—the Mexica, Mayas, Toltecs, Zapotecs, and others were on a cultural level that was in some ways superior to our European civilizations. They had books, great works of art, engineering skills that allowed them to move blocks of stones larger than houses over mountains, a more accurate astronomy, and more mathematically precise calendar. Their roads were safer and more durable than the foul ruts running through many of our locales, and their buildings more solid. In other words, we annihilated civilizations of cultured intelligent peoples."

I stared at the padre as if he were mad. Every Spaniard knew that Cortés had conquered naked ignorant savages who sacrificed virgins and practiced cannibalism. Yet I could see that Lizardi was not as shocked as I by the priest's ignorance. Marina gave me an amused look as I tried to keep my face blank while the padre made the outrageous comments about indios. If she had been my servant, for such impertinence I would have given her a beating . . . after I made love to her.

The padre showed us to an area where clay pottery—bowls, cups, pots, and jars—were baked in an oven. "None finer are made in the colony," he said. He pointed at my leather boots, the ones I was gifted by the lady-in-black, who I was certain was my own sweet Isabella. "The indio workmanship on those boots is finer than anything produced in Spain or the rest of

Europe. The hands that crafted those boots and the pottery are as skilled
with leather and pottery as any in the world. Why, we've even imported
mulberry trees from China. Silkworms will feed off the white fruit, and
we'll in turn use the worms to weave silk."

He enthusiastically explained the process of making silk from worms:
"The silkworms are nurtured from egg to maturity by feeding on the mulberry trees. They build their cocoons by producing and surrounding themselves with a long, continuous fiber. Incredibly, each little cocoon produces
a very fine fiber about a thousand paces long. Several fibers are twisted together to make yarn that's woven into cloth."

The padre beamed at us. "Is it not wonderful? Aztecs producing wine
as fine as the vineyards in Jerez, silks as delicate as those made in Cathay."

"And pottery exquisite as the Greeks," Marina said.

"Bueno, bueno," Lizardi said.

I kept my face expressionless. I would not be surprised if he now told
us that his indios were building a stairway to heaven.

He was different from any priest I'd ever met. Other priests knew and
spoke of little except the narrow precepts of their church. When they dealt
with matters outside those confines, they were often wrong and inevitably
tedious. But the curate of Dolores's church was intelligent, enthusiastic,
and energetic. When he spoke of the vineyard, silk making, and other
crafts, he had the fervor of a merchant and the intellect of a scholar.

And, of course, he was also quite mad. Who but a madman would
teach peons crafts that competed with the work of their betters?

When we were out of the padre's hearing, Lizardi whispered, "Do you
realize everything you see is illegal?"

"What do you mean?"

"Were you educated by moonbeams, señor? Growing grapes for wine,
silk works, pottery—he even has an orchard of olive trees. I've told you,
the colony is barred from the production of all these things because they
compete with imports from Spain."

"Spain sells us wine that tastes like mule piss for extortionate prices.
The priest probably has a special dispensation from the viceroy."

"No, I've heard talk about him in the capital. He's known as a notorious
advocate for indios, but he walks the razor's edge. He won't get away with
these illegal industries forever."

I scoffed. "These projects don't threaten the empire."

"It's their nature, not the size, that threatens the gachupines. The
padre wants to prove that peons are as capable as Spaniards, that they lack
only training and opportunities. How would the gachupines you know react to Aztecs and mestizos being their equal?"

The question didn't require an answer. We both knew that the viceroy
had men strangled in his dungeon for lesser sins.

"'Brother' Juan, one day the viceroy's men or the Inquisition will stop the padre from his folly. He'll die on the scaffold or at the stake. Only the remoteness of this town and his priest's robes have protected him from harm's way thus far."

Lizardi rejoined the priest as Marina approached. She glanced down at my caballero boots. It was a deliberate look. I pursed my lips and locked my eyes on hers.

"You have an amazing facility with language, señor."

I didn't know what she meant, but I took the bait. "I speak French, Latin, and an indio tongue. But how would you know that?"

"I wasn't referring to those but to your command of our colonial dialect and idioms and, as you say, of one of our indio tongues as well . . . all in such a short time."

She gave me a knowing smile that meant many things, none of them good for me. If nothing else, she implied that she had seen through my monk's masquerade.

Averting my eyes, I turned to join Lizardi and the padre when it struck me with hammer force: *I had met the padre before.*

He was the priest with Raquel who had stopped me from beating the lépero-beggar.

 **TWENTY-THREE**

WE HAD DINNER at the padre's, and Marina was there—as a guest. Should I have been surprised that she was not a servant? The entire dinner party was a strange concoction. The padre even had his mistress—an actress he had produced a play for—present.

A priest producing a play?

The other guests were a young Aztec novice for the priesthood from León, a criollo hacendado, owner of the largest hacienda in the area, and two criollo priests from Valladolid who had come to speak to the padre about his indio industries.

The novice, Diego Rayu, was a young man with searching eyes and a bright smile. I learned he had studied for the priesthood and now waited to see if the church would accept him. Indio priests were a rarity in the colony.

Don Roberto Ayala, the hacienda owner, gave Marina and the young novice looks that left no doubt that the only way they would have gotten near his own dinner table was with a serving tray.

One of the visiting priests said the padre's home should be called Francia Chiquita, or Little France. France was the world's guiding light in arts and sciences.

The conversation turned to literature and philosophy, and I felt that I was surrounded by a table full of Raquels—except for Don Roberto, who was as happily ignorant about such things as I was.

After dinner, the padre had his actress-mistress, Marina, and the novice read and act out scenes from *El sí de las niñas* (When a Girl Says Yes) by Leandro Fernández de Moratín. The play dealt with the conflicts between an older, more rigid generation and a younger, rebellious one.

In the play a wealthy fifty-nine-year-old man wants to take a pretty young sixteen-year-old as his bride. Things get complicated because she is in love with a younger man, not knowing that he's the older man's nephew. Nor do the uncle or nephew know each is vying for the girl's hand. The muddle has a happy ending when the rich older man allows his nephew to marry the girl.

The notion of a wealthy man marrying a beautiful girl even though he is four times older than she rang true for me. But that he would hand the hot young señorita over to his nephew rang as false as those chivalric romances that so vexed poor Don Quixote. In the real world, the old man would keep his money, bed the girl, and send the nephew off to be killed in a war.

The padre's guests droned on and on about literature after which Padre Hidalgo read from Molière, a long dead French writer of even deader French comedies. *L'École des femmes* (The School for Wives) the padre said was based on a Spanish story, featuring one Arnolphe, a scholar who never takes his head out of books. When he must marry, he is so frightened of women he chooses a bride who is totally naïve to the ways of the world.

As the padre read the inane utterances of Arnolphe and the young woman, my eyelids drooped, and I reached for the brandy bottle. Arnolphe falls hopelessly in love with the idiotic girl and spends the rest of the play attempting to romance her into bed, making an ass out of himself the entire time.

It took all my willpower to keep from imbibing my brandy straight out of the bottle's neck. I could have told Arnolphe how to handle the woman: I would have ridden up to her on Tempest, carried her off to some quiet place, told her whatever lies she needed to hear, then had my way with her. That was the sort of romancing women respected, not whining sniveling talk.

From small talk between Marina and the actress, I learned that Padre Hidalgo had a child with the actress and had fathered two daughters in another town. Having a mistress and children was not unusual for a parish priest; they were not monks, cloistered in a monastery. But it made the priest even more unfathomable to me.

Dolores was the strangest place I had ever seen. Running Aztec industries in defiance of the king's decrees? Treating peons as social and intellectual equals? Treating women as equals? The priest's mistress reading French plays at the dinner table . . . Was he going to produce it as a play for her?

Meanwhile Padre Hidalgo never intimated that I was the caballero he had encountered in Guanajuato. More than anything else that went on in Dolores, that puzzled me. Why didn't he expose and denounce me as a vicious brute and a fraud? That he recognized me I had no doubt. Why he kept his own counsel I did not know. Even more disturbing he seemed to like me.

While all this was going on, Marina offered her opinion on the Viceroy's recent decree increasing the tax on corn to aid the war effort of our Spanish king. I took it in stride; an Aztec with a mind of her own no longer shocked me. I simply helped myself to more of the padre's admirable brandy. The hacienda owner, however, grew increasingly out of sorts with Marina expressing opinions.

She intrigued me. Despite Marina's literary education, her skill with horses, her considerable beauty, her obvious forthrightness interested yet confused me.

Watching her quick-but-subtle movements, she reminded me of a wild forest creature, not a delicate doe but a menacing feline with the indolent grace of a sated jaguar at rest. A raw power radiated through her. Her interest in the arts and politics matched Raquel's, even though Raquel's reasoning had more depth. Marina compensated in her arguments with primal passion.

She brought out passion in all the guests that night, as they debated the events in the capital and the wars in Europe. After Britain's terrible defeat of the combined Spanish-French fleets at Trafalgar several years ago, the king was again bearding the British lion. This time Spain had invaded Portugal at the behest of the French, who wanted to isolate Britain from its last ally on the continent.

"Tragic," Padre Hidalgo said, "just tragic, so many lives lost, so much of our nation's wealth going into wars. First we ally ourselves with the British and fight the French, now we align with Napoleon against the British, only to court more disaster."

"From what we have heard, we have lost so many ships-of-the-line, we may never be a great naval power again," Lizardi said.

"I blame Godoy," Marina said. "They say he's the queen's lover, no less. First he led us into a disastrous war with France, then another against the British."

Marina's remark provoked an outburst from Señor Ayala, the hacendado. The same age as the padre, the hacendado's rapacious greed and Rabelaisian appetites had endowed him with ridiculous riches, a glutton's girth, and a tyrant's intolerance for political dissent. He had not visited the padre's table to have literate women lecture him on world affairs. The padre's industrious indios he declared beneath contempt. Their lack of basic rights he deemed a cause for jubilation.

I knew him well. He was every aged caballero I grew up around and the sort of gachupine on whom I modeled my own ignoble views.

"Women should breed babies, satisfy their husband's needs in all ways, and refrain from speaking of matters that concern the church and the crown," he fumed at Marina.

"Señor, all men, women, and races are free to express themselves at my table," Hidalgo spoke softly but forcefully.

Most parish priests would pander to a rich hacienda owner and later seek recompense in the name of the church. To side with an india over a grandee was financial folly. The padre, on the other hand, truckled to no man, voicing his beliefs without fear or favor.

Lizardi prudently changed the subject to Diego Rayu, the table's candidate for the priesthood, asking him:

"Do you plan to parish in León?"

Silent for most of the evening, the young novice responded to Lizardi's question. "I am not welcome in León."

While small in stature, Diego had the muscular frame of an indio laborer. As with most Aztecs, he looked to be in better physical condition than Spaniards. With his black hair cropped and large brown eyes, he had a deliberative demeanor and intense gaze.

"Why have you and León become estranged?" Lizardi asked.

"I made trouble for the parish priest who sponsored me for the priesthood. He asked me to speak to the father of a fourteen-year-old servant in a gachupine's house. The grandee had whipped then raped her. When the girl's father confronted the Spaniard, the caballero horsewhipped the father half to death. When the curé told me the Spaniard would compensate the girl and her father in exchange for the church's blessing and absolution, I told the curé bribes would not buy off God or the need for justice. When he disagreed, I complained to the alcalde."

"What did the alcalde do?"

"Threw me in jail."

A silent pall settled over the table.

The hacendado asked, "The servant girl, she was an Aztec?"

"Yes."

He scoffed. "Then what was there to complain about? She was her master's property. Perhaps she was resentful that she did not bear his bastard."

Rising in her chair, Marina caught a look from the padre and sat back down. Diego stared down at his plate, his face working in anger.

"This is my dinner table," Hidalgo said, "and all of you are my guests. Everyone is welcome to express themselves at this table, and I will express myself, too: I hope that this young man enters the priesthood and proves to the church that the Messiah is in all people, including indios, and that we are all God's children and that God does not condone the enslavement or abuse of *His* children." He nodded at the novice. "I hope you can demonstrate to the church that men of your race make fine priests, but whichever path you follow, I am sure you will grace it with dignity and righteousness, with honor and love. Your name already is divinely blessed: Rayu, the Nahuatl word for 'thunder.'"

As I said, Dolores was a very strange place.

Before dinner, Lizardi learned from a discussion with the visiting priests that the padre had once been head of a college. The Inquisition had sanctioned him, however, and he'd lost his seat for his liberal beliefs and his spirited life, which included, it was whispered, gambling and affairs of the heart. But, do we judge a man for his good deeds or his youthful indiscretions?

The hacendado slammed his fist on the table. "You're too damn tolerant, Padre." He glared across the table at Marina. "In my entire life, I have never heard *anyone* permit peons and women to speak their minds on important subjects. You sow insurrection. Men have gone to the rack and the stake for less, even priests."

The padre was undeterred. Instead of shying away from controversy, Hidalgo, indeed the entire table, exploded into another dangerous discourse.

Ignorant of such matters—in fact, not having the vaguest idea what they were talking about—I wisely kept my mouth shut. But for the first time in my life, I had seen caballeros in a different light. No, I suppose it really started back when I was on the streets, hungry and dirty, working like an animal while the "quality" people passed me by, not giving me as much consideration as one would a stray dog. I saw that this old caballero was not the equal of the priest, the novice, and for that matter the women at the table in anything, even his knowledge of horseflesh. I had no doubt Marina knew more on that subject than he did.

I cannot say that I agreed with the padre's radical notions, or that I truly believed that women should speak their minds in the company of men, or even that a woman should be permitted to improve her mind, as Marina and Raquel had, but I didn't like the way the hacendado tried to bully Marina and Diego. I was even more affected by the realization that the two Aztecs were more than a match for him.

"Don't criollos treat peons the same way gachupines treat criollos?" I asked, almost without thinking, breaking my meticulous silence. My remark had been reflexive, and I was guilty of a horrific heresy, which had escaped my lips before I could retrieve it. That statement also provoked a tumultuous debate.

During a pause in the discussions, the hacendado leaned over to me and said, "Brother Juan, I came into town to see the doctor, but he's a quack. He tried to give me medicine I would not swill to my pigs. The padre tells me you are a trained healer. If you can cure me, you would not find me ungenerous."

"What is your condition, señor?"

He reached grabbed his crotch. "I have a hard time passing water. Tonight I've drank a goodly quantity of wine and brandy, I have the burning urge to pass water, but when I attempt it, it's a dribble." He nudged me and gave me a knowing look. "I confess, Brother, I have enjoyed too many india whores." Grinning, he quickly crossed himself.

He had spoken within Marina's hearing, and I saw fury flash across her face. Averting her eyes, she turned her attention to the others.

I felt her anger as my own. Bruto said my mother was an india whore, and I, the son of a whore. What was a whore to a caballero? A woman he took—by force if he so chose—because he could. Rank and privilege conferred on him that right. Nothing else. And those who exposed his rank wrongdoing, he punished brutally.

"Are you in pain right now?" I asked.

"Terrible pain."

"Then come with me."

I stood up. "Padre, your meal was a feast for kings, but Señor Ayala and I have some serious business to transact. You will excuse us, I'm sure."

On the way out Lizardi grabbed my arm and pulled me aside.

"What are you doing?"

"He needs treatment. I'm going to give it to him."

"You know nothing about medicine."

I grinned at him. "You instructed me this morning."

"You'll get us hanged!"

"Can they hang us twice?"

In the room the padre had assigned to me and Lizardi, I selected the proper instrument from our medical bag. I went down the hallway to the hacendado's room and knocked on the door.

He answered the door, and I gave him what I considered to be a professional frown.

"I am ready, señor," I said.

"What are you going to do?" he asked.

"Lay down on the bed. And pull down your pants."

TWENTY-FOUR

WHEN I CAME out of the room, Lizardi, the padre, Marina, and the two visiting priests were huddled in the hallway. I quietly closed the hacendado's door behind me.

Padre Hidalgo stared askance at the door. "We . . . Brother Juan, we heard the screams of Señor Ayala. Is he—"

"You killed him!" my "lay brother" blurted out, white-faced with fear. Ready to bolt, Lizardi's eyes were wide and his legs shaking as he shifted from one foot to another.

I raised my eyebrows. "Killed him? Am I an executioner or a healer?" Without waiting for an answer, I went on. "Señor Ayala is resting comfortably. I think his screaming wore him out."

I smiled at Marina. "I believe, señorita, you had promised to show me the garden."

She hadn't made such a promise, but she reacted graciously. "My pleasure, Brother Juan."

We were nearly out the back door when the padre shouted a question at me. "Brother Juan, what treatment did you give him?"

Lizardi looked ready to detonate. "What did you do to him?"

"I simply gave him the appropriate treatment for his condition." I grinned. "I ran a steel rod up his penis to remove an obstruction."

Marina showed the good grace not to laugh until we were in the garden.

"Is he going to die? His screams were horrible."

"He won't die." I hoped. "But he will hurt like hell."

She picked a rose and smelled it as we walked along.

"You are a very strange person, Brother Juan."

"How so?"

"If I may be so bold, you confuse me. Your horse . . ."

"Given to me by a hacendado who says he threw him once too often. Not the horse of a monk, but as you know, we live on the sufferance of others."

"I suppose the hacendado gave you caballero boots also."

"Of course, a poor man like myself couldn't afford such finery on his feet. My customary footwear is sandals."

I stopped, staring at her in the moonlight.

"Does that satisfy your questions, señorita?"

"One more."

"Sí?"

"You look at a woman as a man looks at a woman. I thought lay brothers had a vow of chastity."

"That depends on the brother."

"But shouldn't they still strive for something less than naked lust?"

I sighed. "I haven't been a Bethlehemite for long, unlike Brother Alano, who, I sometimes think, was born in his monkish robes. I call myself a fraud because I came to the calling in a different way than most. A love affair sent me to the charitable brotherhood." I took her hand and pressed it against my chest. "I was in love with a woman who was far above me socially. She returned my love. Her family found out and demanded she cease our relationship. When she told them she would never give me up, I was forced to flee her father's paid assassins. Locking her in her room, he told her that I had perished under their blades. She believed the lie and . . . and . . ." I couldn't go on. I choked up.

"No, señor . . . She didn't . . . ?"

I nodded. "Yes. She couldn't live without me. She plunged a dagger into her heart. Afterward, I had few choices. I could join the brotherhood . . . or join her. Now, when I see you, I want to rend these monkish robes, be a man again, and taste a woman's lips."

I pulled her closer to me, her lips a kiss away from mine.

"Señorita, my heart has—"

"Brother Juan, I must talk to you!"

I almost jumped out of my monk's habit. It was Lizardi.

"Not now," I snarled.

Marina pulled herself away from me.

"I must go," she said.

She fled, and I grabbed Lizardi by the throat. "You miserable little worm, I should crush your throat and rid myself of you." I shoved him back. "Why are you panicking?"

"The hacendado. You killed him."

"No, I didn't."

In truth, I wasn't sure. I shoved the thin silver tube up his penis and punished him for insulting Diego, Marina, and my mother. I hurt him; he screamed. But kill him?

"Are you sure he's dead?" I whispered.

"I opened his door and peeked in. The candle by his bed was lit, and I could see him on the bed. I heard no noise, no whimpering. That thing you shoved into him—"

"You said it was to clear the penis."

"I told you it was to clear water blockage, but we don't know how to use it. He may have bled to death, or perhaps the pain killed him. He was just lying there, dead I think, with that hideous tube sticking up."

I rubbed my chin. "¡Ay de mi! You have gotten us into another fine mess, amigo."

"Me!"

"If we leave now, this late at night, we'd arouse suspicion. We can't go without awakening the stableman, without the padre and everyone else knowing it. We must escape in the morning at first light. That would arouse the suspicion of no one. We'll just tell them we must continue our journey. We will be gone before they find his body."

"And if they find it first?"

"Is this the first patient to die under the care of a physician? We will examine the body and announce that his heart gave out. We will be saddened, but it was God's will. When his widow comes, we will be kneeling beside the body, opening a path to heaven for the soul."

"You're a madman. I'm sorry I ever got involved with you. I should turn you in and—"

I grabbed him and jerked him close, pulling out my dagger and putting it between his legs. "Listen carefully, amigo. Inform on me to the authorities, the buzzards will breakfast on your eyeballs."

   **TWENTY-FIVE**

A RESTLESS NIGHT without a woman at my side and listening to Lizardi snoring on the bed we shared left me in such a foul mood that I was ready to run one of those silver catheters up a particular part of his body and not where I stuck it in the hacendado.

The sun was barely peeking from the east as I pulled on my boots and grabbed my saddlebag. "Let's go before the rest are up. We'll wake the stableman for our horses and tell him to give our thanks to the padre after we are gone. We'll have him tell Hidalgo that we were called away on a medical emergency."

"Can we eat first?"

"We eat on the way, whatever we can kill. Unless you'd like to stick around and have breakfast with the hacendado's spirit and the hangman."

We slipped out of the room and hurried down the corridor and around the corner . . .

"*Señors!*"

I froze. Lizardi gasped. He looked ready to faint.

Padre Hidalgo and the two visiting priests were in the corridor outside the room the visiting priests had been given. The priests had their bags in hand, too, getting as early a start as Lizardi and I, but of course, they were not sneaking out like thieves. Or murderers.

"Pa—Pa—Padre," Lizardi stammered. "We were just le—le—"

"Leaving," I interjected. "A medical emergency, you see; we must leave immediately."

"I've heard nothing about it," the padre said.

"Nor have we . . . I mean, not until a little while ago."

"But what of the hacendado? How is he?"

"God's will," I said. "It was out of our hands. The Lord acts in mysterious ways." I crossed myself.

The padre stared at me. "You don't mean . . ."

I nodded.

He crossed himself and muttered something in Latin. The other two priests dropped their bags and knelt. One of them began uttering a prayer for the dead.

Lizardi and I exchanged looks, then dropped to our knees. I didn't know the words but quietly mumbled nonsense that I hoped sounded like what the priest was saying.

"What's the matter? Somebody die?"

My blood froze. I slowly turned.

Mother of God!

The ghost of the hacendado stood in the corridor. The specter had a blanket wrapped around him. The blanket stopped at the ghost's bare knees. From that point down to his toes, he was bare.

Padre Hidalgo stepped next to me and addressed the apparition.

"Señor, we were praying for you. Praise the Lord, amigo, we thought you were dead."

"Dead? *Dead!* Yes, I'm a ghost!" he shouted, laughing like a loon.

I was still kneeling as the hacendado came up and stood beside me.

"Señor Doctor," he said, "my water comes out in a fine stream, but can you take this damn contraption from me?"

He opened his blanket to reveal the silver catheter sticking out of his penis.

 **TWENTY-SIX**

WITH THE HACIENDA owner alive and well, we had no need to flee. The "medical emergency" quickly evaporated.

My desire for Marina intensified, so I visited her rancho. Small but comfortable looking, the casa had three rooms, a tile roof, and a pleasant garden. She was not around, but I could see her horses in the distance. They grazed in the field. Good stock, they were not purebloods—certainly not of Tempest's champion lines—but the kind of tough, wiry ponies vaqueros favored.

The sun was high and oppressively hot, as I made my way toward a fragrant frangipani tree beside a pond a hundred paces from the house, its boughs festooned with flamboyant flowers and blossoms.

I leaned under its shaded canopy. Enjoying a cigarro, I thought about Marina. The woman had been on my mind since I first laid eyes on her. I'd gone so long without a woman, thinking about Marina's secret places stirred my desire. Something in her eyes bespoke a sensual hunger that no man had sated, never even brought to full arousal, never truly challenged. Before the day was out, I would rouse her longing from its lair and uncage her savage beast.

Water splashing in the pond distracted my thoughts. Peering through the bushes I saw the naked back of a woman in the water. She had the rich brown coloring of an Aztec, long unbraided black hair flowing down her back . . . the woman of my desire.

I watched in secret as she enjoyed her swim. Annoyed with each other, two birds shrieked and flapped excitedly. Marina tensed and looked my way. I ducked down and watched her through lower bushes. She gave no sign she had spotted me and relaxed in the water once again, lifting her face and upper body to the sun. My eyes savored her nakedness. I dared not move, afraid of causing her to stop. She lazily scooped handfuls of water in a slow and sensual rhythm over her ample breasts and roseate nipples, exuberantly erect in the cool water. The fires of lust levitated in me, desperate to be quenched. I quietly moved closer.

When she emerged from the pond, I came out from the bushes. Wrapped in a white lightweight cotton covering, the thin flimsy cloth only accentuated the lavish curves beneath.

"So, you have been spying on me."

I grinned. "I was just in the same area at the same time you were."

"Then why were you hiding behind the bushes?"

"At first, I didn't want to scare you. Then I couldn't help but look. I've hungered for you from the first moment I saw you."

I didn't wait for her to respond but quickly pulled the thin covering from her body. Stepping forward, she slapped the right side of my face, hard. My right cheek burned hotter than the hinges of hell.

Blinking back tears, I saw that her right hand held a beautifully crafted brass-and-ivory–handled dagger with an ornate four-inch hilt. A twelve-inch blade, honed razor-sharp, scintillated like Satan in the noonday sun.

"What is *that* for?"

"In case you think to rape me."

"Rape you? Señorita, I don't rape women. After I am through making love to them, they bless me for sharing my manhood with them, despising me only when I leave, cursing only my departure and my agonizing absences."

She stood there naked before me, knife in hand. Staring at me, perplexed, she made no attempt to cover her private parts.

I held up my hands in a conciliatory gesture. "I will make you a deal. If my lovemaking is not the best you have ever had, you may cut off my cojones, my garrancha too, and feed them to your pigs."

She shook her head slowly, as if she was trying to puzzle out my soul. She finally said, "You are very sure of yourself, señor."

"No woman has ever complained."

She laughed at that one, and I gave her a boyishly charming grin.

"And how many women *have* you taken to bed?" she asked in a challenging tone.

"I didn't count them, but," I patted my crotch, "I'm told that I have a cannon for a garrancha . . ." The behemoth bulge, even beneath my "lay brother's" robes, was embarrassingly obvious but confirmed my assessment, ". . . and cannonballs for cojones."

She started laughing as if she knew something I didn't. No woman had ever laughed at or derided my machismo before, and my vanity was pricked. I flushed with anger.

"See for yourself, woman!" I slipped off my robes and dropped them to the ground.

She gasped at the immensity of my member.

"¡Dios mío!" she cried out, crossing herself and looking away.

In the back of my mind I prayed that our sainted padre would not happen by. Who knows how many Hail Marys, Our Fathers, and countless other acts of contrition he would sentence my benighted soul to. We were both hopelessly compromised: Marina, her knife pointed at me, and me bare naked with my member at a raging right angle, an angry flag posted at half-staff yet arrogantly erect in a gale-force wind.

I quickly pulled off my boots. I didn't have to force the knife out of her hand. With a sudden turn and a shockingly swift throw she stuck her knife in the frangipani tree, impaling two gaudily fragrant frangipani flowers. She then fell into my arms as eagerly as I collapsed into hers.

With my lay-brother's robes for our sacred bed, we dropped to the ground. She spread her legs wide as paradise.

My garrancha—hard enough to cut diamonds—was furnace hot, thrumming and throbbing like her vibrating knife. Hovering over her own beauteous blossom, however, I was racked by a desperation I had never before felt, and agony of lust so painfully urgent it frightened me.

I had kissed women before but never like her. They weren't kisses so much as a tumbling into an abyss. I had never known lips so soft and a tongue so hot and inventive and lithe. I could have kissed her forever and never enjoyed consummation . . . *that* was how deeply I felt.

I did enter her though, and her flower was lava hot between her legs. I felt her body respond, even as my mouth devoured hers, my tongue ramming at hers as if simulating the ramming of my *cañón*. The bodily tremors increased in intensity and frequency, and I accelerated the power of my stroke to accommodate her pumping, gyrating hips.

The deeper, harder I probed, the more the black fuzzy bush between her legs tickled my lower pelvis. Penetrating deeper, harder, my pelvis palpated her prickly pear, rotating, revolving on and around her clitoral star like a planet orbiting a black yet blazingly hot sun, until running amok, I crisscrossed and crosshatched the little orb, driving her maniacally mad. Rubbing and scraping my pelvis against the heated seed of her now trembling frangipani, I ground at it until not only her budding sprout flowered, but her whole being burgeoned and blossomed, exploding ecstatically into gaudily hued flowers of flamboyant fire.

I was erupting now as was she. All the previous spasms were put to shame by a climactic collective fireworks, an infinite succession of demented detonations blasting us apart, freeing us, as if all the harpies in hell and the demons in our souls were fighting to get out, bringing us ineffably closer together.

None of this slowed or softened my garrancha. He had been so long without a woman—and so embittered by prison—I only worried he might never go down again. He and his flowery friend came again and again. Was it a thunderous thousand-gun salute to heaven's gate or a colossal cannonade from the jaws of hell? I could not say, but my garrancha and his friend were making up for lost time and making their presence known. They clearly had a joint mind of their own. It was as if Marina and I had no say in the matter.

Shuddering with me as the spasms racked her—in time, in tune, with mine, over and over and over—she clenched me tighter, kissing, biting, gnawing, chewing at my lips, like she would never stop, could never stop. Fingernails clawed at my back, thighs, hips, haunches, ass, reaching into the crack of my ass, down to my cojones.

Only once did she make me stop that afternoon, to "cool her frangipani off," she said.

Leading me by the hand into the pond, we gently rubbed each other all over, particularly our tender and much abused . . . friends. She wanted to kiss my manhood, "make it better," she said, fearing she had injured the little bird.

When she took my manhood in her mouth, teasing and torturing its tender underside with her tantalizing tongue, laving and sucking on its hell-hot muzzle, my inconsiderate male part punished her tender caresses with alabaster bursts of blazing cannon fire, milk-white against the nut-brown softness of her cheeks and lips as she gasped for air and my fusillades erupted volcanically out of her mouth, after which I quickly returned for more artillery practice.

Eventually, I returned the favor. Whether I feasted on her fatal flower

at heaven's gate or my tongue stroked and probed the yawning jaws of hell.
I could not say. The caressing and kissing, driving and pounding would not
stop, could not stop. We continued on and on, through the afternoon, even
into dusk.

I'd like to say I taught her the way of a man and a woman, but the best
I can say is I fought her to a draw. She was indeed a *bruja*, a witch, because
for the first time in my life, a woman had me as much as I had her. It was as
if our hips and loins, blossom and balls, indeed had lives, wills, and desperate desires of their own. If I had any concern at all, it was to question
whether we would ever stop, whether anything on earth could interrupt
what we had started, wondering in all sincerity whether death itself could
penetrate and part our ecstatic embrace.

When at last we did lie still, in each other's arms, quiet, exhausted,
spent, innocent-yet-knowing in our nakedness, we said nothing for a long
time. When I at last broke the silence, I did not even know I had spoken.

"It has been a long time?" I asked her.

"Yes, a long time, not since that *bastardo* husband of mine got shot
with his pants down, but even then he was nothing like you."

"Un hombre duro?" A hard *hombre*? I asked.

"Un hombre nada." As a man he was nothing.

As she spoke, her eyes were closed. Opening them, she rolled on top of
me. "You were wrong," she said, as she pulled me back inside her. "Your
manhood is bigger *and* harder than a *cañón*."

Miraculously, my much abused *amigo* had returned to his *duro* stature.
And we returned to our desperate dance.

   **TWENTY-SEVEN**

BEFORE WE MADE our way back to her house, we cooled ourselves off in
the pond. I enjoyed an ease and a comfort with a woman I had never before known. We talked casually of what we would do in the days ahead. I
was enthralled by everything she said. I never even thought about the fact
that she was an Azteca.

I must have cared for her, because I avoided the subject of when
Lizardi and I would leave Dolores.

"I want to show you one of my horses," she said. "I have a buyer for it,
and I have to gentle him for saddle and ride."

She walked the unbroken dun around the field for a time, stroking his
neck, maintaining eye contact, whispering something ineffable to him.
Suddenly swinging onto its saddleless back, she rode the unbroken horse
bareback up and down her field. Bucking and kicking for a moment or so,

snorting, whinnying, shying bites at her arms and legs, the dun quieted down by fits and starts. Finally he broke into a high lope, then a spirited canter, eventually a slow walk.

After a half hour or so of working the dun, she returned with him, now gentled. Throwing a saddle on him and cinching it up, she rode him back out into the field. Eventually she put a bridle on him, and he didn't seem to mind.

I watched awestruck not only by her control over her horses but also by her ease, aplomb, and grace. Few vaqueros could match her horsemanship. None could match her assurance. And at one time I would have dismissed her as a woman. *¡Ay!*

"How did you do that?" I asked.

"I just talk to him from time to time like this . . ." She whispered in the horse's ear, stroking his ear gently, caressing his neck and nose.

"How long did you talk to him?"

"A few days."

I would have required a week of ungentle training to have broken the dun to my saddle: a week of spurs, spade bits, and a well-worn quirt.

After schooling the horse a while longer, she came over to where I leaned against the fence smoking my cigarro.

"Not your type of horse training, is it?"

I shook my head. "I train horses like I train my women—I ride them hard and put them up wet."

She laughed so loud the horse took up the chorus, neighing and whinnying with her. Her up-from-the-gut laugh was utterly different from the crystal-tinkling bell of Isabella, but I enjoyed the sound of Marina's laugh more.

I nodded at the horses. "I thought you'd given up breaking caballos."

"I found a customer who'd buy a horse trained by a woman. The buyer is a woman, of course, the widow of a hacendado." She studied me appraisingly with sharp shrewd eyes. "Speaking of hacienda owners, I understand Señor Ayala is still with us. He tells everyone you are a miracle worker."

I shrugged, trying to look modest. "It was nothing. A brilliant medical procedure with God guiding my hand."

"Then you won't be disturbed if sick people line up at the church for your miracles."

The look on my face started her laughing again.

"If you wish to remain in Dolores, you will have more business than you can handle."

"Only one thing could keep me in Dolores." I took her, rubbing her flower once again, and smothered her mouth with my lips.

●　　●　　●

Again, we fed our hunger.

Afterward I decided to do something constructive. This time I helped her feed her horses, again feeling strangely, inexplicably at ease with her . . . talking with her. We talked for a time about Father Hidalgo.

"The padre is a most unusual priest," I said.

"And a most unusual man. He's a great thinker, yet his head is not in books but with people. He's caring and compassionate toward everything and everyone. He loves all people, not just his fellow Spaniards, but indios, mestizos, chinos, and African slaves as well. He says someday all people will be equal, even indios and slaves, but that it will happen only when the peons are permitted to use all their God-given talents instead of being treated like farm animals. And he respects women, not just for cooking meals and bearing children but for their minds, for the contribution we make in all things, including books and world events. He wants to change the world so that the underprivileged everywhere are treated equally."

"That will only happen when God comes down and runs our lives Himself."

Later, we sat by the creek that ran by her small rancho and fed our empty stomachs. I asked her about her name, curious as to why her mother would give her a name that was not well-respected by the Aztecs in the colony, that was honored only by the Spanish.

She told the story of Marina, the most famous woman in the history of New Spain.

The lover and translator of Cortés, who bore him a son, before the Conquest Marina had been an india princess, the daughter of a powerful leader.

"Doña Marina's" father died when she was young, and her mother remarried. To prevent Marina from laying claim to her deceased father's property, and to seize the estate for her own son, Marina's stepbrother, her mother switched Marina for the dead child of a slave.

Her mother than gave Marina away to a Tabascan tribe. Later, when Cortés landed to conquer the Aztec empire, the Tabascans gave Marina—also called Malinche or Malintzín—to Cortés along with nineteen other women. His priests baptized the women and gave them Christian names—"Marina" was the young woman's baptismal name—and parceled them out among Cortés's men as concubines.

When Cortés learned that Marina had a natural facility for languages—that she picked up Spanish quickly, spoke the Nahuatl language of the Aztecs and the Mayan language of most of the southern region—he took her as both his lover and his translator.

"But she was more than just a lover and translator," my Marina said. "She was a clever, intelligent woman. When Cortés negotiated with the Aztecs, she saw through their schemes and deceptions. While advising Cortés on how to deal with them, she bore him a son, Martín, and he later married her off to one of his soldiers, Juan de Jaramillo. When she traveled to Spain, she was presented to the royals.

"But the indios resented her as a traitor to their cause, arguing Cortés might not have conquered them had she not betrayed them by helping him."

"Maybe they're right," I said.

"Were you ever parceled out to soldiers to be raped? Doña Marina was. Robbed of her inheritance, chatteled into whoredom, then concubinage—first for the pleasure of indios and then for the Spanish—her masters of both races passed her from man to man, forced her to spread her legs, and raped her. Victimized by both races, she turned the tables on her oppressors. She helped the Spanish, only because her own people betrayed and enslaved, raped and oppressed her."

"Then why did your mother name you Marina?"

"My mother was a servant in the house of a Spaniard. He took her when he wanted her and cast her aside when she grew older. But unlike many of the other servants, my mother could read and write. She knew the story of Doña Marina. She gave me the name as a warning, for me to understand that it is a cruel world and that I needed to protect myself because no one else would."

"What about your father?"

"I never knew my father. He was a vaquero who died from a horse fall before I was born."

I thought about the way I had treated my servants over the years. I had often treated them harshly and unjustly to put them in their place. For the first time I found myself wondering what they had thought of me.

 **TWENTY-EIGHT**

I 'M LEAVING," LIZARDI told me the next day.

I was surprised but reconciled. Despite my ardor for Marina, I knew he was right. Both of us had to move on. If we were captured here, the priest would be condemned for his hospitality to us.

Moreover, if I remained in Dolores and the worm left alone for Méjico City, his flapping lips would soon lead the viceroy's constables back to me.

The more I considered that possibility the more I considered silencing the lips permanently but decided against it. Lizardi and I had been through a lot together, and perhaps we had forged a bond, a bond I was reluctant to acknowledge. And my presence threatened Father Hidalgo and Marina either way. Even if I killed Lizardi, I would have to leave.

The old Zavala would have done him in a heartbeat. Letting him live only increased my risk.

Something was happening to me, something that I couldn't define. I just didn't have it in me, and I didn't want the padre or Marina to learn who I was. Strange as it might sound, I didn't want them to think less of me.

Lizardi left, joining a silver train of over a hundred mules passing through Dolores. The train would link up on the road south of Guanajuato with even larger mule trains. Lizardi planned to use his family and friends to plead directly to the viceroy for mercy and a pardon. Everyone knows that justice can be bought, so Lizardi simply had to raise the price. His "sins" were far less expensive than mine. Forgiveness for Zavala would cost half the Inca gold.

In truth, I'd grown attached to Marina and did not want to move on. I could not call my feelings for her love—I had sworn to love forever only sweet Isabella, and that vow I would never break. But my feelings for Marina had passed far beyond lust, and with each passing day the depth and the degree of my caring grew more profound.

Marina had also been right about the consequences of my "medical miracle." People flocked to the church asking for my services. I dodged those entreaties each day less successfully. Once I was backed into a corner and forced to minister to a sick child. Marina heard me tell the mother to give the child hot baths and called me aside to admonish me.

"You don't give hot baths to a child with a fever. Hot water will drive the fever up; you'll kill the child."

¡Ay de mí! Why did I become a medical man?

To clear my head and plan my next more, I saddled Tempest and set out on a three-day hunting trip. In the wilderness, by myself, answering to no one and fearing no one, I would find peace for the first time since Bruto died and left behind a plague of charges and problems.

I didn't feel it sporting to drop a deer with a musket. Borrowing a good hunting bow and a quiver of arrows from a friend of Marina's, I rode into the wilderness on Tempest.

I brought down a deer with an arrow that very morning, hung it from its hind legs, and cut its throat to drain the blood. I was so close to Dolores I decided I'd ride back and drop the carcass off with Marina so she could have it dressed out and hung in the smokehouse while I continued my hunt.

The sky was gray and overcast, the day damp and drizzly, when I arrived at the outskirts of Dolores. As I approached the padre's vineyards, with the deer slung over Tempest's withers, I saw soldiers and constables at the vineyards.

My first instinct was to wheel Tempest around and spur him out of Dolores. I had to leave quietly but couldn't appear to run off.

I saw something that gave me pause. The mounted soldiers and constables began lassoing the trellised grapevines, dallying their saddle ropes around their pommels and pulling the vines out of the ground. While some of the viceroy's men ripped out the vineyard, others were chopping down the mulberry trees. The sound of smashing pottery came from that facility. The constables hadn't come for me; they were destroying the Aztec craftworks.

Lizardi had expressed surprise that the padre had succeeded for so long in improving the indios' lot. Now the viceroy was ending those efforts.

Watching the viceroy's men destroy years of hard work and seeing the sadness and despair on the workers' faces fueled my anger. I wondered where the padre was, whether the soldados had already placed him under arrest.

Marina galloped up to the soldiers who were pulling out the grape trellises. She was too far away for me to hear what she said, but I knew the gist of it. She cursed them roundly for their stupidity.

A mounted soldier lassoed her and pulled her off her horse. She hit the ground hard, crying out in pain. The mounted soldier dragged her into the nearby building, while two of his comrades followed.

A blind man could see what they planned to do. Spurring Tempest hard, I pulled the deer off and galloped straight at their building. In the damp drizzle neither my musket nor pistol were reliable, but then neither were theirs. Taking the reins in my teeth, I nocked an arrow. One of the men, who had pulled Marina inside, came to the doorway when he heard the hooves of the stallion. I released the tri-bladed broad head. It struck his chest with a thrumming *thwack!*, knocking him off his feet and back into the building.

I steered Tempest into the doorway, a new arrow nocked, ducking down as I came through, horse hooves trampling the impaled, supine corpse. A man behind Marina had twisted the rope around her neck into a tourniquet, while a companion was restraining her flailing legs. Both men had their pants pulled down. The men let her go as I came through the door. My triple broadhead took him in his left eye. Slipping the strung bow on my saddle pommel, I charged his companion whom Marina was grappling with. He broke loose from her, and I caught him between the neck and shoulder with the machete blade, sinking it deep.

I wheeled Tempest and grabbed Marina, dragging her up, as she kicked the floor twice, then swung up behind me. Galloping through the doorway, we charged across the yard. I dropped her by her horse. "Ride!" I yelled.

The commotion had attracted other soldiers and constables. Four of them charged me. To draw them away from Marina I rode straight into them, machete swinging like Death's scythe, sending them scattering. As I thundered off in the direction opposite, the one Marina had taken, a horseman tried to cut me off with his sword swinging. I slipped by the sweep of his sword and struck him across the back with the machete as I passed.

Tempest ploughed into another mount. My stallion stumbled but quickly got his footing as the other horse and rider went down. Their flintlock weapons misfired in the drizzle as I galloped through their ranks and another arrow from my bow went true. A musket ball grazed my left arm, but the flesh wound did not crimp my strong sword arm.

I rode out of town with several of the soldiers on my tail. The rain was intensifying, their muskets useless but my bow still lethal. After a hundred meters, I wheeled Tempest around, reins in my teeth, bow in my fist, and thrummed an arrow that hit a soldier's chest.

With Tempest I could outrun them all, their small wiry mounts no match for a purebred stallion. The harder they chased me, the more quickly I turned and fired. Another soldier fell from the saddle. Halting their mounts, the disheartened survivors turned back.

I kept riding until I was sure there was no pursuit. Finally, with Tempest breathing heavily and my left sleeve soaked with blood, I worked my way into thick brush to make camp.

The arm wound was not serious. I cleaned and bandaged it. Fearful of lighting a fire, I ate the last of my tortillas and salt beef cold.

Lying down, exhausted, I still worried for Marina. But she was well mounted and knew the territory. I doubted harm would come to her. She had committed no crimes, and Spain viewed all women as incompetent except for housework and sex. She would be all right; it was the bandido Zavala they would come after and flay whole if they found him. By tomorrow, the constables might pick up my trail.

¡Ay! . . . what kind of man was I? I had handled the bow and arrow not as a Spaniard, but as an Aztec warrior. Many a night I had fallen into a deep sleep during which I had fought and killed Spaniards. This day my nightmare had come true. *What was I becoming?*

I put on my monk's robe to keep warm and fell asleep, wondering which direction I should take in the morning. None seemed promising.

TWENTY-NINE

T EMPEST'S WHINNY BROKE my sleep. Another whinny echoed his, then another. Leaping to my feet, I had taken but a few steps to where Tempest was tied when a group of horsemen crashed into the clearing. Surrounded by six stamping horses, I stared up at a mounted Spaniard who looked as astonished to see me as I was to see him.

"Thank God we've found you!"

Besides the Spaniard, a man who appeared little older than me, five vaqueros had gathered around me. My first instinct was that word of my crimes had traveled fast.

"You are desperately needed, padre."

Padre? Eh, I was wearing the monk's robe.

"Uh, señor . . ." I didn't know what to say.

"My apologies. I realize you're a lay brother, not a priest, Brother Juan. But you are much needed at my casa."

"At your casa?" I repeated.

What the hell was I into now? I hoped his señora was not having medical problems. My knowledge of female anatomy was restricted to bountiful breasts and other voracious private areas.

As we rode, he told me his name was Ruperto Juárez. He was the son of a large hacienda owner. His father, Bernardo, was ill, thought to be dying; an injury to his leg had become infected. Two days ago Ruperto had come to Dolores to find "Brother Juan," the famous "miracle worker," and someone in Dolores told him I'd gone hunting in the wilderness. Ruperto and his men had been searching for me. They apparently didn't know about the raid on the padre's crafts yesterday. They were on their way back to the hacienda and had stumbled upon me by accident.

No, not by accident, but now another time that Señora Fortuna dangled a rack, red-hot pincers, and a blazing stake before my eyes. I had unwittingly camped near the trail that led to their hacienda, and they had camped not far away. Tempest's neighing—no doubt provoked by the scent of their mares—had drawn them to me. At least the Bitch of Fortune had not told them I was a wanted man.

Yet.

"You have an amazing horse for a monk, señor," Ruperto said, as we rode side by side. "I have never seen such a fine stallion."

"A gift from a grateful marqués whose precious life I saved."

"You shall not find us ungenerous when you save my father's life. It is most urgent that he not die, he has matters that must be straightened out. The hacienda naturally should go to me, the eldest son. But after my mother died, my father wed a succubus from hell, a woman only a few years older than me. My stepmother hates me. She tells my father lies about me. She claimed I tried to have intercourse with her." He made the sign of the cross. "¡Dios mío! The woman is a she-demon. Hearing the lie, he changed his will to leave the hacienda to my step-brother, an infant."

He gave me a hard look. "He has to live so he can hear the truth and change his will, making me his heir again. If he does not revive long enough to make things right . . ."

He let the sentence hang . . . like a rope around my neck. It was obvious that I was being rushed to save his father's life not for love but for money. And if I failed . . . This Ruperto was going to send me to hell along with his father.

"I hope we are in time," Ruperto said. "I left my wife to watch over my father and make sure my stepmother doesn't hasten his death. If he passes before I return, I will know they killed him. Then there will be trouble. Half of the vaqueros support me, half my stepmother."

They kidnapped me to fight in a family war.

The reception committee at the house included the father's wife, Ruperto's wife, and vaqueros, all of whom stared at me impolitely. Their faces were a mixture of frowns, disapproval, hope, and expectation. Whatever I did, I was doomed to displease someone.

"How is the poor man?" I asked the wife, hoping he was dead. I tried to look serene and holy.

She gave me a hostile stare. Still I could see why the hacendado was taken by her. She had something I knew too much about: the cold, calculating yet seductive eye of a puta. Her eyes said she could be mine . . . for a price. She would be hard to turn down indeed.

"My husband is sleeping. He will pass very soon . . . unless God grants us a miracle."

It would be a miracle if I escaped the crossfire when it started.

I mumbled something unintelligible in Latin, stared solemnly heavenward, and made the sign of the cross in the air.

"Padre Juan will save him," Ruperto said.

I didn't remind him that I wasn't a priest—it would be a bigger sin to kill a priest than a lay brother, no?

"No one but the padre will be permitted into my husband's room," the lovely wife said. "Come with me."

I followed her, smelling her exotic perfume. She wore a silk house dress that showed more of her figure than was considered modest. Watching the sensuous swing of her buttocks, I found myself getting aroused by the seductive witch. Ay! What kind of man has a pene that swells when his neck is in the noose? I crossed myself as I followed her, knowing I had been raised badly, thinking with my garrancha when the noose is tightening.

For most of my life, I had not found a need to ask the Almighty for help. My parish priest warned me that someday I would need divine intervention. Eh, this was one of those days.

We entered the large bedroom, and she locked the door behind us. She paused and stared at me for a moment, her eyes inviting. I glanced around her, over to the bed. The hacendado was flat on his back, his mouth hanging open, breathing hoarsely, saliva drooling and slavering on his chin. His eyes fluttered open as we approached the bed.

"The priest is here, my love," she told her husband.

He lay silent, the embodiment of death. The only reason I knew he was still alive was the rise and fall of the bedcovers as he breathed.

She pulled the blanket back and I was assaulted by the stench of rot. His leg was swollen and discolored. The wound where the infection started exuded a brownish, foul-smelling pus. Other areas around the wound also erupted with purulence.

I'd seen the symptoms before: The leg of one of my vaqueros had been crushed when he fell under a wagon wheel. When I arrived at the hacienda and saw the wound several days later, it looked and smelled like the rot before me, and he was dead hours later. I was later told that once the poison started to spread, the only solution was to cut off the limb above the poison line.

"You must cut off his leg," his wife said.

I almost jumped out of my monk's robe.

"No!"

"No?" She raised her eyebrows. "Then what is your advice, padre?"

"My advice? My, uh, advice, is to leave the matter in the hands of God. If our Lord has called for your husband, we can do nothing."

"But we must do something to try and save him." Her voice was unconvincing. She didn't want him saved, but I understood her reasoning: If she didn't genuinely try, Ruperto would accuse her of pushing his father into the grave. She knew as well as I did that he was too far gone to survive amputation of his leg. And when he died under my hand, she would have her status as the grieving widow who had done all she could. And Ruperto would roast my cojones over a fire.

And if a miracle occurred and I saved him . . . ¡Ay de mí! I'd face the wrath of this demon-woman.

I was damned if I did and damned if I didn't.

"What do you have in mind?" I asked.

"Everything humanly possible must be done. Naturally, I love my husband and want him to live."

She sounded as convincing as the last puta who told me my garrancha was the god of thunder, lightning, and storms—the Spanish Poseidon.

"I also have a problem with my stepson, Ruperto. My husband's will names my own son as heir. Ruperto will contest the will. Disinheriting the eldest son goes against custom, does it not? If he alleges that I let my husband die without struggling to save him, he may be able to break the will." She nodded at the infected leg. "My understanding is that the leg should be cut off above the wound." She smiled. "So cut it off."

I cleared my throat. "I don't have my medical tools with me. I shall go to Dolores and—"

"There's no time. We have a sharp saw."

A sharp saw. *¡María Madre de Dios!*

"You expect me to . . . to . . ."

The charnel stench was overwhelming. I wanted to gag.

Something tugged at the bottom of my robe and I almost jumped out of the robe again. It was an ugly little mutt.

"This is Piso, my husband's dog. He loves the animal."

Someone knocked on the bedroom door, pounded actually.

"That's Ruperto," she said.

She went to the door with tight lips. I went with her. She opened the door, and Ruperto stepped by her to get a look across the room at his father.

"He's still breathing," Ruperto said.

"The padre will cut off his leg. It's the only way to save him," the soon-to-be widow said.

"Yes, I understand that," Ruperto said. "But what are his chances of surviving if his leg is cut off? Don't most people die when it's done?"

"It's in the hands of the Lord," I croaked.

"When you do the deed," Ruperto said, darkly, touching the sword strapped to his belt, "make sure you are able to call on God for one of those miracles you are famous for."

"He needs a sharp saw," the almost-widow said.

"He needs a barber. I'm not a surgeon."

"You are the only medical man we have," Ruperto said. "We have a saw for you."

A vaquero gave him a saw, and he handed it to me. I almost dropped it.

The wife asked, "Are you all right, padre? You're sweating and shaking."

"A fever I picked up," I croaked. I stared at the saw. A metal blade with jagged teeth and wood handle. There was dried blood on it, no doubt from the last cow they butchered. I'd never used a saw in my life. Now I was supposed to . . . Oh, *¡mierda!*

I needed a priest. I needed to confess my sins, to get absolution. I needed a drink, many drinks.

Four men brought in a long table and laid my patient on it, covers and all, allowing his legs to hang over the edge. They placed a washtub underneath the diseased limb.

"You must all leave the room," I croaked.

After they left, I closed and locked the door. I stood trembling with my back to the door to gather my courage. With saw in shaking hand, I approached the table. As I stood over the man his eyes opened again, and he mumbled something unintelligible before his eyes fluttered shut.

The door exploded with banging. I raced back and opened it, hoping God had answered my pray for salvation.

"Don't you want the brazier, padre?" Ruperto asked. Two men stood behind him holding an iron tub blazing with white-hot coals. A steel rod stuck out of it.

"To stop the bleeding," he said.

"Of course," I said gruffly. "What took you so long?"

Other men brought in a blacksmith's stone table and the men holding the brazier placed the pan of burning coals on it. After the men left, I locked the door again.

Was I really expected to saw off the man's leg and stop the massive bleeding with a hot iron?

I approached the table with the saw as if I were sneaking up on a snake with a club. I pulled down the covers and opened the bandages to expose the leg. The stench of rotting flesh was now incomprehensibly sickening. I gagged, and my knees went weak. Gathering my strength and courage, I held the wood handle of the saw with two shaky hands and lay the saw-toothed edge of the ragged steel blade on the flesh of his left leg, just above the knee. I closed my eyes and began to mutter what I could remember of a prayer I had had to recite in seminary a decade ago. I pulled back and forth, feeling the blade bite into the leg.

Liquid splattered my face. *Blood.* I wiped my face. *¡Ay!* What did I do to deserve this? I swayed, faint again. Determined to see it through, I got a grip on the saw and began sawing again. Soon I hit bone. I kept my eyes shut and kept sawing, working my way through the bone sawing, sawing, sawing. Sweat poured off my face. My knees trembled. I kept my eyes tightly shut as I pushed the saw forward and pulled it back, back and forth, back and forth . . . with each swipe the teeth of the saw ripped through flesh and bone.

When I felt the saw bite the wood table and the leg clunked into the washtub, I opened my eyes and stared down at my handiwork—a stump and a severed leg lying in a washtub filled with blood. The stump itself was ragged and red, with bone and arteries exposed, blood pumping into the blood-filled washtub below.

I grabbed the hot poker and poked it at the bloody stuff to stop the bleeding by broiling the end of the stump. His body had unconsciously convulsed throughout the operation. He did not cease his violent shaking until I touched the stump with the poker one last time, at which point I heard a sigh and then a throaty rattle. The hacendado's features relaxed and a breath expelled from his lungs. His last breath.

¡Santo mierda! He was dead.

He had no sooner given up the ghost then banging started at the door. "I'm not ready yet!" I shouted.

My knees shook so badly I leaned against the bed frame for support. What was I to do? I checked the window. Tempest was below, still saddled, but I had two problems. I'd break a leg in the jump, and standing watch were two vaqueros who would cut my throat while I lay screaming. The only way out of the casa was through the bedroom door, except the grieving widow and loving son were there, at each other's throats and ready to cut mine.

As I faced these decisions of life and death, the nasty little dog lifted his foot and pissed on my pants leg.

I stared down at the little bastardo the hot poker in my hand, ready to stick it in his crotch and broil his minuscule balls. Then a revelation struck me. *¡Madre de dios!* The dog was my savior!

Tearing off a strip of the bedsheet, I tied his jaws shut so he couldn't bark. With more strips, I tied the struggling animal tightly to the chest of the dead man. When I was finished, I pulled the blankets up on the hacendado's chest until the dog was covered. Then I stepped back and looked at my handiwork. The chest area of the man rose and lowered, rose and lowered, just like a man breathing—I hoped.

With a strange sense of calm, I went to the bedroom door and opened it. As the son and widow tried to enter, I blocked them. "The hacendado is resting. He must not be disturbed until I return with medicine."

I let them get a peek past me so they could see the chest rise and fall. I quickly stepped out, shutting the door behind me. I put my finger to my lips.

"*Shhh.* You must be quiet. The slightest noise could kill him. Stay here while I get the medicine from my saddlebags."

I left the familial flock of vultures watching each other at the bedroom door, each one wondering what he or she should do to snare the inheritance. I quickly went down the stairs and out the front door.

The two vaqueros watching my horse came to attention as I came out.

"It's a miracle, my sons, a miracle," I waived the sign of the cross at them. "Kneel, pray, thank God for the deliverance."

While they knelt, I got into the saddle. "Pray, my sons. Praise God for the miracle!"

I gave Tempest his head and rode low in the saddle as the great stallion carried me away.

LOS CONSPIRADORES

PADRE MIGUEL HIDALGO paused in front of his rectory's bedroom door and knocked softly. His housekeeper opened the door. "How is she?" he whispered.

"I'm awake," Marina's voice called to him from the bed.

He went to her bed and took her hand. As a smalltown priest, he had seen murder and rape, beatings and thievery, sins mortal and venal, but the harm had rarely touched those in his immediate circle. Marina was more than an intelligent woman of indio descent. He thought of her as a daughter. Now, as he stood at her bedside and stared down at her swollen, bruised face, he felt the compassion of the priest but also the rage of a man at those who had done this to her.

"Any word of—" she started to ask.

"No, but that's for the best. They won't catch him, that stallion of his can outrun the wind."

"I'm sorry, padre, all your work . . ."

He sat down on the edge of the bed. "No, not just my work, but your work and the sweat of a hundred others."

"Did they destroy everything?"

"No, my child, they can't destroy our will to fight."

Marina took his hand. "I'm afraid for you. I see something in your eyes that I've never seen before. Wrath, padre, the fury of a wolf protecting its cubs."

Padre Hidalgo rode through the night, leaving Dolores for San Miguel el Grande. He left in the dark to avoid detection, accompanied by two vaquero bodyguards. He would not reach San Miguel until midday. He kept an eye on his back trail the entire way.

He would meet with men who, like himself, understood that New Spain would not be saved by the Sermon on the Mount but by the muzzle of a gun.

He knew Dolores, San Miguel, Guanajuato, Querétaro, Valladolid, and the other towns of the Bajío with a vivid intimacy. Born in the Bajío in 1753, now, at fifty-six years of age, he had spent his entire life in the region. Miguel Gregorio Antonio Hidalgo y Costilla Gallaga Mandarte y Villaseñor was his full name. While he was no respecter of bloodlines, his own was purer peninsular Spanish than most of the Spaniards born in the colony. His father, Cristóbal Hidalgo y Costilla, a native of Tejupilco in the intendency of Méjico, had established himself in Penjamo in the province of Guanajuato as the majordomo of a large hacienda. He married Ana María Gallaga.

His mother had died bearing her fifth child when Miguel was eight. Unlike most men of his time, his father, insisting that his children be educated, had personally taught them to read and write. At twelve, his father sent Miguel and an older brother to Valladolid to study at the Jesuit College of San Francisco Javier. Two years later the king expelled the Jesuit order from New Spain, believing their attempts to educate and promote indios a threat to the gachupines.

Miguel and his brother returned to their family at Corralejo. Unable to resume studies elsewhere, in midterm, Hidalgo went with his father to Tejupilco, the place of his father's birth, near Toluca. There, the young Miguel came into contact with Otomí indios. Finding the company of indios agreeable, he befriended them and learned their language. Later he would add two more indio tongues to his repertoire of languages, which included Latin, French, and some English.

Soon afterward, his father sent him to the college of San Nicolás Obispo to study theology and prepare for the priesthood. While at the college, his probing intellect and quick wit earned him the nickname El Zorro—The Fox.

After his schooling, he took up teaching, in the end becoming the head of the college. But his liberal notions were in conflict with those of religious authority. After leaving the college, he served as a parish priest for almost a decade before he was driven from that position, too, for voicing opinions inimical to the church hierarchy.

After several years of eluding the Inquisition, he came to Dolores, where his brother Joaquín was the curate. When his brother passed away in 1803, Miguel assumed the role as curate of the town church.

In all his endeavors, his house and life had been a magnet for literary, musical, and social events. Several nights a week he hosted plays, readings, music recitals, or intellectual discussions.

Much to the chagrin of his church superiors, Miguel read French plays aloud, studied French political essays and often conversed in the language. Studying the Torah and the Koran, he learned of the infidel's singularly tolerant faith and of the many blessings that Jews had bestowed on Spain, the church, and indeed the world. To the church's increasing consternation, he openly voiced such heresies.

Committed to God's service since fourteen, he had spent his entire adult life in the church and had never dreamed he would swerve from the path. But now he feared he'd fallen from grace.

The constables and troops had left after devastating his vineyards and facilities, making no attempt to arrest or restrain him. A stranger, however, had stayed behind. Ostensibly a buyer of hides, Hidalgo quickly divined he was not there for animal skins. He recognized that the man was a *familiar*, a name and profession that, for the padre, had a sinister ring.

Familiars were not priests but members of a hermandad—a brotherhood—known as the Congregation of St. Peter Martyr, named after an inquisitor killed by his victims centuries ago. The secret police of the Inquisition and official protectors of the Holy Office, the hermandad was licensed by both church and law to bear arms. Employed as spies to investigate and apprehend suspects, they often invaded homes late at night to surprise and arrest the accused, then took them to an Inquisition dungeon for "questioning."

Through its army of the night, the church protected its interests, assisting tyrannical governments to suppress free thought and progressive ideas, burying those liberties deeper than any grave.

Father Hidalgo knew the Inquisition's methods—how it concocted false charges—and he knew it was investigating him. In the past, at the Inquisition's instigation, women swore he seduced them, men swore he cheated them in games of chance. Local dignitaries told these hellhounds that he plundered a church dedicated to redeeming the poor and underprivileged. They acted on none of those false charges. They were just a sword to hold over him. Their real concern was that he challenged both church and crown on its treatment of the dispossessed and disenfranchised, on whether the church should dictate what he could read and what his thoughts should be, and on his alleged liberal beliefs.

As he rode, he realized that few men his age, and none in his profession, would have traveled this late at night. Although he might have reached his destination quicker on horseback, he preferred the mule. Mules were more sure-footed, particularly in the dark. Even bandidos avoided night travel; the risk that their mounts would lose their footing and founder was too great.

Angry and depressed at so many years of work destroyed, Hidalgo was willing—even eager—to court the hazards of a night ride. He felt as if he had nothing to lose. The Aztec craftworks had meant everything to him. They were not just enterprises but living proof that brown-skinned indigenous peoples were as innately able as European-Americans, such as himself.

Watching the viceroy's men chop down mulberry trees, smash pottery kilns, tear up trellises, and uproot grapevines had left him in morbid shock. Turning his back on the carnage, he had wandered the woods for hours, sometimes praying, sometimes crying, sometimes cursing, trying to fathom what had happened. When he returned to Dolores and heard of the assault on Marina and others of his flock, an uncontrollable rage seared his soul. He was a changed man.

He was a priest whom his superiors in the church had never understood. A man of God, who seldom found the Messiah in men's "houses of God" but in the hearts and souls of the people he served. A brilliant theologian—he had, in fact, won church honors for his brilliant analyses of religious doctrine—he nonetheless perplexed his superiors.

In truth, the bishops did not care if he deviated spiritually. His burning zeal to improve his parish materially and politically, however, concerned and confounded them. Hidalgo believed the size of a parishioner's soul was a truer measurement of his or her worth than the size of his or her wallet and that truth, justice, and freedom from tyranny were indispensable to spiritual redemption. His mission to free his parishioners from grinding, soul-destroying lives of forced bondage in the colony's mines and haciendas left the bishops anxious.

Whether they approved or not, forced labor was the bedrock on which the church's missions rested, underpinning church missions from the first days of Cortés. From the southernmost regions of South America to Misión San Francisco on the north coast of New California, church-conscripted indios built and fortified church compounds, cleared and cultivated the land.

But Padre Hidalgo had lifted peons above the tilling of corn and mining of ore. In an attempt to break their chains, he had taught them the forbidden arts of manufacturing and commerce.

To justify their oppression by the merchants and grandees, the indio had to be decreed inferior. To their chagrin, Father Hidalgo, in refuting their doctrine, had exposed their fraud. Elevating indios to the economic status of Spaniards would sever their shackles to the land and the mines forever. By offering to free the indio from bondage, Father Hidalgo had threatened to topple a system that maintained the criollo and gachupine in affluence, oppressed the poor of New Spain, and vouchsafed tribute to the crown.

Father Hidalgo now realized Spain would not repudiate that false doctrine until the people of New Spain forced them to, cleansing themselves of terror and tyranny, of lust and lies, of slavery and greed.

"Spain wants slaves, not citizens," he cried to the night wind.

He wasn't a young man, yet in his soul the first fires of rebellion against both church and crown—flames that threatened to incinerate all of New Spain—flickered furiously. And he was in contact with others who had grown increasingly impatient at the gachupines' refusal to share their power and privileges with the less fortunate.

What a fool he had been!

Spain and New Spain's rulers would never change . . . voluntarily. He knew that now. Their treatment of New Spain's peons was not unlike a public execution. The executioner first placed a garrote—a circular iron frame—around the condemned person's throat prior to the hanging. The hangman screwed it tight, bringing the condemned to the point of asphyxiation. Only on the verge of expiration, did the executioner noose the neck and hang the condemned until dead.

In Father Hidalgo's mind, he saw Spain garroting its peons—strangling them to the very edge of death—but never consummating their demise. The torture continued on and on, in perpetuity, into the torture chambers of hell. Shackled, flogged, and raped, the enslaved peons had no hope of improving their lot or even modifying Spain's behavior. Spain's sole goal was infinite exploitation with no end in sight. Nor was the church a candle of hope.

When the padre faced this truth, he felt a spiritual surge. His whole life he had heard priests and parishioners speak of "the hand of God" and "revealed truth." He believed he'd felt them both at that moment. He'd felt Truth's divine touch . . . and that Truth would set his people free.

He knew he could not stop the strangling of the people with words.

As a student of history, of the French and American revolutions, he knew that men had to fight for the rights they enjoyed. And as a Bible student, he knew that the Old Testament prophets—Moses, Solomon, and David—were not mere idealists but warriors who turned their words into swords. Cortés had defeated the indios not with words but with musket and cannon, with hurricanes of fire and tidal waves of blood.

The indios had to reclaim their land the same way: with fire and blood. They had no choice. Their rulers—Hidalgo now knew—were neither ignorant nor innocent. They knew what they were doing and would not change.

 **THIRTY-ONE**

SHORTLY AFTER DAWN, Ignacio Allende and his friend, Juan Aldama, left San Miguel for a rendezvous with Father Hidalgo at a rancho north of town. Departing west, they soon doubled back, continually checking their back trail, covering their tracks, keeping an eye out for the viceroy's spies.

Allende understood the meeting could have cataclysmic consequences, for himself and the colony's 6 million people. Aldama was less prescient but followed where Allende led.

Both men were the caballeros of fine families, of inestimable breeding and considerable means. Full-blooded Spanish criollos by birth, Allende hailed from San Miguel, where his father, Don Domingo Narciso de Allende, a merchant and owner of a hacienda, died during Allende's youth. Bequeathing his family a substantial inheritance, a privileged upper-class existence seemed, for Allende, inevitable.

Handsome and charismatic, Allende was renowned for his courage and caballero horsemanship. His strength was legendary: It was said he could hold back a bull by the horns. His reputation for prowess with women rivaled that of his bullfighting, and his drive to succeed seemed irrepressibly relentless. Even when danger loomed. Stepping into a bullring, he once awed a crowd by openly exposing himself to the charging bull, deliberately leaning into its passing horns, leaning so far in that he was knocked down and left the ring with a broken nose.

He married María Agustina de las Fuentes in 1802, and though their union was childless, three other women bore him children.

Drawn to the military, he had served in the Queen's Dragoons for over twenty years, from age seventeen. He was devoted to its military traditions and camaraderie. Blunt-spoken, aggressive, more competent than many officers above him, he nonetheless failed to rise above captain.

When a Dragoon colonel told him outright that his criollo birth would end all further promotions, adding that people born in the colony were inherently unfit for high command, Allende seethed.

Allende knew of course that if one criollo proved competent in high command, a flood tide of criollos would agitate for promotion. Criollo competence would detonate the myth of gachupine superiority and weaken the gachupines' hold over New Spain, perhaps wounding it fatally.

Eventually, Allende discussed the situation with other criollos: offhanded talks at first, in taverns, at balls, on a paseo, on horseback. Formal meetings inevitably ensued, till they eventually organized, meeting openly as a "literary society." Sometimes meeting in Allende's brother's house in San Miguel, other times in Querétaro, these group get-togethers, sociopolitical in nature, employed the ruse of a "literary society" as a cover.

Of late, at the meetings these dissatisfied criollos increasingly vented their frustration over gachupine dominance. Allende lived his life by the bullfighter's creed. To the matador, bullfighting was not a sport but a test of wills in which the matador courted death, deeming it an honorable price for failure. The bulls used in the corridas de toros were not common cattle but were bred in Spain for savage aggression. Called *Bos tauros ibericus*, violently impulsive, these bulls were instinctively hostile, charging without provocation in tenacious headlong attacks.

To Allende, bullfighting was less a contest between man and bull than a conflict *within* a man. The bull charged out of bloodlust and aggression, but the bullfighter's motives were more complex. Did he enter the ring . . . to kill a bull? To prove something to himself? To impress a señorita? To prove something to the crowd?

If he opted for the last, if he battled a beast solely for the crowd, the fighter's motives were intrinsically impure. Many in the crowd came to see the bullfighter humbled, gored, even killed. Occasionally they were able to shout with glee as a matador disgraced himself by panicking or showing fear or simply by backing away from the bull's charge.

Entering the ring, a man had to ask himself how far he was willing to go to please the crowd, to earn their adulation, to win the gasp of a beautiful señorita. Would he let the passing horns graze his gut or kiss his cojones? Would he die for the adulation of the crowd, for its praise, money, fame? Would he court bloody death with bravura indifference?

More than anything else, Allende's experience as an amateur bullfighter had prepared him for New Spain's moment of truth when he would challenge its people to rise up.

Like most young caballeros, Ignacio Allende had spurned both scholarly and commercial worlds, declining to run his family's hacienda or its merchant business. His interests ran toward the military, with its weapons, its uniforms, its sense of honor, and its devotion to combat, command, and camaraderie. But unlike many of his friends, his male pride was not diluted by mindless machismo. He observed, analyzed, and prepared, then acted upon carefully reasoned judgments rather than lash out in irrational rage.

He understood at last his ambition to rise in rank and lead an army against Spain's fiercest foes, such as Napoleon's France, would be forever thwarted. He now knew this dream of command would only come when he raised his own army.

"What do you know of this priest in Dolores?" Aldama asked.

"I've met him several times. He attended literary club meetings in Querétaro when you were away."

"He has brought the wrath of the viceroy upon him."

Allende shrugged. Over the years, as he observed the corrupt and inefficient viceroyal system, he had grown less concerned about the viceroy's wrath.

"The padre is a man of courage and honesty. Those are traits not often found in men, whether they be kings, popes, or peons. And he transcends those traits when he is rash. He challenged the crown's prohibitions against colonial enterprises, and at the same time he set out to prove the worth of the indio."

Aldama shook his head. "He rubs salt in the viceroy's wounds. The gachupines went to the viceroy and told him to stop this rabble-rouser before the indios overthrew their gachupine masters."

Allende said, "The padre has proven that with proper training the indio is capable of more than tilling the ground and digging in mines."

"Does he expect to train them in defiance of the viceroy? If he does, he'll find himself in the archbishop's prison, if the Inquisition does not break him on the rack."

"I don't know what his plans are. He has asked that the members of the literary club meet and discuss the situation. His message said he's being watched by a familiar, so he asked that the club meet in private."

As they rode, their talk moved from the padre's problems to their own frustrations.

"What of your conversation with Colonel Hernández?" Aldama asked. "Whenever I ask you about it, you look like a dog gnaws your cojones."

"Not a dog but a wolf. The colonel told me what we all have known. The upper ranks are prohibited to criollos." Allende's face reddened. "But this time he gloated, saying the climate of New Spain debilitates our brains, thus disqualifying us from command positions."

Like Allende, Aldama's sole ambition was for a military career. His father managed a factory for others, but Aldama wanted a horse between his legs and a sword in his hand. And, like Allende, Aldama was a captain in the militia and knew how to swear. His blood-curdling oaths ran the gamut of gutter words.

"What did you say to the colonel?" Aldama asked when he had run out of obscenities.

Allende grimaced. "Had anyone but my commanding officer insulted me thus, I would have offered him his choice of weapons and seconds. But what could I say? That he was a fool and a fraud? That the gachupines have commandeered the high command and enslaved New Spain out of hubris, avarice, and depraved ambition? Could I tell him they do these things because they fear not only us but the peons?

"Someday—"

"No!" Allende snapped. "The gachupine will oppose all attempts at reform. If we are to run our own affairs—we must take action."

"What kind of action are you proposing, amigo?"

Allende looked over at his friend. He knew Aldama admired him. In some ways, Aldama looked up to him as an older brother.

"I don't know. It is something to talk to the padre about. But I do know that when two men face each other and only one has a musket, the musket will command indisputable respect."

Allende shared some qualities with the priest of Dolores: Both were restless spirits. Both men began projects, even achieved success, but then moved on to another project before the project achieved its full potential.

One difference between them was the type of knowledge each possessed. Allende knew men and arms; Padre Hidalgo knew the human heart.

Allende said, "You wonder why I encouraged Father Hidalgo to join our efforts for change in the colony. We must recognize what has happened in the past. Forty years ago, when our fathers were young men, the Aztecs rose up, tens of thousands of them, especially in San Luís Potosí, where the inspector general, José de Galvez—"

"Chopped off the heads of nearly a hundred of them and posted them on pikes for all to see and remember."

"Yes, they had no leadership, and the uprising was put down, but imagine what they might have done if they had had leaders guiding them. The indios also remember how ruthlessly the riots were put down. Hidalgo says they remember, and they thirst for revenge for the cruelties."

"I have no confidence in an Aztec army."

"Not even one led by us?"

"How would we raise such a force?"

"That is where the padre is needed. He is famous throughout the Bajío as a friend of the indios. Given the opportunity, I believe they would flock to his banner. Supported by a few thousand well-trained militia, a large host of Aztecs could serve as a military vanguard."

Aldama shook his head. "You speak of insurrection, revolution."

"I speak of change, which will only come by force of arms. Do you want to serve like a peon under the spurs of the gachupines and pass on that heritage of enslavement to your children?"

"No, of course not."

"The winds of change are blowing in the colony. Men speak openly of rebellion. I hear it from other officers throughout the Bajío."

"This has to be thought out carefully. Even loose talk can bring the viceroy down upon us." Aldama was a brave man, but he lacked Allende's willingness to surge ahead despite all dangers.

"We're trained soldiers," Allende said, "as good as any the gachupines can field. If we declare for change and prove we can win, our people will join us. Honor demands that we stand up to the gachupines, that we fight, and if necessary that we die. My blood is as pure as that of any gachupine and I will not be enslaved by them."

Allende grinned at his friend. "Remember, amigo, to the victors go the spoils. If we are the ones to drive the gachupines from New Spain, we will enjoy the fruits of victory—high rank and honors."

 **THIRTY-TWO**

RAQUEL MONTEZ SAT quietly on a coach seat and looked at the woman sitting across from her. Doña Josefa Domínguez was the wife of Don Miguel Domínguez, the corregidor of Querétaro. As corregidor, Doña Josefa's husband was the chief judicial officer for the town and surrounding area. While Raquel had been visiting the señora, a message came from the curate of Dolores, Father Hidalgo, asking to meet privately with members of the Querétaro literary club. Like Doña Josefa, Raquel had attended meetings of the social club to lament the injustices of the colony's political and economic systems.

Raquel and the older woman had spent the night in San Miguel at a friend's home and then set out in the morning for the clandestine meeting.

She enjoyed the company of Doña Josefa, a woman of great intellect and moral quality. Raquel also admired Josefa's husband, Miguel Domínguez. Born in Guanajuato, Don Miguel had risen to a high rank for a criollo. He reminded her somewhat of her father because both men had an intense interest in literature and ideas.

While Don Miguel tacitly supported social change, his strong-willed wife—"La Corregidora," as she was called—actively joined in the literary society's secret meetings. Doña Josefa had lamented the colony's struggles and Spain's troubles in Europe for some time. "Napoleon is a madman driven by insatiable ambition, and no one in Madrid can stop him. He is devouring Europe, advancing to the east now, but he already has a death grip on the peninsula. And that court jester Godoy cannot even slow him down."

"I agree," Raquel said.

Raquel was as knowledgeable and as disgusted with Spain's feckless foreign policy as her godmother, who had inspired her political awareness. While attending school in Querétaro, Raquel had lived with the doña and her family, and Doña Josefa had given her a free run of their library. More important, she engaged her continually in provocative discussions of art, philosophy, history, literature, and the political struggles of their day.

While Raquel's father had encouraged her to study and inquire, Doña Josefa viewed politics and letters as a fiery commitment, and the doña's personal example ignited Raquel's passion for learning as much as the doña's lavish trove of titles, a literary passion that Juan de Zavala had found so singularly unattractive in women.

Raquel's own mother was indifferent to literature but loved music and bequeathed that sensibility to her daughter. A wounded soul, her mother had endured life's vicissitudes with failing health and a weakening will, a tragic fate Raquel was hell-bent to avoid.

Her father's interests, on the other hand, were bolder, more energetic. Loving all forms of the arts—literature, music, painting, and philosophy— he had possessed the finest private library in Guanajuato, an asset that had not served him well when the Inquisition knocked on his door, charging that he was a secret Jew.

An only child, she had joined in her father's intellectual pursuits despite the social convention that women lacked the intellect for serious learning. Recognizing that a woman like Doña Josefa—with her intelligence, erudition, and social status—would exert a positive influence on his daughter, her father encouraged their friendship and asked her to godmother his child. Although Raquel was a mestiza Doña Josefa insisted that Raquel be widely read and demanded a determining role in educating Raquel. Raquel's father acceded to all of the doña's demands.

But that world was gone. The father Raquel adored had been carried home on a door, passing from their lives with merciful quickness. God had not been so kind to her mother. A fragile woman, she had suffered unbearably when her husband died amidst disgrace, suspicion, and tragedy. After his death, her mind and body succumbed as well. She had passed away a month ago. Until her passing, Raquel had cared for her and struggled with the creditors to save something of her inheritance.

The financial struggle was mostly lost, and she was alone in life. Her friends assumed she would enter a convent, the only path available to women who lacked a man's protection and support. A woman could avail herself of no other opportunities except to function as a wife, a whore, or a servant. The convent offered protection, both financial and physical, sheltering many women plagued by an impecunious dowry.

Had Raquel sought the church's protection, she would not have felt alone. She would have followed the path of the historical figure she admired most, a poetess who had died over a hundred years before: Sor Juana Inés de la Cruz.

Sor Juana, "Sister Juana," entered the convent not for spiritual solace but for study and contemplation, the kind of life only a convent could provide her. Sor Juana's exact birth date was not clear (probably around 1648), though at birth she was unquestionably a "daughter of the church," meaning illegitimate, a bastarda.

Sor Juana had been an intellectual prodigy, composing a loa, a brief dramatic poem, at the age of eight. While other girls applied themselves to pleasing men, Sor Juana pleaded with her mother to disguise her as a boy so she could attend a university. Denied an education because of her sex, her grandfather provided the bulk of her instruction.

Despite her beauty, intelligence, and compelling personality, her low birth and her poetic aspirations held her back. Only life in the convent allowed her to write poetry and plays, experiment with science, and develop a large library. When a bishop restricted her studies, however, she rebelled, defending her right as a woman to seek after truth. She was known even in Spain as the "Méjican Phoenix" and the "Tenth Muse."

Ultimately, she was not able to continue her intellectual pursuits; the dogmatists in the church assailed her. Persecuted for her writing and her worldly thoughts, she gave up her books and signed a confession in her own blood. After her famed reply to the bishop, she withdrew from the outside world. She died in her mid-forties after she became ill while nursing the sick during an epidemic.

Lines from Raquel's favorite Sor Juana poem summarized Raquel's views on her own life.

> *The pain and torment of this love*
> *that my heart cannot conceal,*
> *I know I feel, but cannot know*
> *the reasons why it's this I feel.*

> *I suffer greatest agonies*
> *to reach the heights of ecstasy,*
> *but what commences as desire*
> *is doomed to end as misery.*
>
> *And when with greatest tenderness*
> *I weep for my unhappiness,*
> *I only know that I am sad*
> *but reasons I cannot express.*
>
> *First forbearing, then aroused,*
> *conflicting grief I am combating:*
> *that I shall suffer much for him,*
> *but with him I shall suffer nothing.*

She wondered how Sor Juana felt going into a convent. Never to love or be loved by a man. Never to unite with a man, to be in his arms, breast to breast, to be intimate.

She remembered the feeling of having Juan inside of her, his lips on hers, caressing her. She remembered the fear and awe when Juan made love to her, but most of all, the pounding of her blood.

Raquel had told Josefa that she lacked Sor Juana's courage. She could not endure a convent's discipline, abstinence, and abnegation.

She had enough money to leave Guanajuato and its loathsome memories. She would move to Méjico City and purchase a small, respectable house, all that she needed for the solitary life she planned for herself. And she had financial prospects there. A Portuguese businessman who had been a friend of her father's was broadminded enough to ask her to teach his three daughters liberal arts. She might be able to expand her tutelage, though few parents wanted educated daughters. Her best hope was to teach the children of foreigners living in the capital.

It would be a fresh start, getting her away from the Bajío and its memories, while preserving the independence to use her mind. Doña Josefa supported her desire for independence.

The older woman's voice brought Raquel back to the present.

"Godoy has us allied with Napoleon against the British. That's like a mouse warring on a cat. Already we have lost our fleet. How will the colony be defended against an invasion by the British? How long will Napoleon wait before gobbling us up?" She sighed and shook her head. "My dear, not so long ago Spain was a great power. That our leaders betray us breaks my heart, especially when our enemies proliferate, when war festers and spreads in Europe like the pox."

Raquel had only been half-listening to her godmother's lament. They had received word that morning about a subject closer to her heart. She stared out the window of the coach, deep in thought, when Josefa read her thoughts.

"You're thinking about him, aren't you, my dear?"

She didn't need to tell her grandmother his name. "Yes. I was thinking about what María said last night. Months have passed but still people talk about him."

"And why not? Has anything so scandalous happened in the colony before? I've never heard anything like it in my lifetime. An Aztec baby switched for a Spanish one? A peon growing up to be a much admired gachupine caballero? Now he has escaped from jail, and there are reports he has turned highwayman. Oh, how horrified are the gachupines. The irony is exquisite, except for your love of this unfortunate young man."

"I don't love him."

"Of course you do. He's a bad man, and your misfortune is to care for him."

"That he was a changeling isn't his fault."

"Of course not, but his treatment of you is. He exploited, then abandoned you in your time of need."

"I don't blame him. It was an arranged marriage. He never loved me and would never have married me if it had not been arranged for financial reasons, not if I had been the most beautiful woman in the colony, because I'm a mestiza. Besides, he's in love with another woman, one who is said to be the most beautiful woman in the colony. My father's misfortunes and loss of the dowry allowed him to escape a miserable marriage and an unhappy life."

Doña Josefa scoffed. "He's a fool. Her reputation as a flirt and social climber is common gossip, even here in Querétaro. The woman has a face men find attractive, but her husband-to-be will pay dearly for her charms when she demands the most scintillating jewels, the most extortionately expensive houses, only the finest clothes and coaches."

"Well, he need not fear that now. He need only fear the viceroy's constables."

Raquel's tone was neutral as she spoke about Juan, but her heart was not. She loved him from the first moment she had seen him. Because of that love, she had given him the most precious and valuable thing a young woman could give a man, her virginity. He broke her heart when he walked away from her and the planned marriage.

Her stoic features cracked, and she fought back tears. "I do truly love him. I will never love another man. I'm just afraid that I will never find happiness and that I will die in a convent writing regrets with my blood like Sor Juana."

The older woman suddenly chuckled. "I'm sorry, my dear, it's not funny, but I wonder how people would react if they knew that the infamous Juan de Zavala had escaped the Guanajuato jail wearing your father's boots."

AVENIDA DE LOS MUERTOS
(STREET OF THE DEAD)

THIRTY-THREE

MY PLAN, AFTER I left the hacienda—with a live dog strapped to the chest of a dead man—was to head northwest, in the direction of Zacatecas. I had hunted in the Zacatecas area and in the wild country north of it before. At some point, the people at the hacienda would join the viceroy's constables in their search for me. The less populated, ill-protected North was the logical route for a fleeing bandido to take.

Zacatecas was the second richest silver-mining region in the colony. Money flowed there like beehive honey, and the town was wilder and more untamed than Guanajuato. I might even flee farther north; it was hundreds of leagues to the Río Bravo and the settlements beyond. Towns were often weeks apart, and one could journey for days without seeing strangers. With saddlebags full of stolen silver one could stay lost forever.

Yes, going to Zacatecas was a fine plan, and one I carefully avoided. Instead, once I left my tracks for a route north, I did a wide circle of the area surrounding the hacienda and headed south. Zacatecas was the first place my pursuers would look. Even worse, many of the mine owners and suppliers had visited our hacienda and knew my face. They would recognize me the first time I walked down a Zacatecas street.

Other dangers abounded as well. En route to distant settlements like Taos and San Antonio, a lone rider had to fear not only bandidos but also wild indios, some of them still practicing the cannibalism favored by their ancestors. I had hunted with care when I went into those areas, more wary of two-legged beasts than the four-footed kind.

I also knew the unsettled areas of the south and east well, probably better than the constables searching for me. I had hunted the territory that stood at the edge of the great region of mountains and high flatlands we call the Valley of Méjico. I also knew what lay east beyond the mountains: the torrid disease-ridden wet-hot coasts, where, when it rained, the ocean itself seemed to fall from the sky, hot enough to melt a man to the bone. But down that coast also lay the colony's main port, Veracruz.

Hernán Cortés founded a town called La Villa Rica de la Vera Cruz (The Rich Town of the True Cross) when he first landed on the east coast of the colony back in 1519. Eh, he didn't name the town for its "untold riches" since all he had found was swamp and sand. He named it instead after his conquistador dreams, the lust for worldly riches.

Once I was in Veracruz, I would find a way to get on a ship taking me perhaps to Havana, queen of the Carribean.

I had to get out of the colony. I doubted now that if I was captured, I would be sent to the Far East on that infamous Manila galleon. The constables would hang me from the nearest tree. Escape through Veracruz was the only way out.

To get there I would have to cross mountains, descend into the hot zone to the coast, and follow the coast south to the port. Besides the hazards of constables and bandidos, I would have to traverse the coastal areas where mosquitoes and crocodiles abounded, and countless victims died from the dreaded vomito negro lurking in the stinking swamps.

Contemplating that trip, I recalled Bruto's claim that the black vomit transformed me into a gachupine in the first place. If his tale of deceit was true, what would the real Juan de Zavala have become had he lived? More important, what would I have been if he had lived?

Was my mother truly an Aztec puta—a whore? Just because she sold her baby did not necessarily make her a whore or even a bad person. The world was hard on poor women with children. Even harder for a woman with a child outside the marriage bed. She might have sold her baby to give the child a better life.

That lying bastardo Bruto said my mother was a whore, but was he telling the truth? He deliberately set out to disgrace and destroy me after I threatened to take control of my estate. I was certain he lied to bring me down after his plan to poison me and steal my estate went astray.

By the time I had ridden another hour, I was sure he had lied. I had adapted so well as a gachupine my mother had to have been one, or at least a highly placed criolla. No doubt she had become pregnant with me as a result of a love affair with a titled gachupine, a count or marqués, and had permitted Bruto to switch me for the dead baby so I would have a good future.

The main road from the capital to Veracruz ran from Puebla to Jalapa and then down to the coast. Along the coast, the road ran through the sands, wetlands, and swamps that made the torrid region infamously unhealthy. Not always a carriage route, the road in the mountains was at times little more than a mule trail. Yet it was also the most widely traveled road in the colony since most of the colony's imports and exports traversed it.

I was reluctant to take the road since it was also frequented by the viceroy's constables. An alternative was to negotiate precipitous mountain passes, then journey to the coast north of the Jalapa path. I had hunted in those rugged mountains and once went all the way down to the coast. That coastline featured no ports and no ships. The few plantations there grew jungle produce: bananas, coconuts, sugar, tobacco.

Negotiating the steep, narrow mountain passes, the tropical rainstorms, and the disease-ridden swamps along the sweltering coast would be difficult and dangerous. Still I would encounter very few people en route, mostly indios with donkeys and an occasional string of pack mules transporting plantation produce up the mountains and trade goods, such as clothes, utensils, and pulque, back down.

Recalling my previous trip down the coast, I came across the ancient indio ruins of Tajín. I remembered the name from the many boring hours I'd spent listening to Raquel as she lectured me on the glories of the indio civilizations that existed before Cortés landed. The city was now overgrown, but I could make out stone structures. Raquel said that the ancient indios had played a dangerous game in courts like this, a sport played with a hard rubber ball in which the losing team was often sacrificed to the gods.

And I remembered something else about the Tajín area: Along the coast, I had encountered a military post with only about a dozen men, but the crown was bent on fortifying the coast. Other posts may well be deployed with few travelers besides myself to pique their curiosity.

The coast was no good for me. I had no good options. But the thought occurred to me that the least likely place they would look for me was in plain sight, along the crowded roads that led to the capital and Veracruz.

I devised a plan that would have evoked the admiration and envy of Napoleon himself. Disguising myself as a lowly tradesman, I would vanish into the ranks of itinerant tradesmen traversing the roads: indios weighted down with burden baskets, their backs bent, tumplines taut against their foreheads; mestizos hazing donkeys or mules, their backs likewise piled high; and criollo merchants on blooded horses or in sturdy carriages. Mule trains carrying silver or maize often had a thousand or more pack animals. They banned together for protection, and I could easily "lose myself" among them.

But I couldn't hide Tempest. The constables would be looking for me mounted on a fine bluish-black stallion. As Marina pointed out, I hadn't fooled her when I rode into Dolores on the great stallion. To escape detection, I would have to wear the clothes of peons and ride a donkey or mule, the mounts most suited to that class.

Clothing was no problem. Under my monk's robe I wore clothes Marina gave me that had belonged to her deceased husband. I could change my appearance by merely casting the monk's robe off. I rubbed my face. I would be glad to get rid of my beard.

But Tempest was not just my horse; he was the winged Pegasus that carried me away from danger. More than that, he symbolized the life I'd lost but swore I would retrieve. I breathed only because of Tempest's speed and courage.

After I had put two days between myself and the Dolores hacienda, sticking mostly to wilderness, I knew I couldn't keep riding the stallion. I lassoed a mule in a pen on a rancho that raised the animals for work at the mines. I also bought a suitable saddle for a mule from another rancher along the way. After I had the mule saddled and determined that he was not going to be ornery and refuse to let me ride him, I took Tempest aside.

"I'm sorry," I told him sadly. "You have been my amigo and savior, but now we must part. Someday we will be partners again." I turned him loose into a pasture with other mares and left.

Astride a mule and dressed as a peon, I was no longer Juan de Zavala, caballero.

The next day, I bought a load of clothing—mostly serapes that were little more than pieces of cheap blankets—from a mestizo, taking his already packed mule in exchange for mine and the price of the merchandize. It meant I had to walk, but almost all peon merchants except muleteers of long trains walked in order to use every animal they had to carry merchandise.

The one thing I refused to give up were my caballero boots. They were a gift from my beloved Isabella, and I would have sliced off pieces of my flesh before I would part with them. In my heart, I knew that someday I would return, with a fortune and perhaps even that coveted noble title Isabella so fancied. And the first thing I would do is show her that I still wore the boots she had given me. I made one concession however and did not clean them, hiding their quality under layers of dirt.

With my mule, merchandise, and humble attitude, I headed south, toward a place Raquel had described to me. Not that she and her scholarly friends knew much about it. No one did. A place of the dead, where ghosts, gods, and ancient mysteries resided.

   **THIRTY-FOUR**

Teotihuacán

FROM MOUNTAINOUS TRAILS that few people traveled and across wild terrain where I saw no other humans traversing, I finally came to the Valley of Méjico and one of the strangest cities on Earth. The city of the gods.

Teotihuacán (an indio word pronounced tay-oh-tee-wah-KAHN) both fascinated and frightened the Aztecs.

I confess, not much scares me. I have ridden alone on hunting trips into the mountains and forests of our great plateau, down to the jungles on the east side of the mountains, and even beyond Zacatecas, north to the dangerous arid regions that are infested with savage indios. With bow and arrow, I've hunted jaguars, creatures so fast they can deflect arrows with their paws in midflight, so lethal they eviscerate with a single blow. I have fought and killed bad men. While I have met braver hombres, I have faced more dangers than most men my age, and no man has ever accused me of cowardice. But I don't pretend to be brave when it comes to *ghosts*.

I had arrived at Teotihuacán after coming out of the mountains and descending to the tablelands. Located in a valley that also bears its name, Teotihuacán is part of the larger Valley of Méjico. It's about a dozen leagues from the capital. The Spanish name for the place is San Juan de Teotihuacán, but its spirit is in no way saintly.

Walking down the Avenue of the Dead—the broad, empty street that was the central artery of this ghost-city—I sensed the spirits of the long-dead. And shivered despite the warm sunlight.

I leaned against an ancient avenue wall and smoked a cigarro while I watched a crafty lépero eyeing a group of Spanish scholars who had come to study the city of gods and ghosts. Léperos commonly possessed a certain sly and innate cunning when it came to getting money for pulque.

This particular lépero had ingratiated himself with one of the scholars, a pale, sensitive-looking young Spaniard I'd heard other members of the expedition call Carlos Galí. This Carlos the Scholar appeared to be but a few years older than me.

Observing and listening to conversations, I learned that some of the expedition scholars were priest-scholars, others were secular professors at a university in Barcelona. They were in the colony to examine sites of the ancient indio civilizations that flourished before the Conquest.

The name Barcelona had a magic ring in my ear. One of the great cities of Spain, this remarkable city on the Mediterranean in Catalonia was situated not far from the French border. A prized city even in Roman times, it was briefly occupied by the Moors before it became a bastion of Christian power on the peninsula during the centuries-long struggle to drive the infidels back to North Africa. I heard many stories about its greatness from Bruto as I grew up. It was the city of my birth. Or so I was told until a dying madman slandered my origins.

I even spoke a bit of Catalán, a language similar to but distinct from Spanish. Like Spanish, its roots were Latin. I had picked up enough of the language during my childhood to hold a conversation, because Bruto and Zavala family members who visited spoke Catalán around the dinner table.

The expedition employed porters who handled the baggage of individual scholars and the food and supplies of the group as a whole. It had used peons from Veracruz on the trek up the mountains to Jalapa. At Jalapa the Veracruz peons returned home, and new porters took their place. Now the Jalapa porters were being replaced by men who would accompany the expedition on the next leg, south to Cuicuilco, a town just beyond the capital.

If I could join the group as a porter, I would disappear into thin air, at least for the constables looking for me. From sizing up the members, the young scholar whom the lépero finessed seemed the most promising to me. Naïve, he had no idea how the lépero would react to his touching simplicity. He was, in truth, wet-nursing a rattlesnake.

I had noticed the lépero earlier with two other vermin, drinking and laughing, leering at the young scholar with their shifty eyes. I didn't need a cartographer to chart their course for me. They would rob him, and if given the chance, cut his throat for the boots on his feet, even for just his *socks*.

Looking at the dedicated, sincere youth, I felt I was honor bound to save him from this pack of murderous thieves. But I had to tread carefully. The constable from a nearby village had come to meet with the head of the expedition. From the conversations I eavesdropped on, the constable—a fat fool who probably could not read his own name—was describing to the expedition members how the site had once been a great Aztec city. I knew that to be false.

Eh, you wonder how Juan de Zavala, a man who had "read" more horse hooves, and brothel putas than books, would know about an ancient city of indios? Was I not once betrothed to a woman who suckled me at the teat of knowledge? Had I not suffered through Raquel's interminable harangues about the grandeur of indio culture and the destruction visited on it by Cortés's conquest?

Now I was fortunate that she had lectured me on this city of ghosts and on Tenochtitlán, the Aztec capital now occupied by Méjico City.

I approached the young scholar who had moved away from the group, which still listened to the constable explicate the markings the ancient race of indios put on walls. I considered speaking to him in Catalán and telling him I was born in Barcelona and had fallen upon hard times, but I was still pretending to be a peon selling clothes. Anything I told him was likely to be repeated to the others and reach the ear of the constable.

I strode up beside him, removed my hat and addressed him respectfully, putting a guttural edge on my Spanish.

"Señor, I must say something to you but, por favor, keep it in confidence or I will get into trouble. I do not believe the constable is giving your compañeros the correct information about the history of this ancient city."

The young scholar smiled at me. "And what do you know about the history?"

"I know that it was never an Aztec city. For certain, the Aztec emperors visited here each year to pay homage to their pagan gods, but the city was built many centuries before the Aztecs came to the Valley of Méjico. And a long time before the Aztecs rose to power, the city was abandoned. It was that way even when the Aztecs were a mighty empire. They visited the city to worship, but they did not live here because they were fearful of it."

He looked me over. "How did you gain your knowledge of the city?"

"I worked in the home of a scholar in Guadalajara, señor. He had no fame," I said, to ensure he shouldn't expect to know of him, "but he was a learned man. He spoke to me sometimes of what he read."

"Is your master here?"

"No, senór, he died a few months ago. His passing left me homeless and without a master. I have heard you are hiring porters for the trip south.

I am a good worker and obey without too many beatings. I would serve you well if you would so permit."

"I'm sorry, but I've already hired a bearer, Pepe, a local man who not only knows the territory but has many children to feed."

"Perhaps I can serve you in other ways, señor. While I have been nothing more than a lowly household servant, my master did teach me to shoot and to use a blade. There are many bandidos on the road . . ."

He shook his head. "We have men from the army protecting us."

He pointed to where six soldiers were standing around talking, smoking, and drinking wine. If it were not for their dirty, sloppy uniforms, I would have taken the group to be compañeros of the léperos drinking pulque across the way. They would not be mistaken for bandidos only because they were too fat and lazy.

"Are you traveling far beyond Cuicuilco?" I asked.

"We are going all the way to the land of the Mayas."

"That far? To the southern jungles? I am told there are many hazards en route, that the south is even more dangerous than the north, the indios are wild and bloodthirsty."

"The porter I'm hiring," he nodded in the direction of Pepe the lépero, "assures me he knows of safe routes through the jungles."

"Well, señor, as one familiar with the colony, I can say with assurance that you will arrive safely in Cuicuilco."

"What's your name?" he asked.

"Juan Madero," I said.

"Come along with me if you want a day's work. You can assist me by clearing some of the brush from ruins that I want to examine. I'm interested in what other things your former employer told you about the city."

"He told me this main boulevard is called the Avenue of the Dead because many kings and notables—dead since before the time of our Savior Jesus Christ—are said to be buried in the tombs that line it."

"I've heard that story, too, but some question whether those buildings are tombs or temples and palaces. Regardless, it is a ghost city for sure."

"Dead, but not quiet, eh?" I said. "What you couldn't hear with your ears, you feel with your skin as you walk down the roadway between the two great pyramids. You sense them, too, señor?"

He laughed. "If you fear the spirits of the city, you are in good company. Perhaps it runs in your indio blood. As you said, the Aztecs also feared the city. In their pagan tongue, the name Teotihuacán meant something like 'city of the gods.' They believed that it was the dwelling place of powerfully dangerous deities. That's why they pilgrimaged here each year, to pay homage to the gods."

"Señor, why would the Aztecs—who I have been told were bad hombres, who warred and killed at every opportunity—fear a deserted city?"

"They feared what they could see as well as what they didn't see. Look at the incredible ruins. Giant pyramids and brilliantly carved stone temples and palaces. Can you imagine what the city must have looked like in ancient times, when its buildings were brightly painted? I have never heard of a place on earth—except the monuments of the mighty pharaohs in Egypt, and the wall that runs forever through the land of the chinos—that compares to the accomplishments of the ancient race that built this magnificent city.

"What frightened the Aztecs most and continues to alarm people like you who come here, is the fact that no one knows who exactly built the city. Is that not incredible, Juan? We stand in the middle of a great city, with towering pyramids, and no one knows what race of man built it or even what name they gave it.

"As your master told you, your Aztec ancestors didn't build it. They came to the Valley of Méjico thirteen, even fourteen centuries *after* the city was built. Do you realize that Teotihuacán is the largest city that ever existed in the Americas before the time of Columbus? It was larger than the Aztec capital of Tenochtitlán and would have rivaled Rome at its fullest splendor. Not even Méjico City, Havana, or any other city of the Americas today has as many people as this ancient city had."

"How many people do you think lived here?" I asked.

"Some scholars believe over two hundred thousand people populated the city at its height."

¡Ay! That was a lot of ghosts.

We talked as I cleared brush to expose the inscriptions on the side of a wall. I remembered something else Raquel told me.

"The pyramids here, they were what the Aztecs and other indios copied for their cities. At least, this is what I was told."

"You are correct, though the copies are smaller than the Pyramid of the Sun here in Teotihuacán. Think of it, Juan, the great and wondrous monuments of all the indio empires were copied from a city that was built by people no one knows. Look at the Pyramid of the Sun."

The huge structure was on the east side of the Avenue of the Dead, dominating the central part of the ruined city. Carlos told me that the structure was over two hundred feet high and that each of the four sides of its base was over seven hundred feet. From the ground, a man standing atop it looked like an ant on the roof of a hut.

At the north end of the wide avenue was the Pyramid of the Moon.

"The pyramid dedicated to the moon is actually shorter than its sister sun, but it appears to be of equal height only because it's on elevated ground. The Pyramid of the Sun is the third largest pyramid on Earth. While not as tall, it is almost as voluminous as the Great Pyramid of the Pharaoh at Giza in Egypt. Do you realize, Juan, that the largest pyramid of all—one that is even bigger than the pharaoh's pyramid—is not on the Nile, but in New Spain, at Cholula, where we will be journeying soon."

"Why did they build these pyramids? To take people to the top and rip out their hearts?"

"Yes. Human sacrifice was practiced, but other than that heinous institution, the pyramids were really places of worship, as our churches are to us of the true faith. They built them to please their gods. Unlike the pyramids of Egypt, which were built as tombs for kings, religious ceremonies took place atop the pyramids of New Spain. That's why they're flat on top, so the indios could built temples of worship on them. As for sacrifices," he shrugged, "unfortunately, that became part of their religion."

"For blood," I said, remembering the one part of Raquel's lecture that really interested me.

"Exactly. They believed that the sun, rain, and other gods were nourished by blood. The indios relied upon their crops for survival and believed that if they gave blood to the gods, the gods would thrive and bequeath to them weather conducive to raising crops. A blood covenant—human blood for rain and sunshine—was the agreement between the indios and the gods."

"Pure ignorance," I said.

"Perhaps." Carlos looked around to make sure there was no one else in hearing. "But ignorance abounds in many places."

I suspected he was talking about the Inquisition, which burned people at the stake during autos-de-fé.

"I am told that atop the Pyramid of the Sun," I said, "there once was a great gold disk, a tribute to the sun god. It alone was worth a king's ransom. Cortés seized it and had it melted down."

"Sí, scholars confirm that tale. Your master was well informed about the ruins."

"Will we ever know who built this city?" I asked.

"Only God can answer that question. The mystery of who could have built such enormous monuments is as puzzling as why the city's citizens abandoned it."

"You say abandoned, señor. Can it not be that the people simply fled from a stronger enemy?"

"Perhaps, but if war desolated the city, one would expect to see more of war's devastation. One must also wonder why the conquerors did not occupy this prodigious prize."

I shrugged. "Perhaps they did not wish to live cheek by jowl with ghosts."

The scholar studied me with quizzical amusement.

Belief in ghosts was new to me. When I was leading the life of a caballero, I seldom considered anyone or anything, and certainly not anyone in the hereafter. Perhaps I was changing. In the past, an impregnable shield of money and power had protected me, leaving me indifferent to the rest of the world. But now I lived my life, watching my back trail for constables and bandidos, searching the eyes of other travelers to see if they viewed me as their prey or if their suspicions would alert the viceroy's police. Now, on a street named for the dead, in a city long deserted by the living, I sensed the same sort of presence that had made Aztec emperors pay trembling tribute on bended knee to unseen ghosts.

Carlos patted my shoulder as we parted. "I've enjoyed our conversations. I regret that I have already hired Pepe for the journey. But with him knowing the route . . ."

I left the scholar, muttering to myself that he was a naïve fool and the lépero was the Mother of Liars. Other than being sentenced to road construction for drunkenness and theft each time he was scraped out of the gutter, that piece of human garbage had never been more than a league from the spot where he was born. I had told Carlos he'd be safe as far as Cuicuilco because the town was close to the capital. After Cuicuilco, the expedition planned to traveled to Puebla, perhaps a journey of sixty or seventy leagues, along probably the most traveled road in all the Americas. That route was safe, too. But south beyond Puebla, each league took the traveler farther from the heart of the colony until . . . eh, even I didn't know what lay ahead by the time one reached the hot, wet jungles, except that most of those trackless wastes had not been explored.

But I did know that the expedition needed more protection than the soldiers I saw, and only Christian charity impelled me to dignify them with the title "soldiers." If they had actually served in the army, they had been scraped off stockade walls and barracks-brothel floors, then foisted on this expedition by officers who wanted them off the post.

Either way, I had to see that the young scholar got to his destination, at least as far as Puebla, from which the main road to Veracruz runs. From Veracruz, ships plied the Caribbean and Europe sea routes.

The viceroy's constables would not spot me as long as I was part of the expedition. I would be safer traveling in a large well-armed caravan, and if I had trouble duping the constables and customs officials, I could, if necessary, "borrow" the young scholar's documents and dinero for both my journey on the Veracruz road and my passage out of New Spain.

To win employment with the expedition, I had to eliminate the lépero. Preying on Carlos's soft-hearted naiveté, the lépero convinced him he needed his earnings to support a brood of children. Eh, if this thieving scum had had children, he would have sold them into slavery for a jug of pulque. But I couldn't take the risk of alienating the scholar by exposing the lépero's lies and his own naiveté. My only recourse was to ensure that the lepéro could not physically make the trip. A dagger slipped across his throat would do the job.

Who said that necessity is the mother of murder? I believe it was Juan de Zavala.

 **THIRTY-FIVE**

FOR TWO DAYS I watched the lépero, and the constable watched me. I had unpacked my load of clothes from the mule and set them out on the ground in the market where other vendors sold trinkets and goods to the travelers who visited the great pyramids. When the constable came by to question me, I feigned respect for his high office, though he was doubtless hired by a local hacendado and was not an actual government official. I paid the mordida, giving him one of my better shirts as a token of my "respect." But I still sensed skepticism in his eyes. Perhaps my manner was too arrogant, my eyes too shrewd. Taller than most peons, my height may have raised suspicions.

He was approaching me again, probably to extort more bribes and to hammer me with questions I didn't want to answer. I hurried over to the young scholar, who was drawing on paper the carvings and paintings portrayed on the temple walls.

"Are you able to read the pictures, Don Carlos?" I asked. I added the honorific "don" to ingratiate myself with him. He didn't appear to be the type of gachupine who was arrogant about his position, not a wearer of sharp spurs as I had been, eh? But no man is totally without ego, as I well know.

"Unfortunately, I cannot, and neither can my fellow scholars. Several of us can decipher the picture writing of the Aztecs and other indio groups that were present at the time of the Conquest. These symbols, however, predate those hieroglyphs. Also much of the picture writing is illegible, worn away by time and weather or defaced by vandals and curiosity seekers."

"More likely treasure hunters," I said. "Who has not heard the story of Montezuma's lost treasure and lusted for it?" I nodded toward the léperos. "Thieves, not scholars—when those men hear of buried treasure, they come to loot, not learn. These swine would destroy the Parthenon to find a silver spoon."

I thought the reference to the Athenian temple was clever. Raquel had shown me a picture of it when she was talking about places of wonder in the world. I marveled now that I had learned so much from her. Fortunately for me, she had come to Teotihuacán with her father. In her case, a woman's education had not been an entire waste.

"You're a perceptive hombre, Juan. Thieves are truly the bane of antiquity, not just here in New Spain but throughout the world. They've done

more damage to archeological sites than flood, fire, earthquake, and war."
He patted my shoulder. "I'm sorry I've promised the position to another.
You would have made a fine servant."

As I walked away Pepe the Lépero came toward me. He looked like a
man with a mission.

"Stay away from my patrón," he hissed, "or I'll put a dagger in your gullet."

I tried to look frightened but could not keep from laughing. "You
would have to steal one first."

The lépero's fellow swine mimicked his threatening stare. That they
had closed ranks with Pepe was odd. I knew this kind from my time in jail.
Lépero scum were notoriously disloyal. Pepe had no doubt promised them
something of value. After disloyalty, lépero scum favored laziness. Refusing to work, they would not lift a finger for anything except money for
pulque or the means to avoid a prison flogging post.

So Pepe's offer to work for Carlos on the expedition was a lie. Such a
trip would require more work in a few days than the parasite had rendered
in his lifetime. And the notion of traveling to Cuicuilco would have been as
incomprehensible to Pepe as a voyage across the great western ocean to
the land of the chinos or a trip to Jupiter's moons.

Since he would not work for Carlos's money, Pepe and his men
planned to steal it.

I squatted next to my pile of clothes, pretending not to notice what
went on around the site. Carlos continued his work at the stone wall, copying the engravings. Pepe the Lépero huddled with his friends, drinking
pulque. Occasionally, they shot greedy glances at Carlos.

Late that afternoon, the léperos left, all save Pepe. He hung around,
cadging handouts from the capital's visitors. I wandered over to where Carlos was packing up his drawing materials.

"You quit a little early, Don Carlos."

"Sí, the man who is to be my porter wishes to introduce me to his wife
and family before we part for Cuicuilco. I sup with them tonight."

"Ah, supper with his wife and children."

I nodded and smiled like it was the most natural thing in the world for
a lépero to take home a gachupine for dinner. I doubted that Pepe had a
home other than the dirt his filthy body wallowed in when he passed out at
night.

The young scholar wore what any modestly well-off gachupine would
wear: a gold necklace with a pendant, a silver ring with a red stone, another silver ring with a lion's head on it, and a money pouch. Not great
wealth, but to that swine herd, it was a lifetime's worth of thieving and
begging.

I bid good-bye to Carlos and went back to my pile of goods, which I
had paid an indio to watch. I saddled my mule and left the site, starting in

the direction I had seen the pack of vermin go, but veering off so I wouldn't run into them. I climbed a small hill with trees for cover.

I slipped the machete out of its sheath. Spitting on my whetstone, I honed the blade to a razor's edge. Bigger, stronger, and longer than whatever the léperos would wield, I had something else they lacked: I was a trained horseman and swordsman, as skilled in these arts as any caballero in New Spain. Still these léperos were dangerous in a pack. While none of them owned a knife or machete—such items were too valuable to trade for pulque—they would arm themselves with clubs spiked with razor-sharp pieces of obsidian and with obsidian knives. They could also fall back and pelt me with rocks.

Mostly, I feared their obsidian knives. The indios had long used the volcanic vomit for weapons. The Aztecs had refined its effectiveness, embedding it in wood to make swords, daggers, and spears that sliced better than a finely honed sword. Made of sharp black volcanic glass, their obsidian knives would be especially lethal at close quarters. And this was a region in which obsidian was found.

The léperos would use the obsidian to cut Carlos's throat after they clubbed him to the ground. Then they would rob him. The odds were they would be caught later and hanged, but I had met enough of them in jail to know they did not fear hanging the way people whose brains weren't pickled by evil-smelling indio brew.

I watched as Carlos and the lépero came out of the antiquity site, walking together. Since Carlos was not on his horse, the lépero must have told him that they were not going far. A village, which I assumed was their alleged destination, lay just beyond the hilly crest of their trail. A cluster of boulders, bushes, and small trees stood just before that crest. I stared down at it, certain the léperos waited there in ambush. A repeated stirring in the bushes confirmed my suspicions.

I saw their game. They would charge out of their hiding place and kill Carlos, perhaps giving Pepe a small cut to avert blame from him. Pepe would stagger back to the expedition's camp and cry out that he and Carlos were ambushed by bandidos.

No! Not bandidos. That wasn't going to be their cover story. Lepéros survived because they were devilishly clever and manipulative. They'd accuse *me* of the attack. And I had played right into their hands. If I had stayed back at the site, others would have seen me. And where would I be when the attack took place? Hiding alone in the trees nearby.

Now I was doomed if Carlos was murdered.

As Carlos and Pepe neared the crest, I gave the mule a kick with my heels. My mount moved faster but didn't propel itself into a gallop, and I had no spurs or quirt. Slapping it on the flanks with the flat of my machete, I yelled every obscenity I knew at it. It finally picked up its pace as it galloped downhill.

I must have looked like a madman, thundering downhill on a mule, waving a machete, screaming obscenities loud enough to wake the damned. I looked so deranged that the three léperos, charging out of their hiding places and about to stab Carlos, stopped dead in their tracks with weapons raised and stared.

Pepe yelled, "Bandido!" and ran. The other léperos scattered to the wind.

As I galloped toward Pepe on a course that would take me past where Carlos was standing, the Spaniard pulled his dagger and got atop a boulder to meet my charge. I steered the mule away from Carlos, shaking my head in wonderment at him as I went by. Was he was going to fight a mounted man armed with a machete with his dagger?

Pepe was running for his life up to the crest of the hill as I came up behind him. He glanced back in stark terror when he heard my mule hammering up to him. He veered off the road, climbing onto rocks along the edge of the crest of the hill. I went after him, still on the mule, going between the boulders until I couldn't go any farther on the animal. Dismounting, I tied its rein to a bush and went onto the rocks, machete in hand, to follow him. He again glanced frantically over his shoulder before jumping a narrow crevasse, his feet landing on loose gravel. He slipped, teetered for a moment, his arms flailing, and then pitched backward off the ledge, disappearing into the crevasse.

I turned around and went back to the mule, not bothering to see what happened to him. His crazed yell echoed a few seconds up the crevasse, long enough for me to know it was not a short drop.

When I came back down, Carlos had come off the boulder. He still had the dagger in his hand. On his face was a look of consternation and puzzlement. I halted the mule and saluted Carlos with the machete.

"At your service, Don Carlos. As you can see, I've lost my horse and my sword and must fight battles in even a poorer state than the patron saint of poor knight entrants, Señor Don Quixote himself."

Carlos stayed rigid for a moment, not completely certain of what had come down, but the intentions of the léperos were obvious. Pepe's amigos were still racing over the hillside. Not far from us lay a wood club, a limb with a wicked wedge of obsidian embedded in it like an ax blade.

"A crude but nasty weapon," I said. "A well-aimed swipe could decapitate a man."

Carlos stared down at the club, a perplexed smile spreading across his face. He saluted me with his dagger.

"I am in your debt, *Don* Juan."

That night Carlos filled a pot heaping with succulent beef, pork, chiles, and potatoes. And there was also a big chunk of bread—real bread, not corn tortillas, but bread made from wheat flour. We took the food and went a good distance from the camp to share it. I ate ravenously, having supped for weeks on tortillas, beans, and peppers, the sustenance of the poor.

After eating, Carlos opened a jug of wine and nodded at me to follow him. It was after nightfall, but a full moon lit up the city of the dead. We walked slowly along, passing the jug between us.

"A magnificent place, is it not?" he said.

I agreed. Whatever was on Carlos's mind, he kept his counsel. He knew now I was not what I seemed, and I suspected that he was wise enough to understand that some secrets are best kept secret.

If my behavior confused him, I also did not understand Carlos. I had always assumed scholars, like learned priests, were womanly. Since they were indifferent to horses, swords, pistols, putas, and bottles of brandy, I assumed they lacked cojones. Carlos had surprised me. He showed big cojones: When I charged on the mule, waving a machete wildly, he had stood his ground with a dagger.

That he had stood his ground astonished me. I could not think of a single caballero in Guanajuato who would have leaped upon that boulder to face that attack.

I now knew I had more to learn about scholars, at least about this one. He was not a big man nor did he have the agile strength in his legs and upper body to make him a fine swordsman. He didn't ride his horse as if he'd been born in the saddle but as a townsperson more used to carriages. Yet he had stood his ground in the face of certain death. He was much man, despite his book learning.

"I'm not unaware that I owe you my life," Carlos said. He handed me the jug of wine as we walked. "Nor am I unaware that I had been taken in by the lépero."

"Por nada, señor." It was nothing.

"You understand that I personally do not distinguish between the races of men. But tonight, even after saving my life, you could not eat with me because the others on the expedition would take offense. My savior would have to eat with the servants."

I shrugged. "I would naturally eat with the servants, Don Carlos. I know my place."

He took a swig of wine. "You can stop calling me 'don.' My father was a butcher, and the only reason I attended university is because a wealthy patrón thought I had a gift for learning and paid my way."

"The way you stood your ground, you earned the title."

He gave me that puzzled look again. "After today, perhaps I should be calling you 'don' as I did earlier."

"I am a poor man and it honors me that—"

"Stop. You just lapsed into your gutter Spanish. Do you know how you addressed me after you chased the lépero to his death?"

My feet kept moving at an even pace, but my mind went flying. What had I done?

"You spoke Catalán."

My heart pounded. "Of course, my patrón was from Barcelona. I heard him speak in that tongue many times."

"You lapse back and forth between Catalán and Castilian."

"My master spoke—"

"I don't care what your master spoke. It's not your command of the language; it's your tone. One moment you speak with the vulgar tone of the lower classes, the next you sound like the youngest son of a nobleman, the kind who refused to study but who can parrot what others have told him." He held up his hand as I started another protest. "This is the last we will speak of this. Some matters are better left unspoken. You understand that not all the members of the expedition are scholars?"

I understood. Besides the soldiers, priests had come along, one of whom wore the green cross of the Inquisition. The Holy Office of the Inquisition typically sent an Inquisitor on such expeditions to ensure that any aspect of indio artifacts and history that offended the church was summarily suppressed.

In other words, the priest was a spy, constable, and hanging judge, cloaked with the power of the church, an entity that rivaled the viceroy in terms of its dominance in the colony and oftentimes was more powerful.

"We leave in two days for Cuicuilco. I will hire you and your animal at the rate the expedition pays for such services. You will have to dispose of your cargo of clothes because your mule will convey my equipment and personal items. Does that meet with your satisfaction?"

"Completely."

"You are to avoid contact with other members of the expedition. If there are any problems along the road, let the soldiers take care of them. Is that understood?"

"Sí, señor."

"And try to walk without strutting, especially when you see a pretty señorita. You look too much like a caballero."

 **THIRTY-SIX**

FOR THE NEXT two days, I followed Carlos around, carrying his drawing and writing materials. He recorded everything he saw, though some of his observations were solely a product of his imagination. The ruins were heavily overgrown with vegetation, concealing not only their secrets but often their shape.

"Do you realize, Juan, what a wonder this place is?" Carlos said to me, as we ate tortillas filled with peppers and beans. To my dismay, he had packed tortillas and beans rather then steak and trail-baked bread. He found the "peon food" tasty.

"Very nice place," I said, uninterested in the glories of a time and place long dead.

"Ah, *Don* Juan, I can see from your expression that you disdain the forgotten achievements of this ancient city. But perhaps you would care if you knew one of its secrets." He looked around to make sure no one was in earshot. "Can I trust you to keep your lips sealed? I put great trust in you because you saved my life and appear to be a man who keeps secrets."

I wondered if he had found hidden treasure in the old ruins. Eh, a little indio treasure would buy me a grand house in Havana. "Of course, señor, you can trust me."

"Have you heard of Atlantis?"

"Atlantis?"

He grinned like a small boy who knew the answer to a teacher's question at school. "An island in the Atlantic Ocean, it lay west of Gibraltar between Europe and the Americas. Plato—who mentioned it in two of his dialogues—is our sole source of information on this lost civilization. He says the island was beyond the Pillars of Hercules, which was what the Straits of Gibraltar were called in his time. Larger than the lands of Asia Minor and Libya combined, it had the landmass of a small continent.

"A rich and powerful empire, its rulers had conquered much of the Mediterranean world before the Greek army stopped their expansion. But Atlantis's most dreadful nemesis was not the Greeks, or even war, but a cataclysmic earthquake that destroyed the great land and caused it to sink in the ocean."

"What does that have to do with Teotihuacán?" I asked. A more important question in my mind was what it had to do with treasure.

"Some scholars believe that before Atlantis was destroyed, it had sent expeditions to America to colonize the continent and that the indios are the descendants of those people.

"Some argue that indios are descendants of Mongols who came across the Bering Strait in the far north during a time when it was frozen. But the Mongol theory does not account for the differences between the indios of the Americas and the Mongols of Asia. Nor does it account for the fact that ruins here at Teotihuacán, Cholula, and Cuicuilco prove that the indios were very advanced at an early stage.

"The writing of the ancient indios and ancient Egyptians is comparable. They both used picture-writing to communicate. Just as the Egyptians decorated their pyramids and temples with drawings that told stories about their gods and rulers, so did the ancient indios. The Egyptians made books out of paper, and our priests who came here following the Conquest found thousands of books the indios made from paper. Sadly, in a rush of religious fervor, almost all of the books were destroyed."

"So did the indios swim here from Atlantis or across the northern strait?"

He shrugged. "Some of my scholar friends have another theory, one that takes into account the resemblance between the indios and the Egyptians. They believe that the pyramids were built by a lost tribe of Israel that—driven by war and the desire for a homeland—crossed Asia and the Bering Strait. These people would have known the shape of the Egyptian pyramids and could have duplicated them in the New World."

Suddenly still, he glanced at the inquisitor-priest who stood nearby.

"Do you know that Teotihuacán played a famous role in the conquest of the Aztecs? Of the connection between the Pyramid of the Sun and Cortés?" Carlos asked me, changing subjects.

I shook my head. "No, señor. I apologize for my ignorance."

We climbed partway up the Pyramid of the Sun. Covered with cactus and other thick vegetation, the ascent was rough-going. When we were halfway up, over a hundred feet from the ground, we paused, and Carlos told me the story of Cortés and his connection to the pyramid.

"The Aztecs feared this city of ancient, inscrutable peoples, long dead would one day help the Great Conqueror.

"The connection between Cortés and the pyramid began soon after he arrived in what is now New Spain, landing on the coast with his small army. He won battles and recruited indio leaders who hated the dominance of the Aztecs. After he made his way to the Aztec capital, Tenochtitlán, Montezuma received him with great pomp. Even with indio allies, however, Montezuma's men vastly outnumbered Cortés's small force. In the end, the Great Conqueror subdued the indio empires by force of personality as much as he did by force of arms.

"While in Tenochtitlán, he received word that another Spaniard, Pánfilo Narváez, had arrived with an armed force to relieve Cortés of his command. Cortés set out with most of his men, leaving behind in the Aztec capital about eighty of his soldiers and several hundred indio allies under the command of Pedro de Alvarado. Cortés then proceeded to the coast, defeated Narváez's force, and brought the survivors under his own command.

"He returned to the capital to discover it seething and Alvarado's force under siege. Alvarado was the most rash and brutal of Cortes's lieutenants. Suspecting a plot, Alvarado attacked the indios during a religious festival, massacring them with cannon fire.

"Cortés saw that the entire city was rallying against the Spaniards. That night, he and his army fought their way out of the city, absconding with priceless treasures, retreating to the plains near what is now the town of

Otumba. As he peered out over the plains from a great eminence, Cortés saw thousands of indio warriors, stretching as far as the eye could see.

"Do you see what I'm getting at?" Carlos asked me. "The only elevated mounds from which Cortés could have surveyed the plains were either the Pyramid of the Sun or that of the Moon. Were they as overgrown with vegetation as they are today, he might not have even known he was climbing a pyramid. But the indios, who revered this place, would have known.

"As the vast indio army closed in, Cortés knew he could not prevail through military power alone. From his towering pyramid, he spotted the captain-general of the Aztec forces marching with banner unfurled. Díaz, who fought alongside Cortés in the battle, described the Aztec commander as garishly garbed in golden armor, gold and silver plumes rising high above his headpiece. Ordering his men to attack the Aztec commander, Cortés led the charge, sweeping through the Aztec ranks on his magnificent warhorse, plowing through them until he reached the commander.

"Cortés struck the commander with his horse, knocking his banner to the ground while Cortés's lieutenants crashed through the lines behind him. Juan de Salamanca, who rode beside Cortés on a fine piebald mare, killed the Aztec commander with a lance thrust and took from him his rich plumes.

"When the indios saw their commander fall, his banner trampled, his plumes of regal power usurped, they broke ranks, fleeing in panic and confusion. Several years later, our king gave the symbol of the plume to Salamanca as his coat of arms, and his descendants bear it on their tabards.

"This battle marked the beginning of the Aztec empire's end. Following the battle, Cortés and his indio allies returned to Tenochtitlán. After months of fierce fighting, they retook the city, battling Aztec warriors street by street. Think of it, amigo, we may be on the very same spot where Cortés stood when he saw the Aztec army approaching."

Carlos was a very knowledgeable scholar, even more learned than Rachel. Like her and Padre Hidalgo, his head was full of the people, places, and events of history. Unfortunately, all his information didn't bring any treasure to assist in my escape. But he was also full of both mystery and surprises. One of those mysteries would surface before we left this great city of the dead.

THIRTY-SEVEN

THE NIGHT BEFORE we were to break camp and head south for Cuicuilco, the members of the expedition went to an inn at Otumba to meet with a colonial savant, Doctor Oteyza, who was studying and measuring the pyramid. Carlos had paid our mule train's head driver to take the porters to a pulquería in San Juan. He also treated the camp guards, who stayed behind, to a feast of wine and roasted fowl. And he sent me to a village to bring back putas for the soldiers. Upon my return, he gave me dinero and told me to go back to the village and enjoy myself with a bottle and a woman.

It was providing putas for the guards that piqued my interest the most. Ay, the Barcelonan scholar was not a man to procure whores, even through an emissary. His actions seemed to center around having the entire encampment of scholars to himself.

I decided to stay around, inconspicuous, and see why Carlos wanted the run of the camp. Pretending to be off to the village pulquería, instead I took a jug of wine from the cook's tent, cigars from Carlos's tent and climbed up on the Pyramid of the Sun to relax, drink, and smoke my purloined cigars, hiding the tobacco's glow with my hat.

I was dozing off when I saw a figure on a mule approaching the camp from the direction of Otumba. I stared, trying to make out who it was in the darkness. The moon was three-quarters full and lit the site with surprising luminosity.

The person got off the mule before the camp, tied it to a bush, and walked to the tent of Roberto Muñoz, the expedition's military engineer.

I had had no dealings with the engineer. In fact, I hadn't had dealings with any members of the expedition except Carlos. But I had heard that the king had commissioned Muñoz to draw diagrams of the colony's fortifications and report on their condition.

I recognized the man who entered Muñoz's tent—it was Carlos. He had left the mule a considerable distance from the tent. Approaching the tent surreptitiously, he didn't reveal his presence to the soldiers who were gathered at the other end of the camp, sampling the wine and whores he had so generously provided.

Very curious. Getting everyone out of camp so he could enter the engineer's tent? There was some skullduggery afoot, no?

After leaving the tent with papers in hand, Carlos disappeared into his own tent. A candle lamp illuminated his tent walls.

I worked my way down the pyramid and crouched behind a bush near the tent to wait. A few minutes later the light went out. Leaving the tent, Carlos returned briefly to the engineer's tent, then, carrying a pouch, he headed back for his mule.

It was obvious that Carlos had copied something belonging to the military engineer. That he did it covertly indicated that he played a dangerous game.

I mounted my mule bareback and set off after Carlos, keeping enough distance behind so he would not be aware I was following him. I had not thought out my purpose for following him. I liked the young scholar from Barcelona and bid him no ill will. My own position, however, was precarious. I needed to know if I would profit—or suffer—from Carlos's mysterious agenda.

I followed him for over an hour when I saw a carriage approaching. More mystery. Few people would risk an animal's broken leg or a broken wheel on a carriage by traveling at night, not to mention the danger from two-legged animals with pistolas.

I got off the mule, tied its reins to a limb, and quietly sneaked through the brush. Carlos was waiting by the roadside as the carriage rumbled slowly over the rutted road toward him. Then he did another curious thing: When the carriage came to a halt, Carlos moved away from the roadside, steering his mount up a hillock to a copse of trees. Having devised my own clandestine movements to avoid jealous husbands and constables, I realized he had moved away to avoid letting the carriage driver see his features.

The carriage came to a halt, and a man wearing a cloak that covered him from head to foot stepped out. Without hesitation, he went up the hill and into the trees where Carlos was waiting. Emblazoned on the side of the coach was a coat of arms, but I couldn't discern its exact design.

I made my way on foot around the side of the hill, keeping low to the ground, crouching, and finally crawling on my stomach. Having stalked many animals on my hunting trips, I now moved as stealthily as el tigre, the jaguar, through scrub brush. I got close enough to see through the trees. I heard Carlos's voice, but could not make out his words, though I recognized that he was speaking French and, judging by his excited hand movements, very animatedly. I spoke French, although not as fluently as the scholarly Carlos.

Carlos waved the papers he held, which I assumed were a copy of the military engineer's drawings. When the cloaked person reached for them, he jerked back and said, "No!"

The other man pulled a pistol out from under his cloak and pointed it point-blank at Carlos. I froze. My own pistol was back at the camp, hidden in my possessions. Armed only with a knife, I was too far away to throw it with any accuracy.

Carlos threw the papers on the ground and approached the cloaked man, seemingly unafraid of the pistol. Then something else surprising happened: The man put the pistol away, he and Carlos hugged, and they exchanged more words, quietly, almost whispering to each other. Then their heads went together—*they kissed.*

Carlos and the man were sodomites!

Shortly thereafter, Carlos left, leaving the papers on the ground. The cloaked man picked up the papers and started back to where his carriage was waiting. But I was waiting closer to him than to the carriage. As he drew abreast, I came out of the bushes and hit him with my shoulder, sending him reeling back with an exclamation—the sound a woman would make.

Before the person could recover, I grabbed the cloak and jerked off the hood to reveal a pale pretty face and golden locks. I got a whiff of perfume. Immediately, the pistol came up in her hand, and I stumbled back as she fired, replacing the perfume scent in my nostrils with the acrid stench of black-powder smoke. The ball wheezed by me. I kept going back until, tripping on a bush, I fell on my rear.

She ran, yelling in French for help to whoever was waiting back at the carriage. Leaping to my feet, I raced through the brush to my mule.

As I rode back to the encampment, many thoughts buzzed in my head, but none of them made sense. Obviously, Carlos had made a copy of something the engineer had done and had delivered it to the woman. But why had he gotten angry and thrown the papers on the ground? Who was this mystery woman with golden locks, a cocked pistol, and the will to use it?

I felt like everywhere I stepped since Uncle Bruto had died was a pile of cow manure. Now once again there was some intrigue going on.

The most provocative thing about the situation was not Carlos's deeds or motives but the lingering scent of the woman's perfume in my nostrils. I recognized her scent. It was called Lily of the Valley. My darling Isabella and some of her friends in Guanajuato wore it. The sweet female scent caused a bulge in my pants, although once in a while, rather than sweet perfume, the lingering stink of her black-powder smoke burned my nostrils.

THIRTY-EIGHT

Cuicuilco

WE DEPARTED TEOTIHUACÁN, abandoning both the gods and the ancient dead, on the road that would take us south. Méjico City was about a dozen leagues from the City of the Dead. In most countries a league was three English miles, but in our lands it was slightly less. In any event, the road to the capital was well traveled, and many sturdy, heavily laden indios, burden baskets strapped to their backs, tumplines taut against their foreheads, walked the entire thirty-two miles to the capital. And since our expedition served many interests and purposes, we stopped at almost every town so the scholars could collect data and study artifacts. Our journey would stretch to several days.

"We're not going into the capital," Carlos told me, as we set out from Teotihuacán. "We visited there earlier. Going around the city, we will visit the town of San Agustín de las Cuevas. We will examine the pyramid at Cuicuilco, which is less than a league from San Agustín. Our expedition leaders also wish to meet with the viceroy, having missed him during our earlier visit. He'll be at San Agustín for a festival."

I didn't care where or why we traveled as long as I was a muleteer on the expedition. I had been to the capital several times but, unlike many wealthy gachupines, didn't own a house there. Bruto didn't favor the capital's pretentious social life and neither did I, preferring to spend my time outside Guanajuato on my hacienda, working with the vaqueros, or in the wilderness, hunting.

As for the town, I knew the festival by reputation, though I had never been there. I feigned ignorance when Carlos spoke to me about the festivities.

"San Agustín, I am told, is a quiet village all but the three days of the year when the capital's gentry come to gamble. The viceroy will bet on the cocks, perhaps even enter his own birds in the competition."

I didn't volunteer that besides the capital's wealthy, St. Agustín would swarm with thousands of thieves and léperos, putas, pícaros, tradesmen, and merchants who came for the visitors' clinking jingling coins. Nowhere in all the colony did gold, silver, and copper change hands so promiscuously as during the three days of the festival.

I had never mentioned to Carlos his meeting with the woman in the carriage. Nor did he indicate he knew of my attempt to assist him. The woman probably thought I was a highwayman.

The road leading to San Agustín was congested. We veered off to establish our campsite before entering.

"The town inns are full," Carlos said, "we'll camp here. I'm staying with a friend from Barcelona who has a house on the other side of town. You can assist me by carrying my overnight pack. After that, you're free to enjoy the festival."

Yes, free unless I was recognized by a visitor from Guanajuato. But that was not likely—or so I hoped. I had a beard and long hair and was dressed as a muleteer. Spaniards invariably ignore peons, as if they were used furniture or browsing cattle.

As we made camp, a rider showed up. Our men gathered around him. I was out of hearing range, but I saw him speak to the men, then depart for another camp site.

"What did he say?" I asked Carlos.

"News from Spain, something incredible. A mob at Aranjuez, where the king has a palace near Madrid, forced the abdication of King Carlos. They placed Prince Ferdinand on the throne and nearly killed Godoy."

He saw the lack of interest expressed on my face. I didn't find politics exciting, and news from Spain was usually a couple of months old; things had often changed by the time we heard about an event.

"Events in Spain mean little to you, but be assured, they affect us all. Many people in Spain distrust Carlos. He's incompetent, and the queen's lover, Godoy, who was once nothing but a young palace guardsman, runs the country. By allying Spain with Napoleon, Godoy had antagonized those who spurn French influence.

"Napoleon boasts that he will rid Spain of a corrupt government run by an imbecilic king and the queen's lover. After ridding Spain of the church's tyranny and its Inquisition spies, Napoleon says he will establish a more enlightened regime, introducing intellectual freedoms." Carlos spoke low, in a whisper. To utter such words, even to a servant, was to risk imprisonment. Torturing the servant to get a confession of the master's guilt is an old trick of dungeon masters.

Why did I suspect that our Carlos also favored a French influence in Spain's affairs? His mysterious visitor had obviously been French.

When we finished making camp, I walked Carlos into town, carrying his bag. He slung a small pouch from his shoulder. I held out my hand to take it from him, but he shook his head. "I'll carry it myself," he said.

On the way into town, Carlos could not get the recent events in Spain out of his mind.

"Imagine it," he said, almost muttering to himself, "people mobbed the streets, took the crown from a king, and installed his son. I always believed our people to be too cowed by church and crown to oppose tyranny or religious oppression, but they did." Grabbing my arm, he stopped and looked me in the eye. "Juan, don't you see the importance of these events?"

"Of course, señor," I said, in complete ignorance as to the significance of replacing one tyrant with another.

"The French Revolution started the same way twenty years ago. People packed the streets, first in small, brave bands, demanding liberty and bread. As their courage and numbers grew, they stormed the Bastille, deposing a weak, corrupt king and installing their own government.

"You're indifferent to who governs you and your people, Juan, but to the rest of us a king is society's bedrock. Kings don't govern, as viceroys and prime ministers do; they *are* the government. Our people long for security in the now and in the hereafter. They turn to their king for one and their priest for the other. From the king they get their bread on the table and protection from thieves and rampaging armies. Their priest is God's messenger, ministering to their birth, marriage, death, and their place in the hereafter.

"Deposing a king is like a child killing his father—"

He suddenly broke off. Veering toward a quiet alleyway, I followed beside him, steering him through the growing mob, converging on the town square.

He spoke again, his voice a low quizzical mutter: "Spain is a country of much greatness—for a thousand years, we have been the western bulwark against the infidel Moors who sought to conquer Europe and stamp out Christianity's flame. The English boast of their Magna Carta and the rights it bestowed on the English people. But Spanish kings granted those rights to us long before the Magna Carta. The British and French boast of their empires, but the sun never sets on Spain's colonies, and we are still the greatest empire on earth, encircling the globe, encompassing more territory than even that conquered by Genghis Khan. Spain was the first place where literature and art flowered after the Renaissance, where the first novel was penned.

"But look at us now," he whispered angrily. "After centuries of atrocious kings in which the nobility has strangled economics and the church has castrated thought, we are condemned first to an imbecilic king and now perhaps to his son, who is said to be both imbecilic *and* tyrannical. We are condemned to inquisitorial hounds who suppress any thought outside the strictest confines of church dogma."

He stopped and grabbed my arm. "But the people have spoken. They have smashed the chains imprisoning their thoughts and have mobbed streets as in France, striking sparks that can inflame the world. Do you know how hard it is to extinguish the fires of truth? Do you see how important the events at Aranjuez are?"

"Sí, señor, very important. Now we must make our way through this crowd, or you will arrive at your friend's house for breakfast instead of dinner."

Returning to the main street, we headed toward the town square. Pass-

ing an inn, a lavishly accoutered coach pulled by six fine mules drew up beside us. As we approached, I sensed Carlos stiffening.

A coat of arms was emblazoned on the side of the coach door. I wasn't
sure it was the one I'd seen the night I watched Carlos pass the engineer's
papers to the woman with golden locks, but the question was soon solved.
Garbed in an exquisite dress of black Cathay silk, her ivory skin and long
honey-hued hair dazzlingly adorned with gaudy glittering jewels, the
golden goddess descended from the coach.

Poor Carlos! Stumbling like a bumpkin, he bounced off the person
next to him. Grabbing his arm, I steered him on. As we approached, the
woman's eyes slid by us without a flicker of recognition. But she was the
one.

It wasn't the golden hair or the ivory skin that betrayed her or the carriage and six with its coat of arms or Carlos's lost composure but what I
sniffed as I walked by: lily of the valley. The scent filled my nostrils, and my
manhood burgeoned in my pants as she swept by.

 **THIRTY-NINE**

AS SOON AS I had deposited Carlos at his amigo's casa, I returned to the
main square. A guard was posted at the door of the inn. I showed him a silver coin, a half reale.

"My patrón saw a beautiful woman with golden hair get out of her
coach and enter the inn a while ago. He wishes to know her name."

"Your patrón has a good eye," he said, palming the coin. "Camilla,
Countess de Valls. She's French but married a Spanish count. I have heard
her husband is dead and that he left her with mucho dinero."

A man on the street passing paused when he heard the word *French*
and jabbered at the inn guard. "They're trying to steal our country."

The speaker moved on, and I asked the guard, "My patrón will desire
to have a small token of his appreciation delivered to the countess. In
which room is she staying."

"All deliveries are to be deposited with me."

I flashed another silver piece, this time a full reale, and lowered my
voice. "My patrón is an important man with a jealous wife. He will want to
make a discreet visit himself."

"Up the back stairway. Her room is at the corner of the building, the
room with a balcony, there," he pointed. "But the countess will be out this
evening. Her coach is returning after dark to take her to the viceroy's ball."

I gave him the coin. "If my patrón finds the backdoor unlocked when
he comes tonight, another silver piece will join his brother in your pocket."

Thinking about the French countess, I slowly made my way through the crowd pressing into the main square. From Bruto's occasional dinner table political discussions and the many discussions I'd overheard among the expedition members, I now knew for certain that Carlos played a dangerous game.

Many in New Spain feared the French or British would invade the colony. Combined with Napoleon's boasts that he would liberate the Spanish masses, people in the colony saw foreign spies under every rug.

That I should involve myself in the scholar's intrigues was madness, but I could not get the woman's scent out of my head. I have heard of aphrodisiacs that drive men mad and turn their minds to jelly—the very effect the countess's scent had on me. But her presence also stirred an emotion as old and vital as lust—my survival instinct. For better or worse, I had cast my lot with Carlos. In hopes of escaping New Spain, I now considered accompanying him on the entire expedition. It would take me as far south as the Yucatán and perhaps ship me to Havana, where they would dock en route back to Spain. I still had my eye upon the Cuban capital as a refuge from the colony. And I couldn't afford to have the machinations of this French countess spoiling my plans.

Carlos's intrigues with the countess had placed him in extreme jeopardy. If the viceroy even suspected Carlos of scheming against the crown, he would end up on the wrong end of a rope . . . after the viceroy's jailors had loosened his lips with persuasions only the devil himself would employ.

And if Carlos's tongue was loosened sufficiently, his faithful retainer—namely, me—would join him rack by rack, noose by noose, stake by stake. To protect myself I had to probe the countess's plot and keep my friend from harm—a difficult task, considering how the scent of her petticoats aroused memories of things past . . . stirring my garrancha as well.

The rest of the afternoon I wandered the festival. In celebrating the Fête of Pascua—what the British call Whitsunday—St. Agustín commemorated the Holy Spirit's sanctification of the disciples, after Christ's death, resurrection, and ascension. The church called that day the Pentecost and celebrated it on the Sunday that falls on the fiftieth day after Easter. In St. Agustín, however, the holiday gained an added dimension. This event, holy among the most Catholic of peoples, existed in St. Agustín almost solely as an excuse for intemperate gambling, most notably cockfights and monte, a popular card game.

The city fathers emptied the main square—the Plaza de Gallos (Plaza of Cocks)—and set up seating so that the viceroy and notables could watch cockfights. Standing in the rear, lowly peons like myself could watch, too. By midafternoon, the plaza was packed with people, wagering frantically on various games of chance but most frantically on the cockfights.

I don't consider cockfighting a sport, a contest in which men fasten sharp steel spurs to the chickens' feet for the purpose of murdering their feathered opponents amid shrieking explosions of feathers and guts, blood and balls. Yet its popularity among all classes of people cannot be denied. Even women crowded around the roosters, many of them smoking cigarillos and cigarros. The wealthier women were lavishly attired in extortionately expensive gowns, gaudy gold rings, and glittering jewels.

I understand our love of el toro. A man entering a bullring wagers he can keep his *own* belly from being ripped open by several thousand pounds of horned fury spawned in hell. But where is the sport watching chickens slice each other to ribbons?

I spent a few minutes, pretending to be interested in the cockfights, then, working my way through the throng, I drifted back to the inn.

I waited near the inn until the countess's coach took her to an evening ball. Having changed from black silk into a fawn-colored satin dress with a beige-black mantilla—the light scarf women in the colony and Spain wore over their heads and shoulders—she was now adorned with diamond earrings that almost touched her shoulders and a necklace of pear-shaped pearls. New Spain was a place where women and diamonds were inseparable, where no man, down to the lowest mercantile clerk, entered into marriage without giving his wife diamonds. Even the beauty of rubies and sapphires were not judged to be as exquisite as that of diamonds.

As I feigned interest in the gambling, I watched the countess's balcony window. She would have a maid, of course, and I waited until I saw the lamp go out in the countess's room, calculating that the maid would return to her room or, more likely, come out onto the streets to enjoy the festival.

After a couple of hours of losing at cards, I saw the lamp light go out. I casually strolled to the back of the inn, intending to enter the countess's room and wait for her return.

As promised, the back door was unlocked, and, as one would expect, the room door was also unlocked, except for a sliding-door bolt that one could throw before going to sleep. No one would ever have considered leaving jewels or money in an inn room, so no one needed locks while they were away.

The room was dark. The countess, however, had lit a small, long-burning oil lamp, which provided enough illumination for her to light the other lamps and candles when she returned. The room smelled sweet, like the countess. Sí, as weak as I am when it comes to petticoats, the smell warmed my blood more than the cockfights heated the blood of the aficionados below.

I discovered the prize almost immediately: the pouch Carlos had insisted on carrying to his friend's house earlier. Inside was a paper drawing. In the dim light I could not discern much detail, but it was clearly the layout of a fortification. I shook my head. "Carlos, you are a fool," I said aloud.

What I held in my hands was more deadly than a hangman's rope. Hanging was considered too gentle a punishment for treason—and spying on your own country was an even more heinous crime than being a foreign spy. Before they put the noose around your neck, they made sure every part of your body had suffered the tortures of the damned.

I lit the corner of the paper with the lamp and burned it in the fireplace. "Why, Carlos?" I asked. The fool risked both our necks by playing the spy, even if he was not aware of the risk to me. I knew from our conversations that he was an *afrancesado*, one of those Spaniards who was attracted to the ideals of the French Revolution: liberty, equality, and fraternity. But spying was different from intellectual discourse.

Was he playing this game of death for love of liberty or petticoats? The woman, this Countess Camille, was an attractive woman. Did she recruit him in bed? Of course, Carlos could be the leader in the scheme, but my common sense balked at the idea.

The countess's involvement was bad news, no? I have never fought, let alone killed, a woman. Could I frighten her away with a knife to her throat and a warning that I would cut off her head if she didn't leave Carlos alone? I thought for a moment about the woman who had nearly blown my face off with a pistol the last time we tangled and decided that a warning would not scare her away.

Maybe I would have to kill her.

I was hidden behind the balcony curtains just inside the open door when she returned to the room, sooner than I expected. Midnight had not tolled, yet as soon as she entered, she undressed. I realized she had returned to change so she could go to another ball in a different dress, which was the current vogue. She muttered aloud about her "stupid maid." No doubt the maid was out enjoying herself.

As I watched her remove the dress and her layered petticoats, I could understand why Carlos would steal secrets for her. Eh, if I were less concerned about the Inquisition's red-hot pincers and the viceroy's dungeon, I would kill and steal for a woman like this.

The balcony door was open, creating a draft. I stood paralyzed behind the curtains as she suddenly came over to close it. She shut the door and with one jerk, moved the drapes to cover it, exposing me!

I flew at her before her hand had even left the drapes, getting my hand over her mouth. She bit my hand and kicked me in my most sensitive extremities.

¡Ay de mí! What a devil this woman was! We fought across the room until I had her on the bed and was atop her.

"I know what you're up to," I gasped. "Call for help, and you'll hang as a spy."

Her teeth clenched down on my hand again. I yelped and let go. She stared at me, getting her breathing under control, and I continued to hold her down. Her scent filled my nostrils and clouded my reasoning. I felt my manhood rising and my eagerness to do battle fading. Once again my male part took command of my judgment.

"Who are you?" she asked.

"A friend of Carlos."

One of her breasts had come loose from her inner garment, and I stared at it like a man stranded on a deserted island spying a fresh-water spring.

My eyes met hers. I wasn't proud. It had been a long time since I had lain with a woman. She read the desire in my eyes, the lust in my heart, the weakness in my soul.

My mouth eagerly found her breast. Her hands went to the back of my head.

"Suck harder," she whispered.

Her nipples grew hard and firm as my tongue wrapped around them. Many times I enjoyed sticking my garrancha in a puta's mouth, then firing fusillade after fusillade. Now I had the sensation of this woman's large nipples growing against my tongue.

My hand found the moist treasure between her legs. I could feel the little garrancha burgeoning between her legs swell. I had never experienced a love button that was this long and hard—or this eager. I had to taste it. I moved down, sticking my head between her legs. I was sucking on heaven when I heard a pistol cock.

I rolled off the bed, pulling her with me, catching the wrist of the hand that clutched a pistol. I twisted the pistol out of her hand. "Bitch."

"Take me." Her mouth found mine.

¡Ay! What can I say in defense of myself? The woman despises me, tries to kill me, insults me, . . . and like a dog, I take the whipping and continue humping her leg.

While I contemplated my depraved debasement, she leaped on top of me and pulled my garrancha out of my pants. Straddling my manhood, she catapulted herself up, then, tightening her legs and squeezing my manhood like a vise, she allowed gravity to drop her down.

She rose and fell, rose and fell, my manly sword detonating in time, in perfect union, in harmonious concord with her rising and falling, over and over and over again, a symphonic cannonade from hell. My vision blurred, then exploded again, this time with a thousand crimson comets colliding with one another, bursting into fireballs, into flames . . . red . . . red . . . red . . . as . . . *blood*?

Blood was pouring down my forehead into my eyes. The puta had brained me with a brass urn she'd knocked off a nearby table.

Twisting her viselike treasure between her legs violently on my male part, the pleasure in my crotch turned to blinding agony, and I feared she would rip my penis from my body even as she again picked up the pistol.

I hammered her across the side of the head with my fist. She went off me, rolling across the floor. I grabbed the pistol and pulled up my pants. She sat up rubbing her head, her eyes burning, her upper lip bleeding.

"¡Ay! Woman, you're a man-killer. Why can't you just lie back and enjoy it?"

"Enjoy it? You think I could enjoy coupling with Aztec trash? I've seen more manly members on squirrels."

I was speechless. I considered hitting her again, but staring at her there, fire in her eyes and blood in her mouth, I wondered instead whether I might lure her back into bed for a second round. In short, my weakness for women defeated me.

"Puta!" was the best I could muster. It was an impotent remark, sí, but it was all I could think of.

I turned away from her, and for the first time in my life I had my tail between my legs. You can kill a man who insults you, but what can you do to a woman with a vile mouth?

I was at the window when I looked back and saw her fumbling with another pistol. This she-devil had more guns than Napoleon's Praetorian Guard.

I leaped out the window and went over the edge of the balcony, gripping the railing for a second to help break my fall to the alley below. I hit the ground and was running when I heard her shouting "Rapist! Thief!" and a shot sounded. Fortunately, the alley was deserted, and the celebration on the crowded streets would drown out cannon fire.

Twisting my foot in the fall, I limped back to camp, humiliated by the defeat I had suffered at the hands of this woman. But my shame faded when I remembered my pleasure pumping out of me over and over and over again. I always lacked basic moral fiber when it came to women.

 **FORTY**

THE NEXT DAY, Carlos and I rode the short distance to the pyramid at Cuicuilco. Once again, had he any knowledge of my meeting with the countess, he kept it to himself.

I expected Cuicuilco to be another prodigious pyramid, like those of the Sun and Moon at Teotihuacán. Significantly smaller, it was perhaps a fourth the height of the Pyramid of the Sun. Still a formidable structure, basaltic lava blanketed at least a third of it: Overgrown with jungle vegetation, it was taller than a dozen men.

Because of the lava and vegetation, it looked less like a pyramid than a stony hill. Had I not been told it was a man-made structure, I would have thought it a small volcano. Not eerily haunted like the great pyramids of Teotihuacán, it was grimmer, starker. A gloomy foreboding enveloped it.

"Cuicuilco, in the tongue of the indios, means 'the place of song and dance,'" Carlos said.

"Much lava surrounds it," I said.

"True, but mystery shrouds it, too, like the pyramids at Teotihuacán. We don't know who built it or even why it was built, though one would suppose it had religious significance. And you must understand, Juan, older than any other of the colony's pyramids, it commands our respect." He pointed at the mound. "The oldest man-made structure in the entire New World, this pyramid is older than the time of Christ, perhaps even older than the pyramids of the Nile River valley. A mighty people bequeathed it to us.

"You have never been to Spain, but we have great cathedrals there, magnificent monuments of our great past and others in the colony that are also glorious, but none are as old as this pyramid. It was here a thousand years, perhaps even two thousand years, before they were built."

He waved a hand at the magnificent edifice. "Think of it, Juan, in New Spain there is blood of two great civilizations, the indios of the New World and the Spanish of the old. What do you say, Don Juan the Aztec?" He looked at me intently. "Are you not proud of your blood?"

"Very proud."

Sí, I was proud that my blood still coursed through my veins and not across the floors of the jail from which I'd so recently escaped or on the walls of an Inquisition torture chamber. But I said nothing, letting the scholar go on about the accomplishments of people on both sides of the Atlantic.

When I cease fleeing the hangman, perhaps I will appreciate my blood's past wonders.

 **FORTY-ONE**

Cholula

WE MADE GOOD time traveling to Puebla from San Agustín, a distance of thirty leagues or so.

A wealthy town, Puebla de los Ángeles—Place of the Angels—lies on a broad, flat plain in the foothills of the Sierra Madre Oriental. In terms of size, Puebla, east-by-southeast of the capitol, claimed to be the second city of New Spain. When the mining villas surrounding Guanajuato are included, however, Guanajuato marginally exceeded Puebla's population.

Positioned en route between the capital and the colony's main port in Veracruz, Puebla had been a potential chokehold for enemy forces. It would be a small wonder if the military engineer had not drafted drawings of those fortifications for the crown, and if Carlos was not stealing them for the countess and Napoleon.

Still, no mention was made of my carnal encounter of her. Earlier, I had half-expected Carlos to offer me my choice of pistols or swords and demand satisfaction on the field of honor, but he offered and demanded nothing. Nor was I certain that his motivation for stealing the plans of the colony's fortresses had a sexual aspect. Obsessed with politics, history, and science, Carlos struck me as too scholarly and idealistic for mad, passionate love. His lack of romantic interest in the legions of señoritas we encountered seemed to confirm that. His work preempted everything.

In Puebla, unlike Guanajuato, with its mining-town terrain, the roads broke up the town into a classic colonial pattern. A patchwork of broad, straight streets intersecting each other, Puebla had paved them in either checkered or diamond-shape designs.

It reminded me of the capital. As we approached the central plaza, I could see that most of the houses were three stories. Some were painted with vivid, vibrant colors, their balconies—rimmed with black wrought-iron railings—overreaching the streets. Tiled roofs overhung the streets.

Grand carriages manned by liveried servants and pulled by fine, tall mules, some of which stood sixteen hands, demonstrated that, like Méjico City and Guanajuato, Puebla was a rich city.

Carlos and I quartered in a private home: he in a room on the third floor and I in the back of a leather shop on the first.

As we were walking to the main cathedral, Carlos said, "Puebla's fine architecture is said to be similar to that of Toledo, one of the great cities of Spain."

I could have told him that I had something of a connection myself with that famed fortress-city. Raquel's father was from Toledo, his fortune founded upon the fine blades that had long been produced there.

From the cathedral's high tower, we studied the two volcanic peaks: dominant Popocatépetl, "the smoking mountain," and its smaller companion, Iztaccíhuatl, "white woman." From that height we studied another imposing house of worship, this one surmounting a distant pyramid.

"Cholula," Carlos said, pointing to it, "the largest pyramid in the world. Its base and volume exceed even those of the largest Egyptian pyramid."

"It looks like a hill with a church on top."

"Sí, it's even more densely covered by vegetation than even the pyramids at Teotihuacán. We'll look more closely at it tomorrow."

I shook my head. "I can't believe it's a pyramid."

"It's the king of pyramids. Indio structures were either torn down so the building materials could be used for churches, or the jungle was allowed to reclaim them so the indios would never know the true splendor of their extraordinary heritage."

We came out of the cathedral and into the main square. The church, which forms one side of the square, had a simple exterior with little architectural ornament. Its interior and furnishings, however, were elaborate: a magnificent altar of silver and lofty columns with plinths and capitals of burnished gold.

"With sixty churches, numerous religious colleges, and over twenty monasteries and convents," Carlos said, as we walked in the main square, "Puebla is known as a city of churches."

Too many churches, his tone implied. That would not be a surprising conclusion for an admirer of the French emperor, who was known for his war on churches.

I lacked his contempt for religious institutions. Churches provide comfort to women, old people, small children, and those who fear the final reckoning. Knowing that my own soul was irrevocably and inescapably damned, I, of course, had never felt the need for religious solace.

Once we had arrived in the square, we purchased mango and lemon fruit juice. The female vendors kept the juices, along with pulque and chocolate, in small jugs contained within large red earthenware vases filled with water and buried in sand. Flowers, mostly poppies, were stuck around the drinks.

Carlos was very taken by Puebla. "I find the slower pace more charming than the frantic pace of the capital."

After satisfying our thirst, we went to the bishop's palace, where Carlos had arranged to view the library. The library, a truly handsome room, was quite enormous, at least a hundred paces long and perhaps twenty wide. As one who prided himself on never having read a book—a fact I never volunteered to the scholarly Carlos—I found the library to be overstocked with interminable tomes, many bound in vellum.

A monsignor, who identified himself only as the bishop's chief librarian, showed us around the room. One area—off limits to even the priests of the diocese—contained books and other writings considered too indecent for good Christians to read. Carlos later told me that many of the materials had been seized from colonists or by Inquisitors who met ships and checked their cargo for what the church considered to be improper materials.

"I understand that there are thirty-two volumes of indio hieroglyphic pictures, dating back before the Conquest," Carlos said to the librarian.

"Those materials are not available for inspection," he answered in a monotone.

Carlos stiffened and met his eye. "I have a commission from the king himself to examine and catalog items of indio antiquity."

"Those materials are not available for inspection."

"What do you mean? I have a royal privilege, a commission from the crown, to inspect them." Carlos was so angry, he stammered.

"Those materials are not available for inspection."

We left the library, and Carlos did not speak all the way back to our house. I wanted to inquire what was so important about some old Aztec picture-books but wisely kept my counsel, knowing that his interests extended beyond mine, which seldom strayed beyond women, wine, horses, and weapons.

Carlos later notified me that he would remain in his room for the rest of the day and read. At loose ends, I attended to two of my four basic needs: I visited an inn for vino and a puta.

The next morning we returned to the great square, where small mule-drawn coaches were available for hire. Even early in the morning, the market vendors were busy, selling everything needed for a household, from food to clothing. Many of the indios placed their merchandise directly on the ground or on blankets, and protected themselves and their goods from sudden downpours with crude umbrellas.

Unlike the capital, where léperos befoul the streets, here the indios were clean and neatly dressed.

We purchased items for our lunch later. Carlos was hungry for fish, which was not plentiful in Puebla, since it was far from the sea, but he was able to purchase a coarse paste pie filled with fish that was carried to the city only half-baked from a great distance. The baking process was finished while we filled out the rest of our lunch needs with wine, cheese, a roasted hen, and fresh-baked bread.

Carlos was in a lighter mood than when we left the bishop's palace the previous afternoon.

"I owe you an apology, Juan, for permitting my anger to dominate me yesterday."

"You owe me no apology, Don Carlos. I am merely—"

"Don't give me that poor peon servant act; your breeding is evident. And despite your efforts to appear humble, you're cockier than those gamecocks we saw in San Agustín." He held up his hand, silencing my protestations. "I don't want to know your life story, the hearing of which would no doubt compel me to call the constable or risk imprisonment myself. Those are choices I don't want to make, but Juan, do not misjudge me, I'm neither ignorant nor naïve. The only truth you have thus far uttered is your unmistakable disdain for all things important: history, literature, politics, religion. Were it not for brandy and swords, pistolas and putas, your head would be as empty as your heart. Don't ask me why, but I would still like to fill that howling void between your ears with something other than violence and lust."

I gave him my best, most scintillating grin. "Frankly, amigo, you're not the first to call me ignorant or the first to encourage book learning. Only through great perseverance have I prevented the dead weight of books from weakening my strong sword hand."

"Juan, Juan," he shook his head, "you weaken your brain, not your sword hand, with your fear of truth and of learning."

"I fear nothing."

"No, Juan, you don't fear the great beast you Aztecs call jaguar nor a bad hombre's pistol leveled at your dead-empty head. When it comes to books, however, you're like a cat on a fiery grid who won't leap into a puddle below because it dreads the unknown. Do you know what I mean when I refer to that movement called the Enlightenment?"

"Of course," I said, annoyed at his condescension. I thought Raquel or Lizardi had mentioned the word, but, in truth, I wasn't sure. A reading lamp, perhaps? Fortunately, Carlos didn't wait for me to expose my ignorance.

"It refers to the rebirth of learning, which has transformed European culture. Starting over a century ago, it has grown in scope and intensity ever since. A way of thinking logically, it's a new faith based on reason. By examining a subject and asking questions, we can reach conclusions, rather than relying upon superstition or the restrictive dogmas of religion. If we understand the world we live in as it is, if we are not trapped by the narrow thinking that has dominated so much knowledge of the past, we will attain the knowledge that truly sets us free. Do you understand, Juan?"

"Sí, knowledge sets us free." I tried to look intelligent, but our carriage had rolled by a group of pretty girls, and I was grinning and waving at them as we passed.

He sighed and shook his head. "Perhaps you are a lost cause. Pistolas and cojones instead of a soul."

"Eh, señor, I'm not without education. I don't make my mark, I sign my name. I am half a priest, no less. I attended seminary school as a teenager and learned the Latin of priests and French of culture."

His jaw dropped. "You speak French?"

"C'est en forgeant qu'on devient forgeron." One must forge over and over again to become a blacksmith. In other words, one must work hard at a trade to succeed at it.

Carlos started to jabber in French but quickly stopped as the driver looked back. Carlos's look to me said that we shouldn't flaunt our knowledge of French while Napoleon occupied most of Spain.

"If you had a teacher, who taught you French, you must know about the *Encyclopédie*," Carlos said.

"*Encyclopédie?*"

"A word from the Greek, it means 'general education.' It's an attempt to compile all the knowledge known to man in one set of books—in a single encyclopedia. It was prepared in France before we were born." His voice had dropped to an eager whisper. "But encyclopedias have existed since Speusippus; a nephew of Plato, compiled the knowledge of his day. In Roman times both Pliny the Elder and Gaius Julius Solinus created such works, but Spain has yet to even attempt a modern compendium of knowledge. We've long been under the iron heel of repressive kings and religious dogma."

Carlos grabbed my arm. "Juan, there's no reason why other countries should be ahead of us in producing encyclopedias. Spaniards have made many contributions to the compilation of knowledge. St. Isidore, the archbishop of Seville, as far back as the seventh century, founded schools in each diocese that taught the arts, medicine, law, and science. He wrote the *Etymologies*, an encyclopedic compilation of the knowledge of his day. His history of the Goths is still the prime source on that ancient culture. *That was over a thousand years ago!*

"Other Spaniards have made major contributions. Juan Vives's *De disciplinis* taught the great thinkers that were to come the practice of inductive reasoning. Does it surprise you that he fled Spain with the hounds of the Inquisition snapping at his heels?"

Carlos shook his head and grimaced. "Pedro Mexía and Fray Benito Jerónimo Feijoo, both denounced to the Inquisition. Gaspar Melchor de Jovellanos wrote from an Inquisition prison. Pablo de Olavide, Juan Meléndez Valdéz, Sor Juana here in the colony—they all lived in mortal fear of the Inquisition. Would it surprise you if I told you that the *Encyclopédie* itself, composed by d'Alembert and Diderot, was banned by the Inquisition?"

I muttered something I hoped would sound sympathetic. Frankly, after finding out that I was a changeling and plunging from gachupine heaven into lépero hell in a matter of hours, nothing surprised me.

Shaking with righteous fervor, Carlos took deep breaths to get his breathing under control. "Do you understand now why news of the Aztec books so devastated me."

"Did I miss something?" I asked, still not sure why he had become incensed when he was denied access to the manuscripts.

"The monsignor lied. They've destroyed the manuscripts. Just as Bishop Zumárraga and Landa set out to destroy all vestiges of the indio civilizations of the New World after the Conquest, those fools at the bishop's library have destroyed the manuscripts left in their custody. They destroyed them because they feared the writings; they feared the writings because they didn't understand them. Do you know why they didn't understand what the indios said? Because they never deciphered the writings.

"Do you realize what harm religious zealots like Zumárraga have done? The consequences of their acts? The Aztec culture prior to the Conquest was a mature civilization, a society advanced in government, commerce, medicine, and sciences. They had books, just as we do, even though their writing was different from ours. They studied the sun and moon and stars and composed a calendar more accurate than the one we use. They had medicines that actually healed, not the rat dung that so many of our ignorant doctors prescribe.

"Our priestly zealots set out to destroy every vestige of the indio culture in order to replace it with their own religion. What they did to the indios when they destroyed their places of worship, their statuaries, and writings is equivalent to the Moors invading Europe and *destroying every church, burning every book, and smashing all the statues and artworks in Christendom.*"

We both sighed.

I was beginning to feel as bad about what happened to the Aztecs as Carlos. Did that mean that I was becoming *educated*?

 **FORTY-TWO**

THE CARRIAGE CARRIED us through a maguey plantation as we approached the pyramid. Maguey plants were the source of the Aztec beer, pulque.

"An indio legend says that Cholula and Teotihuacán were built by a race of giants," Carlos said, "sons of the Milky Way. The giants enslaved the Olmec nation, the first great indio nation, but led by their own clever chief, the Olmecs threw a banquet for the giants and got the giants drunk on pulque. After they passed out, the Olmecs slew them."

I grinned at Carlos. "Being a man of reason, not dominated by superstition and old wives' tales, I do not believe in giants."

"That's too bad," Carlos said. "Our best witness from that period, Bernal Díaz, did. A soldier of Cortés, he wrote a history of the Conquest. He said that Aztecs showed him the bones of giants, convincing him the story was true." Carlos laughed at the look on my face. "But don't worry, amigo, we don't know what kind of old bones the indios showed Díaz."

I nodded up at the yellow and green–tiled church atop the pyramid. "That church was built on the very spot that blood sacrifices took place?"

"Amazing," Carlos said. "Already you are becoming a thinker, a questioner, a seeker of truth."

I tapped the side of my head. "How can I not use my brain when you keep stuffing it? What were these people you call my ancestors really like? I have heard many stories of their savagery. Are those stories not true?"

"Many of the tales are true, probably most of them. We discussed the reason for the blood sacrifices, the covenant with the gods—"

"Blood for rain and sunshine so corn and beans will grow."

"Blood sacrifice is not something to glory in, any more than Christianity's bloodlettings are a source of pride. But you cannot judge a civilization solely by its mistakes. If that were true, we would condemn Europeans from the time of the Greeks and Romans for their many savage massacres and forget about their contributions to civilization. Speaking of massacres, are you aware that one took place here in Cholula?

"It happened when Cortés was first making his way toward Tenochtitlán, the Aztec capital, after landing on the coast. The facts are controversial because the Spanish and indio versions differ so radically."

I listened to the tale of murder and bloodlust as we neared the largest pyramid on the face of the earth.

The name Cholula meant "place of springs" in Nahuatl. The city was famous before the arrival of Cortés for the artistic beauty of its pottery. Montezuma and other indio kings would only eat out of Cholulan dishes and cups.

Cholula was on the route Cortés took as he made his way from the coast and over the mountains to Montezuma's city. He stopped en route to investigate Cholula before going on to confront Montezuma in Tenochtitlán. He had made indio allies on the coast, and he thought he could persuade the Cholulans to join forces with him, since they were old enemies of Montezuma.

Cholula dazzled Cortés with its beauty. He called the city "much more beautiful than all those in Spain . . . well-fortified and on very level ground." From the top of the great pyramid, Cortés said he saw, "four hundred towers, all of mosques," in reference to indio temples and pyramids.

Cortés was wrong in thinking he could enlist the Cholulans in his bid to conquer the Aztecs. They believed that the invaders would anger the indio gods. Their priests told them that their gods would protect them from these strange men, that if the intruders desecrated their temples, the Lord of Waters would create a huge flood and drown them.

The Spaniards invited the prominent people of the city into the main square but made them enter unarmed. After they arrived, Cortés's men sealed off all the exits, and the slaughter began, with thousands killed before it ended.

Cortés later claimed that the Cholulans—to please Montezuma—were plotting to attack and kill the invaders, leaving only a few alive for sacrifice.

Cortés said an old woman told his translator, Doña Marina, about the plot.

The Cholulans had enlisted the old woman to befriend Doña Marina and get information about the foreigners from her. Because Doña Marina was a woman of beauty and had grown wealthy from Cortés's gifts and payments to her, the old woman told her about the murder plot, hoping Doña Marina would escape death and marry one of her sons. Instead of going along with the treachery, Doña Marina reported it to Cortés, who set a trap for the indios.

Carlos said, "Bartolomeo de Las Casas, a Dominican monk and one of the great historians of the era, wrote that the massacre was an act of cold-blooded murder, designed to inspire fear and terror through the indio nations. He said Cortés committed the massacre so that the Aztecs would be too frightened to attack them after they heard about it."

"So which is it, señor?" I asked. "Did my ancestors plot to murder my Spanish ancestors, or did Cortés slaughter thousands of innocent indios in cold blood to terrorize the Aztecs into submission?"

Carlos smiled. "You will find, amigo, that all words of men long dead must be given respect."

 **FORTY-THREE**

IT WAS TIME to leave Puebla. The expedition hired new porters for the next leg of the trip south to replace those from Teotihuacán who were returning to their homes. I was the only "old hand" continuing on the journey.

Carlos went into town to walk in the main square he liked so much, while the rest of us gathered at a campsite on the edge of town to organize the goods and equipment for the long trip south. I had finished packing my mule with Carlos's gear when a priest struck me on the back with his walking stick. "You. Come with me."

Eh, I leave it to your imagination where that stick would have been placed had he done that to me when I was a caballero.

The priest's name was Fray Benito. He was a detestable creature: thin, stoop-shouldered, hatchet-faced, with a bulbous nose and bulging eyes. He was the most disagreeable member of the expedition.

"Help this other peon load my supplies."

Poor but respectable laborers, most of the indios and mestizos in the colony were called peons, but the fray's new helper was neither respectable nor a laborer. He was a thieving lépero. I saw that after one look at the shifty-eyed bastardo. Had he touched Carlos's supplies, I would have sent him packing with the imprint of my boot on the back of his pants. I didn't care if he stole the fray blind, however, and cut his throat. The man was rude to porters and had wrongfully whipped more than one.

I was arranging the fray's things when a book fell to the ground. I knelt down to pick it up, and my eye caught the French title on a page inside the cover: *L'École des Filles*—The School of Girls. It claimed to relate the tale of how a "knowledgeable" woman instructs a virgin on how to give and take sexual pleasure and makes reference to a position it called "woman on top." But the title on the cover proclaimed that it was a history of St. Augustine.

¡Ay! It's the type of book called by the church *pornos graphos*. They're known on the streets as books that can only be read with one hand because the other hand is succumbing to the sin of Onan.

Eh, the fray was a pervert, at least as much as any of us, except he concealed his perversity behind holy robes.

The book was suddenly ripped from my hands. I stared up at Fray Benito. He glared down at me, the nervous bird for once speechless.

"I'm sorry, Fray. I saw the book." I pointed at the cover. "I like to look at the words that you learned men read. Perhaps someday I will be taught to read, no?"

"You don't read?"

"Of course not. Few of my kind can read."

He buried the book deep in his pack but still looked at me with suspicion.

Worthless little toad. He didn't know what to do because he didn't have the courage to confront me head-on. If I had lied about being able to read . . . eh, not even his holy robes would have saved him from the Inquisition.

He moved away, and we continued working. We were nearly finished when I saw the lépero put something into his pocket. As I said, if it had been my amigo Carlos's, I would have exposed—and punished—the thief on the spot. I kept quiet, but the fray came out from behind a tree where he'd been hiding and screamed like a squawking bird at the lépero, "Thief! Thief!"

Others soon gathered around, and the fray dangled a chain holding a silver cross in front of the sergeant in charge of our military patrol.

"You see! These beggars cannot be trusted, they would steal the holiest of relics for a cup of pulque." He pointed at the lépero. "Give him twenty lashes and send him back to town." Then he glared at me. "Give them both twenty lashes."

"But I did nothing!" I said.

"You're both lépero trash. Whip them."

I stood, unsure of what I was going to do. If I fought back, I would have to flee the expedition and lose my cover. But to accept a flogging when I had done nothing . . .

Soldiers led me to a tree adjacent to one selected for the lépero. My wrists were strung from a low-hanging tree limb.

I listened in tense anticipation as the lépero got his lashes. He screamed with each blow. Twenty lashes would bloody a back and scar it for life. I struggled with the rope holding my wrists, sorry that I hadn't resisted. I wished I'd killed a couple of the gachupines and fled.

Finally my turn came. I tensed as the man with the whip got behind me and cracked the whip. The sergeant played with me, cracking the whip next to my skin twice to tense me even more than I already was.

The first lash cracked, and I felt like hot irons had been laid across my back. I grunted, holding back the screams the lépero had made.

The second lash cracked, and I gasped, barely able to keep from screaming. I jerked harder on the ropes, anxious to break them and kill some of the fools who reveled in my pain.

Ay! Another lash ripped my back. I jerked harder on my bonds, but no sound came from my lips.

"This one thinks he is mucho hombre," the sergeant told his audience. "We shall see how tough he is."

The whip cut deeper than before. I gasped. It struck again, digging in. I could feel the blood running down my back.

"*Stop!*"

The voice was that of Carlos, but I couldn't twist around to see him. I leaned my weight against the tree. My back felt like it had been clawed by a jungle cat.

I heard arguing, but I couldn't follow it. Carlos was suddenly at my side.

"Did you help the lépero steal the cross?"

I grunted between my teeth. "Of course not. Why would I help such trash? I could take what I wanted myself."

He cut my bonds.

"I'm very sorry," he said. "Punishing you for another man's crime is outrageous."

Fray Benito was across the way talking to other members of the expedition. His darkly intense disposition had been replaced by one of grinning animation. Spilling blood had lifted his spirits.

Ay! I couldn't exact revenge and stay with the expedition. I had to play the peon and keep my mouth shut. But, as God above rules and the devil below knows, this fray would pay for the blood of my flesh that he wrongfully spilled. I didn't know when or how I would strike, but the day would come when I would put the man's cojones in a vise and twist them.

Deep in thought, I suddenly realized the inquisitor-priest Fray Baltar was staring at me. He pointed a fat finger at me. "I saw the demon in you just now. Beware! Beware! I can sniff out evil. I will be watching you."

FORTY-FOUR

Palenque

WE SET OFF toward the jungles to the south and the ancient Mayan city known as Palenque, from which we would journey to Chichén Itzá and other treasured Mayan sites in the Yucatán.

"We could go to the coast and take a boat south, shortening the journey, but no one wants to return to Veracruz," Carlos told me as we walked together. As an expedition member, he had a mule to ride but frequently walked in order to talk to me. I couldn't ride my mule, which was bent under mountains of equipment and supplies.

"They fear the vómito negro. After arriving from Spain, we escaped Vera Cruz with only one death, but no one wants to risk the yellow fever again. So we will proceed south by land. Besides, we would have nothing to catalogue or investigate aboard a boat."

He showed me on his map where our route would take us. "From Puebla, we proceed down to the Istmo de Tehuantepec, the narrow neck of New Spain that lies between the Gulf of Mexico on the Atlantic side and the Gulf of Tehuantepec on the Pacific side, and then on to San Juan Bautista. From there, we will turn inland and proceed to the ruins at Palenque, which are about thirty or so leagues from San Juan."

I nodded. "The map, however, does not show the difficulty of the terrain. We will journey from this high plateau to the colony's jungle heart, from temperate mountains to the hot-wet, tropical jungle and rivers of the Isthmus and Tabasco. By the time we reach these indio ruins you seek, we may discover that the black vomit of the coast is less dreadful than the sweltering jungles we will face."

Most of the journey toward San Juan Bautista was uneventful, but we were only days from the town when the rains started. After we descended from the plateau, rain came down continuously in showers, deluges, and mists, but this time the floodgates of heaven opened and water thundered down on us as if the Mayan gods cursed us for violating their territory.

In mud up to our knees, our mules would sink up to their bellies, and we would struggle to extricate them from the muck. ¡Dios mío! Insects ate us alive like rabid beasts; snakes, dangling from tree limbs, hunted us even as we walked beneath their bows. Those big, brutal, dragonlike demons of the rivers and swamps stalked us at every turn.

When your mount is up to its belly in mud, you have no choice but to get off and battle the muck yourself. Soon even the gachupines got their feet wet.

The wounds from the whipping were still raw and painful when we reached the dense tropics. Each night as I squirmed in agony from their itch, or bled when the wounds reopened, I thought about the fray who caused them.

We crossed floodplains, rivers, lagoons, marshlands, and swamps, sloshing through the mud, swimming river fords alongside our mules. At some of the streams, when their horses couldn't carry them, we porters hauled the expedition members across on our shoulders. Only Carlos crossed all the streams on his own feet.

Often we hacked our way through vegetation so thick that only birds in flight could have negotiated our route. Swelteringly hot, dripping wet every moment, day or night, we were too far removed from the northern mountains and the great seas that hammered the coasts to breathe clean, cool air. We saw few people of European stock, encountering only an occasional mestizo trader and once a hacienda's criollo majordomo, but mostly we encountered indios from the scattered villages. A people time has forgotten, they lived no differently from the way they did when Cortés landed three centuries before or when God's Son trod the shores of Galilee.

The savages wore scant clothing and spoke no Spanish. Not that I called them "savages" in Carlos's presence. He regarded them as the "indigenous people" whom we had conquered, ravaged, raped, and exploited and whose culture we had shamelessly annihilated.

I personally cannot judge or evaluate their cultural achievements, but I must assert that the indios I met were physically impressive. Modest in stature, they were nonetheless powerfully built and obviously fit—all this despite the sickeningly hot climate, pestilential insects, and ubiquitous predators, such as alligators, jaguars, and pythons, which dogged them— and us—at every turn. Still, I could not share Carlos's glowing admiration for them. Their conspicuous absence of clothing, their ludicrous lack of weaponry and horses, combined with their pervasive profusion of blood-red body tattoos, which they colored with a foul-smelling ointment made from gum tree residues, inclined me to view them as less than civilized.

I found their criminal justice system barbaric as well. To punish the unjustified killing of a person, the killer was sentenced to be delivered to the relatives of the deceased. Once in the hands of the victim's family, the killer either had to pay his way out or was put to death. A thief had to pay back not only the value of what he stole but was indentured as a slave to the victim for a period of time, his internment determined by the value of the theft.

"An eye for an eye," Carlos said.

"Not if you buy your way out of it," I muttered under my breath.

For adultery, the guilty men were tied to a pole and delivered to the aggrieved husband. The husband had a choice of forgiving the crime or dropping a large rock on the adulterer's head from a goodly height, thus killing him. Abandoned by the husband, the unfaithful wife lost the protection of her village, which led inevitably to slow, agonizing death.

I found it odd that in most villages the young men did not live in the same households with their parents. Instead, they were housed communally until they married. When Carlos asked a priest why they lived that way, the priest denounced the practice rather than provide an explanation.

This ignorance incensed Carlos. "The priests try to convert the indios to our faith, but the priests refuse to understand their old gods. Maybe if the priests knew the reasons for the customs better, they would convert more of them."

Tempers were short, food moldy, and—except for the local indios— whomever we hired fell victim to fever and returned home. I endured the unendurable cheerfully, which surprised Carlos. I couldn't explain to him, of course, that living on the run, continually looking over my shoulder, accepting insults and humiliation from my inferiors, made our jungle trek seem relatively bearable.

I also assumed a new role, one that freed me from the camp's petty problems. The soldiers had proven so singularly inept at both tracking and marksmanship that Carlos had handed me a musket, powder, and ball and commanded me to bag the camp's fowl and game.

The rain, which now showed no sign of letting up, prevented our clothes and boots from ever really drying. It did give us temporary reprieve from the pestilential mosquitoes that plagued us day and night, biting and sucking our blood until our exposed hands and faces were covered with lividly inflamed, wickedly infected sores.

Each night before darkness fell, I hung an oiled tarp for Carlos to eat and sleep under. He invited me to share it with him, even though the inquisitor-priest and Fray Benito both frowned at Carlos's kindnesses to a peon.

I soon discovered that Carlos wanted me close by at night so he could talk. I knew more than he suspected but kept my tongue still. I asked few questions and mostly listened. A burden in him fought to escape, devils he had to exorcise one day.

Drinking more and more, Carlos leaned sideways on his bedroll, talking and sucking on a brass brandy flask. Brandy loosened his tongue, so much so that I sometimes feared he would get us both in trouble. Sitting up with my back against a tree, I listened to his whispered confidences and the buzz of mosquitoes.

As he stared up at the starry sky, he told me something that made me wonder if he had completely lost his mind.

"You know six planets circle the sun, don't you, with Saturn being the farthest from Earth?"

I didn't know, but I pretended I did.

"Despite the nonsense they speak in churches about heaven above,

astronomers with telescopes have discovered an incalculable number of
suns, solar systems, and worlds like our Earth in the universe. The astronomers state with perfect logic and clarity that if life thrives on our
Earth, then life must exist on other planets as well. Let me read you something from a set of knowledgeable books published by the British a few
years before I was born called the *Encyclopaedia Britannica.*"

He read from a piece of paper:

To an attentive confiderer, it will appear highly probable, that the
planets of our system, together with their attendants, called satel-
lites ör moons, are much of the same nature with our earth, and
destined for like purpose. For they are solid opaque globes, capable of supporting animals and vegetable.

He was so excited, his voice trembled. "Juan, there are people on other
planets. Listen, it goes on to say that people even live on the moon!"

On the surface of the moon, because it is nearer us than any other
of the celestial bodies, we discover a nearer resemblance of our
earth. For, by the assistance of telescopes we observe the moon to
be full of high mountains, large valleys, and deep cavities. These
similarities leave us no room to doubt, but that all the planets and
moons in the system are designed as commodious habitations for
creatures endued with capacities of knowing and adoring their
beneficent Creator.

He stared at me, wonder enveloping his face. "Don't you find that incredible, Juan? Scholars with telescopes have discovered that we are not
alone in the universe. The church doesn't want us to know this, that's why
they prosecuted Galileo after he asked the bishops to peer through his tel-
escope. The bishops weren't afraid they would see heaven; they feared
sighting habitable planets."

I didn't tell him I found it more frightening than incredible. People on
the moon and Mars? An infinite universe rather than heaven? If the
inquisitor-priest got his hands on the paper Carlos had read from, he'd rack
us both right there in the jungle and broil us at the stake.

"I told you about encyclopedias, about how scholars in many nations
are following the lead of the French and producing them, compiling and
organizing the wisdom of the ages so that all may access and learn from it.
What I didn't tell you is that I am working on two Spanish encyclopedias."

"Two? At the same time?"

"Yes, two. One for the king and the other for all mankind. The version
the king gets will have been censored by the Inquisition and the pack of
narrow-minded court hangers-on who find it to their advantage to keep the

people in intellectual darkness. But the other, Juan, the one I compile in secret will be the truth. Do you know what that is, what I mean by the truth?"

I shrugged. "As things are, señor?"

"Yes, as they *really* are, not what the narrow dogma of the Inquisition says is truth, not what the professors who teach lies in our schools and universities say is the truth because they are too ignorant or too afraid to speak the truth."

I rubbed the stubble on my chin and looked around the camp. Most of the men were sweating in their tents, suffering the heat to hide from the mosquitoes.

My friend Carlos was getting more complicated every day. It would be better if I carried the bags of a priest rather than those of a heretic.

"I know what you're thinking, Juan, that I am bait for that Inquisitor over there." He jerked his head in the direction of the inquisitor-priest's tent. "But I don't care; I'm tired of being afraid, of hiding in the dark. Because of men like him I have had to hide knowledge like a thief hides his plunder. Do you know what they did to my teacher, the man who first took me by the hand and showed me the light beyond the darkness of religious dogma? One night they came to his house and took him to their dungeon, the place the Inquisition maintains to frighten us. They accused him of giving forbidden books on the Church's 'Index Librorum Prohibitorum' to his students to read—"

"A lie, of course."

"No, it was true. He gave us forbidden fruit. But do you break a man's bones for reading a book?"

 **FORTY-FIVE**

AS WE NEARED the ruins of the ancient city, Carlos told me that like Teotihuacán, the true name of the place had been lost in time. "It's called Palenque because that's the name of the nearest settlement of any consequence, San Domingo de Palenque, an indio pueblo three or four leagues from the ruins. If the bishops had not been so intent upon destroying every vestige of indio history and culture after the Conquest, we would know the real name of this great city."

Nearing the ruins, we traversed a less relentless country, part savannah, part forest. We crossed streams and a small river, a respite from the swamps and mires we had trudged in for days.

One night we stayed at the casa of a hacienda, camping against the outer wall. Like other haciendas in underdeveloped regions, the amount of ground owned by the hacendado was vast, but only a small fraction of it could be used for crops and cattle. A hospitable gentleman, he roasted two cows over an open fire for our dinner.

That night as we lay in the darkness, Carlos expanded on the culture that built Palenque and the other Mayan centers.

"The Mayas rose as a great civilization hundreds of years before the Aztecs," Carlos said. "In terms of the history of the indios, the Aztecs had been a mighty empire for only a relatively short time, perhaps a century or so, prior to the Conquest. But many scholars believe the Mayas had been a powerful empire centuries before, reaching back to the time of our Lord Christ."

He explained that the Mayan culture rose to power sometime after Christ's birth and reigned supreme up to the beginning of Europe's Dark Ages.

"The first stage of Mayan civilization lasted up to around 900 A.D. During that time, at least fifty significant Mayan cities dominated this region, places like Copan, Tikal, and Palenque, some with populations of fifty thousand or more. After that period, most of the great Mayan centers were abandoned for reasons we don't know.

"During the next stage, the wondrous city of Chichén Itzá became a Yucatán center, along with the cities we call today Mayapán, Uxmal, and others. The civilizations of the Mayas extended from the neck of territory between the two great oceans, the isthmus, to the Yucatán Peninsula and down to the Guatemala region."

The Mayan society had rituals similar to those of the indio civilizations to the north, he said. "Like their cousins the Mexica, Toltecs, and other indio civilizations, the Mayas practiced human sacrifice as part of the blood-for-corn covenant with the gods. They frequently fought savage wars, yet like the other indios, the Mayas were also passionate seekers of knowledge. Their observations permitted them to construct an amazingly accurate calendar. Like the Aztecs, the Mayas preserved their great wells of knowledge in books and encriptions. And, just as the zealots of the church destroyed the evidence of other indio accomplishments, they committed the same sin against the Mayas."

He shook his head. "Do you not find it unbelievable that our knowledge of the rich culture of the Mayas is lost because of zealots?"

Having lost everything, including my bloodline, not so long ago and having learned that my life had been a folly and a fraud perpetrated by a man consumed by grotesque greed, I found nothing my fellow man did unbelievable.

FORTY-SIX

AS WE CAME to our destination of the ancient city, Carlos said, "I found out from the majordomo last night that Cortés had passed near here several years after the Conquest of the Aztecs. A fascinating man, I suppose the great conquistador exemplified what it took to discover, conquer, and exploit new worlds. Are you familiar with his Honduras trek?"

"Once again, I confess my ignorance."

"Like so many events in the era of the Conquest, it is a tale of adventure, murder, and perhaps even a bit of madness. It began when Cortés sent one of his captains, Cristóbal de Olid, to start a colony in Honduras. Far removed from Cortés's supervision, Olid swelled with ambition, and his good senses took flight. Cortés learned in Mexico City that his captain would no longer obey his commands, that he was now acting independently.

"I tell you, Juan, Olid was foolish. He knew how tough Cortés was, knew the conqueror was so tenacious that he burned his own fleet to force his men to fight the Aztecs after they became frightened and wanted to return to Cuba."

No guts, no glory, eh.

"Olid thought that, given the distance between himself and Cortés, he could defy him. He was wrong. Cortés first sent a trusted captain, Francisco de las Casas, to show Olid the error of his ways. Shipwrecked on the coast, las Casas fell into Olid's hands. Even though he was held captive, las Casas still rallied Olid's men, raised an insurrection, arrested Olid, and beheaded him. However, only word of the shipwreck reached Cortés in Mexico City, so he set out for Honduras with an army of about a hundred and fifty Spaniards and several thousand indios along with a troupe of dancers, jugglers, and musicians. Still the rough terrain made the journey a miserable one.

"Guatemozín, the last emperor of the Aztecs, was with Cortés, possibly because Cortés feared leaving him in the capital.

"When the men became exhausted and near starving, Guatemozín and other indio notables, plotted to kill the Spaniards and to parade Cortés's head on a stake all the way back to Mexico City, stirring the indios to rally against the Spanish.

"Cortés learned of the conspiracy, again through Doña Marina. Holding an impromptu trial, in which Guatemozín protested his innocence, Cortés had him and other leaders hanged."

Carlos shook his head. "Whether Cortés was correct about Guatemozín's guilt, the Cholula plot, or the many other victories and atrocities attributed to him, for certain he was a man of decision. He shared three attributes with the Emperor Napoleon, character traits that have made Napoleon the conqueror of Europe—decisiveness, boldness, and utter ruthlessness."

Each time Carlos mentioned the amazing feats of Marina, I was reminded of the touch and courage of my Marina.

When we finally arrived at Palenque, I felt like Columbus when he spotted land after his nightmarish voyage. Another city of the dead, long abandoned by its occupants, perhaps even centuries before, Palenque had been swallowed whole by the jungle. Unlike Teotihuacán, whose towering pyramids dazzled everyone, even from a distance, the ruins had to be cleared of their entanglement to be observed.

It would have taken a small army to hack the city free of the jungle's grip, a luxury we were short of, forcing the scholars to choose only specific parts of edifices to be cleared and studied.

Carlos told me these ancient ruins were discovered shortly after the Conquest, but two centuries passed before a priest, Padre Solís, was sent by his bishop to examine the site. Little came of the mission; like so many of the antiquities of the New World, no one cared about the sites once they had been stripped of treasure.

How large had the city been? It wasn't possible for us to tell, but we discovered structures overrun by jungle for a league in each direction.

"They call this the Palace," Carlos told me as we examined a huge complex. An enormous oblong structure with tall walls surrounding buildings, courtyards, and a tower, the Palace, like other structures of Palenque, was covered by a coating of a stucco that dried hard and kept its shape for long periods. The structures were dark and dank, with many halls and rooms, including a series of underground storerooms.

"It's huge," I said to Carlos, as I slowly grasped the Palace's scope and significance. "You could put Méjico City's whole main square into it."

"It may have been the administrative center of the empire the city ruled," Carlos said.

Near the Palace was the Temple of Inscriptions, a pyramid consisting of nine successive terraces, the ancient indios used to communicate and record important events. Over fifty feet high, it contained hundreds of hieroglyphic carvings.

A smaller pyramid, the Temple of the Sun, almost matched its vertiginous height when the spacious chamber at its top was included. To the left and right of the entrances, life-size human figures were sculpted in stone. The sun was sculpted in bas-relief, ten feet wide and over three feet high. Carlos called it a "masterwork of art."

Immersion in the ancient indio culture was slowly transforming me. As I stared at the magnificent edifices from the past, I realized that, starting weeks ago at the Avenue of the Dead in Teotihuacán, a new world had begun to open up for me. I now understood that everything I'd been taught about the indios was wrong. Rather than the dray animals and jungle savages I thought them to be, they were a magnificent people who had been horrifically harmed. I also finally understood why the padre in Dolores insisted that, given the chance, the Aztec was as capable as anyone else.

Too bad I came to these revelations one step ahead of the hangman.

 **FORTY-SEVEN**

Río Usumacinto

AFTER TALKING TO a trader, I informed Carlos that the only practical way to return to the coast was by boat. "We can trudge through muck for weeks, chopping our way through jungle, or we can hire boats and have a smooth trip down the river that would take just a few days."

No one wanted to hack their way back to the coast.

"How big is this river you would have us take?" Carlos asked.

"I'm told it's muy grande. The Usumacinto is wide and deep and has a strong current to the sea. It will be a pleasure trip, amigo."

I didn't mention that I was also told the river was infested with indio pirates who swarmed boats in canoes, crocodiles two or times as long as a man, mosquitoes said to be as huge as humming birds and voracious as vultures. Eh, I was tired of hacking through jungles, pulling mules out of mud, and carrying gachupines on my scarred back.

It took several days to sell the mules and arrange passage on three long river boats, each about forty feet long and crewed by three men who used long poles to push their boat through calm waters and push off from the riverbank and sand barges.

We began the journey not in the mighty Río Usumacinto, but a small, shallow, muddy waterway. The men manning the poles pushed us along the brown water while we baked in the sun and were bitten to the point of madness by the relentless mosquitoes.

In that moment of temporary madness, I asked the inquisitor-priest why God would create mosquitoes, and he snapped at me, "To question God's acts is a sacrilege!"

We finally linked up with the big river and began to float down it, with a light breeze keeping us mosquito-free. Things were quite pleasant if you did not count the hundreds of crocodiles that lined the riverbanks or stared darkly at us from the water.

"¡Ay de mi!. They are monsters," I told a pole man.

"Truly," he said. "Once in a while we lose a passenger overboard. Unless he gets back aboard instantly, he is pulled under, and the water boils red with his blood. Some of these creatures are big enough to swallow a person whole. One hunter killed a big one, and when they cut it open there was a fully clothed man inside."

In the middle of the afternoon, the sky quickly turned black as Hades. A strong wind rose without warning, whipping stinging rain at us. We were only a couple feet above the water, and the wind whipped the river into a furious frenzy that nearly capsized the boats and sent us all into croc-infested water. But the violent storm passed as suddenly as it had risen. One moment the Furies flogged us; the next, brilliant sunlight shattered the Stygian gloom, and the sky was blindingly bright.

Like the jungle, the air on our River Styx was hot and humid, so thick you bathed in it. But we found no hint of shade, no vestige of relief.

We passed no towns our first two days down the river and viewed nothing on the banks save crocs, endless vegetation, and random scatterings of indio hunters and fishermen.

On the third day downriver, we reached a village called Palisadas, a depot for logs cut on the river, where an unpleasant surprise greeted us. A posse of constables with indio guides was waiting as our boats slid up to the embankment. I was almost ready to take my chances with the crocs when I saw them. Almost, I say. Only the inevitability of being ripped to pieces by those giant fiends kept me from diving into the water.

Believing I was to be arrested, I shrugged and shot a "sorry, amigo" look at Carlos, who gaped at the constables and then at me, his face filled with questions.

"Manual Díaz, step forward," the chief constable said.

As I stepped forward reflexively, I caught myself; *He was asking for Díaz the military engineer,* whom they soon had in their custody, chained, and whose baggage they began searching while Díaz stared about dazed, a cow culled for slaughter.

Long conversations took place among the constables, the engineer, and Señor Pico, the head of the expedition, before we cast off again and started downriver. After we were underway, Carlos and I found a private space at the rear of the boat, where we lay upon baggage as he explained what happened.

"There is shocking news, a great deal of it," he said. "The military engineer Díaz has been arrested for spying." Carlos stared at me with a mixture of raw emotion—fear, horror, wonderment—"The customs inspectors searched a man trying to board a French ship at Veracruz and found plans for New Spain's military installations in his possession."

Shades of Countess Camilla. They obviously had found only a messenger, not the true spy. The countess had probably vouchsafed her passage by bedding the viceroy.

"Díaz has been arrested for treason, accused of supplying the French with the secrets of the colony's defenses." He spoke as if the words were being pried out of him, as if someone other than himself were speaking. He knew Díaz was innocent, and it was ripping him up inside.

"We also have news from Spain. Something terrible has happened. The French have seized the country." He stared at me, his face a mask of anguish. "Napoleon has taken both King Carlos and Ferdinand captive and is holding them in France, at Bayonne. Then he commanded that all the royal family be brought to France. In Madrid, the people learned that the king's nine-year-old son, Prince Don Francisco, was to be taken to France. Disturbed by the French takeover of the nation, and with their leaders doing nothing to resist it, the citizens gathered by the royal palace. When the carriages pulled up to carry the young prince and his party away, the people intervened." Carlos began to sob.

"It occurred on the second day of May. People barred the French from kidnapping the prince, and the French troops opened fire on them with muskets and cannons, killing butchers and bakers and store clerks who were only trying to protect their country," he said tearfully.

"When word of the massacre spread, people—men, women, and even children—grabbed whatever weapons they had. With kitchen knives and ancient muskets, clubs and shovels, and some with only their bare hands, they faced the finest troops in Europe, soldiers of the Emperor Napoleon, and fought them. For two days it was a terrible massacre. The French army slaughtered thousands of my people."

Carlos broke down. I could see the same news was being discussed on all the boats. Some men cried, others shouted angry words, others just stared out at the river. But the tears did not last long; a cold rage seemed to settle down among the Spaniards.

Ay, if they knew Carlos had spied for the French . . .

My friend and mentor fell into a deep depression and remained in that black abyss most of the day. He did not speak to me again until late afternoon.

"I must tell you something," he said.

"You should tell me nothing."

In truth, I wanted to forget the subject. Carlos was too emotional. He might decide to confess to spying and get us both arrested . . . No, we would not be arrested, considering the present mood of the men on the expedition; we would be given a Viking funeral . . . while still alive.

He stared at me. "For some reason, I trust you. I know the face you show to the world is, like mine, a mask." He waved away mosquitoes, a useless gesture that all of us made. "I am the spy they seek, not the engineer." He blurted out the statement, expecting a reaction.

I gave him a sigh. "From your admiration of Napoleon and his reforms, I knew you had French sympathies. But why spying?"

He shook his head. "I told you about my professor, the one who died in an Inquisition dungeon. He introduced me not only to forbidden literature but to others of a like mind, people who had read the literature of revolutionaries. We met in secret and discussed ideas that could have been expounded upon in any coffee shop in Paris or Philadelphia but could have sent us to the rack in Spain.

"Do you understand my frustrations, Juan? We were only permitted to read books approved by the king and church. Those books taught the infallibility of kings and popes, traits we knew to be lies! And across our borders, a man had sprung from the fires of the French revolution and was transforming Europe."

I had never thought of Napoleon as a savior for justice and truth, but as a man dedicated to conquest and power. He put the crown on his own head, not the people's. But Carlos was in no condition to have his ideals challenged.

He rubbed his face with his hands. "We started out posing as a literary society, but we weren't just a book club, we met to discuss forbidden ideas. Some of these meetings took place at the home of a noblewoman, a person of high rank."

Yes, and I had met her. She had stabbed me once with her knife, and I had stabbed her back with my own tool.

"She is a woman of great . . . persuasion and great passion, for many things."

Poor fool, I thought. She must have bedded him, and he thought she loved him.

"When the opportunity came to join this expedition, she called on me to stand up for my ideals."

She did "call" upon him: She coaxed him into bed, grabbed his garrancha and humped it as she whispered in his ear. Men are fools when it comes to a woman's wiles. When the countess got through with him, he would have sold his mother and sisters to French soldiers.

"It is my duty to confess my treason."

I gasped aloud, feeling the rope they would put around his neck also tightening around mine. I instinctively made the sign of the cross to let Our Savior know I was still one of His needy sheep.

"That would be foolish, amigo."

"I can't let Manuel Díaz take the blame, he'll be hanged."

I waved aside Manual's stretched neck. "That's not true. You copied his fine drawing in a rough hand, no?"

He stared up at me. "How did you know?"

I shrugged. "Just a guess. Your awkward copying will save the engineer. How can they accuse him of giving drawings to the enemy when it is obvious that they were not done in his hand? As soon as they compare the engineer's drawings with the ones seized from the spy, they will see that the plans are the stolen ones."

His face lit up. "Are you certain?"

"Certain?" I leaned toward him. "Don Carlos, it happens that I have some considerable knowledge and experience with the work of constables in the colony. You may rely upon my word as if the Lord God Himself chiseled it in stone."

"So Manuel will come to no harm?"

"Mi amigo, rest assured, Manuel will get special treatment."

Very special treatment. The constables were probably already breaking his bones because they were not getting the answers they wanted. As for comparing the original and stolen sets of drawings, if Manuel had money and family, they might eventually intervene and save him from being drawn and quartered, the punishment for traitors, but only after he had been broken on the rack and he had rotted in a prison dungeon for years.

But I saw no point in bothering Carlos about such things and having him regurgitate confessions that would get us arrested and do nothing to help Manuel. I was surprised that Carlos didn't know that I was aware of his spying. For whatever reason, the countess had not gotten the information to him.

Carlos shook his head. "I don't know, Juan. I'm still afraid for Manuel—"

"Be afraid for *her*, amigo."

"Her?"

"Your noblewoman. If they take you and torture the truth out of you, as they surely will, what will happen to her?"

He gasped. "You're right. They would arrest her. They—"

He couldn't say it so I made a cutting motion across my throat. "First they will take advantage of her, each of the jailers, those stinking, filthy creatures that are born and die in dungeons. When they are finished, they'll pass her around to any prisoner who has the price. Then, when it is time to carry out the king's justice, they'll draw and quarter her, tying each of her arms and legs to a different horse. Whipping the horses to the four cardinal directions, the beast will rip off her limbs, dragging away only her bloody stumps—"

He turned pale as a ghost, and his breath rasped like a death rattle. I thought he was going to faint, and I was prepared to catch him. Instead, he leaned over the railing and gagged into the river. I sucked on a foul-tasting indio cigarro and held his collar while he puked.

Did I not tell you what fools men are when it comes to petticoats? Now, Carlos would never confess to the king's men and jeopardize the countess. But I would be fortunate if I could just keep him alive; like any good man with a conscience, his next thought would be suicide.

¡Ay! Those hellhounds had sniffed out my trail once again and would soon be snapping at my heels. I would have to move fast, and the expedition moved very slowly. As soon as we reached the right place, I would flee the scholars and mosquitoes and board a boat bound for Havana.

 **FORTY-EIGHT**

The Yucatán

WE CONTINUED DOWNRIVER, poling and flowing from the broad Río Usumacinto and Río Palizada to the Laguna de Términos, a large, shallow lagoon separated from the sea by a narrow bridge of land some called Términos and others called Carmen.

Though many leagues in each direction, the lagoon was only about seven feet deep. While its depth was shallow, its dangers were many: one side of it was mangrove swamps infested with crocodiles. El norte storms routinely battered the lagoon, capsizing boats and fattening its flotillas of crocs, but we made the crossing on an uneventful day.

As soon as we cleared the mud banks of the swamps, we hoisted our sails and caught a fresh breeze. The island of Términos came low on the horizon, its white houses vividly visible.

"Many pirates have held Términos," Carlos told me. "English, French, Dutch, even Spanish ones took turns holding the island in the century following the Conquest. Less than a century ago, a Spanish don expelled the pirates. Most of the interest in Términos, besides as a base to attack shipping, was control of the wood that was cut upriver and brought down by boats."

The island's main town consisted of two long parallel streets of houses and other buildings, with a fort guarding the entrance to the harbor. Ships drawing more than nine feet had to stay a distance offshore, where they were loaded and unloaded with small craft called ships' tenders.

In town, I found no ships making the Havana run. Instead I would have to take a coastal boat to ports where the ships visited more frequently, either to Veracruz or to the ports of Campeche or Sisal in the Yucatán.

I didn't want to ship out of Veracruz, which was no doubt packed with the king's constables, all of whom were on the lookout for spies. The expedition's plan was to proceed by boat to Campeche, the closest Yucatán port, then travel overland through various ancient Mayan cities before terminating the journey at Mérida, the main city on the peninsula, and its port of Sisal. My only recourse was to stay with the expedition as far as Campeche, for sure, and perhaps even on to Sisal if there was no ship available at Campeche.

For the trip along the coast to Campeche, the entire expedition was loaded into one boat, called a bungo, a two-masted flat-bottomed craft of about thirty tons that carried logs downriver and along the coast. Once again, mules were left behind, sold to a mule trader for a much lower price than they would have brought at Campeche.

Carlos had little to say after his confession on the river. Most of the expedition members had taken badly to the jungle conditions, Carlos among them. The whole bunch looked sick and wane, and most were plagued by fevers. I found it interesting that the porters, myself included, suffered through the jungle miasma better than the gachupines.

Two days of sailing along the coast toward the Yucatán Peninsula took us to Campeche, a town built on the coast between two raised fortified areas. We landed at a long stone pier that extended about 250 paces out into the bay.

Before the Conquest, Campeche was a major town of the province of Ah Kin Pech, which meant "serpent tick," in reference to a pest that infested the Yucatán region. The community that existed before the Conquest was said to have been sizable: several thousand dwellings.

Spaniards took longer to subjugate the Yucatán than they did the heart of the colony. It took two years of bloody contention to conquer the Aztecs. In the Mayan Campeche region, battles raged over a couple of decades before Francisco de Montejo conquered the area in 1540–1541 and founded the town of Villa de San Francisco de Campeche on the site of the Mayan village of Kimpech. Campeche became one of the main ports on the Gulf, controlling the Yucatán trade in its own region, with salt, dyewood, sugar, hides, and other products passing through it.

Pirates had routinely pillaged the town. In the seventeenth century, Sir Christopher Mims took the town for the English, and other buccaneers took it twice more over the next twenty years. In 1685, pirates from Santo Domingo set fire to the town and ravaged the surrounding countryside for five leagues. They burned enormous stores of hardwood because the authorities would not pay the ransom they demanded for the wood.

To ward off pirate attacks and defend against England's threat on the high seas, Campeche developed into a well-fortified town. Surrounded by a wall and a dry ditch, Campeche had four gates, including one that opened on the pier. Well protected against attack by both land and sea, forts to the east and west—with two batteries beneath the western one—commanded the high ground.

Entering the town, I found it to be a handsome community with some buildings in the Old Moorish and Spanish style: buildings surrounded a square in the center, with piazzas on each side of the square and a fountain and tropical garden in the middle.

Carlos and the other expedition members were settled into two inns across from each other, near the main square, while I was given a room at a nearby stable.

"You are privileged to sleep among the animals," Carlos said, grinning. "Did not our Lord Jesus first come to us in a stable?"

While I wandered the town, I ate a local favorite, a taste I had not experienced before: young shark stewed with garlic and chile. I drank a bottle of wine and leered at lovely señoritas. Soon, I found myself at the port, inquiring about boats to Havana and was told that one would be leaving tomorrow at first light.

I would be on it. The ship, which drew much more water than the flat-bottomed bungo that brought us to the town, could not moor closer than a couple leagues. I arranged for a small boat to row me out to sea so I could board before dawn. It took nothing to book passage but my presence and dinero. I was short on money, but I had served Carlos well, saved him from the hangman, no less, and my conscience would not be offended if I helped myself to some of his gold.

When I went to the inn where Carlos was staying, I found him in bed and suffering from the fever that had plagued many of the expedition. His skin was burning hot, and he was shaking and suffering shakes and chills. The attack could go on for hours, perhaps until the next morning. I gave him a dose of the medicine we used for the fever, a substance obtained from the bark of the cinchona tree.

Coming down the stairs, I heard words spoken among expedition members in the main room that put a chill worse than malaria down my spine.

Constables! Díaz, the engineer, had convinced authorities that his plans had been stolen and copied. A search was going to be made of the baggage of all members of the expedition.

I rushed back upstairs. Was it possible that Carlos still had the plans in his baggage? Not even he could be that naïve and foolish, I told myself.

I was wrong, *María Madre de Dios!* He still had the drawing of a fortification near Puebla. The fool should never have left Spain; he was a danger to himself when he stepped outside the hallowed halls of a university.

Alternatives flew through my mind, including climbing out the window and getting to the port to find a rowboat that would take me out to the Havana-bound ship immediately. But I couldn't leave Carlos sick and helpless; he'd become my amigo, and I didn't have many in my brief life. I couldn't leave him to face the danger alone.

I thought about burning the papers, but that would leave tale-tell ashes, not to mention I had no fire going in the room. By the time I got one lit, the constables would be at my side. Even if I ate the paper, the constables would be relentless unless they had their criminal and the evidence. They needed to complete their mission.

The only thing to do was to give them the evidence and the culprit and hope that would satisfy them. If the constables were still around tomorrow asking questions, and Carlos had broken the fever, fool that he was, he would end up telling them his sins, and we'd both get arrested.

Taking the contraband plan, I left Carlos's room and quickly went down the hallway to the door from which I had seen Fray Benito exit earlier. He was now downstairs with the other expedition members, speaking to the constables. His arrogant tone as he discoursed on what should be done to traitors carried all the way up the stairs.

I rummaged through his baggage and found the book that bore the false title about a "saint's" life. Slipping the book out of its cover so the pornographo contents would be obvious, I put the plans between the pages and put it back into the baggage.

I left the room and barely got back to Carlos's room when I heard the stamp of the boots of the constables coming up the stairs. I was sitting beside Carlos, wiping sweat off his face, when the constables opened the door.

"My patrón is sick, señor," I told the constable standing in the doorway. He looked back at another man behind him. Neither man looked eager to enter a sick man's rooms.

"Tell the servant to throw out the bags," the other man said. "We'll search them first, then have the man moved so we can search the room."

With a couple "Sí, señors," I put Carlos's bags in the hallway. They were going through them when another constable came rushing out of Fray Benito's room.

"I found them!" he shouted. "And look at what else I found. A pornographos!"

I can't tell you how watching the fray being dragged from the inn, his hands and feet in chains, soothed the scars on my back. I made the sign of the cross as they led the stunned fray by me. The head of the expedition and the sergeant in charge of the guard saw me, and they both made the gesture. No doubt they thought I had asked God to save the poor fray's soul. Truthfully, I was *thanking* God; I knew now that, for certain, heaven sided with me.

I admit that I amazed myself every time I survived some demonic plan that could bring a hangman's rough rope against the soft flesh of my neck. The only thing I could attribute my abilities to was the many times I hunted wild beasts. None of the two-legged animals I had encountered were as hard to anticipate as a jaguar or a wolf.

The ship to Cuba sailed without me, and I was at Carlos's bedside the next morning. He felt well enough to sit up and drink chocolate. I could not flee and leave Carlos to find out that another man had been arrested for his sins. I had to be there to explain what happened.

I told him about the fray. "Don Carlos, I confess I was driven to do this thing in part because I knew he was an evil man. And besides my desire to protect you, I knew it was necessary to once more give the viceroy's men a diversion so they did not seek out the countess. We both must pray—" I made the sign of the cross. I felt it implied I had God's blessing.

He listened quietly, quite surprising me by the calm manner in which he took the news. After I was finished, he said, "I have met many good priests, often finding that those at the parish level have led lives of hard work and sacrifice for their flock, but Fray Benito was the worse kind of priest, as bad as the Inquisitors. The world will benefit if they take his robes. I am just relieved that Díaz, the engineer, has been cleared of the charges."

I breathed a sigh of relief. "I, too, am relieved. Now, let me get your breakfast."

I got up, but he stopped me as I opened the door.

"How did you know she was a countess?"

I paused and raised my eyebrows. "Señor?"

"I don't recall mentioning her title."

"You did it when you were delirious." I lied and started out.

"Don Juan."

I stuck my head back in. "Señor?"

"You are a very dangerous man."

"Sí, señor."

I closed the door and went quickly down the steps.

Now what did he mean by that?

 **FORTY-NINE**

FRAY BENITO WAS shipped to Veracruz, and I wanted to put distance between us and Campeche in case he talked his way out of being a spy. Carlos told me that the inquisitor-priest had written a letter to the bishop at Veracruz, vouching for the fray and asserting someone had planted the map and porno-graphos on him. I don't think the Inquisitor wrote the letter out of friendship; I had seen him and Benito huddled together with books, and I'm sure he feared the fray would implicate him.

Before we left Campeche, we heard stories that a rebel chieftain had taken the name of a warlike Mayan king of old, Canek, and had been terrorizing the Yucatán, practicing the "old ways": war and human sacrifice. The governor in Mérida had sent soldiers to capture him but stated publicly that the chief and his followers had fled to Guatemala.

I told Carlos he should argue for more soldiers to accompany us, but he said the expedition didn't have the dinero. "Besides, the warring chief has fled."

"The same two feet that took this bloodthirsty devil south can bring him back again—if he left in the first place."

Carlos ignored my concerns. As I've said, he was very intelligent . . . when it came to *book* learning.

"We'll encounter many ancient sites in the Puuc Hills region on our way to the ancient city of Chichén Itzá," Carlos told me when we were en route. "We'll examine only a couple of them because the expedition can't go on forever. Many of us are anxious to return home now that our country has been invaded. You understand, don't you, what side I'll be fighting on?"

He was one hundred percent Spanish and would fight the French. I noted that he had stopped talking about Napoleon as someone he admired and now referred to the emperor's armies as "invaders." Still weak from his bouts with fever, I insisted he ride a mule. Faithful servant that I was, I walked beside him, occasionally stepping in the droppings left by the mules ahead.

At night, mosquitoes so plagued us that we sewed our sheets into a bag and slept inside the bag, hot and sweating as if from a raging fever. Tiny black fleas swarmed my pants bottoms whenever I took a step. Worse than fleas and mosquitoes were the blood-sucking ticks, called garrapatas, that attacked us from the bushes and vegetation.

Added to the horrors of the insect kingdom were armies of ferocious black ants that had a bite to equal beestings and large, lethal-looking, hairy black spiders that crossed one's path looking very much like a walking hand. If the insects didn't get you, there were snakes that brought death in a heartbeat with a single bite.

I must admit the evening fireflies were beautiful. Never had I seen ones to match those legendary luminaries we encountered en route to Palenque and now in the Yucatán. Shooting down dark corridors, they were a dazzling spectacle. Carlos claimed one could read a book by the light of three or four of them, and I believed him.

The first stop we made was the ruin called Labna. The most prominent structure at this ancient site was an overgrown pyramidal forty-five-foot-high mound. We climbed the pyramid, clinging to vines and branches, until we reached a narrow pinnacle. An imposing structure twenty paces in width and ten front to back surmounted the pyramid. Partially in ruins now, one section had collapsed, but three doorways and two large chambers remained inside.

What was most curious about the temple on the crest were the stone carvings of skulls. I didn't know the answers to the scholar's questions about the name of the people who built the city, but there was one thing I knew about their character: "Their religion seethed with violence and death. Why else would they have carved death heads on their temple?"

"Skulls and skeletons play a role in the artwork of many Christian churches, too."

I guess that is why I called him the scholar. He had an answer for everything, even the mysteries of the ages.

Forty paces from the pyramidal structure was an impressive building with an arched entrance. The structure, which Carlos simply named the Gateway at Labna, was of such artistic merit, it could have served as a cathedral entrance.

"Amazing," Carlos said, as we stood back and gazed at the impressive stone edifices. "This kingdom of snakes and spiders was once a proud city, as were many like it in this region. But we face the same puzzle we did when we stood before the pyramids at Teotihuacán: Who built it? Here we are, in the middle of what was once a city, a community built by an intelligent and talented race, and not one word about it appears on the pages of history!" He was so excited, he almost jumped off the ground. "Think of it, this place will be known for eternity by what I write about it in the encyclopedia! I will mention your name, amigo, as one of the first explorers of the site."

Wouldn't the viceroy's constables love that.

We camped in the midst of the ancient ruins but couldn't get any indio to enter the ruins at night, much less camp beside us.

"Ghosts," their headman told us, "spirits of the long-dead dwell here. The stone places are their homes. They don't come out in the daylight, but at night they seek those who trespass on their domain. We hear their music. I once sneaked up to see why the music was playing and saw warriors of the long-dead dancing."

The truth was the indios knew little about the past except a few stories passed along around the fire at night. This became evident when an indio clearing brush saw the stone features of an ancient god and began striking it with his ax.

Carlos stopped him and demanded an explanation. The man said that he was told by his priest that the ancient figures all represented evil and he was to smash them.

Carlos walked away, shaking his head. "Don't they understand they are destroying history?"

We spent two days exploring Labna before moving on to large caves the indios called demon caves.

Using lamps burning with tree pitch, we descended into the caves through a rift in the ground. I had been in caves before on hunting trips but nothing like what I beheld while descending to the demon's lair. A couple hundred feet below the surface, we came to eerie formations and fantastic shapes, cones resembling huge icicles hanging from the ceiling and erupting from the floor. Carlos called them stalactites and stalagmites, "from a Greek word for 'dripping,'" the scholar said, deposits of dripping minerals.

The cones and other fantastic shapes seemed to take life as the flickering light from our fiery torches struck the strange formations.

Carlos and the other expedition members made much fuss over the beauty of the caverns, but I found them haunting and was relieved when I again saw the light of day.

I came out of the caves chilled despite the hot-wet jungle air. The eerie caves reminded me of the Aztec hell I had nightmared about so many times. Perhaps the Aztec gods were trying to tell me something.

 **FIFTY**

CARLOS TOLD ME more of the grisly history of the early Spanish in the Yucatán region as we moved across the peninsula. "Columbus never set foot on the dirt of the American continent, his movements were restricted to the islands of the Caribbean. The Yucatán Peninsula itself was discovered around 1508 by Juan Díaz de Solís and Vincent Yáñez Pinzón. Pinzón had commanded the *Niña* for Columbus in the original discovery of the New World. Solís and Pinzón sailed along the coast of the Yucatán and down to the area of Central America in search of a passage to the Spice Islands. Fortunately for Pinzón, he and Solís disagreed, and Pinzón returned to Spain. Solís went ashore while exploring a river region of South America. Charrua Indians attacked and captured him and his men, eating them one by one in plain view of the other sailors. Only one man escaped to tell the tale."

Ay! What thoughts went on inside the heads of the sailors as they watched their shipmates being cut up, cooked, and eaten . . . *knowing their turn was coming?* More important, what was the character of the one man who escaped to tell the tale?

"After the defeat of Montezuma, the crown gave one of Cortés's captains, Don Francisco Montejo a royal commission to conquer the people of the 'islands' of Yucatán and Cozumel. Montejo was soon to find that the Yucatán indios were the most fierce and warlike in all of New Spain. Everywhere he went, he encountered resistance. Foolishly, he sent one of his captains, Dávila, to Chichén Itzá, from which Dávila ultimately retreated with many casualties. After more years of fighting—and losing—by 1535, the indios had driven the Spanish out of the Yucatán.

"Around 1542, sixteen years after Montejo first received the royal license to conquer the Yucatán and twenty-one years after the fall of Montezuma, the Spanish had subdued enough of the region to occupy with some confidence the areas around Campeche and Mérida."

•   •   •

We left Mayapán and began a trek through the tropical forest to the city Carlos most desired to see: Chichén Itzá.

Carlos educated me about the city as we traveled. "Chichén Itzá is a large site, I'm told," he said. As we walked, he pushed a serpent tick off his pant leg. "As we have seen, the Yucatán possesses little water. Violent deluges frequently fall during the rainy season, but the peninsula's terrain doesn't hold water. The only year-round water source for much of the region are cenotes, sinkholes in limestone formations. Chichén Itzá was built on the site of two such water sources. And those sinkholes gave the city its name: *chi*, which means 'mouth' and *chen*, which means 'wells.' *Itza* refers to the tribe that lived there."

"So, the name means 'the people at the mouth of the wells,'" I said.

"No one knows for certain how long the city had been inhabited, but we estimate it was founded over a thousand years ago, about the time barbaric hordes were overrunning the last tattered remnants of the Roman Empire and Mohammed's armies were conquering North Africa and the Iberian Peninsula. By the time we conquered the region, most of the major cities had been abandoned and people were living in smaller communities. Once again, we don't know the reason for the inhabitants' flight."

Nothing had prepared me for the wonders of the ancient city called Chichén Itzá. The ruins covered more than a square league, and the vegetation that hid much of the other sites had been cleared from magnificent edifices in the heart of the ruins.

"Strange," Carlos said. "Someone has gone through the great effort of clearing El Castillo and other structures of growth."

The city was a feast for our eyes, with amazing structures, including an observatory for studying the night sky. I was once again struck by the power and glory of an ancient civilization that could build such monuments, and, as Carlos pointed out, they did so without metal tools for carving and beasts of burden and wheeled carts for hauling.

We stood in an incredible sports arena, a place for playing a ball game Carlos called *pok-ta-pok*. The arena was over two hundred paces long and about a hundred wide.

"Pok-ta-pok was even more dangerous than bullfighting," I said, pointing out a sculpted relief on the wall that showed the victor of a game holding the severed head of a loser.

The name for the Chichén Itzá pyramid, El Castillo, didn't originate from the indios but from the Spaniards who found the structure to have a castlelike appearance.

I found the naked stone edifices as strange and eerie as the dark, twisted formations in the caverns we had explored. Picking our way through brush and vines to see previous structures had distracted me from the magnificence of the sites, but with the center of an ancient city laid out before us, its grandeur left me thunderstruck. How could the indios, whom I had always thought of as common savages, have built this magnificent city that lay before my eyes?

The Castillo pyramid, Carlos said, was about eighty feet high. "Ninety-one stairs at each of its four sides and another step on the top platform, for a total of 365. That this equals the number of days in the solar year, the time it takes the earth to revolve around the sun, was no accident. Mayan astronomers of that period were more advanced than their European counterparts. See that elegant building over there? It's called the Observatory, and it may be where sky watchers gazed at the heavens and made their calculations."

He pointed at the carving of a plumed serpent at the top of the pyramid. "Quetzalcóatl, the god called the feathered serpent, was known to the Mayas as Kukulcán. During the spring and autumnal equinoxes, shadows cast by the setting sun give the appearance of a snake slithering down the Castillo's steps. It's said to be an eerie sight."

We paused by a cenote among the ruins. More a sunken lake than a well, it was oblong, over 150 paces in length and a bit less than that in width. The sides were 60 feet high from water level to the ground surface we stood upon.

"The cult of the Cenote," Carlos said.

"Señor?"

"Just as other indio nations believed the gods had to be fed blood to appease them, the Mayans also practiced human sacrifice. Tying their victims up, they threw them into this cenote as well as others in the Yucatán. They had priests, called chacs, who held onto the arms and legs of the sacrificial victims. A moment ago we passed a life-size stone figure of a man lying on his back with his head up and his hands holding a bowl, the god named Chac Mool. Human hearts were deposited in his bowl after they were ripped out of the victim's chest."

Carlos said the Romans, Huns, and other European tribes, crusaders, perpetrators of the Inquisition, infidels of Mohammed, and Mongol hordes all had violent pasts. What was it in mankind that sought satisfaction in bloody slaughter?

Even before we set up a proper camp, the sergeant and other soldiers joined Carlos and the rest of the expedition in rushing to the cenote to take a swim in the cool, dark water. They could have their swim. I didn't care how long it had been since someone had been sacrificed in the pool; it was haunted as far as I was concerned.

While they swam, I took a walk to the Castillo pyramid. The steps up were not for the faint of heart, being nearly vertical. Although most vegetation had been cleared, a twisted vine could still snarl a foot and send one tumbling down.

I was three-quarters of the way up when I saw something that caused me to stop and stare. Splattered on the upper steps were bloodstains. Dried blood, but in this hot climate, blood would dry almost as soon as it hit the warm stone.

I turned and looked behind me as if expecting to find my nocturnal hounds of hell at my back.

They were.

Hundreds of indios had crept into the cleared area between the Castillo, where I climbed, and the cenote where the rest of the expedition was swimming. They had come silently, not breathing a word or snapping a twig.

Besides their large number, the first thing that struck me was their battle dress, their spears, shields, and elaborate headdresses. I had seen them before; at least I had seen their spiritual brothers. Etched on many of the walls of the indio ruins we had examined, were these warriors of the past, from the days when great indio empires ruled what they called the One World.

In the center of this indio mass, one figure stood out, a warrior with the most elaborate headdress, a great spray of brilliant feathers, green and yellow and red.

I didn't need an introduction; he had to be Canek, the rebellious Mayan warlord who had gathered an army and was reviving the "old ways." He raised his spear and yelled. Immediately, a great roar erupted from the warriors. They charged up the steps of the Castillo for me and rushed for the cenote.

I pulled the machete out of my backsheath. As the warriors raced up the steps screaming like ghouls from the indio underworld, my last thought was to wonder what it would be like to watch my companions being eaten one by one while I awaited my turn.

 **FIFTY-ONE**

CANEK'S NEGATIVE VIEW of life was understandable; while most Spaniards viewed the indios as a physically attractive race, Canek was the exception that tested the rule. A mortally homely brute, he had a broad nose that dominated his face, below which his front teeth protruded like flat fangs over his lower lip. His massively menacing upper torso and his abnormally long arms gave him a serious advantage in reach. The loathsomeness of his appearance was exceeded only by the surliness of his disposition.

We were taken captive and put into wood cages like beasts penned up for the slaughter, which was exactly what we were. The cages were lined up in a long row, with three and four of us to a cage. I was caged with Carlos and the inquisitor-priest, Fray Baltar.

Late that afternoon, they opened the first cage in line and pulled the three occupants out. They removed the men's shirts and pants.

"It's starting," I told Carlos.

Carlos didn't look. He sat in a corner with his face covered with his hands. Baltar gaped in wide-eyed horror. I knelt, with my hands clutching the wood bars, and watched it with grim determination. Somehow, some-way, I would get out and take my amigo with me.

Instead of taking the men up the steps of the pyramid, they were dragged to a fire. One of the men had his face forced down close enough to the flames to breathe in the smoke of whatever they were roasting. And as soon as he was pulled back, he appeared weak kneed, unable to stand without resistance. I could see that his face had lost the terror that had twisted his features a moment before.

"What are they doing?" the Inquisitor asked.

"Killing his resistance." I didn't know which of the mind-stealing substances the Mayans were using, but once it was inhaled, the men became passive and manageable.

They took the first man to the steps of El Castillo, a warrior at each arm, holding him up, half-dragging him because he couldn't keep his feet under him. At the base, two other warriors grabbed his feet and helped take him up. Waiting at the top were three Mayans, one dressed almost as splendidly as Canek. I took them to be the high priest and his assistants. The man was laid, face up, on a curved stone slab.

My hands shook as I realized why the slab was curved upward: It forced his back to arch, shoving his chest up. As the warriors held the man down, the high priest stepped up, screeching incantations that were alien to me as he waived a dagger with a razor-sharp obsidian blade.

Carlos began saying a prayer. Fray Baltar shot a look back at him but was too morbidly preoccupied with the horror unfolding before our eyes to remember his duty toward the dying.

The high priest reared back, then lunged down, plunging the blade deep into the victim's chest, blood spraying from the wound.

I gasped, and my head swirled as the high priest stuck his hand into the hole and pulled out the man's still beating heart, lifting the blood-dripping organ high overhead to the roar of the assembled throng.

Carlos sobbed behind me. All along the cages came cries of panic, shouts of anger, wailing prayers. I let go of the bars and turned my back to the madness as one by one, the Spanish scholars, their minds filled with great thoughts and the knowledge of the ages, were led up the steep steps of the pyramid to be sacrificed by savages.

After the "religious" ceremony, in which their blood was proffered to the "gods," they held their feast. They lay the bodies on the ground in sight of those of us in the cages. Using obsidian knives, they methodically began to cut them up, snapping bones to break the pieces apart. I didn't watch but couldn't get out of my mind the image of the sawing I'd done on the hacendado's leg.

They sacrificed and ate some of us each night for several days. Carlos, the fray, and I were the last victims . . . and not by chance. They had identified Fray Baltar as a priest—he was in his church robes when they captured him—and priests were considered special. I suppose it was like saving the best bite for last.

Among those at the cenote, Carlos had been the only one near enough to a weapon—and brave enough—to fight back. He killed one of the heathens before he collapsed under their blows. In their pagan minds he was a worthy warrior.

And Don Juan de Zavala . . . Why was I chosen? My flesh was highly prized because I had put up the most ferocious fight. I had killed four of them with my machete and given violent wounds to five more before they took me down.

Carlos understood snatches of their devilish Mayan tongue. Canek, he said, had personally staked a claim to my heart and that the rest of me, the edible parts, he would distribute to the savages who finally brought me down.

These creatures believed that eating the flesh of brave men instills that person's courage in them. The warriors we had killed were also eaten, to pass on their courage to the living.

"We'll be dressed as Mayan warriors when they sacrifice us," Carlos said. "That way the gods will know we're worthy warriors."

"I must thank the pagan bastardos for the honor," I said.

After watching them eat the members of the expedition and their own slain warriors, I regretted not having cut my own throat with the machete instead of fighting back.

One of Canek's underlings, a warrior who, we had already learned, spoke a little Spanish, came to the cage. I discovered the inquisitor-priest also spoke a little Mayan because he started jabbering away in the mixture of the two languages.

I asked Carlos what he was saying. "He's telling him that it's okay to eat us, but he should be spared because he's a holy man."

He didn't get across his message very well because the guard just gave him a stupid stare.

"Is that what they taught you in the Inquisition, to save yourself at the expense of your sheep?" I asked.

He was bent over, his hands on the bars of the cage, his back to me. He turned to me just long enough to make a street-gesture I hadn't used since I was kicked out of the seminary. I kicked him in the rear, not in but *under* the buttocks, my boot toe hammering his cojones. His head crashed into the cage, and he went down, grabbing at his male parts, groaning.

The indios at the cage enjoyed the violence. I couldn't quite stand up but did the best I could and took a bow.

"Miserable bastards," I said. "Him *and* those savages."

"He's just trying to save his own life," Carlos said.

"You're too damn forgiving. He took an oath to minister to us all when he put on the cloth."

"He took an oath to save souls, not lives," Carlos corrected.

"And what about these creatures . . . What oath did they take?"

"The blood covenant. They're simply doing what they believe will please their gods. Isn't that what our churches do when they burn us at the stake for our real or imagined transgressions? What infidels do when they kill people for not bowing to Mecca eight times a day? What—"

I leaned over and grabbed the front of his shirt. "Amigo, this is no time to be scholarly and understanding. These savages are going to rip out our hearts and eat us alive."

"To defeat your enemy, you must know the enemy."

He was pale and weak. He'd been cut in the fight with the indios and had lost blood. I had removed the flint point of an arrow from the side of his leg.

"My point is that deriding these people as mindless savages wins you nothing. Did our conquistadors treat their ancestors any differently than they are treating us now?"

"Yes . . . maybe they robbed, raped, and killed them, but, Señor Scholar, Cortés didn't eat them!"

Arguing with Carlos was pointless. Since he learned of France's attack on Spain and the uprising it had provoked, he'd changed. He was an unqualified admirer of all things French, but he was also a Spaniard. In his own mind, he justified spying for the French on the grounds that it might rid us of an incompetent Spanish king and help to inspire an Age of Enlightenment in the country. But Napoleon had put his own brother on the throne and murdered those Spaniards who opposed the foreign king. Eh, that would make the blood boil in any patriot.

For Carlos, Napoleon's betrayal of the Spaniards who supported him had been devastating. Perhaps in his own mind, being murdered and cannibalized by the savages was just punishment. For me, the world was simpler. I had no interest in kings and wars, in who was right and wrong, good or bad. I just didn't want to be eaten. I had to come up with an escape plan. And, because Carlos had always stood up for me, I included him in it. As for Fray Baltar . . . he could poison the indios with his toxic soul.

The warriors drifted away from the cages and gathered at the cenote, the deep watery pit where the expedition members had been swimming when they were captured.

"What's going on?" I asked Carlos as I heard excited yelling.

"One of our people, Ignacio Ramírez, a scholar of primitive art, has wavy hair. Because the waves mimic waves in water, the indios believe that the water gods are especially pleased when someone with wavy hair is sacrificed. To please the water gods, they are ripping out Ignacio's heart and then throwing it into the pool of water."

Carlos spoke with little emotion. He could have been describing the pictures on the wall of an indio temple. Again, he seemed resigned to his fate, as if he deserved to be eaten alive. The last thing I wanted for myself was my just deserts.

Late in the afternoon the indios took us out of the cage and dressed us in the ceremonial garb we would wear for our sacrifice. After we were put back in to await our turns, there was still a cage of expedition members ahead of us. I whispered to Carlos, "Rub dirt on the exposed parts of your body so you're not white."

"Why?" he asked.

"So you can pass for an indio, at least under the cover of darkness."

Fray Baltar overheard me. Since my well-placed kick, he had stayed at the opposite end of the cage, looking in my direction only to glare balefully at me.

"I'm going with you."

"No, Señor Inquisitor, we need you to stay around and get eaten while we make our escape. You don't mind sacrificing yourself for your fellow man, do you? Maybe if you sacrifice yourself, God will forgive you for all the evils you've done in His name."

"God will punish you," he snarled.

"He has. Being caged with you is hell."

I would have enjoyed throwing the fray to the savages piece by piece, but I had to let him come along to keep him from exposing my plan.

While we half-dozed in the afternoon heat, Carlos told me about an early expedition of Spanish conquistadors who invaded the Yucatán in search of treasure. Tales of gold and silver lured part of the army to Chichén Itzá, where an indio force attacked them.

"The battle raged all day, and 150 Spanish were killed while the others took refuge in the ruins. That night, the Spanish waged periodic assaults on the indio camp to disturb their sleep. Finally, in the wee hours, with the indios exhausted, the Spaniards tied a dog to the clapper of a bell and put some food slightly out of reach of the dog. Earlier, the Spanish had rung the bell at odd intervals, to let the indios hear that they were still present. But this time, while the dog rang the bell as it tried to get to the food, the Spanish silently slipped away."

That evening as the indios worked up an appetite, dancing and drinking jungle beer, I used the piece of flint I had removed from Carlos's leg to cut the vines that were used like rope to hold the cage together, opening up one side. I urged Carlos and the inquisitor-priest to follow me, and we crawled to the mountainous supply of corn and discarded husks near the cages.

I used the flint again, this time with the metal of my belt to ignite the dried husks. We quickly spread the fire, which a fortuitous breeze whipped into an inferno. Indios from all around raced to it. Dressed as Mayan warriors, we melted in with them, making our escape through the drunken confused masses.

We were away from the main body of indios and about to break into the dense jungle when Fray Baltar bumped into a sentry. The indio stared at him. The priest turned and pointed at Carlos and me. "There!" he shouted in Mayan. Ay! I should have followed my first instinct and slit the priest's throat.

Carlos and I ran into the darkness, into the jungle, with the sentry trailing us with his spear. Under cover of the brush, I suddenly whipped around and went low, letting the guard fall over me. He rolled, raising his spear as I leaped on him. The blade sliced me across the left shoulder, but when he twisted onto his hands and knees to rise, I got on his back. Tightening my forearm around his throat, I shoved a knee in his back and broke his neck.

But now more indios were thrashing through the foliage. I grabbed Carlos by the arm. "Run!"

We ran, tripping and falling along the way, making slow progress. Luckily the savages behind us fared no better and were hopelessly confused as to where we were. I pulled myself loose from the clinging bush and continued leading Carlos deeper into the thickets.

When Carlos could no longer run, I helped him up a tree and climbed up after him. We sat high in the branches and listened to the shouts and footfalls of the indios. The sky opened up, and a great downpour engulfed the jungle, concealing us and our trail. Hopefully, soon the indios would tire of sloshing in the water.

We stayed in the tree until the break of light, uncomfortable but occasionally dozing. I had not heard any movement for hours and decided it was time to climb down.

Carlos fell the last ten feet. His leg wound had ripped open, he was trembling from malaria, and I discovered he had another wound in his back. He had taken an indio arrow there, and I didn't realize it until I examined him in the light of day. ¡Ay! His shirt and pants were soaked with blood. He had lost too much blood to go on. My own wound was superficial . . . as long as it did not become infected.

"Go," he said. "Hurry, they may still be hunting for us."

"I won't leave you."

He grabbed the front of my shirt. "Don't be the fool you have always believed *I* am. I know who *you* are, Don Juan de Zavala."

"How—"

"In Teotihuacán, the constables asked for a man by that name. I knew from the description it was you. Besides, you strutted like a damn caballero. And those boots," he whispered.

I grinned. "Then for certain I cannot leave you. I have to get you to Mérida so you can claim the reward."

He coughed, and blood spilled from his mouth. "The only reward I will get is a season in hell for betraying my country," he said with great pain. He hung on to my shirt, pulling me down. "You must go there . . . to my city, Barcelona. Take my ring, my locket . . . give them to my sister, Rosa. Tell her that I was wrong . . . what she's done is not a sin . . . It's God's will . . . the path . . ."

He never told me what God had willed for his sister before he coughed one last time and his life left him in a single protracted sigh.

I dug a hole as best I could and covered him with limbs. The animals would find him, but I didn't think he'd mind. He had given up the ghost, and now his only care would be for his soul. I took Carlos's rings, locket, identity papers, and money pouch. I said good-bye to my amigo-scholar, saluting him for his courage and his ideals, and fled into the jungle.

I knew that Mérida was somewhat east of the ruins, several days journey even for a man in good health. As I pushed through the jungle, thickets ripped at my flesh, opening my shoulder injury, giving me a bleeding wound. I was baked by the heat, soaked by great downpours of rain, and starved. I grew weaker and even more miserable when I came down with fever. Staggering through the jungle, I was hardly aware of who I was or where I was. Finally I fell to the ground and was unable to rise. My mind slipped its moorings, and I vanished into a black void.

When I awoke, the earth was trembling. Strange noises filled the air. I panicked, believing that the earth was opening up, that a volcano was exploding under me. I pushed myself up and saw a horned beast charging. I crawled out of its way and found shelter behind a tree. The "horned beast" was followed by dozens of others—cattle—being herded by vaqueros.

One of the vaqueros spotted me and almost fell off his horse. He shouted in surprise. *"Fantasma!"*

"No!" I shouted, "not a ghost, but a Spaniard!" And then I passed out again.

FIFTY-TWO

I AWOKE IN a hut outside the casa of a hacienda. The owner lived in Mérida, and the majordomo was visiting him. The majordomo's wife, a lonely angel of mercy, tended to my wounds. As soon as I was strong enough to sit up, she climbed into my bed to assure that my manhood was intact.

When I could stand, a vaquero helped me onto a mule. Riding behind him, he took me to the nearest village. The only doctors in the entire Yucatán were in Mérida and Campeche, so the village priest ministered to my injuries as best he could.

He believed me to be Spanish, one Carlos Galí, a gentleman and scholar from Barcelona. Word had come of the ill-fated expedition. The priest knew of no other survivors.

For a week I lived in a village hut, one room built of upright poles, with a steep roof of thatched palm leaves. I slept in a hammock and drank water from a pot, after waiting for the insects to sink to the bottom.

A quiet village, it was little different from many others the expedition had passed through. During the hot afternoons, siesta time, indios swung in hammocks in the shade of their huts while a man in a doorway thrummed a homemade guitar. Dogs, chickens, and naked, dirt-encrusted children played in the street.

When I was able to travel, four village men transported me to Mérida on a hand-carried "coach" of cut poles, horses and mules being more valuable and expensive than men. The villagers laid two poles side by side, three feet apart, connecting the spread poles to crossbars at each end with unspun hemp. They secured a grass hammock between the poles. When they finished, the four men raised it to their padded shoulders.

On the way to Mérida, we passed large carts loaded with hemp and drawn by mule teams. Hemp, which would be later woven into rope, was the region's staple crop.

Mérida was an attractive town with well-constructed buildings and large houses with balconies and patios, some two-storied with balconied windows. Many houses were built of stone and were only one tall story high.

Like most colonial towns, Mérida had a large plazuea in the center that measured over two hundred paces in each direction. The plazuea featured a church, the bishop's palace and offices, and a palace for the governor and his officials. Mérida's main streets, which radiated out from the square were lined with homes and businesses. Nearby was the Castillo, a fortress with battlements of dark gray stone.

One of the city's more unusual features was its carriages. I had seen similar vehicles in Campeche and was told they were unique to the Yucatán. Called calesas, they were the only wheeled carriages in the city, large wooden structures, commonly painted red, with bright, multicolored curtains. The awkward-looking vehicles were drawn by a single horse with a boy riding it.

When they plied the alameda, the carriages each carried two or three ladies, Spanish of course. The women rode without hats or veils but had their hair trimmed with flowers. They comported themselves with a modesty and simplicity that women lacked in the larger cities to the north. The many india and mestiza women on the streets—always unpretentious, often pretty—again lacked the sophistication of the women in the larger cities, such as the capital and Guanajuato, but made up for it with their sincerity and simple charm.

Mérida welcomed me as a hero. They believed I was Carlos, and since the king authorized the expedition, they also believed the viceroy would reimburse the local government for any bills I incurred.

After a week in Mérida, I was transferred by diligencia, a calesa coach, to Mérida's seaport, Sisal. The trip would take a full day, and I was anxious to get away from the city. News traveled slowly to Mérida, which was at the far end of the colony, but I heard many stories of French conspiracies to seize New Spain. I was now Carlos, the man I knew to have spied for the French. I was anxious to leave before they hanged me for his crimes . . . or my own were exposed.

No ships were departing for Havana. My next best choice, though by no means a perfect one, was Spain itself, and at Sisal the ship's tender transported me to a Spanish-bound vessel.

Spain, in many ways, was like saying "heaven." As a colonist, I was raised in the belief that the Iberian Peninsula, home to Spain and Portugal, and the Garden of Eden were one and the same. However, I would have boarded the ship with more enthusiasm if I hadn't feared for my European reception.

War raged in Spain with the people of Spain battling the dreaded Napoleon, one of history's greatest conquerors. And I was going to Spain in the guise of Carlos Galí, a scientist on an expedition of monumental scientific importance . . .

A man who had made a heroic escape from a horde of cannibals . . .

And who was a French spy.

NAPOLEON'S ULCER

The Spaniard is brave, daring, and proud; he is a perfect assassin. This race resembles no other—it values only itself and loves only God, whom it serves very badly.

—General de Beurnonville,
Army of Napoleon

FIFTY-THREE

Madrid, Spain, May 2, 1808

As PACO, a twelve-year-old street urchin, left his slum hovel and walked up the street, he gnawed at a small morsel of fatty meat on a bone, given to him by a neighbor whose chamber pots he emptied. His mother was dead, and he was mostly on his own. He lived with his father, who shoveled manure in a stable, but his father was at best an absentee one who often failed to return home after work. Paco was accustomed to going out in the morning to find his father sleeping off a drunk in the gutter.

The boy was tall and gangly for his age, almost as tall as most men, but rail thin because he rarely had enough to eat. As he walked toward the central plaza, the Puerta del Sol—Gateway of the Sun—people converged on it from all directions. From the plaza, the mass of people moved up Calle Mayor and Calle Arenal, streets that led toward the royal palace.

While Paco followed the flow of the crowds, he heard excited talk, heated words, as people lamented the seizure of the Spanish king, queen, and crown prince after Napoleon had invited them to France on a pretext and the next French move against Spanish sovereignty: the seizure and transport of a child-prince to France.

As he listened to the angry words swirling around him, Paco was unaware that he and those around him would soon initiate six years of brutal warfare on the Iberian Peninsula, warfare that would smash the dreams of an empire of one of the greatest conquerors in history.

Under the pretext of preparing for a joint invasion of Portugal, French troops had occupied Madrid and other key points throughout the country. Now the people's passions blazed at French treachery. They jeered and booed General Murat, head of the French occupation of the city, as he entered the city in his golden coach. Murat had thirty-six thousand French troops under his command in the city, as compared to Spain's three thousand. Moreover, the king's administrators had ordered the Spanish army to stand down and not to oppose the French takeover.

"For shame, for shame," people cried at the news that their army wouldn't fight to defend their nation and that the royals had renounced their rights in return for generous pensions.

Spain's wealthy grandees compounded the cowardice of the royals by also acquiescing in France's conquest of the country, in part because Napoleon had promised them they could keep their assets, privileges, and power. Of Spain's political institutions only the church, which Napoleon degraded and looted in other parts of Europe, strongly opposed French occupation.

"They're taking our Paquitito!" the boy heard repeatedly.

Prince Francisco, the youngest son of King Charles, was housed at the royal palace. Word had spread through the crowd that the young prince was to be taken by coach to France. The nine-year-old prince was a particular favorite of the people of Madrid. He was called by an affectionate nickname: Paquitito.

Though he was called Paco by his father, the twelve-year-old street urchin, like the prince, was also actually named Francisco.

As Paco flowed with the angry crowd, he saw French troops, cavalry and infantry, moving into position along with a line of cannon. Although some people expressed fear at the sight of the soldiers, this day the impressive body of troops only inflamed the crowd's wrath.

When he reached the square, Paco climbed atop a statue across from the palace to get a better look. To one side, lines of French troops deployed in musket squares, muskets at the ready, and a line of dragoons with their horses prevented the crowd from expanding. Behind the soldiers' lines were cannons.

Coaches lined the front of the palace entrance. Shouts of "They're taking Paquitito!" rang through the crowd. People near the coaches began to cut at the harnesses with knives. With no warning, the French squares opened fire, the front line of troops firing, then dropping to their knees to reload as the second and third lines followed the same pattern. The musket balls ripped into the crowd, a ball going through one person and then another and sometimes even killing a third. After all three lines had fired, the musketeers melted back behind the cannons.

French cannons thundered point-blank into the densely packed crowd, shrapnel and shell blasting people to pieces. Holding onto the statue, Paco froze, his mouth gaped. Blood, bone, and flesh of men, the blasted bodies of women and children lay spread across the cobblestones.

As quickly as the cannons quit firing, the musketeers stepped forward and fired another series of volleys, knocking down hundreds of people. When the last volley sounded, the cavalry surged forward, chasing the people as they ran in panic, cutting them down with their sabers, trampling those who fell.

After the mounted troops had passed his statue, Paco jumped down to make his way toward home through the panic and chaos. People on the street were bloodied, frantic men searched for their wives, women screamed for their children.

Soon, however, he saw another spirit rise from the masses: As the panic faded, a ferocious fury rose. Men and women came out of their dwellings wielding kitchen knives, axes, clubs, anything they could fight back with. Women and children stood on balconies and rooftops to rain street stones down on the advancing troops.

The boy watched in wonderment as people whom he recognized as bakers and store clerks, stable workers and barmaids, challenged the crack French troops with kitchen utensils, stones, and sometimes just their bare hands. Soon his wonderment turned to anger and horror as he saw people falling under the barages of musket fire and trampled by horses or cut down by the sabers of charging dragoons.

Paco followed a group that ran toward the barracks of a small artillery unit of the Spanish army. A Spanish captain met them, shouting at first that they were under orders not to engage the French in battle. As French cavalry stormed into the area, trampling and cutting everyone that got into their way, the Spanish captain relented and ordered five cannons directed at the advancing French troops. His cannon tenders sent off first one, then another volley that cut into the ranks of the attackers and sent them reeling back.

The Spanish cannons kept up the fire until a white flag of parley was raised by the French, and the Spanish captain was invited to talk. A senior French officer stood at the front of a detail of musketeers with bayonets at the ready and awaited the Spanish artillery commander. The commander, whom Paco recognized as a captain named Laoiz, went forward to discuss terms with the French officer. The French officer, a general, suddenly shouted a command. Musketeers with bayonets stabbed the Spanish officer to death, and French cavalry charged the Spanish cannon positions, catching the batteries by surprise.

Numb and in shock, Paco left the carnage at the artillery barracks and made his way toward the tenement where he lived with his indigent father. Even as fighting erupted all around him, civilians with crude implements and makeshift weapons were fighting the finest troops of the greatest military power on earth. As he neared the tenement, he heard another cry of outrage explode around him. *Mamluks!*

He stood rooted and gawked as they charged into the crowd, the infamous infidel troops whose very name sowed terror in Spanish hearts. The wild, murderous French Moslem troops from North Africa charged into the crowd, cutting people down with their curved scimitars.

Muslim troops attacking Spaniards! He had been raised to believe Moors were demons. Spanish kings struggled for seven hundred years to drive the infidels from the peninsula. Now the French were sending them to kill Christians.

Paco never went to school, but from street talk, he knew a little of the history of the infamous warriors, though he didn't know that the word *mamluk* itself meant "slave" in an Arabic tongue. The original Mamluks were slave units that fought for the sultans and sometimes became their palace guards. Often they were Christians, captured and enslaved. Like the praetorian guards of the Caesars, the Mamluks eventually became the real rulers of the Turkish and Arabic kingdoms, and the sultans merely figureheads. Sometimes Mamluk generals even assumed royal thrones.

Napoleon encountered the fierce fighters during his Egyptian campaign and eventually incorporated small units of them into his armies. However, the Mamluks were so fierce and uncontrollable he had never deployed them in force.

Paco watched as women on the rooftop of a house threw rocks down on the troops. Three Mamluks dismounted and invaded the house. Paco knew what would happen in the house: The women would be raped and murdered. It was the house of the woman who had given him the bone.

His eyes went to a kitchen knife in the gutter. He picked it up and shot into the house. On the stairway a screaming woman struggled with a Mamluk who tore at her clothing. A young man whom Paco recognized as the woman's brother was crumbled at the bottom of the stairs, dead.

Paco ran up the stairs and aimed his knife-thrust at the infidel's spine, the blade instead sinking into the wide leather belt around the Mamluk's waist. He pulled the blade back as the Mamluk twisted around. Paco saw the cutting edge of the curved sword coming at him, just a flash of light off the blade before it connected with his neck.

 **FIFTY-FOUR**

Zaragoza

IT WAS ALMOST midday. María Agustina had heard the continuous bombardment as she made her way down an alley and onto the boulevard that led to Zaragoza's Portillo Gate. She was twenty years old, and the French siege of the city was her first memory of war. She carried with her a freshly made bucket of stew and a jug of watered-down red wine for the young artilleryman she had fallen in love with.

Zaragoza lay on the Río Ebro, Spain's longest river, about two hundred miles northeast of Madrid. Portillo was not the only gate in the city besieged; the city was being attacked on all sides. The war had come to Zaragoza in the middle of June, less than two months after the people of Madrid rose up against the French invaders. *Dos de mayo* was that day, when madrileños had fought bravely but futilely against trained troops, men fighting with little more than sticks and stones, women and children throwing rocks and pouring hot water from rooftops and balconies. The next day the angry French had taken revenge on the city, grabbing people off the streets or dragging them out of their homes capriciously, dragging them to death behind horses or hanging and shooting them with hastily assembled death squads. Thousands of madrileños died, but the French general's belief that if he killed enough civilians, the rest would be cowed, proved to be seriously flawed.

Instead of frightening the people of Spain into submission, when news of the atrocities swept over the nation, a spirit of defiance rose. The dates themselves—*dos de mayo* and *tres de mayo*—became rallying cries of resistance. Across the nation, in cities, towns, and villages, the common people of Spain faced the invaders not as a population intimidated by the French troops but as citizen-warriors ready to fight and die for their country.

Like everyone else in the city, María had heard of the atrocities committed by the French not only in Madrid but throughout Spain as the people rose against the invaders. French soldiers attacked homes, churches, and convents, torturing and murdering the occupants for their valuables and raping the women. Cities that tried to close their gates were attacked and ravaged. French generals loaded onto their personal transport the national treasures of the Spanish nation and its great cathedrals.

While the stories frightened her, they also fueled her anger and determination. And the presence of the violent invaders had unleashed something else in her as it had in most of the common people of the country: a fiery passion to drive out the enemy.

Coming out of the gate, an unseasonable north wind, El Cierzo, bit at her exposed hands and face. She put down her head and crouched low to get to the artillery battery where her lover was stationed. As she approached the unit, she stopped and gasped. The battery was silent. Her lover was on the ground, dead. The entire crew that manned the cannon were either dead or stricken with serious wounds.

She dropped the provisions and ran to her lover. As she did, musket shots sang past her ears. With the artillery battery silenced, a column of French troops advanced on the exposed gate, firing in the traditional one-two-three order as they advanced. The outgunned Spanish troops and irregulars kept their heads down.

One of her lover's comrades on the gun crew, unable to talk because of his wounds, gestured at the "match" used to fire the cannon. The piece of metal with a wood tip was lying on the ground next to him. María grabbed the match and lit the end of it in a coal brazier kept glowing for that purpose. With musket balls smacking the ground around her, she ran for the cannon and put the match to the powder charge.

The cannon was primed with powder and loaded with iron horseshoe nails. When it fired, a lethal hail of the nails cut down the advancing column, lined up twenty men wide and forty deep, like a scythe. The shrapnel had blown a big hole in the ranks of the French column, The cannon had annihilated much of the front of the column, killing or wounding ten deep. By the grace of God and Lady Luck, it had been a perfect shot that mowed down the French ranks.

The noise, concussion, and buck of the cannon as it rocked back knocked María off her feet. She got off the ground and to her feet as the smoke cleared. In a daze, hardly conscious of what she was doing, she picked up a heavy musket. She didn't know how to load one or even if the one she grabbed was loaded.

"We have to fight!" she yelled at the Spanish soldiers who had been hiding their heads. She stepped forward, advancing alone toward the French column. All around her, Spanish soldiers stood up and followed her lead.

"You're telling me that a young woman rallied the men at the Portillo Gate and led the fight that saved the city?"

General Palafox, commander of the Spanish troops and irregulars who were defending Zaragoza, stared at his adjutant.

"It was a miracle," the aide said. "God willed it."

"Another miracle," Palafox muttered. "The city is a place of miracles, not the least of which is that the French haven't managed to take the city and kill us all."

He had been met with the news as he came out of church. Now he walked away from the church, his aide keeping step with him.

"I wish I could leave the defense of the city to God," he grumbled at his aide, "but I've learned that God expects us to fight our own battles."

Palafox had been wounded and unhorsed in an earlier fight against the French when he tried to stop them in an open battle as they advanced on the city. But he was a man of indomitable spirit and took up the defense of the city despite his wound. He was one of a small group of Spanish generals in the nation who had put together makeshift armies to face the invaders. He cringed at the thought of the regular army troops of Madrid who had stood by and let the French butcher people. Outnumbered a dozen to one, they were under orders to stand down, but they never should have permitted French troops to kill civilians.

Leaders who failed to resist the invaders were no longer in command. All over Spain, the people had risen up and deposed—or killed—leaders who were too timid with the French or who sided with them.

Prior to Spain, Napoleon had pitted his troops against the professional armies of other monarchs and characterized the wars as a crusade to spread the gospel of revolution. In Spain, they encountered mass resistance from the very people Napoleon claimed they were "liberating."

Few Spanish career officers of high rank had joined the people's war against the invaders. Most of the regular troops that fought the French were the junior officers and common soldiers. The insurgents had drafted Palafox himself when they rose up in fury after the royal family had abandoned Spain. To combat the French, the common people of Zaragoza—mostly students, small merchants, and the working classes—had thrown out the city's administrators. The upper classes had accommodated the invaders, in exchange for which they were allowed to keep their wealth, power, and privileged positions.

Two other miracles also occurred before the Portillo Gate incident: one nearly two thousand years before. The city's name of Zaragoza derived from a corruption of its Roman name, Caesar Augusta. Not long after the Crucifixion—at a time when the Roman Empire was at its glory and Christianity was at its lowest ebb—the Apostle James had a vision in Zaragoza of the Virgin Mary descending from the heavens. She stood on a marble pillar. She disappeared when the pillar touched the ground, but the pillar remained.

The pillar was now enthroned in the city's main cathedral, the *Basílica de Nuestra Señora del Pilar*—Church of Our Lady of the Pillar. The people commonly referred to the church simply as "the Pilar."

The second miracle had occurred shortly before the French besieged the city. During a daytime mass at the Pilar, people claimed that a "royal crown" appeared. Palafox had not been present, but some people told him that the vision materialized out of a cloud above the cathedral, while others said it appeared above the altar. In any event, the vision had a profound effect on the city. Rebels and anti-Bonaparte clergy said that the crown was a sign from God that He supported Ferdinand for the crown of Spain. Some people even claimed that the crown bore an inscription that read: "God Supports Ferdinand."

Insurgents went into the streets, attacking the military governor's residence, taking him hostage and seizing the castle of Aljafería, which contained a supply of arms. The demonstration of anti-French, national unity ended at the house of Palafox with a demand that he take charge of the defense of the city.

As Palafox had listened to the news that the heroics of a young woman had stopped the French at the Portillo Gate, a surge of pride shot through him. But he knew that stopping the French here and there was not enough to save the city. If they didn't breach that gate, with their professionally trained and equipped troops and artillery, they would soon breach the city's defenses somewhere else.

As he entered his headquarters, a panicked messenger rushed in with news that the French army, after pounding the city unmercifully with forty-six cannons, had broken through at the Carmen Gate and was pouring into the town. Praying for another miracle, he went to the battle front to rally the defenders. The defenders resisted, making the French pay dearly for every foot they advanced.

Over the next days, the battle for the city was fought street to street, building to building. Day after day, the street battles were ferocious. Every house had to be taken, often with the family who lived there fighting to the last, with women and children joining the fight alongside the raw recruits that composed most of General Palafox's army.

Palafox's frustrations at defending a large city against Napoleon's well-trained troops with his ill-equipped, poorly trained volunteers were legion. He had put together a defense with superhuman effort. That their foe had brought most of Europe to its knees was psychologically intimidating.

Immediately after the siege had begun, Lefebvre-Desnouettes, a French general, had attacked and taken Monte Torrero. By deploying his batteries on that commanding height, Lefebvre-Desnouettes could rain shot and shell on the city. Palafox was so enraged by the failure of his Monte Torrero commander, he had the man hanged in Zaragoza's public square.

When nearly half of the city was taken after the breach at the Carmen Gate, the French general, Verdier, who had assumed command of the siege, sent a messenger under a flag of truce of General Palafox, bearing one word: surrender. Palafox stared at the word scribbled on a piece of paper. Taking a quill and ink, he scribbled his reply: *Guerra a cuchillo*.

When General Verdier read Palafox's reply, he shook his head and asked the messenger, "What does he mean, 'war to the knife'?"

"No surrender," the messenger said. "No quarter asked or given. The fight will be to the death."

Once more the fighting erupted, with the people of Zaragoza attacking the French literally en masse. No quarter was shown, and blood ran in the streets. Men, women, and even children cried *"Viva María del Pilar!"* as they charged the French musket-and-cannon fire or threw stones and hot water from upstairs windows and rooftops. They were urged on by priests who often led counterattacks. The French cried *"Vive l'empereur!"* to proclaim the omnipotence of their emperor.

Finally, exhausted, dispirited, awed at the bravery of city people who fought them *to the knife*, the French withdrew. Verdier, angry at the defeat, bombarded the city ruthlessly with the last of his artillery munitions before he left.

French General Lannes wrote Napoleon: "The siege of Zaragoza in no way resembles the type of war that we have waged in Europe until now. It is a craft for which we need great prudence and great strength. We are obliged to take one house at a time. The poor people defend themselves there with a desperate eagerness that one cannot imagine. Sire, it is a horrific war . . ."

LORD BYRON'S ODE TO THE MAID OF ZARAGOZA

LORD BYRON WAS in Spain during part of the Spanish war against the French. After he heard the story of how María Agustine had saved the city by leading an impromptu attack after she found her lover dead, he wrote of María, "the Maid of Zaragoza," in his autobiographical poem, *Childe Harold's Pilgrimage:*

> Ye who shall marvel when you hear her tale,
>> Oh! had you known her in her softer hour,
>> Mark'd her black eye that mocks her coal-black veil,
>> Hear her light, lively tones in Lady's bower,
>> Seen her long locks that foil the painter's power,
>> Her fairy form, with more than female grace,
>> Scarce would you deem that Zaragoza's tower
>> Beheld her smile in Danger's Gorgon face,
> Thin the closed ranks, and lead in Glory's fearful chase.

> Her lover sinks —she sheds no ill-timed tear;
> Her chief is slain —she fills his fatal post;
> Her fellows flee —she checks their base career;
> The foe retires —she heads the sallying host:
> Who can appease like her a lover's ghost?
> Who can avenge so well a leader's fall?
> What maid retrieve when man's flush'd hope is lost?
> Who hang so fiercely on the flying Gaul,
> Foil'd by a woman's hand, before a batter'd wall?

> Yet are Spain's maids no race of Amazons,
> But form'd for all the witching arts of love . . .

 **FIFTY-FIVE**

Andalusia, Southern Spain, December 1808

IN THE RUGGED Sierra Nevada mountain region of Andalusia, in Spain's southern region, a priest paused along a road to pray. Before him, from a low-hanging bough the French had hung an entire family—a man, woman, and their two teenage sons—in retaliation for the killing of a French courier. Napoleon's troops had not hanged the family because they attacked the courier but because they were . . . available. The French forces retaliated against such targets of convenience with routine ruthlessness.

Seven months after Dos de mayo, the battle for Spain had become a war of attrition, with death and retribution on both sides the order of the day. In Pamplona, the French summarily shot three Spanish patriots who they discovered had been secretly making weapons in a church, hanging their bodies where the town's people would have to see them. The next morning, the French commander found three of his men hanging with a sign notifying him: YOU HANG OURS; WE HANG YOURS.

Not to be outdone, the commander hanged fifteen priests.

And so it went: *war to the knife.*

After praying for the family, the priest moved on. He didn't cut the bodies down and bury them, because the French would find another family to replace them in the tree if he had.

A few hours later he joined a guerrilla group hiding in the high rocks above a mountain pass. The men and women awaiting him were common people: peasants, small farmers, and village clerks. Now they were a military unit, an unorthodox one that no officer educated at a war college would have recognized.

Nearly the end of 1808, much had happened in the months following Madrid's *dos de mayo* uprising. Napoleon had declared his brother, Joseph Bonaparte, king, but Joseph fled weeks later after the French army suffered battlefield and siege reversals from one end of Spain to the other. In Catalonia, Andalusia, Navarre, Valencia, Aragón, Castile, León and everywhere else in Spain, the Spanish forces had beaten the French back, forced them to hide behind fortress walls or to flee back to France. Both sides had perpetrated horrors, but the French were the invaders, bloodying the soil of another people, allies whom they'd betrayed.

Under names like partides, guerrillas, somatenes, and corso terretres— land pirates—the Spanish waged a war to the death with Napoleon's armies. Outmanned and outgunned by the well-armed enemy troops, the guerrillas avoided open battle. Instead they hid behind rocks, crouched in gullies, and lay in wait in thick foliage. They practiced ambush, assassination, sabotage, hit-and-run. When the enemy least expected it, they annihilated smaller units or inflicted hit-and-run damage on large ones. As soon as their ammunition or advantage ran out, they melted back into their hiding areas to await the next set of French troops.

Their tactics terrorized the French military, who had never faced "ghost brigades." The French generals had forgotten the lessons of their own revolution less than twenty years earlier, when the citizens of Paris stormed Versailles and the Bastille.

Early in the afternoon, the target of the priest's group—a French military unit—came down the mountain. They expected a French courier escorted by thirty dragoons. Instead the unit was much larger: about two hundred hussars. The hussars were light, fast-moving cavalry. The dragoons were slower and more heavily armed.

The priest studied the hussars through a spyglass. He had nearly three hundred guerrillas, but they were untrained soldiers and poorly armed, lacking everything but courage. He was their commanding officer, but seven months earlier he had been their parish priest. The French had come to his town, robbed his church of its silver and gold icons, fed their horses at his altar, raped women, and killed every father, brother, and husband who objected.

The priest had once baptized their children and forgave their sins. Now their kill rate was more important than their souls.

He had bloodied his own hands, pulling an officer off a thirteen-year-old girl and breaking his neck. He fled the town and hid in the rocky hills. As the months went by, men and women from the nearby towns and villages joined him, some on the run from the French, others just anxious to fight back. He had been their leader in peace, in times of need and plenty, and now he had become their leader in a war of liberation.

At the moment he had to decide what to do about the French unit that was approaching.

"We can't risk a fight," Cipriano said, "they are too many." He had been a shoemaker before he became second in command of a guerrilla unit.

"Then we won't risk a fight with *all* of them." The priest laid out his plan, scratching terrain and troop movements in the dirt. "We still have that cannon we bluffed with before." The "cannon" was nothing more than six feet of foot-thick oak tree trunk that had been painted black and mounted on a pair of wagon wheels.

"We'll put ten men on the road, *here*, and they'll pretend they are hauling the cannon."

The maneuver would allow the French to spot the cannon in a ravine while the guerrillas hid on both sides. "The commander's mission is to escort the courier, but he won't be able to resist capturing a rebel cannon. He'll send some of his hussars, maybe forty or fifty to kill the rebels and take the cannon. We'll be waiting. When they come charging into the ravine, we'll fire and run."

"Run" meant to melt into the rocks and hilly terrain where the mounted hussars wouldn't follow them.

They might get a dozen with the single volley he ordered and more than that in dead horses. It was often harder for the French to replace trained war horses than men. The losses to the French would not win the war, but it would be another bloody nose for them.

Not long ago, the priest had captured a French general who was on his way back to France after another general had replaced him. The fool had an escort of just a hundred, and the unit was slowed down by the general's insistence that his war wagons, packed with booty, go with him.

To elicit tactical information—and to exact retribution for his atrocities—he ordered the general lowered into a cauldron of boiling water . . . slowly. While the general parboiled, the priest had ten captured French soldiers and officers castrated in retaliation for the rape of Spanish women. Whether the men being punished had actually raped any women was irrelevant. He turned them loose to convey their agony to their fellow soldiers.

Guerrillas routinely left captured French soldiers by the wayside, their eyes gouged, their tongues cut out, their limbs broken but still alive so they could think about the atrocities that had been inflicted on Spanish men, women, and children. It was up to their comrades to put them out of their misery.

As he waited to attack the French unit, he thought for a moment about the schism between what he once was and what he was now, but he quickly shrugged off the thought. He was a shepherd, and he had to protect his flock from wolves.

CÁDIZ

FIFTY-SIX

Cadiz, 1809

WHEN WE WERE in the Golfo de Cádiz, two days from the great port city, a passing ship dropped a floatable packet for us, which our captain fished out of the sea. In it were newspapers and pamphlets reporting on the war in Spain. The captain and crew knew something of the events already—and I'd heard many discussions during the voyage—but as the news indicated, the situation turned more critical each day.

Since the central junta governing Spain was in Seville—because Madrid was in French hands—Napoleon's army had besieged the city, and it was expected to fall any day to the overwhelming forces. The junta had relocated to Cádiz, because that city was easier to defend. Lying on a long, narrow peninsula, Cádiz was vulnerable by land from only one direction, and the British navy controlled approaches by sea.

Gerona, in the far north near the French border, and Zaragoza, along the Río Ebro, both suffered under long, murderous sieges. Each time they defeated a French army, another came over the Pyrénées and began another siege, battering the cities and their defenders with the world's finest artillary.

"Ay!" I muttered under my breath. I was entering another hornet's nest. The Spanish battled a French invader who seemed to have the upper hand. Almost the whole country was in French hands. Napoleon himself had led an enormous army into Spain to restore his brother Joseph to the throne after the Spanish had sent Joseph racing back to France.

I didn't care if the country was in the hands of the devil. I owed the Spanish nothing but grief and had nothing against the French. I just didn't want the war to affect me. Eh, I might as well have pretended to be Napoleon himself, as much good as my current guise might do me. Carlos was a French spy, and the authorities in New Spain might very well have uncovered that fact by now. A hangman with a rope could easily await my landfall when I got off the ship.

The newspapers and pamphlets demonstrated that any support for the invaders—even dressing in French fashions—could be deadly. Since the French massacre in Madrid on the second of May, from one end of the country to the other, Spanish patriots had executed traitors and malingerers.

The ship's captain told me Cádiz had been one of the major cities where the people seized control of the government because the city's notables refused to act.

"It was the common people who took to the streets, not the rich or the nobles," the captain said. "They marched on the Marqués del Socorro, the captain-general of the city, when he failed to immediately declare for Ferdinand. When he called out the garrison to drive them off, the marchers broke into the armory to confiscate weapons. Then they returned to the marqués's house, dragged him out, and executed him as a traitor. When they finished with the marqués, they aimed artillery pieces at the homes of the wealthy along Calle de la Caleta. The priests only barely persuaded them not to massacre the city's elites. Since that time, the people of Cádiz have been leaders in the war of independence."

The captain told me that all across the country the common people had taken control in Zaragoza, Seville, Córdova, León, Mallorca, Cartegena, Badajoz, Granada, La Coruña. In Valencia people took to the streets and crowded in front of the municipal offices, demanding that their leaders recognize Ferdinand as king and reject the French usurper, Joseph. But the civil leaders refused, perhaps as fearful of enfranchising the common people as they were of French retaliation. The insurgents exploded when faced with such treason, killing hundreds of people they believed to be in league with the French.

"In the city of El Ferrol," the captain said, "the site of an important naval base and arsenal, a group of women insurgents seized the governor and distributed weapons to the people."

Holy Mother! Petticoats with muskets. What was the world coming to?

A decree of the junta legalized the attack on the French by the bands of what were being called "land pirates."

"More accurate to call them *privateers*," the captain said, "on land."

Privateers were civilian ships outfitted as war vessels and given commissions to attack enemy shipping and keep whatever they were able to steal as spoils of war. The attacked ships considered them nothing more than pirates. In essence, the junta authorized the guerrillas to attack the French units and take any material goods as "prizes."

The captain told me that the goods taken from the dead French soldiers had in turn been stolen when the French ravaged Spanish cities.

He went back to his duties while I remained at the railing and read. The decree vindicated—even validated—the "land pirates" because French soldiers had violated Spanish homes, "with the rape of mothers and daughters, who had to suffer all the excesses of this brutality in sight of their dismembered fathers and husbands . . ." It went on to describe how French soldiers impaled Spanish children on their bayonets and carried them around in triumph as "military trophies." They sacked convents, raped nuns, defiled monasteries, and murdered monks.

Dios mío.

"It's how he pays his soldiers," a voice next to me said.

"Señor?"

The speaker was a fellow passenger, a merchant returning from a trip to the Caribbean. He gestured at the proclamation.

"Napoleon rewards his generals and his soldiers with booty," the man said. "That's why they're raping our country. From generals right down to the lowest musketeer, they're stealing everything they can get their hands on because that's how they get their pay." He wagged his finger at me. "But it will bring them down in the end. Have you ever tried to aim a musket or run for cover when you're loaded down with loot?" The man jeered. "We'll kill them all, first the French invaders, and when we've cut the throat of the last of them, we'll go back after the lovers of the French who betrayed us and rip out their throats, too."

My hand instinctively went to my throat.

When the ship docked at Cádiz, custom inspectors came aboard. They searched my meager possessions, as they did everyone else's. I was tempted to give another false name to the inspectors, but a ship's officer who knew my name was standing nearby. I waited tensely, half-expecting the man to put me in chains, but he just wrote down my name and said nothing.

I left the ship a free man, stepping into a strange city in the midst of a war. My only plans were to stay alive and out of the hands of the authorities.

As I wandered down city streets, Cádiz appeared to be a fine city, smaller than México City, and hemmed in, nearly surrounded by water. The city was compact and pleasing to the eye, with a tall watchtower and many white buildings in the Moorish style, the city having been occupied by that infidel people for many centuries. I learned aboard ship that Cádiz was one of the oldest cities in Europe, founded by the Phoenicians nearly a century before the birth of Christ. Since that time it had been occupied by the Carthaginians, Romans, Moors, and Spanish. It had replaced Seville as the main port for trade with the colonies, but with that wealth came attacks by pirates and the British. Now, of course, it was the turn of the French to test the city's defenses.

From the docks I strolled to the center of the city and took a room at an inn. I was in a quandary as to what my next move should be. An ocean's distance from the viceroy's men would not protect me from them forever. Ships continually brought dispatches from the viceroy's administration. Authorities in Cádiz would learn that a notorious colonial bandido had fled to their jurisdiction. And there was the problem of money. I would have to turn to thievery when my last piece of eight was gone.

I ordered wine and something to eat and was chewing on a tough piece of beef when I looked up at two men wearing military uniforms.

"Carlos Galí?" one inquired.

I shook my head. "No, señor, I am Roberto Herra. However, I know of this man you ask about, his room is near mine." I pointed up the stairs. "Second floor, first room on the right."

The two soldiers started for the stairway, and I started for the front door. I was halfway to it when the landlord pointed at me. "That's him!"

The devil take him for not minding his own business.

One of the soldiers pointed a pistol at my face. "You are under arrest, Señor Galí."

"For what crime?" I demanded.

"The one the executioner whispers in your ear."

FIFTY-SEVEN

To MY SURPRISE, I was not taken to a dungeon but to the city's military headquarters. A frenzied facility, staff officers and couriers came and went, always in a hurry, some bristling with self-importance, others with worried expressions as they brought word of the war's progress. Officers took me down a stone stairway into the bowels of the building and shoved me into a dark room. The door slammed behind me, and I was in complete darkness. I hadn't seen anything in the room except stacks of papers, as if the room was used for storage of records. I made myself comfortable on the papers and tried not to think about my predicament. Not thinking about it was as easy as forgetting to breathe.

Was I to be taken out and summarily shot? If I were given the chance to explain myself, I might buy some time. I could confess to being a fraud—as well as a notorious colonial bandido and murderer—rather than a spy and traitor. That might buy me a few hours while they decided the best way to execute me.

I don't know how long they kept me in the storage room. I awoke when I heard the lock clicking.

"Come with me," an officer said. He spoke with the arrogance and authority of a soldier who had spent his military career in staff assignments rather than facing an enemy in the field. Two soldados flanked him.

"Where are you taking me?"

"Hopefully to hell."

"When we meet there, I'll be mounted on your wife, giving her a taste of a real man."

The devil must make me say these things. The officer stood perfectly still, frozen in place. His face went pale. The two soldiers gawked.

The officer's pale color faded, and his face went red. "You—You—I'll have you—"

"Whipped? Hanged? You wish to redress the insult? Give me a sword, amigo, and we will settle the matter of your wife's affection for my manhood."

"Put him in chains!"

A moment later I was taken into a room on an upper floor of the headquarters building—chained. Behind a desk sat an officer, this one in a uniform that told me he outranked the dog I had insulted. Unlike the pansy, this one looked like a man who would have my male member cut off and stuffed down my throat if I spoke ill of his wife or daughters.

"Unchain him and leave," the ranking officer told the men who had brought me in after the young officer had conferred with him in private. He glared at me as soon as we were alone. "I should put you immediately before a firing squad for your insults to my lieutenant."

I sneered. "He's a woman."

"He's my son."

Santo mierda! "I apologize, Señor General." I didn't know his rank, but calling him a "general" sounded like a good start. "I find that when I am falsely accused of crimes, I must defend myself against whomever is closest. Your fine young son was unfortunately the closest target available when the door opened."

"And exactly what crimes have you been falsely accused of?"

"I'm not a spy!"

"And why do you find it necessary to defend yourself against such a charge?"

"Well I—I—"

"Perhaps you come prepared to defend against such a charge because you are in fact guilty of it. Is that the case, Señor Galí?"

Frantic strategies for getting my foot out of my mouth flew through my head, but none reached my tongue. I tried a lie. "The soldiers last night, one of them called me a spy."

"You're lying. They didn't know why they were arresting you."

"Sí, I am lying." I leaned forward and spread my hands on his desk. I could not fool the man, so I resorted to the truth . . . or at least a small piece of it. "I have been an admirer of France, an afrancesado, as they say. I believed that some factions in Spain restricted free speech—even the freedom to think—and those are still my feelings. But now I spit on the French!" I banged my fist on the desk. "When the people of Madrid rose up and fought the invaders with their bare hands, I could no longer call myself an admirer of the French. I am first a patriot of Spain. Give me a sword, señor, and you will see French blood running down our gutters."

He stared at me and pursed his lips. "A report from the viceroy in New

Spain names spies who conspired to send to the French plans for our fortifications."

"I know of this matter. While on a scientific expedition in the colony, two of our people were arrested as spies."

He grinned like one of the sharks I ate in Termino. "Your name is one of those accused."

I made the sign of the cross and gestured to the heavens, somewhere above the cracked plaster ceiling overhead. "Señor General, may God strike me dead if I lie. I swear to you, I know nothing of these foul deeds except what I heard." I hoped the good Lord realized there was more than a little truth in what I said. *Personally, I had never spied!*

"I suspect you're lying. Something about you shouts to me that you're a bad hombre. Before you were brought before me, I expected you to be a timid, frightened scholar, a man of books and ideas. Instead, you have a foul mouth, you challenge an officer to a duel, and you lie as easily as if you were raised by gypsies."

"I come from a good Catalán—"

"Which is the only reason you are alive."

I looked at him in puzzlement. "Señor General?"

"I am a colonel, not a general. My name is Colonel Ramírez, so please stop inflating my rank. You come from Barcelona, where you're known to have French sympathies, perhaps even to have been a spy for the French before you went to the New World."

"I—"

He held up his hand. "Please stop thundering your innocence. There were suspicions about you, not proof, from the colonial authorities. But now that I've met you, I wouldn't be surprised if the accusations had included acts of murder, banditry, blackmail, blasphemy, and the defilement of women, to say nothing of treason. So let's not waste time with protestations, which will simply tighten the noose I wish to loop around your neck."

I involuntarily felt my neck and cleared my throat.

He shark-grinned again. "Yes, that very neck. But you may be able to save it if you cooperate."

"What do you want of me?" I assumed he wanted me to implicate my alleged coconspirators. I didn't know any, except for the countess, and I was ready to name her and make up a few others just to make it sound good.

"You have qualities that we need at the moment. You're from Barcelona, and you speak Catalán and French fluently."

"Sí, most excellently." I was suddenly elated. They wanted me to translate for them! What a soft job that would be, especially when the alternative was to be ripped apart by a team of horses. My mastery of both languages was questionable, but I could fake it.

"We need you for a mission," he said.

"A mission?"

"We must obtain information from Catalonia. We need a man who can travel to Barcelona and beyond, to Gerona near the French border."

"Gerona?" I squeaked. I knew enough about the geography of Spain to know that Cádiz was near the southern tip of the Iberian Peninsula and Gerona was hundreds of leagues away, beyond Barcelona, near the French border on the northern edge of the country. In between, several hundred thousand French troops ravaged the country. The French occupied Barcelona and were storming the gates of Gerona.

His grin tightened. "I can see that your passionate feelings of patriotism immediately ignited when I mentioned the need of your country. As you said a moment ago, just give you a sword and French blood would run in gutters."

"Of course, General—Colonel—Naturally my first thought was to ask myself . . . what can I do for my country? And I'm sure there are many valuable things I can do," I cleared my throat, "right here in Cádiz—"

"Your choices are to go north or be executed immediately."

I nodded and smiled. "Naturally, the atrocities those French bastardos have committed has inflamed my patriotic fervor. I am eager to go north for my country. What exactly is it you want me to do?"

"Several things. The first step is that you will be transported to Barcelona by boat."

"By boat? What of French warships?"

"The British are our allies, and their ships dominate the sea."

"What happens after I reach Barcelona?"

"You will find out the next step after your arrival there."

Icy fingers ruffled the hackles on my nape.

He read concern on my face. "I told you your choices. Cooperate and make up for your treasonable conduct, or find yourself summarily executed. You have been chosen because we know who you are, what you are, and where you will be. If you disobey orders, you'll not survive until the next dawn."

He got up and stood at the window, his hands clasped together behind him. "These are dark days, señor. Men and women die each day as heroes from one end of the country to the other. Sometimes they die alone, other times with hundreds of their fellows falling beside them. Tailors and shoemakers, kitchen maids and housewives are fighting the invaders. The names of their cities are sung and heralded across Europe as citadels of courage and determination by a people who will not surrender in the face of murderous aggression by a foreign invader." He swung around and glared at me. "When I thought you were a spineless but idealistic scholar, I doubted you would be of any use to me. Now I can see that you are an opportunist who would sell his soul to the highest bidder . . . and I am that bidder."

"What have you bid, Señor Colonel?"

"*Your life.* I see in you the incarnation of human corruption, a worthless, scheming, lying, violent, drunken, fornicating swine. If you survive this mission without our own people cutting your throat and hanging you up to bleed like a stuck pig, I will be unpleasantly surprised."

What could I say? That I was not a French sympathizer, but merely an ordinary bandido and murderer?

I stood and puffed out my chest. "Rest assured, Colonel, I will accomplish this mission in the name of the people of Spain."

"I would rather send the rawest recruit than someone like you who can't be trusted, but you two are all we have."

I blinked. "Two?"

"Your compadre is going with you."

"What compadre?"

"The one who saved your life in the Yucatan when the savages were attacking: Fray Baltar."

María Mother of God. *The inquisitor-priest was alive.* I crossed myself for real.

Justice is dead in this world. I have known that since Bruto slandered me on his deathbed.

That good-hearted, idealistic Carlos should die at the hands of savages, while that mongrel hound of Satan's Inquisition should live was evidence of God's negligence that day in the Yucatán.

I would have to remedy the situation.

 **FIFTY-EIGHT**

BEFORE I LEFT, the colonel mentioned that Fray Baltar had not attended our first meeting because the cardinal was awarding him a holy medal for his "bravery" in the Yucatán. While I had escaped by shipping out through Sisal, the priest had gone in the opposite direction, getting to the southern coast of the Yucatán Peninsula near Tulum. There he boarded a coastal boat that took him south to Cartagena, where he caught a Cádiz-bound ship.

He had first told the authorities that no one survived the expedition, *despite his heroic efforts to save them.* When he found out "Carlos" had survived, he took credit for his escape from the savages. I suspected he had deliberately avoided the meeting at the colonel's out of fear that "Carlos" would have exposed him as the cowardly cur he was. Thank God he had not been there to unmask me. But the issue was still coming to a head; we had to meet with the colonel tomorrow.

Colonel Ramírez obligingly told me of the location of the monastery where my "compadre" was staying. The colonel released me with orders to meet him and Fray Baltar at his office the next day. There, he would give us final instructions.

I found my way to the religious complex. I took up a position at an inn window, ordered food and wine, and watched the priests coming in and out of the church grounds. Most of them crossed the street for a cup of wine, and I noticed one occasionally disappeared upstairs with one of the inn's putas. I learned from a barmaid that by dinnertime, the place would be crowded with priests, as would the upstairs.

The landlord brought me a fresh jug of wine after I had finished the first. I asked him if the priest, who was the "hero of the Yucatán," favored his premises, and he assured me the man was a regular visitor.

He asked if I wanted a woman.

"Send your most beautiful one over," I told him. The putas I'd seen were ugly enough to make a wolf drop a pork chop, but one could still hope.

"I am Serena," the woman told me, as she swaggered up to my table. "You wish to go upstairs? I will cost you two escudos."

Long black hair, black flashing eyes, a black skirt and blouse, a black heart, and a disposition to match, she was perfect for what I wanted.

I raised my eyebrows. "Am I speaking to the Queen of Sheba? I could buy a mule with that kind of money."

"You could buy two mules, but they have all been requisitioned for the war. So have most of my sister putas." She tossed back her hair. "You are lucky to even find one willing to give you pleasure. I support the war effort by sleeping only with heroes and high-ranking officers."

I lowered my voice. "Are you a patriot, Serena?"

"I am willing to die for Cádiz. Have you not heard of how women like María Agustine in Zaragoza have fought alongside men?"

"You need not die, but I have a mission for you of great importance."

She stared at me, at my slightly unfamiliar clothes, which conveyed that I was not from Cádiz. She threw back her head. "Who are you to make such talk?"

Keeping my voice low, I told her, "I work for Colonel Ramírez, who is in charge of sorting out French spies. Do you know what we do with French spies when we catch them?"

"I know what I would do to them." She pulled a wicked dagger from somewhere under her clothes. "I would cut out their guts and feed them to the dogs."

I believed her. I could slip a knife between the ribs of that Inquisitor bastardo myself, but that would raise many questions, not to mention that the Inquisition would be out in force after my sorry hide. A better idea was unfolding in my mind and off my tongue.

"Serena, I am on the trail of a French spy who is posing as a priest."

"A spy posing as a priest?" She crossed herself. "May the devil shit out his soul."

"Sometime today or this evening, he will come in here. This is what we need to do to make sure he does not compromise our city's defenses . . ."

I sat in a dark corner of the inn, half-hidden behind the end of the bar, and watched the action. The inquisitor-priest had been inside for an hour, pouring a steady deluge of wine down his gullet. I noticed that none of the other priests appeared eager to socialize with him. He moved from one table to another as his drinking companions faded away. I easily understood the reaction of the priests: no one wanted to say something that might launch an investigation by the Holy Office of the Inquisition.

When Baltar had drunk enough wine to dull his senses, I signaled Serena. The puta sat down at the table and poured him a mug of wine. She leaned close and spoke in his ear. It didn't take long for her to convey the message I'd given her: As a patriot, she wanted to honor Fray Baltar the best way any woman could.

I waited a moment after they disappeared upstairs, then went up after them. I had rented adjoining rooms . . . at double the landlord's usual rate. I went into the vacant one, moved quickly across, opened the door to the balcony, and stuck my head out. The balcony to the room I had rented for the puta and Baltar was unoccupied. Grasping the iron rail, I slipped over my balcony and leaned across to get a handhold on the railing on the other balcony before I put my foot across. Nothing lay below but a dark alley filled with garbage thrown out the back of the inn or tossed from its windows: the stench of thousands of emptied chamber pots mixed with the smell of the rancid beef the innkeeper served.

I listened at the balcony door and heard the sound of a woman's screech and laughter. Then the stamp of feet toward the door. *Good girl!* I stepped to the side of the door as it burst open, and Serena flew out, naked and giggling. The priest came out after her. She ducked under him and started to slip by but he got a handhold on her hair.

"Buenas noches, amigo." I grinned at him in the darkness.

He let go of her hair as if it was on fire. "What—Who—"

"It's me, your old friend from Chichén Itzá. You remember, the one you saved from the savages."

Baltar squinted at me, trying to see my face in the darkness of the night. The puta flew inside as I stepped toward him, the light from the lamp in the room highlighting my features for him.

"I came by to thank you for what you did to Carlos."

He was quick for a man with a belly full of wine. I don't know where the dagger came from, but it was suddenly in his hand as he lunged at me. I leaped back and twisted sideways as the blade snagged and tore my shirt.

I grabbed both his wrists, trying to keep the knife in his right hand away from my flesh and pushed him backward, jamming him against the wrought-iron railing. He was stronger than I realized, and he pushed me back against the wall. I let go of his left hand and hit him across the side of his head with my fist. I didn't get much power behind the punch or his head was hard, because my fist bounced. The next thing I knew, the hand I had let go of was a fist pummeling me. Still gripping his dagger hand, I bent my knees and pushed off from the wall behind me, shoving him toward the railing. He staggered back, hitting the railing with his big ass. I heard the crack of metal parting, felt him falling backward off the balcony when . . . *he grabbed my shirt and took me with him.*

I was flying, no, dropping like a rock. Someone screamed as we fell into the alley's darkness. I didn't know if it was me or the bastardo Inquisitor. Maybe both our souls were screeching in terror.

When I hit the ground, my breath whooshed out of me. For a long moment I was engulfed by a void, drowning in a sea of black ink. Some primordial instinct got me off the ground. Swaying on my feet, I stumbled over someone: the priest. I realized I had ridden him all the way down and that he had broken my fall. He didn't move when I stumbled against his prone body. I gave him a kick. Nothing.

"I hope your everlasting soul burns in the fire of hell," I told the body.

I appeared in Colonel Ramírez's office at the appointed time the next morning, sore and aching from my fall but with what I hoped was a look of eager anticipation at the prospect of being sent on a mission that I would probably not survive.

"I have terrible news, Carlos. Your amigo, the priest who saved your life in New Spain, had a terrible accident."

"An accident, señor?"

"He fell from a balcony at an inn. He may die."

"He's not dead?"

"I can see from your reaction that you are shocked by the news. No, he is not dead but is not expected to live out the day."

"I should hope not."

"Señor?"

"I mean, because of his injuries, I don't want my friend to suffer."

"Yes, I can understand that you will mourn your friend, after he saved you from that host of savages. I regret that I can't let you race to his bedside. A fishing boat awaits you and must sail with the tide." The colonel came around and patted my shoulder. "Do not worry, Carlos. Fray Baltar is unconscious and would not know you were at his bedside. When he passes, I will see to it that he gets the funeral he deserves."

I crossed myself. "May God send his soul to the place he deserves so well."

I left his office and was crossing the anteroom when the colonel came out his doorway and called after me.

"I forgot to tell you. There will be a surprise waiting for you in Barcelonia."

¡Ay de mí!

 **FIFTY-NINE**

THE *SEA CAT* was the name of the fishing boat. It was also a phrase used to describe Catalán sailors: gatos del mar—cats of the sea.

As I approached, a woman standing at the bow lifted her skirt to expose her naked private parts to the sea. One of the sailors, repairing a net on the dock, grinned at my reaction. "The captain's woman. It is bad luck to have a woman on a voyage, but the sea loves women. It calms the waters and makes for a good voyage when a woman gives the sea a glimpse of her privates."

"Let's pray that his wife has calmed the sea for us," I said.

"She's not his wife but his Cádiz girlfriend. His wife in Barcelona will calm the sea for the return trip."

The captain sounded liked my kind of hombre.

I stayed out of the way while the captain and his three-man crew got us underway. The sailor I spoke to on the dock stayed behind. I had taken his place: his bunk, clothes, identification papers, everything. He was chosen because he was the closest to my own height.

There were times when I wondered what Carlos would want me to do. Had he lived, he would have returned to Spain and joined a guerrilla band. That is a certainty. I owed him my very life, though some people would say that my miserable life was not worth much. But I could not whip myself into a passion about this war. My survival instincts and anger over Spanish insults and assaults on my life had left me a lone wolf.

I was frowning about the cruel way the world had treated me when a voice beside me said, "They've all invaded Spain before." It was the captain.

"Who has invaded her?"

"The Phoenicians, Greeks, Carthaginians, Romans, barbaric hordes, Moors, and now the French. The peninsula has seen one invasion after another for thousands of years. But we have always shown our strength against the dark forces that try to enslave us."

"History is rife," I said, "with wars of conquest."

"My apologies, señor, but I saw on your face that you were thinking about the fate of our great nation. In our case, history will record the conqueror's defeat. Do not fear, these French are just another invader whom we shall defeat because we are a strong people. No other nation has repelled so many invaders, so many who thought they could break us to their will."

He described for me the situation in Catalonia, from Barcelona, which the French controlled only because the Spanish government had let them occupy a fortress in the heart of the city, to the guerrilla fighters the Catalonians called somaténs, who made life hell for the French in the countryside. Barcelona had one hundred fifty thousand people, about the same population as Méjico City.

The captain spoke to me in Catalán, and the more he spoke, the more the language came back to me.

"For freedom fighters like Mílans del Bosch," the captain said, "somaténs is also a battle cry. And not just for our guerrillas, who are fighting and winning. We have army units that are beating the French. The French general in command of Catalonia recently left the city with an army but was harassed, defeated, and chased into hiding back behind the thick walls of his fortress in Barcelona with his tail between his legs."

I learned that Napoleon kept increasing troop numbers to smash the guerrillas, but it was useless. "Most of Catalonia is in the hands of our people," he said.

Listening to him and others talk about the war and about the history of his nation, I was struck by how better informed the people of Spain were than those in the colony. Other than well-read thinkers like Padre Hidalgo, Raquel, and Marina, most people in the colony have the misconception that all of Europe is under the dominion of Spain and that the French emperor is an upstart challenging Spanish rule. England, France, Italy, Holland, Germany—these and the other countries of Europe are just paltry states or provinces for which the king of Spain appoints governors to rule. No doubt such thinking harkens back to the days when Spain cast a giant shadow in Europe.

As night fell, I spotted a white sail for a moment on the horizon. It quickly sank out of sight. "It's not French, is it?" I asked a seaman.

He shook his head. "No, it looked like a Spanish galleon to me. We spot it sometimes, usually on moonless nights. It carries the souls of the dead that have been rejected in heaven and hell. They have offended God with their arrogance and the devil with their refusal to fear eternal damnation. It's mastered by a captain who once commanded a ship in the slave trade. You can hear him sometimes, cracking his whip. You can hear the scream of the souls."

Eh, just what I needed, a tale of retribution, tortured souls, and eternal punishment. Was that my fate? Was I to find the doors of both heaven and hell closed to me because I had offended God *and* the devil?

SIXTY

Barcelona

A SHINING CITY set against resplendent hills, Barcelona boasted one of the world's most beautiful bays. As I studied that picturesque seaport from the ship's prow, however, all I could think about was how to get out of it.

Again, I considered my escape plan. The colonel had instructed me to go to a waterfront inn called the Blue Fish and wait for one of his agents to contact me. I planned to head in the opposite direction.

I struggled with my conscience over my promise to Carlos—to give his sister his message and jewelry—but it was a brief tussle. I would not risk my life to search for Carlos's family, which would be the first place the colonel's men would look for me. Besides, the locket and ring I wore to honor Carlos were valuable. I was branded as a thief, no? Should I not live up to my reputation and rob my dead amigo's family? I could not sully my soul in the eyes of God any more than I had already.

As the fishing boat neared the city, the colonel's comment that a "surprise" awaited me at Barcelona weighed heavily on my mind. Sighting the port only heightened my nervousness, especially when the captain grinned knowingly at me. He definitely knew something that I didn't know, and I knew in my bones the secret didn't bode well for me.

Other than getting away from the waterfront, I had no idea of where I should direct my feet. Barcelona was a big city, but how thoroughly I could disappear into it was still unknown. At any time Spanish resistance fighters could slip a dagger between my ribs for betraying them, or the French could arrest me as a spy.

I was careful to ask only general questions about the various regions of Spain, not giving any clue that I might want to flee to another area. The captain told me Barcelona was only thirty-odd leagues from the French border. He had never visited Madrid but knew it to be an even bigger city than Barcelona. The sheer size of the capital attracted me. Furthermore, the road between the two large cities was well traveled, permitting me to melt in with legitimate travelers.

I would get out of Barcelona as soon as possible, not even spending a night in the city, pausing only to sell the locket and ring and buy a mount. Once in the capital, I would try to make enough money through honest labor—or dishonest, more likely—for passage to Havana.

I was deep in thought, devising and revising my plans, when the captain leaned beside me on the rail.

"It is the most magnificent city in the world, my Barcelona," he said. "It is the city of discovery, too. On his return from discovering the New World, Columbus raced the *Niña* to Barcelona, where the king and queen were holding court, outsailing the treacherous Captain Pinzón aboard the *Pinta*. The men were racing to be the first to claim credit for the discoveries. Columbus brought six Carib indios and took them with him to the royal place in the Barri Góti, where he presented them to Isabella and Ferdinand."

I told him about something curious I had seen earlier: fishing boats throwing large pieces of wood weighed down with iron and dragging a net overboard.

"Red coral," the captain said. "Very valuable but too deep for a man to dive down and chip off. The boats are dragging the wooden rams along the coral, breaking off pieces which are then picked up by the net."

We passed a French patrol boat, and I saw a man on board examining us with a spyglass.

"They are checking the name of the boat. When the *Sea Cat* sailed out of the city, they made a note of it. Now they will check to see how long the boat was gone. If more than a couple of days, the captain and crew are arrested and accused of carrying information to our forces at Cádiz."

"Won't they realize you've been gone a couple weeks when they check their records?"

"The *Sea Cat* has only been gone overnight," he said, grinning. "That is what their records will show."

"You have someone altering their records?"

"No, señor, we of the resistance just have more than one boat named the *Sea Cat*. The other one was noted by the French when it sailed out of Barcelona yesterday, and we take its place on the French rolls today as returning from an overnight fishing trip."

"Clever." *But risky*, I thought.

"We'll dock near the Baceloneta district," he said. "It is like a small village itself, a village of fishermen and dockworkers, even though it's part of the city. Your inn is near there."

Again, the captain's knowing grin made me uneasy.

When we docked, I grabbed my sea bag of clothes and gear—I would have looked suspicious without it—and jumped down to the dock as soon as the crew had the lines secured. I waved good-bye to the captain and tried to keep my stride casual when I really wanted to break into a run. The wharf area was a busy one, bustling with fishing crews and fishmongers.

As I waved, the captain's grin got wider. He pointed at me and yelled, "There he is!"

Two women waiting at the end of the dock stared at me: an older woman who was recognizable as the mother of a younger one standing beside her. My eyes froze on the old woman because of the intense look she gave me. She wore widow's black from the scarf on her head to her shoes.

As my feet drew me involuntarily closer, I realized it wasn't my face she was staring at but the locket dangling from the chain around my neck. Her resemblance to Carlos was unmistakable, and just as the enormity of my dilemma sank in, she screamed: *"Murderer!"*

I ran, and Carlos's mother gave chase, still screaming: *"Murderer!"*

I dodged fishmongers with sharp knives and ran into the arms of two constables.

The widow and her daughter caught up with us. The king's men held me as the older woman pointed an accusatory finger at me.

"He murdered my son!" she shouted.

"How do you know, señora?"

Carlos's mother pointed at the locket and the rings on my fingers.

"He murdered my son and stole his jewelry."

 **SIXTY-ONE**

THE CONSTABLES TOOK me to the Barcelona jail. My first fear was that I would be turned over to the French, but the captain had been right when he described the French's occupation as only being effective where the French stood. They occupied the massive, pentagonal fortress that dominated the city but left the day-to-day policing of the streets to the city police.

I spent my first night in jail, contemplating my options—everything from escape to confession—when in the morning a jailer released me from my cell.

"You're a lucky one," he said, as I followed him up a dim set of stone steps. "Your lover arranged your release."

I mumbled my appreciation and wondered who the hell my lover was. And if she would start screaming when she saw I wasn't Carlos.

I couldn't keep the wonderment off my face when I was brought into a room and came face to face with the young woman who had been with Carlos's mother on the dock. Her sisterly resemblance to Carlos was indisputable.

She gave me a hug. "I'm sorry, Carlos, but now we're together again."

A grinning constable handed me my sea bag. He slapped me on the back. "I know what you'll be doing tonight!"

I was glad he knew; I certainly didn't.

I followed her out of the jail, neither of us saying a word. When we reached the street, her affectionate demeanor evaporated. She said, "This way," and walked briskly down the street.

I followed her toward the heart of the city, questions with no answers buzzing in my head. Did she still believe I murdered her brother? Why had she rescued me? Was I being rescued only so her family could wreak blood vengeance on me?

"I didn't kill your brother," I said.

"Not now," she hissed.

Despite her clear resemblance to Carlos, her personality was different, more assertive. She exuded a hardness Carlos had lacked; I didn't doubt she was capable of putting a blade in my gut. Perhaps living under foreign occupation had toughened her up. She was an attractive woman who no doubt had to resist the unwanted attention of French soldiers who thought Spanish women were spoils of war.

She led me into a maze of crowded streets intersected by narrow twisting lanes. The surrounding buildings had been built in the Middle Ages, but they didn't seem medieval; the atmosphere was too hectic, the district a frenzied hive of activity.

Carlos's sister had taken me to the Barri Gótic, the old Gothic section in the very heart of Barcelona. It was the oldest part of the city, dating back to Roman times. The area was filled with small businesses that manufactured many kinds of merchandise. In each a master craftsman employed an apprentice or two, producing wares such as wood casks, furniture, or iron goods. Generally the master and his family lived over the shop, while the apprentices slept wherever they could find room. The area contained the main cathedral and the Palau Reial Major, the royal palace where Columbus had appeared before the king and queen.

The street names mirrored the commerce of their shops. We passed a street called Boters, and as its street sign suggested, it housed wine cask makers. Agullers Street, true to its name, employed needle makers, and Corders featured shops full of rope spinners.

"A blind man could make his way through the Barri Gótic and know where he was with every step," the captain had said, "just from the manufacturing sounds and smells."

When we came to the royal palace, the woman—whose name I knew to be Rosa only because Carlos had told me—glared at me and said, "There's a room in the palace where the Inquisition used to conduct trials. They say the walls trembled when people lied."

Was she trying to tell me something?

We came to a knife grinder's shop on Dagueria Street. Two young apprentices grinding blades did not even glance at us as we walked through the shop and to a stairway down to a cellar. I followed meekly—a lamb led to the matadero—conspicuously short on options. When we reached the bottom of the steps, two men appeared from out of the cellar's shadowy corners. Two more came down the steps behind me. All four men had daggers out.

"This is the bastardo that murdered my brother," Rosa said.

SIXTY-TWO

I THREW UP my hands to show I had no weapons. "I was Carlos's friend, not his murderer."

"Kill him," she hissed. "He's a French spy."

"Don't listen to her. I was sent here on an important mission by Colonel Ramírez in Cádiz. I'm here to contact the guerrillas fighting the French."

"Murderer!" She lifted her skirt and pulled a dagger from a sheath strapped to her leg.

"Stop it!" one of the men commanded.

"Casio—"

"No, we need information before we draw blood. You can take your revenge later."

"I'm only here to serve," I said, smiling. "Question me, and then she can kill me."

The man called Casio stepped closer to me. I suspected he was only a few years older than me, perhaps around thirty but already world-weary. The hands holding the dagger were large and scarred from some sort of manual labor. Perhaps he'd been a smith. Stocky, powerfully built, he was a formidable presence.

I said, "I came here to help the resistance, not be killed by it."

"What happened to Rosa's brother? Why are you pretending to be him?"

My life was on the line. Such moments arose now with numbing frequency, so numbing I did something shockingly out of character for me: I told the truth.

"My name is Juan de Zavala. I'm a colonial, from Guanajuato in the Bajío region of New Spain. I'm a liar and sometimes a thief by necessity, but not a murderer. I have only killed in self-defense. I didn't kill Carlos. He was my amigo. I tried to save his life when indios attacked us in the Yucatán. I nearly did so. He gave me his locket and ring to return to his family."

Casio chuckled without humor. "And you came here, halfway around the world, to return them." It was not a question.

"I came to Spain because I was mistaken for Carlos after I escaped from the savages. I had his identification on me when I was found. I was wanted in New Spain, not for capricious crimes, but for ones I was forced to commit because Señora Fortuna had stacked the deck against me." I told them the sad tale of the caballero who woke up one day to find that he was a changeling, of how I met Carlos at Teotihuacán while running from constables and stayed with him as his servant until he died in the Yucatán. I left out a few details, among them the countess in New Spain and the killing of the inquisitor-priest in Cádiz.

When I finished, silence filled the room. An uncomfortable silence. Casio looked at me as if I were one of those people Carlos had believed lived on another planet. He slowly shook his head. "I don't know if I should cry because of your sad story . . . or cut your throat because you are the biggest liar in Christendom."

"No one could make up such a story," the man beside Casio said. "Not even Cervantes could have dreamed up such a tale."

"We shall see," Casio said. "Get the indiano."

I'd heard the word before. Men who had gone to the colonies in the Americas and returned after making their fortune were called americanos or indianos in Spain. We called them gachupines in the colony.

When the man left to bring back the indiano, I turned to Rosa. "I'm sorry about Carlos. I truly came to think of him as my own brother. I would have given my life for him . . . and almost did."

She said nothing. I couldn't tell if she was still ready to kill me or not. One thing was for certain: she was not a compromising woman. While Carlos was a person of reason, his sister struck me as one who would make quick judgments and not change them.

After an hour or so the man returned with the indiano. Older than the men in the room, who were in their twenties or thirties, the so-called indio had grayish hair and was perhaps in his fifties.

"Tell him your story," Casio said.

I started through it once again, slowly. I got as far as breaking out of the Guanajuato jail when Casio interrupted.

"What do you think?" he asked the indiano.

"Who is the intendent of Guanajuato?" he asked me.

"Señor Riano."

"Anyone can know the governor's name," Casio said.

"What's his oldest son's name?" the indiano asked.

"Gilberto."

He asked me directions from the center of town to roads leading to other areas, from the largest cathedral in the city to two other prominent ones. He asked me the best place to buy jewelry in the city, and I confessed my ignorance. "Ask me who makes the best saddles," I said.

"Tell me what your uncle—what Bruto looked like."

"Not like me. His skin, hair, and eyes were lighter, but the most important thing was a mark here," I touched the side of my head near my right temple. "He had a brown mark. He called it a birthmark."

"He's Juan de Zavala," the indiano said.

"Are you certain?"

"Without doubt. He's lived in Guanajuato, that's for certain. I met Bruto over ten years ago but don't remember him well. I don't remember the birthmark at all. But I know the changeling story from a letter my cousin sent me. It is the biggest scandal in the colony." He shrugged. "Besides, he is obviously a colonial; he has their accent. But the most convincing proof is his boots."

We all looked down at my boots. And his.

"Indios also make my boots. The boot makers of Spain cannot match their craftsmanship."

"Thank you, señor," I said, truly grateful.

The indiano left, and Casio faced me again.

"How do we know you are not a French spy?"

"I care as little about the French as I do about you Spanish," I said. "Besides, I didn't spy for the French. Carlos did."

"That's a lie!" Rosa snapped.

"It's not a lie," Casio said. "That Carlos was a lover of the French is well known. Do they know in Cádiz this story of the changeling?"

"No, the colonel thinks I'm Carlos."

He nodded his head. "Then you will be Carlos."

I almost sighed with relief.

"We can't trust him," Rosa said. "You heard him, he's not loyal to us."

"But he's not loyal to the French either. He only cares for his own hide, so we know where he stands. Right now we need him. He was sent here because he reads French, and his face is not known to the French military here."

"Rosa is right," I said. "You need someone who is loyal to the Spanish cause. If you will permit, I will leave the city and never—"

"Our people watch every road in and out of Barcelona night and day. Not a mouse gets through unless we permit it. If you try to leave the city, we will give you the special treatment we reserve for traitors to our cause."

I bowed in surrender. "Señor Casio, consider me a soldier in the war of independence from the French devils."

"I don't trust him," the she-demon said. "I think we should kill him,"

"Then you are the perfect person to watch over him. Let's go. I'm tired of this dark place," he said to his companions.

As he started up the cellar steps, he paused and looked back at Rosa. "Don't worry, señorita, it's an extremely dangerous mission. He will more than likely be killed."

SIXTY-THREE

I'M HUNGRY," I said, when we came out of the knife-grinding shop.

"You can starve as far as I'm concerned."

Such sentimentality for a man who was her loving brother's amigo. I stopped and faced her. "When I said Carlos was like a brother to me, I wasn't lying. I would have given my life for Carlos and he for me. I don't care if you like me or not, but you have no right to be angry at me."

She stared at me for a long moment, no doubt pondering whether she should put a knife in my ribs.

"I know a decent café at the square around the corner," she said.

We drank *vi blanc*—white wine—and ate *arrós negre*—black rice—a dish with rice and pieces of monkfish, shellfish, onion, garlic, tomatoes, olive oil, squid, and squid ink. As we ate, we watched people on their afternoon siesta dancing the sardana, a dance uniquely Catalonian. The dancers held hands and formed a circle as they performed intricate and rather sedate steps. It was a dance of deliberation rather than the wild passion of a flamenco.

"Flamencos are for mindless gypsies," Rosa said. "The sardana is for inner contemplation. The dancers have to concentrate to do the steps correctly, counting their short and long steps, skips and jumps."

Later, as we listened to the guitarist Fernando Sor, Rosa said he was the best guitarist in Spain. Something about the way she spoke caused me to ask, "Is he a guerrilla?"

She didn't answer, but her lack of response left me with the impression that this famous plucker of strings was also a partisan in the patriotic cause.

So far I had only one tiny clue as to what my mission was, other than Casio's pronouncement that I would probably be killed. The clue came from Casio's mouth. These people needed me because I read French, but what I was supposed to read was still a mystery. And I had to wonder whether there weren't other people in a city so close to the French border who read French.

I would be wasting my breath asking her, so I kept my mouth shut about the subject, hoping she would warm to me. As it was, she loosened up and began to explain some things. She said, as had the fishing boat captain, that they were fighting to bring Ferdinand, El Deseado—the Desired One—back to Spain and restore him to the throne. I held my tongue and didn't mention Carlos's opinion that Prince Ferdinand was an ignorant tyrant who would make a bad king.

She explained why she had taken me to the knife shop. "The master of the shop is my uncle," she said.

"Does he make knives to put into the hearts of the invaders?" I asked.

"He is careful to make nothing but kitchen knives, because his shop serves other purposes. I work for him, making deliveries to his customers all over the city. You will be going with me when I make deliveries, so you should know what I do. The deliveries give me a chance to carry messages. And the French patrols get to know me as well, so they don't question my presence wherever I am."

"I haven't seen any French yet," I said.

"Oh, they're here. They avoid the Barri Góti unless they move in large numbers. The streets of the Barri are narrow, and a housewife is likely to pitch a cobblestone out of an upper window at them or douse them with a chamber pot. But they patrol other parts of the city, at least in the daytime. They retreat to the Ciutadella at night."

"The captain on the fishing boat said the Ciutadella is a mighty fortress."

"It's the curse of Barcelona. They say it's impregnable, and it is for our guerrilla fighters. We'd need a large army with artillery and siege equipment to take it. That's why we haven't driven the French from Barcelona; they hide behind the walls of the citadel. From it their cannons could turn the entire city into rubble before we breached a single wall. Do you know why it was built?"

I confessed my ignorance.

"It was built about a hundred years ago to house a Spanish occupying army after the city was on the losing side of the War of Spanish Succession. The war brought Felipe V, the first of Spain's Bourbon monarchs, to the throne, and he hated Barcelona for opposing him. He considered Catalonians radicals and troublemakers. To punish us and control the rebellious region, Felipe erected the huge, five-sided, star-shaped citadel.

"You see how his curse has come back to haunt us? Foreign invaders now hide behind the fortress walls, and we can't drive them out. His name is spit upon in Barcelona. When people relieve themselves, you'll sometimes hear them say they are 'going to visit Felipe.'"

"So they control the fortress but not the city?" I asked.

"It's a stalemate. Our people avoid too many violent confrontations with the French, because we don't want them shelling the palace, cathedral, or any of our other beautiful buildings. But when they leave the city, they're fair game for our somatene units. We also have regular and irregular army units still operating in Catalonia. Did your captain tell you about the victory at Bruc?"

"No."

She smiled broadly. "It has made the invaders a laughingstock. A small Catalonian unit, less than two thousand fighters, attacked a much larger

French army. As always, the French units had the best equipment and were highly trained. Our people had an advantage in that they ambushed the French from a rocky enclosure. They intended to attack, kill some French soldiers, then retreat into the rocks and scatter when the French came in pursuit. But we had a little drummer boy who was overly enthusiastic. He beat a ferocious drumroll that echoed so thunderously off the high rocks and escarpments, the French thought they were surrounded. As our people advanced, the French troops panicked and ran."

I shared her laugh at the drummer-boy story and offered a toast to the brave somatenes like herself who were fighting the French. I could see she was warming up to me . . . and I to her—it had been weeks since I had had a woman, and my male member was telling me that it needed a woman's warmth.

As the wine and conversation relaxed her, she told me more about her city. I pretended complete ignorance even though I had heard some of it from the *Sea Cat's* captain. According to tradition, Barcelona was founded by either the Phoenicians or their descendents, the Carthaginians, who built trading posts along the Catalonian coast. The city was called Barcino during Roman times, and during three centuries of Visigothic occupation it was known as Barcinona. The Islamic Moors arrived in 717. Christian Franks about a century later. The counts of Barcelona consolidated their influence over Catalonia in the tenth and eleventh centuries.

"The hero of the city is Guifré el Pelós—Wilfred the Hairy. He started the dynasty of the Counts of Barcelona, who ruled for five hundred years. He died heroically, fighting the Moors. Before that he fought dragons and had other adventures. You saw the Catalonian flag: four crimson stripes on a gold field. That flag commemorates Guifre. Fighting for Louis the Pious in his siege of Barcelona, the Saracens wounded him severely. As he lay in his tent after the victory, the king came to him and noticed Guifré's shield, covered in gold leaf but without a blazon. Louis dipped his fingers into Guifré's blood and dragged them across the shield."

I had heard the story on the fishing boat but didn't tell her that many doubted its authenticity because Louis had died before Guifré was born.

She suddenly stopped talking and glared at me.

"What is it? What have I done now?" I asked.

"Stop looking at me like I am a receptacle for your disgusting lust. Touch me, and I'll cut your peneocha off and shove it down your throat."

¡Ay! I wondered how much the city putas charged.

SIXTY-FOUR

I SLEPT IN an inn that night, the same one that I was supposed to have stayed at upon arrival. From the looks I received, I'm sure that everyone in the place was assigned to watch me. Rosa woke me at the break of dawn. "You have time for some bread and wine, and then we are off."

"Off where?"

"To make deliveries." She had two packs loaded with kitchen knives.

"You're off to spy," I said.

She raised her eyebrows. "Say that loud enough, and you'll quickly be in the hands of Bailly, the French general in charge of the secret police. He's in charge of collecting both taxes and Spaniards who oppose the French. He puts the heads of guerrilla fighters in the same baskets as the taxes he collects."

It was good to have someone like Rosa around to keep me from losing my head because my tongue wagged too much.

Toting one of the bags, I accompanied her along the city streets and up a long, wide boulevard called Las Ramblas. She would occasionally stop at a home or shop to make a delivery. I waited outside and never knew if she was passing information or knives.

We passed a French patrol, and she greeted the men with a smile and stopped to introduce me as her cousin to the corporal in charge. She spoke fluent French. As we proceeded on, she said, "They feel safer on Las Ramblas than in the Barri Gótic. You can't fire a cannon around corners."

"Pardon?"

"Las Ramblas was once a riverbed, in fact the word means something like that in Arabic. In the old days, the avenue followed the meandering course of the dry bed. It was turned into this broad, straight street by the king to keep us Barcelonans in line. Many small, narrow streets were razed to make a broad thoroughfare that is almost as straight as an arrow."

When we went past the Ciutadella fortress, bodies were hanging from high gallows outside the massive gates. Across the road, people were lined up before a guard station. Few young men were among the group, which was made up mostly of women, children, and the elderly. Like mourners at a funeral, the people were tearful and grief stricken. They waited in line to learn the fate of relatives in French hands.

"They execute people every day," Rosa said. "The French think they can control us with fear, but it only infuriates us and escalates the violence against them. You see the grief of our people everywhere, not just in the city but in the smallest towns and villages. All over Catalonia people grieve for their loved ones: fathers and sons and even daughters taken out of their house, then killed, raped, or imprisoned where the families can't find them or even know if they're alive. The French can jail you for any reason, even a sullen glance at a Frenchman or a complaint that a loved one is missing. Sometimes a whole village is summarily executed in retaliation or carted off en masse to a prison.

"Bailly's spies are everywhere: on street corners, in inns and taverns. You cannot even be sure that the priest you whisper confession to isn't a French spy. The invaders are especially brutal toward the family of anyone they suspect sympathizes with the guerrillas. If they harbor the slightest suspicion that a family member is a guerrilla, the entire family is arrested and tortured for information. I've sent my own mother out of the city to stay with her brother in case my activities are discovered. I only permitted her to come into town when we thought Carlos was coming home."

"Is Casio the leader of the guerrillas in Barcelona?"

"No, he's just one of the leaders in the Catalonian region."

I was truly impressed by the courage and resolve of the people resisting the invaders. "It must bother Casio and you and the others to know that you risk not only your own life but also the lives of your family."

She stopped and locked eyes with me. "Casio has no family to worry about; he found his wife, children, and elderly father hanging from a tree on the outskirts of their village."

She told me more about the life of a guerrilla. They lived like wild animals in the forests and mountains, always on the move, frequently on the run, cold in the winter, melting under the summer heat. The leader got volunteers when the weather was good and the fighting went well, but few takers when the wind or battles turned bad. Sometimes no one would fight because they had to return home and harvest the crops.

In the same way the French tracked the fishing boats, their spies reported if a son or husband from a village was missing from home for long periods. When such reports came in, the families were arrested and sometimes arbitrarily murdered.

The instinct for violence was rampant on both sides.

"The resistance fighters must both admire *and* fear Casio and other leaders," Rosa said. "The bands are run like wolf packs: any sign of weakness by a leader and someone who covets the leadership will slip a knife between his ribs. Casio got his first musket when he killed a French soldier with a kitchen knife. The man had raped Casio's wife." She shook her head. "Unlike my brother who fought revolutions in his head rather than with his hands, guerrilla leaders are sometimes more akin to bandit leaders than political scholars. But they have to know how to deal with people on all levels.

"That is especially true when seeking support from the villages and small towns. Just as the French tax these places, so do the guerrilla bands in order to have money to buy food and weapons. If the leader is too harsh—and some bands have become nothing more than brigands robbing and murdering our people—the communities close their doors to them. Casio had to kill one of his own lieutenants, a childhood friend, because the man was excessively brutal toward villagers when he collected taxes. If he hadn't done it, that village and its neighbors would have frozen us out. And it's not just food and money we need from the towns and villages, we also need intelligence about troop movements and a place to hole up when the pursuit is hot.

"The same thing is true about dealing with the church. Most common priests are anti-French because of Napoleon's anticlerical policies. His troops have turned monasteries and convents into barracks and stables, murdered priests and raped nuns. But the priests have to be careful, too, because they're watched closely by the French. Given the slightest provocation, the French will hang the village priest."

I never thought about the logistics, the need to recruit, train, pay, and supply guerrilla forces. In my mind, a guerrilla was a man—and sometimes a woman—who left home in the morning with a musket to fight the French and returned home that night. But in truth they had the same problems with supplies and arms that regular armies had. Their needs were fewer but their resources were more strained.

Rosa said her first assignment had been making musket balls in a chicken coop behind a French army officer's mess.

"Obtaining supplies is a constant struggle," she said. "Less than half our men are equipped with muskets, and we rarely have sufficient ammunition for them. In Navarre, the guerrilla leader Mina employed a one-bullet strategy that Casio and other leaders have adopted. When they ambush a French unit, they move in as close as possible before firing. Then, as soon as they've fired their muskets *once*, they rush the French with bayonets and fight hand to hand. Some of our men are kept in reserve. When we need to disengage, the reserves fire another volley to cover the retreat.

"Even when we have enough musket balls, we continue the same strategy because we are better off with a quick attack, engaging the French with bayonets rather than sitting back and exchanging musket fire while the French wait for reinforcements to arrive."

"The French came to Spain expecting to live off the land, stealing what they could, paying only when they absolutely had to. They have found that they have to tighten their belts. Our people flee into the hills with their herds rather than let the French take them, and our guerrilla bands buy the grains as soon as they are harvested and burn the rest to keep them from the invaders.

"Another advantage we have is speed. Because our units are small, lightly armed, and know the territory, we can move much faster. Our biggest advantage is always in the mountains. Either the Spanish army never had good maps or they hid them from the French, because the French rarely know the mountain passes like we do. Wherever we go, the partisans show us the secret routes over the mountains and the best places to ambush the enemy.

"The most effective tactic has been to hide in the high rocks and shoot down on the French troops below," she said. "All rough terrain— mountains, hills, forests—work to our guerrillas' advantage because it hinders the enemy's cavalry."

I listened in silence while Rosa described their tactics. All the while, my admiration for the guerrillas was growing. A French officer requisitioned muskets, lead balls, and powder from the quartermaster, while patriots like Casio fought with a kitchen knife against a musket . . . and fight the guerrillas they did, with rare courage and determination, the kind that sent David armed only with a sling and stone against Goliath.

 **SIXTY-FIVE**

ROUNDING A CORNER, we approached a house where Rosa was to make a delivery. She grabbed my arm and whispered, "Soldiers!"

Ahead of us a group of French soldiers with muskets milled in front of a house. I turned around; more soldiers came up behind us.

"Here." She pushed open a wooden gate that closed off a narrow alleyway between the walls of two houses.

I followed her in, telling her that they'd spotted us. The passageway was no more than a few paces long, dead-ending at the wall of a house. We were trapped. She dropped her pack and pulled a knife from it.

Knives wouldn't work against a French patrol armed with muskets. Surrendering was also not an alternative. They hanged most of the people they got their hands on, letting God sort out the innocent from the guilty.

She bent over, looking through a crack in the gate, her rump shoved back at me. I don't usually get aroused when soldiers with muskets are breathing down my neck, but having her well-rounded bottom shoved against my manhood put me into an instant state of excitation. I knew this was a character flaw on my part, but my garrancha had no morality. My libidinous urges, however, did give me an idea that could save our lives.

I grabbed her dress from behind and lifted it.

"What are you doing?"

"*Shhhh,* act like a bitch in heat."

Like most women of her class, Rosa was naked under her petticoats. As a man who considers himself an expert on women's derrières, I can attest that Rosa's was of the finest quality: smooth and firm, warm to the touch. Hearing boots approach, I did not have time to fully examine her prurient bounty. Backing her up against one of the houses, I instead unbuckled my pants.

The sword of my lust was hard enough to cut up diamonds, but—ay! still it could not penetrate the vise of her vixen's treasure. She was tighter than the garrote the French would throttle us both with if they arrested us.

The gate crashed open from a kick, and I was staring into the muzzle of a French musket. The soldier gawked at me, his eyes like saucers, as our hips pumped and gyrated in a lurid display of simulated sex.

"Es-tu, le mari?"—Are you the husband?—I asked, our hips still pounding, writhing, and rotating, while Rosa moaned with electrifying authenticity.

Shouting erupted on the street. Giving me a sly grin and a knowing wink, the soldier slapped me on the back and grunted, "Trés bien!"—Very good—and left, letting the gate swing shut behind him.

"We have to remain in this position," I whispered. "They may return . . . if nothing else just to watch."

"French bastards," she snarled under her breath, shaking with fear but, as much as she detested me, still too frightened of the soldiers to risk withdrawing from our embrace. She even continued to move her hips, though not as provocatively as before.

"They would have killed us," I whispered in her ear. "We did the right thing."

Relief was also flooding my body, which, in combination with our simulated sex act, made my aroused manhood rise even higher. In fact the hammer of my love was now throbbing poignantly, painfully with pent-up desire.

She must have felt the same way, because her flower suddenly, magically opened. Since it was unwise to separate—the French soldier could return at any moment—we had to make it look good, no? My garrancha, having a mind of its own, decided to make it look *very* good. Her secret treasure seemed to have the same idea. Her blossom not only opened but reflexively tilted up just as I instinctively leaned forward. Excitement once again overwhelmed my survival instincts, and before I knew it I was in her.

I moved my left hand onto her breast; the other went down between her legs to her trigger of passion. There, I teased and tantalized the tender bud of her passionflower with my finger. Moving my left hand to her delectable derrière, I was now lifting her off the ground a full foot at a time with each bump and pump of my powerful hips.

Perhaps we were relieved at having survived the French dragnet, energized by the thrilling sense that we might live after all. Whatever it was, our desires and needs had overwhelmed us. We did not like each other—her hatred of me was indisputably homicidal—but that somehow made it better.

Dropping her to the ground, I fell on top of her in the alley. We had more leverage this way, and we were instantly banging at each other like hammer and anvil, as if all the demons in hell were struggling to escape our libidinous loins, as if our pelvises were weapons, battering rams in the siege-war of lust. She felt like she had steel plates in hers, and she pounded mine so hard it swelled and turned livid. None of which slowed me down . . . not with spasm after spasm after spasm of lecherous lust pumping out of me and out of her over and over and over and over.

Breathless, exhausted, covered with dirt, we finally rose, straightened our clothes and waited for the French to clear out of the street.

Kneeling, with my back to the wall, I closed my eyes and sighed when a knife was suddenly at my throat. Without moving, I gaped at the woman holding it.

"I would kill you for raping me, but Casio would be angry."

Rape? Shades of Marina! I wanted to correct her false impression of our lovemaking; she had thrust her frangipani at me. I decided, however, not to argue with a woman as quick with a knife as she. Most women are soft and pliable after lovemaking. This one only got meaner.

I gently pushed the blade away from my throat. "I forgot to tell you Carlos's message for you. Just before the ghost left his body, he said to tell you that you're doing God's will, not committing a sin, but following the path God chose for you."

She glared at me. "What more did he say?"

"That was all." I grinned. "He never told me your sins, if that's what you are wondering."

Rosa tapped the knife blade against her palm. "I have no sins, Señor Pícaro."

Eh, I had a new name. A pícaro was a low-class rogue and scoundrel, a vile thief and defiler of women. She thought she was insulting me, but after having been called a lépero, bandido, traitor, murderer, and worse, being labeled a pícaro was not a slander.

 **SIXTY-SIX**

GOOD NEWS," CASIO told me effusively. "You can at last be a hero for your country."

Associating with Spaniards had taught me that in their lexicon *dead* and *hero* were often indistinguishable.

"I am ready to serve the cause of liberty," I lied.

"You're lying, of course. Rosa has already reported to me that you are a worthless scoundrel. Under ordinary circumstances, I would cut out your liver and feed it to my dog, but . . ." he paused and grinned, "your ability to dupe others and survive is phenomenal. You've managed to avoid the colony's hangmen as well as those in Cádiz and, so far, even those in Barcelona. Being a thief, a murderer, and a confidence man could be invaluable in this small war we wage against an overwhelming adversary. We will have abundant time to deal with your crimes after we've driven the French back over the Pyrénées."

He told me that most of the battle plans Napoleon sends to his generals in command of armies in Spain come over the Pyrénées and through Barcelona.

"The emperor keeps his hands tight on the Spanish throat," Casio said. "He allows his commanders little leeway, because they've suffered so many defeats at the hands of our regulars and guerrillas. We have information from a source at French headquarters inside the Ciutadella that a major campaign to sweep the resistance from our province will begin shortly. A general will carry Napoleon's orders to his field commanders in Barcelona. He'll attend a ball in his honor. The next morning he will assemble a group of high-ranking officers and give them their orders.

"The general, Habert, goes nowhere without his attaché case, which contains copies of the emperor's commands. We need to obtain a copy of those orders. The simplest method would be to ambush him and his escort, but then the French would know we had their plans."

"You want to copy them without him knowing," I said.

"Exactly. We need to slip one out of his attaché case, quickly copy it, and return the original. Naturally, it would have to be copied by someone who is fluent in French."

"Many people in Barcelona speak—"

"True, but we asked for someone from Cádiz because of the high risk that our own people would be recognized. Besides, while we have many people who can speak a little French, few can read it."

I now realized why Colonel Ramírez had chosen "Carlos" for the mission. Carlos had had a talent for slipping plans out of an attaché case, copying, and putting them back. Because of his known French sympathies, they wouldn't suspect him. If the plans included drawings of fortifications, Carlos could also duplicate them. Drawing was a talent I didn't have, and I, too, didn't read French as well as I spoke it. But these were not points to urge upon a man when my life was hanging by a thread and he held a dagger. To refuse the mission would be suicidal.

"How do I get my hands on the plan?"

"A noble woman who the French believe is sympathetic to their cause—will give a ball in the general's honor. She is also, shall we say, a woman"—his smile at this point scintillated—"of charismatic charm and irresistible beauty. She will see to it that the plan is removed and replaced after you are through with it."

I didn't like anything about his scheme. Where the general went with his attaché case, troops of French dragoons would follow close behind. I also suspected that Casio had other plots up his sleeve, and my survival wasn't part of the plan. My own suspicious nature and lack of confidence in the innate goodness of my fellow man led me to suspect friend and foe alike. Among other things, if the guerrillas really wanted the French not to know I'd copied the plans, they could dispel that possibility by killing me.

I felt a little like I did when the Mayan war chief ordered my heart served blood-rare as his main entrée.

 **SIXTY-SEVEN**

WE'RE POSING AS servants," Rosa told me.

The noblewoman's palace was half a day's journey from the city.

"French guards will watch the palace. Only servants will be able to move freely, and even we will be scrutinized. Their mistress is known for her . . . projets d'amours, as the French say."

"She likes to bed men?" I asked.

Rosa growled something unintelligible but disparaging.

These Spanish noblewomen must be lusty wenches, I thought to myself. I had already bedded one of them in the colony, though she was of French blood. Could it be the same woman? I asked Rosa the name of the woman whose palace we were going to.

"That's not your concern."

I didn't argue the point. For certain, the woman I'd met was not a Spanish patriot.

"You'll be working as a wine steward," Rosa said. "Late in the evening, you'll carry brandy to her bedchamber and remain there in an adjoining room. She will entertain General Habert privately. She'll slip a sleeping powder into his brandy and call you when it's taken effect. You'll remove the campaign plan from the attaché case, quickly copy it, and put it back." She grinned at me. "It's a very simple plan."

I smiled and nodded, as if I were artless enough to believe her. I was to steal a military plan from a French general surrounded by French officers. A simple plan? My feelings about the plan could be expressed by a single word: *gallows!*

For one thing the plan presumed that the French were fools. I didn't assume that French generals who had conquered most of Europe were incontrollable cretins.

"The French officers will be gambling and whoring." Rosa eyed me narrowly. "Unless you want me to cut out your apple, you will behave yourself."

What is it about me that made this woman's bloodlust boil over one minute and her passion ignite the next? I had incited many señoritas to amorous feats and peaks, but this was the first woman whose lust for me was intrinsically homicidal.

The noblewoman's home was palatial. It would have humiliated the viceroy's palace in Méjico City almost as badly as a servant's uniform humiliated me. It didn't fit.

"It's not my size," I told Rosa. The jacket was too small, the breeches too tight and short.

She stared down at my male parts bulging in the crouch. "Can't you hide that thing?"

"It's being strangled."

"Keep it under control, or I'll cut it off."

There she went again, wanting to turn me into a *castrato*, a church choirboy who has had his cojones cut off to ensure he will never lose his sweet soprano voice. Women were not permitted to sing in church choirs, so the church turned men into women. Perhaps she desired men who sang with a voice higher-pitched than mine?

"Take this tray of wine goblets into the great hall," she said.

As I came into the huge room, a French officer brushed by me as if I were invisible, arrogantly bumping my tray, spilling the wine. He walked away—no, strutted—without acknowledging his discourtesy.

Rosa was immediately in my face, hissing like a snake. "Stay in character, you fool. You look ready to challenge him to a duel."

She was right; I should be looking for an escape route, not preparing to fight the French army. I put a blank-eyed smile on my face, hoping it would make me look harmless and stupid, and circulated.

What a life the conquerors had: fine food, fine wines, and the best-looking putas I'd ever seen. In one of the rooms, card tables had been set up. I noticed that most of the bets were placed with jewelry, gems that had obviously belonged to Spanish households. One officer, a captain of cavalry, announced as he threw a ring on the table that it was still bloodied from the finger he'd cut it off. The table erupted with laughter.

To the victors go the spoils, no? But from the way the guerrillas fought back, many of these arrogant bastardos would soon dine with the devil.

I was on my third tray of goblets and humility when the roomful of officers parted like the Red Sea and a woman of inexpressible beauty floated across the room toward me. Honey-hued hair down to her waist, dazzlingly bejeweled, eyes that scintillated like sin itself, she was exquisitely accoutered in a silver gown of sheer pongee silk fit for a queen . . . or a countess.

The earth vanished beneath my feet. I stared into my open grave, certain my hell-forged soul had vacated my body.

"Keep moving with that wine," Camilla, Countess de Valls, snapped at me. She stared at me, with that noble eye that sees through servants but doesn't acknowledge that they're human.

Swaying on my feet, I had difficulty breathing. Rosa was suddenly in my face again. "You heard the countess: keep the wine moving.!"

Two women in the room who wanted to flog, castrate, and kill me. I shouldn't have been surprised, but I had convinced myself it wasn't possible that it could be the same woman.

The countess's eyes, of course, flickered no hint of recognition. Was it possible that she didn't recognize me as the intruder who searched her room in the colony, then ravished her senseless? With due modesty, she might not remember the face of the man with whom she wrestled in the dark . . . but would she forget the finest loins on two continents? Yes, she might conceivably not recall my much-abused face, but she could never forget the love hammer that pounded her passionflower into a fiery frenzy of lewd lascivious lust. ¡Ay! Much to my embarrassment, my cañon rose obscenely against the taut seams of my too-tight servant's trousers.

Perhaps she knew exactly who I was and didn't want to give me away to the French. What had Casio said about the countess? The French thought she was on their side? She had been spying for the French in the colony, that was a certainty. Or was she? She could have been a double agent, only pretending to spy for the French while she ferreted out Spanish traitors. And using poor Carlos as her tool. Or, perhaps, like Carlos, the French atrocities committed against the Spanish people turned her against the Bonapartes.

Or perhaps I had walked into a trap, and by morning the general would gibbet me in front of the Barcelona fortress and the buzzards would breakfast on my eyeballs.

Rosa was suddenly in my face again. "Stop thinking about your pene and serve wine."

"Did you know the countess is a French spy?"

"She's a patriot. Now start serving."

A patriot, yes. But for which country?

By late evening, I was tired and sick of serving French officers. Finally Rosa ordered me upstairs with bottles of the best wine and brandy from the countess's cellar. I went up the steps that led to the countess's chambers. Rosa came up behind me and served common wine and a good meal of beef and potatoes to the guards at the corridor. The guards hardly looked at me as I passed by with the spirits for the countess and her special

guest, General Habert. The top two buttons on Rosa's blouse were un-
done, and the guards were busy staring. I ogled her, too. Men are swine.

I had seen the general arrive earlier and was not impressed with his
bearing. His stomach ballooned over his belt, but I suppose that as a general he had little need for physical fitness.

However, I was impressed with his attaché case. Hand-crafted leather
elaborately embossed with a gold coat of arms, it never left his side, according to Casio. He carried it himself rather than have the aide at his
heels handle it. He disappeared upstairs soon after arriving. The countess
went up shortly after him. The plan was for her to divert the general, drug
his drink, then let me into the room to copy the papers by candlelight. But,
like I said, something about their scheme bothered me. And now that the
countess turned out to be my old nemesis, my thoughts were even bleaker.

By the time I mounted the stairs, the French officers were drunk,
many had passed out, others were carousing with whores or playing cards
in a smoke-filled room.

Following Rosa's instructions, I waited outside the countess's chambers
by a side door that led into a private alcove. Rosa told me I was to wait in
the alcove and out of fear that I would snore, to not fall asleep. Of course I
wouldn't snore; I would be too busy spying on the countess and looking for
an escape route.

I had never been tempted to take a whip to a woman . . . until I tangled
with Rosa.

Kneeling at the keyhole did not give me a good view of the countess's
bedroom. The bed was too far off to the left for me to see anything but its
foot. The room was not dark but dimly lit, shadowy, half of the candles extinguished. I quietly opened the door just enough to poke my head in. I
heard the telltale heavy breathing and guttural grunts of lovemaking but
still didn't have a view of her bed. Keeping low, I snaked across the floor on
my belly to a table and peeked around it.

The countess was mounted atop the general. She was bare-ass naked,
and even in the dim light I recognized her bountiful bottom, the concupiscent curve of her breasts, and knew it was she. General Habert was flat on
his back, with his behemoth belly ballooning up like a hairy beast. She was
the only one working, pumping and groaning, as if his manhood filled her
with blind passions and insane cravings. From experience, I recognized her
ecstatic gasps as false cries by a fulsome whore to fool vain men into believing they have garranchas of steel.

The prized attaché case was on the table next to the bed.

A strange sound came from the bed. I strained to listen. It was a sound
that I recognized yet could not place. Then it hit me: the general was snoring!

The countess's mendacious moans subsided. Finally she stopped her
sexual charade and stared down at the general's flaccid features.

"Général?" she asked in French.

He responded with a painfully stentorian snore. She gently slapped his face and called his name again.

"Did you drug him well?" I asked.

"*Akkkk!*" She swung around, the twin muzzles of her magnificent melons targeting me like artillery pieces.

"*Shhhh.* The guards are outside."

She careened off the snoring walrus. As I suspected, the brandy and drugs had spiked and crumpled his cañon. I wondered how long it had been that way.

"You aren't very good at obeying orders, are you?" she hissed.

I shrugged. "When did you stop spying for the French and start whoring for the Spanish?"

She didn't hide her nakedness from me, not even a modest hand over her breasts. Nor had I tried to hide the fact that I desired her. The burgeoning bulge in my breeches amply attested to that reality.

"I watch which way the winds blow. Right now, it's blowing the Spanish crown off Joseph Bonaparte's head."

She opened the attaché case, exposing a thick ream of papers, and pulled out a one-page document. "Copy this." She indicated a quill and a pot of ink on a table.

I sat down and hurriedly skimmed the document. It contained instructions to three different commands concerning troop movement. The instructions were brief and to the point and in simple enough wording even for my limited grasp of written French. It gave the name of the commander and the exact movement the unit was to make. It gave routes, dates, and troop strength in a few concise paragraphs.

"Just copy it," she said. "The information means nothing to you, you lépero scum, but the guerrillas will make good use of it."

Rosa entered just as I was finishing the copy. The two never spoke to each other. Both hung over me until I had written the last word.

"Go now," the countess said. "Leave this way."

I followed her across the room. She opened a secret door that led into another alcove. Across the alcove was another door. I knew immediately what it was: a way for her lovers to make their way in and out of the bedchamber without being seen.

"Take the stairway behind that door to the ground level and leave through the door to the garden. A horse is saddled and waiting. The French guards at the front gates have been told to expect a messenger. See that the war plans get to the hands of our people immediately. They'll be waiting for you by the forest road."

I felt like saluting the French woman cracking the orders but merely gave her a "Oui, madame."

I rushed through the door, my boots banging on the steps. I paused at the bottom, but instead of going out to the garden where a saddled horse awaited, I silently crept back up the stairs.

Many things bothered me, the most humiliating of which was that Rosa and the countess treated me as if I were inconceivably stupid, a naïve colonial bumpkin, at best. While my education was mostly in the saddle, as Casio pointed out, I had had the agility of a cat in adversity.

I was told the countess wouldn't copy the war document because she feared that the handwriting would expose her as a Spanish spy if the messenger was caught. Ay, that rang true enough, I suppose. *But how did she know exactly where the document was in the attaché case?* She reached in and grabbed it without even searching for it.

A high-ranking officer would be carrying more in his attaché case than a single piece of paper. In fact, I saw a thick stack of papers when she opened the case. Yet she blindly pulled out the exact sheet we needed. The only way she would have known its exact location was if she had been shown where to find it. Or if she had planted it in the case herself.

And what had she said about the guards at the gate? They would be expecting a messenger to ride through. Who had the authority to give them such an order? Only a high-ranking French officer.

My final suspicion had been the way Rosa entered the room. Rosa was at best a daughter of the working class. The countess was high nobility. But their body language, their silent acceptance of each other's presence, not a word between them . . . their actions connoted to my dense colonial mind an informality, even a familiarity I found paradoxical for two women worlds apart on the social and financial scale

Back upstairs, I listened at the door but heard nothing. I quietly opened the door a crack and listened again. Once again I heard the sounds of a woman in sexual ecstasy. Had the general awoken? I wondered. I could not get a view of the bed from the doorway. I crawled back into the dimly lit room. As I came around the corner of a chest, I stopped and stared, stunned.

It wasn't the countess and the general making the love noises; *it was the two women.* The countess was lying on her back on the bed, naked. Her legs were spread, and Rosa knelt between them, her face palpating the countess's undulating passionflower.

"What are you doing?" I snarled out loud.

My question cracked in the room like a pistol shot. Both women looked at me, startled. Rosa recovered first. She flew off the bed with the speed of a jungle cat, grabbing her dagger from a pile of her clothes on the floor.

She came at me in a low crouch to stick the blade up between my legs. I stepped sideways and hit her. I had never hit a woman before, but Rosa was no mere woman, she was a wild she-demon exploding out of hell.

My roundhouse punch, thrown off a pivot, hammered her temple. She went down like a thunder-smitten oak and would not rise for a while.

The bathroom door suddenly opened up, and General Habert, as naked as the two women, appeared in the doorway. I rushed him. As I grappled with him, the other she-devil assaulted me, leaping on my back and clawing at my eyes. Normally I wouldn't find it offensive to have a naked woman clawing at me, but the momentary distraction gave the general the opportunity to hit me in the nose. He made a dash to get around me as I staggered back. I flipped the countess over my shoulders, slamming him to the floor with her body. While they both floundered on the floor, I kicked the general in his Adam's apple. The countess bolted like a banshee and ran screaming for the bedroom door.

While the general rolled on his back, gagging and clutching his throat, I ran back toward the lover's alcove and grabbed the attaché case, knocking over a table and lamp as I rushed by. I swatted another oil lamp with the attaché case, sending it flying into the drapes before I went through the secret doorway.

Coming off the steps and into the garden, the saddled horse was waiting for me. With hell detonating in my wake—screams, flames, and a barrage of boots thundering down the stairway—I swung into the saddle and wheeled the horse around, sending it back toward the door to the stairway. As a guard came out the door, I hammered him in the head with the attaché case.

I raced for the front gate at a high lope. To the rear, flames shot out of the windows of the countess's upper-level bedchambers. As I galloped at the guards lining up at the gate, I yelled, "We're under attack! I'm going for reinforcements!"

I rode by them but one of them, brighter or deafer than the rest, fired his musket. The shot missed, but a mounted patrol was quickly on my tail. I had to stay on the road because of the darkness. I rode faster than I should have, any pothole could have sent the animal head over heels with me crushed under him.

The patrol was closing the gap, almost on my heels, when I rode into a blaze of musket fire, and my horse went down.

 **SIXTY-EIGHT**

YOU COULD HAVE killed me!" I yelled at Casio.

We were at a house an hour's ride from the palace, a peasant's cottage in a village of a dozen such houses. Casio and his men had waited for me. They had ambushed those French hellhounds dogging my heels. I wasn't angry because they had accidentally shot my horse out from under me but that they were blithely indifferent to the peril they'd put me in.

"If I was not certain of your loyalty to me as a fellow freedom fighter," I said, "I would suspect you had orders to kill me along with the French."

Casio shrugged. He clearly did not care whether I lived or died. However, after I went through the attaché case with him, reading to him the French emperor's real orders because he couldn't read French, the guerrilla leader's attitude toward me changed. He was almost affectionate.

"As you can see, my suspicions were correct," I said, smugly. "The countess is *still* a French agent. The report she arranged for us to steal was a trick. When you compare the emperor's seal on the other documents in the attaché case, you can see that the report she gave me is a forgery. These real orders here to the commanders from the emperor differ from her fraudulent order. Rosa and the countess were part of the plan to dupe us. This poor colonial pícaro before you," I grinned modesty, "is a greater patriot than those two seditious strumpets."

"I am greatly disappointed in Rosa," Casio said. "I can understand the countess—she is Spanish only by marriage—but Rosa was one of us. I suspect that after she was raped—"

"The French raped Rosa?"

"Our own guerrillas raped Rosa or at least a bandido gang who claimed to be partisans. She carried a message to them from me, and they rewarded her for risking her life by passing her around the camp."

"The bastardos should be castrated."

"The bastardos are dead. Rosa saw to that. And she will join them if we catch her. For her sake, I hope she flees to France with the countess."

I had not told him of Rosa's lovemaking with the countess. I kept quiet out of loyalty to her brother, Carlos. He would have wanted it that way. His mother had lost a son. Carlos would not have wanted me to further compound the old woman's inevitable disgrace at her daughter's treason . . . with lewd lurid gossip.

"Our knowledge of their plans will be a serious setback for the French," Casio said. "They plan a major campaign against Gerona, a surprise attack after feigning that they will simply keep it under siege."

"They'll just change their plans," I said.

He shook his head. "It's not that easy. The emperor keeps tight control over troop movements, despite the fact that he's far away and our guerrilla activity constantly disrupts his lines of communication. His generals will have to follow his standing orders. Besides, General Habert will not disclose the theft of the plans. Napoleon would have him shot for such a blunder."

"What are you going to do about Gerona?" Gerona was the major town between Barcelona and the French border. It had held out heroically against French assaults.

"Warn them. The emperor's orders are for a French division to join with the present army besieging the city and for the bulk of the force to take the fortifications at Montjuic, part of the city's defensive perimeter. We need to warn our defenders there of the impending action. Manuel Álvarez, who commands the city's defenses, knows that Gerona will fall someday, but each day he keeps the French tied down in the siege reduces their forces in the rest of the peninsula."

Casio left me alone while he went to another house where his lieutenants were quartered. "I must tell them the news," he said.

I was grateful for the respite from his watchful eyes. I had found something else in the general's case: besides messages shuttled back and forth between the Catalán command and the emperor, were two velvet pouches. I opened the pouches after Casio left. One pouch contained an assortment of scintillating jewels: diamonds, rubies, and sapphires. I could easily imagine the source: France's General Habert, their top-ranking commander, who extorted "gifts" from Spain's traitorous nobility as well as the booty from the marauding troops.

The second pouch contained an even more stunning surprise: a gorgeous gold necklace strung with large diamonds. A note in the pouch explained that the necklace was a gift arranged for Napoleon's new wife, the Austrian princess Marie Louise, from the now disgraced Spanish prime minister, Godoy. Godoy was being held captive in France along with the Spanish royal family but had arranged for the necklace to be sent to Napoleon, no doubt to curry his favor. The necklace had once belonged to the similarly named Spanish queen, María Luisa of Parma.

I slipped the pouches under my shirt. These royal gems were now the property of a disgraced caballero-lépero-pícaro named Juan de Zavala; and I had earned them. Was I to risk my life battling two hell-forged vixens, a French army, an ungrateful gang of kill-crazed guerrillas, the Spanish crown, the Holy Inquisition, New Spain's viceroy, and my gachupine persecutors, then walk away with my pockets empty as my hell-black heart?

I had a slug of brandy straight out of the jug, congratulating myself on both my successful mission and my newfound riches. The door opened, and Gusto, a lieutenant of Casio's, entered.

"Where's Casio?" he asked.

"Looking for you and his other commanders," I said.

He was tense, his eyes darting around the room. "Is there anyone in the other room?"

I picked up the brandy jug, suddenly tense myself at the tone of his question and his stiff body language. "Join me in a toast to celebrate my success."

He grinned. "I have something for your success."

He pulled out his blade, and I flung the brandy jug. It caught him not in the head but only on his shoulder. His thrust diverted, he cut only my side instead of gutting me like a stuck pig. I shouldered him in the gut, and a shot went off. I froze, stunned by the sudden explosion in the room.

Gusto dropped to his knees and pitched forward onto the floor, face down, hemorrhaging from the throat. I stared at Casio, who was framed in the doorway. The guerrilla leader stepped in, pulled another pistol from his waistband, and shot Gusto in the back of the head.

"Another French spy?" I asked.

Casio shook his head. "Cádiz sent an order that we were to execute you after we finished using you. They believed you couldn't be trusted. We believed you would cooperate on the mission because we had your sister and mother—Carlos's family, of course, not actually yours—in our grasp. I have countermanded that order for two reasons: your actions were heroic, and they sent the order to Gusto as an affront to me. They refuse to recognize me as a leader of the Barcelona movement because I refuse to recognize them as having authority over Catalonia."

Ay, Raquel was right. Politics were wonderful, especially when it worked to my advantage.

SIXTY-NINE

Cádiz

YOU HAVE ANOTHER chance to martyr yourself for the resistance," Casio told me three days later, when I thought I was shipping out to Cádiz.

To keep enemy communications across the Pyrénées in disruption, Casio led attacks along the route from Barcelona to Gerona.

"The maneuver will show you first-hand how a small band of motivated fighters can inflict damage on larger forces," Casio said. The guerrilla target was a French courier escorted by a company of light cavalry.

At an obvious ambush spot that provided excellent defilade for the ambushers, Casio deliberately exposed one of his men to the courier's advance patrol. The advance scouts would rush back to the main body. After their report of an ambush ahead, the entire unit would wheel around and retreat back *in the other direction*, right into an ambush of 150 guerrillas.

"They thought we were ahead of them," Casio said, "and that the route behind them was safe. Of course, this strategy only works if you leave no survivors to spread the word of how we do it."

I learned something of soldiering and battle tactics running with the guerrillas. I already knew about small arms, the tools of that trade. My hunting weapons, however, were better treated, of higher quality, and had greater accuracy than their military arms. But they were not as lethal in battle. The French and the better-equipped Spanish units used a muzzle-loading, smooth-bore, flintlock musket. The muskets were a little over forty inches long and weighed around twelve pounds. The lead ball they fired weighed an ounce.

To load the musket, a soldier would take a wrapped cartridge that held a ball and black powder from a belt pouch and rip off the part with the lead ball with his teeth. Keeping the ball in his mouth, he would pour a little of the black powder into the musket's flashpan, which was on top of the weapon. He then poured the rest of the powder down the barrel and packed it down with his ramrod. The musketeer then spit the lead ball into the barrel and rammed that down. When he squeezed the trigger, the flint snapped down, struck metal, sparking and igniting the powder in the flashpan, which in turn ignited the powder in the barrel. The explosion blew the ball out the barrel.

The musket fired the ball about a half a mile but with very poor accuracy. But, eh, they were not shooting the eye of a hawk but firing into lines of men. Loading and firing was a slow process, which is why they shot in rows, with one row firing, then ducking down to reload as the row above them fired, after which the third row of troops discharged their muskets. They repeated the drill as long as necessary.

A three-deep line was the order of battle for most infantry and cavalry. If the lines were only two deep, gaping holes appeared, and if they were four or more deep, movements were too awkward.

"When the weapons are fired by the hundreds, it creates a scythe of death that mows down line after line of men," Casio said. "But the worst death is not from a lead ball or from the long bayonet at the end of the musket, but from a ramrod."

"A ramrod kills?"

"In the rush of battle, a musketeer will sometimes forget to remove the ramrod from his barrel, which then comes flying out. During one battle a French musketeer left the ramrod in when he pulled the trigger. The metal rod flew through my compañero's throat like a bayonet."

Occasionally the weapon with the ramrod exploded in the face of the shooter.

I fought alongside the guerrillas when we faced the armed invaders, but I turned away when the French who surrendered were killed. I didn't fault the guerrillas for their revenge. Many of the guerrillas had lost loved ones or close friends to the invaders. Both sides fought a war without quarter, without mercy, what they called "war to the knife." But it was their war, not mine. I no longer thought of myself as Juan de Zavala, a Spanish-born caballero. I no longer cared who or what I was. Having dealt with so many different people and so many different kinds of hate, I no longer respected birthrights, bloodlines, religious creeds or inherited titles. People like Carlos and Casio worked harder for Spanish freedom than their kings and nobles.

They believed that Napoleon's legions would never defeat the spirit of the Spanish people.

"We will drive them from our country," Casio said, "and then we will go over the mountains and loot their churches, rape their women, steal their treasures. Then Señora Justice will smile, no?"

I was returning to Cádiz a hero. Of course, the search for me was still going strong. The French desperately wanted the rogue who fled the countess's palace with the general's attaché case and who ambushed their courier's military escort, so I hid for two weeks at the monastery at Montserrat, the "sacred mountain" northwest of Barcelona. The monks concealed me despite the continual threat that the French cannons would level the monastery if they ever discovered that the monks were aiding the resistance.

When the threat cooled down, a fishing boat returned me to Cádiz as a hero, no less. A stellar reward for subduing two tempestuous temptresses and an obese French general with a limp manhood, then absconding with the emperor's battle plans, no? And an even better reward was in a pouch I hid near my own "family jewels." The "king's ransom" in gems would keep me in fine wine, roast beef, and passionate putas in the years to come, long after the Spaniards' praise rang cold.

Aboard the boat, I gave my first thought to what I would do in Cádiz. I wanted to return to the colony for sure. The war between Napoleon and the Spanish rebels was too dangerous for a poor colonial outcast. Cádiz was still the only place in Spain not under titular French control. Who knew what my next assignment from the Cádiz authorities would be? The last one they sent me on was not only suicidal but homicidal on their part . . . just in case I survived.

Well, Casio did protect me in the end. He now assured me I would get a hero's welcome and I could parlay my hero's status into a return ticket to New Spain, pardon in hand. There, I would reunite with my darling Isabella. I still took loving care of the boots she'd lavished on me.

I knew my fate as soon as I saw Baltar on the Cádiz dock, the inquisitor-priest I thought I had killed. Last time I saw the bastardo, he was lying in a foul alley after flying face-first off a whore's balcony. As he stood on the wharf and pointed me out to Colonel Ramírez and a squad of soldiers, I could see that the priest's near-death experience had not improved his ugly disposition.

"He's in league with the devil," I told Ramírez. "Either that or he has the lives of a cat."

Baltar howled that I should be taken immediately to the hangman, that he would arrange for my summary execution.

"I will deal with him like the knave he is," the colonel assured the priest. As soon as I was in a coach alone with Ramírez, he grinned at me.

"Your services to Spain are the toast of Cádiz." The colonel waved his hand. "Don't be concerned about that idiot priest. I had to pretend to arrest you or he would have denounced me to the cardinal. However, the fact that you have tried to kill a son of the church—and more particularly, a son of the Inquisition—does make things difficult for you here in Cádiz. I fear I must ship you back to New Spain. A proclamation decreeing you a hero of the War of Independence and a full pardon for your lifetime of crimes is already on its way to the colony. No doubt, you will find a hero's welcome when you step on the dock at Veracruz." The colonel eyed me narrowly. "Of course, I understand that your own preference would be to stay here and continue your fight against the invaders."

I put my hand over my heart. "But of course."

 **SEVENTY**

Veracruz

IN A SMALL, fast packet, we raced across the great sea in less than a month. On the voyage, I enjoyed the company of a woman who was on her way to join her husband, a grain merchant in Puebla. I was sure a month in my bed had ruined her for all other men.

When the ship from Cádiz dropped anchor in Veracruz, for once I knew I could disembark at a port without fear of arrest and execution. Life was good. I was happy, rich, and a hero. The colonel had sent a copy of my pardon ahead on a dispatch boat to the viceroy in Méjico City. He included with the pardon an official proclamation enumerating my death-defying deeds in the war against Napoleon

We dropped anchor in the bay, within sight of the massive fort that had protected the city for three centuries, el Castillo de San Juan de Ulúa. Before we were allowed to leave the ship, a familiar from the Holy Office of the Inquisition and a customs official were rowed out on a ship's tender. As soon as they finished going through the passenger list, luggage, and goods, they asked to speak to me.

"Juan Zavala, you are to report immediately to the governor," the customs official said.

I climbed down the rope ladder to the ship's tender, whose crew was instructed by the customs official to take me to the dock. I grinned like a monkey as we headed toward land, where I saw a reception committee gathering on the dock for me. What did the governor have in mind for me? A parade through the streets for the hero of the Spanish War of Independence? Perhaps he would fête me at a grand ball, where caballeros would envy my courage and women my garrancha. Or would the viceroy himself be here to honor me for my services to the crown? Would Isabella be at the dock to hurl herself into my arms?

As soon as I climbed up the ladder and onto the dock, an official stepped forward.

"Juan Zavala, you are under arrest!"

I spent the night in the governor's jail, a stinking cell that made the Guanajuato confines palatial by comparison. I was taken before his excellency the governor the next morning.

My warders had confiscated my fine sword and dagger. I had slept in silk clothes fit for a prince, and now they were smelly, foul, and soiled. Much of my wealth had been converted into a letter of credit for a Méjico City bank, and luckily I had sneaked the paper somewhere they would never search.

"Is this the way a hero of Spain is treated?" I demanded of the governor the moment I was led into his office, having decided to go on the offensive immediately. "Did you not receive word of my feats and pardon from Cádiz?"

The governor scowled at me and pushed aside what I recognized as my pardon certificate on his desk as if it were a horse apple.

"You may have fooled the authorities in Cádiz, but in the colony we know you as a brutal bandido and cold-blooded killer."

"I have a pardon for crimes, even the false ones that you just mentioned."

"Don't use that tone of voice with me," he said, "I'm in charge here in Veracruz, and only the viceroy has greater authority than me. You would have been better off staying in Spain, where your crimes weren't known. Now that you've returned in silk to a place where you're not wanted, you'll find that you aren't any more welcome than when Bruto de Zavala exposed you for the lépero scum you are. Take this as a warning: we're going to be watching you, as will the archbishop. The church knows of your heresies. Revert to your old ways, and our constables will convey you to the gallows or our Inquisitors to the stake."

I was seething. "My possessions—"

"Return his possessions and escort him out of my compound," he told the sergeant who had brought me in. "And send in a servant to air out this room."

My luggage from the ship was in the jail entry area. I refused to take possession of the bags until I checked and made sure everything was there. The only items missing were the fine sword and dagger I was wearing when I came ashore. I asked the sergeant for them.

"You are not permitted by law to carry weapons," he said.

As he escorted me to the gate to the compound, I glanced over at him. He was a mestizo.

"They're doing this, because they believe I'm a peon?"

He looked at me out of the corner of his eye but said nothing. I knew that I had hit upon the truth. Had I been a pure-blood Spaniard, I would have received the grand reception I had expected. But I was back now in a world where Spanish blood counted for more than purity of soul . . . or anything else. The entire political and economic system was based upon the myth of bloodlines.

A peon who had been accepted as a gachupine caballero had offended and frightened the landed gentry of the colony. Now I had returned showered with honors from the mother country herself. I laughed aloud as I stepped out the gate.

"When the viceroy and the governor found out the colony's biggest hero was a peon," I said to the sergeant, "they must have shit giant green avocados."

He avoided my eye, but I could see he had to struggle to keep his features rigid.

"Listen, amigo," I said. "I want my sword and dagger back. They're wetted with French blood in the war I fought to keep the gachupines in power. How do I get them?"

"If I can locate them, it will cost you a hundred reales for their return."

"Bring them to the best inn in town tonight, the one with the loveliest señoritas."

There's no justice, eh? The people who dispense it profit from their abuses by keeping the poor down and themselves up. Had the governor and notables of Veracruz been mestizos or Aztecs, they would have paraded me through the city, amid glittering showers of flowers and gold. Instead, they treated me like a leper, except they don't salivate to hang lepers.

I went to the inn, drank too much, took two putas to my room, and made love till they were panting with exhaustion.

When the passive-faced sergeant knocked on my door after midnight, I was still awake, lying on my bed smoking a cigar and drinking brandy from the neck of the bottle.

"Your sword and dagger, señor."

He laid them at the foot of the bed. I threw him a pouch containing a hundred reales. He carefully counted the money, then dropped ten reales on the bed.

"What's that for?" I asked.

"My commission from the officer who took your weapons. He said I could keep one part in ten for my services."

"You earned it."

"No, señor, you earned it. I couldn't show my pride in your actions when we were at the governor's. Rest assured, however, while the gachupines may fear you for your accomplishments, to people of your own kind, you are a hero."

"Wonderful. I am a hero to peons. Do you know what that does for me?"

"I am a mejicano, like you, not a peon. You are a hero to mejicanos," he said. "And you should be proud of that."

He left me puzzling over his remark.

Mejicano? What was that? I'd heard the word used before but never by someone with such pride. Most often it was used in the colony to describe people living in the capital itself and the surrounding Valley of Méjico.

I had heard people, including Father Hidalgo, a criollo, and Marina, an india, call themselves americanos because they were born on the American continent and didn't like the official designations of race. The word americano in fact was very popular among educated people. But it was geographically ambiguous; a person in the United States, in Spanish possessions in the Caribbean, Peru, Argentina, and the rest of the Río de la Plata region and in Portuguese Brazil were also americanos.

The word Méjica had been used by the Aztecs to describe themselves. That was why the capital was called Méjico City after the Conquest, because it had been a city of "Méjicans." The sergeant, however, had not used the word to indicate he had Aztec ancestry but to express his pride that, regardless of his bloodline, he was proud of his colonial birth. No doubt, if I spoke to Marina or Father Hidalgo, they would understand immediately that the sergeant used the word *mejicano* to convey equality: *Mejicanos were all equal and inferior to no one.*

Glossing the sergeant's statement was probably the most complex sociopolitical exercise I had ever managed. It gave me a headache. Hands trembling, I once more upended the brandy bottle. Fortified by the return of my weapons and the fresh infusion of spirits, I opened my door and shouted down the stairs for more whores.

 **SEVENTY-ONE**

I BOUGHT THE best horse in Veracruz. He was not of Tempest's quality, but I was not going to ride into the capital as a peon. I knew I'd be watched. I had already learned from the innkeeper, who appeared to know all the business of everyone in the colony, that Isabella had married a margués and now lived in Méjico City. My heart bled at the news, and I was certain that she had only married—and not buried herself in a convent with a broken heart over me—because of some terrible need of money.

My anger rode with me as I left Veracruz. Bandidos sometimes assaulted travelers on the road, and since I journeyed alone, I rode with my pistols loaded and a sheathed sword lashed to my pommel. I hoped some fool would challenge me, but the only bandidos I saw were two crucified along the roadside as I neared Jalapa.

I was shocked by the brutality. I was told that the crucifixion was the work of a hermandad, a brotherhood of citizens who formed civilian posses with the unofficial approval of the authorities. These posses sometimes decapitated bandidos, nailing their heads to the tree nearest the crime scene. I saw nothing wrong with hanging brigands. I even understood savages ripping out a man's heart and eating it. But to nail a criminal to a cross as our Lord and Savior had been crucified seemed almost to honor them.

I needed a shave, and in Jalapa I searched for a barbershop and its traditional storefront display: the burnished brass basin representing Mambrino's helmet. Cervantes made famous this emblem of the barber's profession. His knight-errant, Don Quijote, saw a man riding an ass and wearing what appeared to be the magical gold helmet of the Saracen king Mambrino. Naturally, the rider was no Saracen king. A simple barber, he sported not headgear but the brass pan he used for bloodletting.

As the barber shaved me, he talked about the highwaymen who'd been crucified. "The bandidos were heroes of the common people," he said, "taking from the rich and giving to the poor."

I had heard such tales of the charity of highwaymen many times before, and they always seemed to apply to *dead* bandidos rather than to the ones who were currently robbing and killing. I am sure the Bethlehemite monks that Lizardi and I found tied to trees with their throats cut didn't think bandidos were heroes.

But I was still angry at the crucifixions I saw. They again exemplified the gachupines' excessive and unnecessary cruelty against races they deemed inferior. The gachupines would have hanged murderers and rapists of Spanish blood, not nailed them on a tree to die. They saved such brutality for peons. It was as if they'd heard tales about the bandidos' popularity among the people and crucified them as a brutal warning.

The talkative barber also told me a tale about the face of a man he had been shaving.

"You see how the soap stays wet on your face?" he asked. "When I put it on the man's face last week, it dried quickly. I told him that he would be dead within two days. It happens every time I shave a man and the soap dries so quickly. They are soon dead from the black vomito. The man was dead the next day."

If the barber thought he could prophesize death, I didn't want to disabuse him. However, as one who has had considerable experience as a healer and physician, I knew the shaving soap dried quickly because the man was hot from fever.

To get to Jalapa, I had had to pass through the corridor of death: the sand and swamps of the coastal plains, the dreaded region where breathing miasma from the swamps infects one with the black vomit. Naturally, thoughts about my parents, whoever they were, collided with speculations on the life I might have led had the real Juan Zavala not perished from yellow fever.

It was true, I no longer considered myself a gachupine. But the purity or even the impurity of my blood no longer mattered to me. I was Juan de Zavala, and I would kill any man who sullied my honor.

Soon I was approaching the capital itself.

Méjico City was in the great Valley of Méjico, on the plateau region the Aztecs had called Anáhuac, a word I was told meant "Land by the Water" because it had five interlocking lakes. In the midst of that water had stood the Aztec capital Tenochtitlán, a large city served by three causeways. It was on the broken bones and ashes of Tenochtitlán that the conquistadors had built Méjico City.

The mining treasures of Guanajuato, the arid far reaches of New Méjico and Texas, the nearly uninhabited region of New California, the hot-wet jungle regions of the Mayan south—none of these were the prize of New Spain. Méjico City was not just the gem of the colony, not just the greatest city of the Americas, it rivaled the great cities of the world. One could damn the Spaniards for many things—and they committed wrongs in the colony in ways too numerous to enumerate—but they truly excelled at city building.

Raquel had called the capital a metropolis, a word that she said was from the Greeks and meant "mother city." The word applied to Méjico City because while 150,000 souls lived inside its limits, ten times that many dwelt in the surrounding area, all of whom were dependent on it.

I stayed at a small inn an hour from the city because I didn't want to arrive anonymously, like a thief in the night. I wanted to ride tall into the city, proud and defiant in case a reception committee pounced on me as the one in Veracruz had.

My return to the colony was to terminate in the capital. I had no desire to revisit the maddening memories of Guanajuato. Isabella was the object of all my desires, and now she lived in the capital. I intended to make my mark in the city before long and reclaim my woman.

I still wore the boots she had given me when I was a prisoner in Guanajuato. They had taken me through jails, jungles, deserts, and wars, and I'd had them repaired innumerable times. Even now, however, they were serviceable. When she saw them, she would know my love was true. Naturally from time to time in the presence of a pretty señorita the beast in my pants had soiled her sainted memory, but my love for her was pure.

In the early morning, the route to the city was already a fervent hive of frantic activity a league back from the causeway. The energy of the awakening city was like no other I had experienced. Long mule trains and armies of indio carriers transported food and supplies to the city's merchants, who flung open their shop doors to hawk these myriad wares. The streets swarmed with beggars and merchants fighting for space on the sidewalks and streets. It was everything I remembered about the brief but memorable visits I had made to the city with Bruto many years before: noisy, smelly, violent, crazy, and chaotic but also vivid, thrilling, and alive.

A newspaper I picked up in Veracruz posted the population of the capital according to a census made five years earlier as 3,000 gachupines, 65,000 criollos, 33,000 indios, 27,000 mestizos, and about 10,000 africanos and mulattos, giving a total of 138,000 back then. The figures were not representative of all of New Spain, of course. Because it was the center of wealth and power, there was a higher concentration of Spanish in the city than in the colony as a whole. And a higher concentration of africanos used as servants by the wealthy.

As I approached the causeway, the landscape flattened and turned arid, despite the gloomy, melancholy marshlands where sparkling lakes had stood before the Conquest. Nearly three centuries of "civilization" had almost drained the lakes and filled in many of the lakebeds.

I entered the city with the incredible migration that crossed the calzadas each morning—indios piled high with goods like beasts of burden, two-wheeled carts and four-wheeled wagons, long trains of mules commanded by arrieros—all competing with droves of cattle, flocks of sheep, herds of pigs, and packs of dogs for shoulder room.

The congestion didn't end once I was off the causeway and on city streets, even though the capital was well laid out with many straight streets running east-west and north-south. When the city was awake, the peddlers and porters began their day's work. Peddlers walked down the streets loaded with merchandise that they hawked to people on the business and residential streets. Sellers of fruits—mangos, lemons, oranges, and pomegranates—cheese and hot pastry, salted beef and tortillas, rivaled the retailers of tubs of butter, cans of milk, and baskets of fish.

The streets were so hemmed in by peddlers and makeshift wooden stalls that porters were more adroit at carrying merchandise across and down streets than four-legged beasts of burden pulling carts. The porters carried mountainous stacks of goods in burden baskets strapped to their backs and held in place by tump lines stretched tight across their foreheads. Porters, acting as human aquadors, transported large clay jugs of water from the two great aqueducts connecting the city with the mountain springs to the west to dwellings that lacked access to the city's public fountains.

Goods that weren't transported over the causeways arrived in hundreds of canoes loaded with fruits and vegetables and handicrafts. Few of the craft were paddled. Instead, long poles were used to push them along in the shallow marshy lakes that had not been filled yet.

At this time in the morning, women were coming out of their dwellings and emptying bedpans into the channels of water that ran down the middle of streets. Waste and rubbish was simply thrown into the streets, most of it ending up in the shallow water channels. Once a week street workers removed the refuse from the water and left it along the banks to dry, eventually carting the stinking mess away.

The government and wealthy merchants congregated in the plaza mayor. The viceroy's palace was the finest looking building on the square. It served not only as the residence for the ruler of New Spain and his family but also as government offices for many of the officials and agencies that administered the colony. On another side of the square stood their great cathedral.

The differences and inequalities of the classes were most evident in the main plaza. I rode by bronze, near-naked indio men with a ragged blanket or a serape covering their upper body, their women modestly dressed but often in little more than rags. Their poverty contrasted with the well-to-do Spaniards attired in handsome clothes embroidered with silver and gold and riding blooded horses. In carriages so brazenly expensive they would have even embarrassed the high and mighty of Cádiz and Barcelona, Spanish women were carried to the jewelry and clothing shops that provided them with the dazzling gowns and gems they needed for the balls that dominated their lives.

The laws that prohibited mixing of the classes prevented indios from even dressing like or living among Spaniards and prohibited the Spanish from residing in indio areas. But commerce brought the peons and spur-wearers shoulder to shoulder in the crowded main plaza.

I rode aimlessly through the city, reacquainting myself. The police carts that hauled drunks away like stacks of dead bodies were gone before dawn. The lepéros who hadn't gotten removed lay passed out in the gutters or deployed themselves on the sidewalks screeching for alms. Some of the drunks who had been hauled away unconscious during the wee hours were also back, cleaning the streets.

I could have given them lessons.

My circuitous odyssey took me past four bloody gibbets festooned with dead prisoners. I casually rode past the main jail as well, where last night's murder victims were laid out in front so families with missing members could come and search among them. I journeyed past the noise and smells of vegetable and meat markets to the place where the Inquisition used to conduct its autos-da-fé, burning the "unfaithful" at the stake, "mercifully" garroting those who had repented their sins, before the flames devoured them. And finally down Calle San Francisco, one of the most pleasant and attractive streets in the city, with its fine houses and shops.

I explored the alameda, a rectangular-shaped green park at least three hundred paces across where many of the city's notables enjoyed the shade of the many trees and shrubbery, most of them refusing to ever step out of their carriages and walk; everyone had feet to walk on, but to ride in a carriage was a sign of distinction. In the middle of the park a handsome fountain geysered water. Once considered a dangerous place after sundown, menaced by wolves—both the four- and two-legged variety—I wondered if the city constables still allowed the park to become a jungle after dark.

I headed up Paseo de Bucareli, the long, broad path that had become more popular than the alameda among the city's gentry for promenading their fine carriages and horses. But it was too early in the day for the señoritas, young señoras, and dandies to come out to socialize and flirt.

Was I half-hoping I would run into Isabella, la Señora Marquesa? Of course I was. But were I to meet her by "accident," I would prefer to encounter her at the paseo instead of the alameda, which attracted the older gentry. Most of the people on the paseo usually took their promenade from four in the afternoon until near sundown. During that time, ladies filled two long rows of carriages while countless caballeros traversed the promenade on horseback.

When I was prepared to present myself as the caballero I once was, I would return to the paseo and find Isabella.

I took a room at an inn around the corner from the Plaza Mayor, then left to explore the great square on foot. When I heard a familiar voice shouting, I looked over and saw someone I knew hawking pamphlets.

"Hark the words of the Mejicano Thinker! Laugh! Cry! Be angry at injustices!"

"Does the viceroy know you were once a bandido?" I asked Lizardi.

He gaped at me.

"Shut your mouth; you're gathering flies." I slapped him on the back. "It's been a long time, no?"

"Juan de Zavala, as I live and breathe. Dios mío, the stories I have heard about you: you have been hanged at least six times for your crimes, seduced wives and daughters, stole from widows and orphans, fought duels, and even vanquished Napoleon himself on the battlefield."

"Just Napoleon? No, amigo, it was Napoleon, his brother Joseph, and a thousand of his best troops that I single-handedly bested."

"I've been excommunicated," was the first thing out of the pamphleteer's mouth as soon as we were seated in the inn and he had swallowed half a cup of wine in a gulp. "When a plague hit the city, I wrote a pamphlet in which I advised the government to clean up the streets, burn all refuse, quarantine the sick, bury plague victims outside the city rather than in the churchyards, and to use monasteries and the homes of the rich as hospitals."

"Your plan would cost the church their death tribute."

"And make the rich give something of which they stole back to the people. It did not make me popular. I've published more bombasts under the name The Mejicano Thinker. Do you like it?"

There was that word mejicano again. But Lizardi used it to refer to himself as the greatest mind in Méjico City, not as a reference to race or birth.

"It sounds worthy of a scholar such as yourself."

"Yes, I agree," he said. "I've also put out a pamphlet in which I called our viceroyalty the worst government in the Americas, stating that no civilized nation has had a government as corrupt and illegitimate as ours. I called the viceroy a cursed monster who leads an evil government."

I made the sign of the cross. "Have you gone insane, Lizardi? Why have they not hanged you? Burned you at the stake? Drawn and quartered you?"

"They are too busy protecting their own ill-gotten enterprises ever since Napoleon overran Spain. Besides, the junta in Cádiz has decreed freedom of the press, not that the viceroy permits it, of course. And they consider me a madman. They arrest me occasionally and hold me until friends buy my way out."

The little bookworm had not changed since I last saw him. He was still ghostly pale as if he lived in a cave and never saw the sun. Still as unkempt as a lépero, his cloak looked as if he used it as his dinner table and his bed. I had no doubt that when the police confronted him, he informed on everyone around him. He had great courage, but he fought with a quill, not a sword, and was not above sacrificing someone else to save his own skin.

I listened to him boast of the caustic broadsides he had written, scolding criollos for having the same vices as gachupines, condemning the Spanish for plundering the colony and giving nothing in return, and even excoriating the lower classes as thieves, beggars, drunkards, and malingers.

I listened to his boasts and diatribes for an hour before I asked him about the subject closest to my heart: Isabella.

"A typical society woman with too many jewels, too many dresses, and too few brains. Her husband, the Marqués del Mira, is very rich, though I've heard he has had some financial problems due to an investment in a silver mine that flooded. Water is the bane of mining, no? So many fortunes get washed away. She has the usual love affairs for a woman of her decadent and mindless class. Her latest indiscretion is said to be with—"

He saw my face and stopped.

"Of course," he muttered, avoiding my eyes, "those are all just baseless rumors."

"And what do you hear about me, señor? Other than how I bested the French emperor."

"About you?" He blinked as if he had just become aware that there was a living, breathing human being across from him. "They're afraid of you."

"They?"

"The gachupines. First you humiliate them in Guanajuato, then you come back to the colony as its only hero of the war against France." He shook his head. "There has been talk . . ."

"Of what? Killing me?"

"Yes. Rumors that García, the finest duelist in New Spain, would challenge you, but the viceroy quickly squashed the idea."

"He's protecting me?"

"No, he doesn't care if García kills you. He's afraid you'll kill García or whomever else they send against you, that you will humiliate the gachupines even further, proving once again that a peon can be superior to Spaniards. He's forbidden anyone to challenge you to a duel. He has even tried to quash news of your feats and the commendation from Cádiz, but too many eyes saw the communiqué, and word was soon out. News of your heroism spread only among the educated class, naturally. You will find that few of your own class will admit to having heard of you, unless it is as the notorious bandido—"

"And his amigo," I interjected.

He glanced around the room. "I have received a pardon for my political sins but would not want to remind the authorities of any other indiscretions." He cleared his throat. "Having ruffled the feathers of the gachupines, you should go somewhere smaller, where there is less resentment. This is their city, not yours. Nor should you return to Guanajuato. You will not be welcome there. Perhaps you should consider a place like Dolores with that curate Hidalgo. He's known to be tolerant of the lower classes."

"Señor Mejicano Thinker, I am always amazed that just when I come to respect your opinion about the state of the world, you say something breathtakingly stupid. If you refer to me again as of the lower classes, I will cut off your cojones. Now tell me what else is going on, what is the temper of the times?"

"The colony seethes with the frustrated political ambitions of the criollos," he said. "Resentment toward the gachupines has increased since the French invaded Spain. Taxes for the war have bled the colony white. The junta has granted the criollos political rights, but the viceroy blocks their enforcement, resisting any and all criollo enfranchisement. The gachupines still treat us like ignorant, incompetent children."

Criollos and gachupines had abused me for so long, I couldn't commiserate with their woes. As far as I was concerned, Lizardi and the rest of the colony's criollos deserved to be treated as children because they didn't stand up for themselves.

As usual, his notion of liberty, equality, and fraternity only included criollos.

SEVENTY-TWO

PATRONS OF THE city's inns used them primarily as places for drinking and whoring rather than as residences. I couldn't stay at an inn and maintain the image of a caballero. So after hiring Lizardi, who knew the city better than I did, to represent me, I began looking for a house.

I knew that as a peon I would have a difficult time renting a house in a respectable neighborhood. When he found one that suited me, I instructed Lizardi to rent it in his name, with a generous payment for the use of his criollo bloodline. When Lizardi saw that my stay in the capital would profit him, he stopped impugning it.

Meanwhile, I sent a messenger to the region where I had turned Tempest loose and offered a reward for information about the stallion. He was easy to spot; few horses in all the colony stood as tall. I soon stole the stallion back . . . not that the current owner could complain. He had no title to him.

Believing Tempest too dangerous to ride, the owner had put him out to stud. Now the stallion had not only suffered the loss of his harem, he bore the indignity of my weighty frame on his back. The beast showed his gratitude by trying to throw me. I bought a mare to keep him company, and it calmed his temper.

No person of quality in the capital went without a carriage and fine mules, some of which went sixteen hands. I debated whether I could stand riding in a carriage and concluded it was transport for women and merchants, not caballeros. I would ride Tempest when I traveled through the city.

The house I rented in Lizardi's name was small: only two stories in a city where the better homes were almost all three high. However, I didn't need much room. Most large homes not only housed the family on the upper floor—with the servants, kitchen, and storerooms below them—they also had a floor devoted to the master's business.

A high stone wall surrounded my house, and the courtyard featured a spacious fieldstone patio and a stable. The main casa had several verandas, a bountiful garden, and a cascading water fountain.

Once I was settled, I climbed upon the roof with a brandy jug and my silver cigarro box. Lying back, I listened to the night. The righteous chords of a church organ drifted toward me from one direction and a haunting choir of harmonious monks intoning a "Te Deum" wafted in from another. The viceroy required that at dusk, when a house was occupied, an oil or candle lantern had to be hung in front and kept lit until an hour before dawn, so each house had a light near the front door. The viceroy believed the lights reduced crime, but, to me—someone who had lived a life of crime—his system merely alerted the bandidos as to whether anyone was home.

I heard our night watchman pass by. At nightfall, serenos posted themselves every few hundred paces and stood guard for the homeowners. Armed with only a club to beat off street dogs, the serenos were to shout warnings if they spotted thieves. In reality, most serenos subsisted on homeowner handouts and spent their nights passed out from pulque in doorways.

The night was pleasant with a light breeze. Like Guanajuato, the temperature of the capital did not vary drastically during the year, gracing us with perpetual springtime rather than freezing winters followed by sweltering summers. I was relaxed but not at peace. I still did not have my Isabella.

Had Bruto been standing there, he would have shouted I was twice the fool I'd been in Guanajuato. *Was she not married to a rich nobleman?* he would have fumed.

But I couldn't see a future without Isabella. I was obsessed. I dreamt of running off with her to Havana and starting a new life. I had enough money for a comfortable life but not the fortune she would require. Since I could not offer proof of ownership, I had sold the gems in Cádiz short of their value but like the ranchero who had pastured Tempest, I couldn't complain. Now that I had Tempest back under me, I would ride the Paseo de Bucareli and approach her.

From Lizardi, I had learned more about Isabella's husband. He'd gone broke in Spain and had come to the New World, where his title was worth more than a silver mine. Marrying into wealth, he inherited a fortune when his wife died. Twice as old as Isabella, he was arrogant, ignorant, small of frame, large of waist, and financially incompetent. He was your typical gachupine.

But he was still Isabella's husband and had more to offer than I. Short of slitting his throat—something I gave serious thought to—I didn't know how to win her from him. Still I was determined to win her back . . . or to die trying.

What I didn't know was that *dying* for Isabella was not far from what Señora Fortuna had in mind for me.

SEVENTY-THREE

RIDING ALONG A street near the main plaza, I caught the silhouette of a woman in black walking in the distance. A vision of the woman in black who disappeared around the corner in Guanajuato after providing me with boots flashed in my mind. *Isabella!*

I urged Tempest on. Hearing me coming, the woman turned to face me.

"Raquel!"

"Juan!"

We stared at each other until I remembered common courtesy and dismounted to stand beside her.

"I can't believe it's you," I said. "I thought—"

"Yes?"

I grinned at her. "It doesn't matter. What are you doing in the capital?"

"I live here."

My eye immediately went to her ring finger.

"No, I have not married."

I blushed from the shame of my past sins.

She smiled sweetly. "Take refreshment with me. Stories of your adventures have more tongues wagging than the wars in Europe."

We retired to her house, a small, pleasant dwelling facing the Alameda. She lived alone, served only by an india who came during the day to do her shopping and household chores. She still had property and friends in the Bajío and visited the region each year.

"Living alone suits me," she said, as she poured coffee for me and chocolate for herself. She had a busy life, teaching girls music and poetry. "I throw in a little education about the world around them, too," she said, laughing. "But not so much that their parents will think I am ruining them for marriage. I always watch what I say to them about politics, not wanting the Viceroy's constables to arrest me as a subversive. I also refrain from criticizing the church's suppression of thought. The Inquisition's nocturnal knock still hammers on our doors."

We talked about Guanajuato and about my travels since I left the city. Naturally, I gave her a heavily censored version of how I left the colony as a bandido and returned as a hero. And the subject of how I jilted her, walking out on her when troubles pounded on her family's door, never came up. I've never been proud of my actions, but now in my own mind I can argue she was better off without me. Had we married, the attacks on me—that I was the son of a whore—would have disgraced her.

We talked about people we knew in common. She knew Lizardi and that he was an acquaintance of mine.

"We are members of the same literary discussion group," she said. She said Lizardi was considered brilliant but unreliable. "He's tolerated to an impossible degree by his friends. There's no question he's very progressive in his political thinking, but we are careful not to talk openly in front of him because he's known to offer up his friends when he faces the viceroy's wrath.

"A few months ago the viceroy's constables played a cruel joke on him. They put him in a cell reserved for those scheduled to be executed in the morning. One of the guards borrowed a priest's robe and pretended to take his confession. They say he offered the names of everyone he knew who ever spoke derisively of the viceroy in hopes that it would save him from the gallows."

I started laughing.

"What's so funny?" she asked.

"Me, my stupidity. I suddenly realized why the viceroy's men showed up in Dolores when I was there. Lizardi betrayed me."

"The constables arrested Lizardi en route to Méjico City—after he left you in Dolores—but he didn't betray you. He informed on the padre instead. He told the authorities about Padre Hidalgo's illegal activities. They already knew about them, anyway, but I suspect they decided to act out of fear Lizardi would publish stories about the padre's success."

"That miserable cur . . . after the padre treated us with such generosity."

Raquel shrugged. "The padre has forgiven him. The padre's heart is an infinite repository of unqualified love."

I started to ask if she knew Hidalgo personally but then remembered that the padre was in her coach when I struck the lépero who had brushed against my horse.

She stared down at my boots.

"I know," I said, "they're patched almost beyond further repair, but they have great sentimental value to me. Isabella gave them to me when I was held prisoner in the Guanajuato jail."

She stared at me for a moment, her lips frozen in a smile. She said, "I can understand your feelings. My own father had a similar pair, which I have always cherished."

I revealed my plan to contact Isabella, to thank her for the boots and find out whether she was still fired by her love for me.

When Raquel walked me to her gate she made a remark that I puzzled over but didn't comprehend. "You have changed greatly, Juan de Zavala. You're no longer the caballero who knows horses better than people. You have traveled widely and picked up knowledge everywhere you have gone." She paused and met my eye. "You have gained insight into everything but yourself."

SEVENTY-FOUR

I WAS ONCE again a caballero.

I paid Lizardi to find out when Isabella paraded in her coach on the paseo and purchased with great care the finest caballero's clothes available. Staring into my bedroom mirror, I combed my hair straight back, parting it in the middle and tying it off with a ribbon of spun silver. Clean-shaven, I didn't favor a mustache but in the style of the day flaunted wide sideburns that covered half the side of my face.

I chose a white shirt made of the best linen and had it trimmed with silver thread. My black hat was low crowned, rising about four inches off my head into a flat crown. Rather than a simple silver trim, I had the leather band that circled the bottom of the crown clustered with pearls. Under my hat, with the sides showing because I wore my hat in a rakish cock, was a black handkerchief.

Jacket and breeches followed the black and white of the rest of my outfit. I permitted fine detail on the deerskin coat and breeches but only in silver and only of a subtle pattern. Even my waistcoat was made of silver silk, with a brocaded pattern that was subtle because the weave was silver thread.

I dressed in grim colors. Unlike the dandies who paraded on the alameda and paseo, and unlike the way I had dressed when I was a caballero in the Bajío, I chose black and silver. I stayed away from bright colors.

Lizardi shook his head when he saw the finished product. "You look more like a killer than a caballero."

"Good," I said.

I rode out on the paseo, tall in the saddle but torn inside. Raquel had been polite, but I had sensed her disapproval of my adulterous intentions.

Lizardi had been more blunt: "You're insane."

When I spotted Isabella's carriage, I approached her casually, but my heart raced. The carriage stopped while Isabella and a woman sitting across from her conversed with two women in another coach. All eyes turned to me as I rode up to the side of her carriage.

I saluted her, touching my fingers to my hat brim. "Señora Marquesa."

She fluttered her fan before her face and stared at me as if I was a complete stranger. "And whom do I have the honor of meeting, señor?"

"An admirer from the distant past. One who has crossed an ocean twice since the last time he laid eyes on you."

She laughed. "Oh, yes. I recall you were once a boy in Guanajuato. I remember seeing you on the paseo there. Your horse is familiar."

That brought a titter from the women.

"I've heard that a peon from that town made a name for himself fighting the French. My husband, the marqués, is a great patriot of Spain. If you are that person who contributed to our Spanish cause on the continent, perhaps he will employ you as a vaquero on one of our haciendas."

My face became hot. I indicated my boots. "These boots have not just crossed oceans, they've stomped through jungles, swam rivers full of crocodiles, and fought wars. I've kept them because they remind me of the woman who blessed me with them in my hour of need."

Isabella laughed her gay, melodious bell-tinkle of a laugh, which, from the first time I heard it, rang in my heart and sang in my soul. "I heard you came back as rich as Croesus, but that must be a false story if you can't afford new boots. Perhaps I can get my husband to buy you a new pair of boots if you go to work for him. Those are in a terrible state."

She ordered her driver to move on. I sat still and watched the carriages move away. *What a fool!* I had been stupid to approach her in public, riding up to her in front of her friends. What else could the poor woman do except pretend that I meant nothing to her? She was a married woman and could not afford even the hint of scandal.

But the realization that I had acted foolishly did little to soothe the hurt and humiliation I felt.

Peon. The word was a knife slashing to my heart.

A horse neighed behind me, and I turned in the saddle. Three young caballeros on horseback faced me.

"A lépero dressed as a gentleman is still gutter scum," the one in the middle said. "Such sons of whores are not permitted to ride on the paseo. If you come here again we'll take whips to you. If you speak to our women again, we'll kill you."

A black rage roared through me. I spurred Tempest, galloping straight at the three riders. They parted before my charge, but I still caught one of them by the throat and pulled him from the saddle. I attempted to throw him to the ground, but his left rowel hooked his saddle's latigo. His horse bolted, dragging him up the street at a full gallop. I wheeled Tempest and turned on another one foolish enough to pull his sword on me. I was without my own saber but feared no dandy's blade. I drove the great stallion full-tilt and straight at him. His own mount shied, spooked by Tempest, who was half a head taller. I unlimbered the triple-plaited quirt—the one with the shot-loaded whip-spring buttstock—that I kept lashed to the pommel by its wrist loop. As the caballero tried to gain control of his horse, I rode up behind him at full gallop. Whipping its triple-plaited lash around his neck, I slipped its wrist loop around my pommel.

Tempest and I had roped hundreds of longhorns, and he knew the

drill. Halting hard, he rocked back on his rear legs and dug in. The caballero flew from his saddle, clutching his throat in pain-wracked terror,
crashing onto the street like a collapsing bridge. With his face turning purple, I shook the lash off his neck but only after I'd dragged him a couple of
dozen yards.

When I wheeled Tempest to the third insolent dandy, the caballero
turned tail and ran, which was a mistake. Not only did he prove himself a
coward—a tale that would sweep the city within hours and follow him to
his grave—but in yielding his horse's rump he gave up his own.

I came up behind the horse at a hard lope and grabbed his mount's tail.
Jerking it up, I gave Tempest the spurs. A bull-throwing sport, Tempest,
my vaqueros, and I had done it to my hacienda bulls in the Bajío. The maneuver throws the animal off balance and flips it. In this case, the horse
flipped onto its back with the rider still on board, pinning him underneath.

Leaving the three caballeros in my wake—vanquished, humiliated,
and in excruciating pain—I rode out of the paseo. Two dozen pure-
blooded Spanish horsemen watched me go, but none dared call me out.

As I passed Isabella's carriage, my love stared at me with wide eyes. I
saluted her one more time.

Lizardi met me at an inn later for food and wine and to advise me of
the city's reaction to my actions in the paseo. He left soon after stuffing
himself, because he had a meeting to attend but then gave me his assessment.

"You will be dead within a week."

SEVENTY-FIVE

RAQUEL KNEW THAT the discussion at her literary circle that night was
going to be about the sensation Juan de Zavala had caused at the paseo.

To hide their true purposes, the group called themselves the Sor Juana
Literary Society. While they in fact met and discussed books, they also frequently used their meetings for discussions of political and social issues
that were on the prohibition lists of the viceroy and cardinal. The members
were of like political minds. The Enlightenment and the great revolutions
in France and the United States had shaken all of them intellectually.

Some clubs used the names of saints for their clubs, but Raquel and
her close friend, Leona Vicario, thought it was hypocritical to name their
society after a saint when one of its purposes was to debate and complain
about the restrictions in free thought the church wrought. Instead they
chose the name of Méjico's great poetess.

Andrés Quintana Roo, a bright young lawyer who was attracted intellectually and romantically to Leona, considered Sor Juana's name for their society as a joke on the church. "She wrote her resignation from intellectual life in blood because of criticism from the church," he said.

Eleven members of the society were present that evening, including the self-proclaimed Mejicano Thinker. As Raquel had intimated to Juan, the members put a reign on their political tongues on the occasions Lizardi showed up. Tonight, however, the talk was more personal than profound.

"All of the homes of the city tonight are discussing the actions of Zavala," Quintana Roo speculated.

None of them knew that Raquel had once been betrothed to Juan, not even Lizardi. Juan had told Raquel that he had never mentioned to the writer that he knew Raquel.

"The gachupines are very upset," Leona said. "The junta in Cádiz has offered the colony full political representation, but the viceroy and his peninsular minions have ignored their decree, not wanting their colonial-born to have rights equal to theirs. But this adventurer, Zavala, has caused them no end of worry. A peon who first is a hero of Spain and who then humiliates three caballeros who assaulted him in the paseo? The gachupines will not—cannot—let such rebelliousness go unpunished."

Lizardi said, "The gachupines fear that Zavala, by demanding an equal place at their table, will inflame and inspire peons everywhere."

"Four caballeros he has offended," Leona said. "He approached the wife of the Marqués de Mira besides humiliating the three caballeros. It's a major embarrassment for the marqués because it is known that his wife, Isabella, permitted Zavala to woo her when they both lived in Guanajuato. Had a Spaniard approached her, it would have been grounds for a duel."

"I've heard the marqués is in financial difficulty, not only as a result of his bad investments but also his wife's extravagances," Lizardi said. "The woman overindulges her expenditures—and her lovers. It is rumored that Augustín de Iturbide, a young officer in a provincial regiment, is her current lover."

"Iturbide's a Spaniard; so the marqués can look the other way about that affair," Leona said, "but he can't with a public affront by a peon. And he can't challenge Zavala to a duel; a Spanish nobleman can't fight a peon. It would be a socially unacceptable match."

"He would also lose," Quintana Roo said, "as will anyone else who calls Zavala out. The man is said to be indomitable with gun and sword."

"But the marqués must have his honor restored," Lizardi said, "as well as the caballeros Zavala humiliated. They will have their revenge."

Raquel knew that that was the conclusion of everyone in the room and probably every Spaniard in the city, and it ripped her heart. Even as he made a fool of himself over another woman, her feelings didn't change toward him.

"Zavala will pay," Leona said, "and it won't be on the dueling field."

"He will be assassinated," Lizardi said.

"You mean murdered." After Raquel spoke the words, she got up and left the house.

 **SEVENTY-SIX**

HUMBERTO, MARQUÉS DEL Mira, entered his wife's bedroom and came up behind her as the maid finished dressing her. Isabella wore a silver silk dress elaborately embroidered with spun gold and lavishly festooned with jewels. While Isabella admired her own golden mane of lustrous waist-length hair, her maid draped a black mantilla over her head and shoulders. Isabella viewed herself in her dressing mirrors approvingly. Light blonde hair was all the vogue now, and Isabella had imported from Milan an alchemic elixir that had turned her tresses a dazzling gold.

Marriage had been good to Isabella. When she was an unwed girl in Guanajuato, she had been thin. Since marrying, she had gained ten pounds, which had filled her out in the right places, making her even more stunning.

Studying his wife, Humberto felt pride of ownership, the same sort of pleasure he felt when he contemplated his palatial home and his stable of thoroughbred horses. He considered Isabella the most beautiful woman in the colony, a wife fit for a Spanish nobleman, even for a king.

Scion of a noble family that had fallen from royal favor before his birth, Humberto came to the colony to use his social status to regain his family fortunes. He was only twenty-two years old when he married a wealthy widow twice his age. Unfortunately, the widow had lived another quarter of a century, so he was forty-seven before he came into full control of the large estate left by her first husband, a gachupine who used his position as an assistant to the viceroy to make a large fortune speculating on—and manipulating—the corn market.

Humberto's strong point were his dress, speech, mannerisms, and presentation of himself as a nobleman. He knew nothing about the management of money and had wisely left the widow's fortune in her control. She had managed to make a modest increase in it during her lifetime, but since her death and his remarriage to the beautiful Isabella the fortune had deflated. Unwise investments on his part coupled with his wife's extravagant lifestyle and gambling losses had substantially reduced his income and assets. He had not shared his financial woes with Isabella because it was not a proper matter for a man to discuss with his wife. Anyway, she knew less about financial matters than he did.

"You are stunning, my dear," he told Isabella. "But it is not the clothes. You would be the most beautiful woman in the colony even if you were dressed in rags."

"You are too kind, Humberto. Did the jeweler send over my new necklace? I want to wear it to the theater tomorrow night."

He winced at the mention of the jewelry. He was having a difficult time covering the purchase. "It's coming mañana."

He gestured for her to send her maid out. After the servant left, he said, "I'm sorry you're being asked to meet with this hombre." He puffed his chest up. "I'd put a bullet through his heart on the field of honor, but as you know, the viceroy has instructed that no Spaniard is to stain his hands with the man's tainted blood."

She sighed. "It's just so strange. Juan was a fine caballero one day, a peon the next. But I suppose that was God's wish. Darling, would you have the jeweler make diamond earrings to match my new necklace?"

 **SEVENTY-SEVEN**

MY GREAT DAY had finally come. A bribe to her maid had gotten a note into Isabella's hands, and she wrote back, agreeing to meet me. The parchment contained her rose scent. The smell of it brought back visions of Isabella in her carriage in Guanajuato and her sparkling laugh . . . and of Juan de Zavala, caballero, Prince of the Paseo, riding tall.

Bruto, may you rot in hell, a hammer pounding your cojones over and over again.

No, instead, on my deathbed, I'll pray to God for just a few minutes in a room alone with him.

The meeting place she selected was away from the city, on Chapúltepec Hill, an hour's ride west of the heart of the city. Chapúltepec meant "Hill of the Grasshopper" in the barbaric Aztec tongue. Rising a couple hundred feet, it afforded an astonishingly detailed view of the city and valley of Méjico from its summit: the canals and causeways, dying lakes, innumerable churches, houses, great and small, priestly seminaries and convents for nuns, and the two great aqueducts that snaked across the plains. An Aztec temple once stood on the hill. A summer palace for the viceroy was built there, but everyone knew the structure was actually a fort, a place for the viceroy to retreat to when the political climate got too "hot."

As I rode toward the meeting place, I thought about Isabella's husband. During my time in Spain, I had grown to admire much about the Spanish and the culture they gave the colony. But I respected the people, not their rulers and landed gentry. After the gachupines had spurned me as a leper in the colony, and after watching upper-class Spaniards in Europe hoard and hide their fortunes while common people who owned nothing but their courage fought Napoleon tooth and claw—"to the knife"— without their help, I had neither respect nor awe for Spain's ruling class.

From talk in the streets and at the inn, I learned that the marqués was a typical Spanish nobleman, full of macho vanity and pretentious superiority. I knew his type well, having rubbed shoulders with men like him in my gachupine days. His notorious vanity reminded me of the tale of two haughty gachupines who entered a narrow alley in their carriages at the same time. Proceeding in opposite directions, both men refused to back their carriages up, each insisting that the other back up. Come nightfall, each was still there, refusing to leave his coach.

Friends brought in food and also stocked their coaches with blankets and pillows, and the two Spanish peacocks settled in to outwait the other. As days passed, the incident became a cause célèbre that attracted thousands to the area. After five days of the nonsense, the viceroy intervened and ordered the two to back up, each matching the other's speed.

A real man would have settled the matter with hombrada—a manly deed or an act of valor—and my way would have been on the dueling field with sword or pistol.

Isabella chose for our meeting a stone cottage, a house that once belonged to a family who tended the park's gardens. The park had been a project of Viceroy Iturrigaray, but after the viceroy was sent back to Spain in disgrace for toying with the notion of making the colony his own fief, the park and the keeper's house had been abandoned. I knew something of it because I had visited the area earlier in the day to ensure I knew the way; the meeting with my love was set for sunset, and I didn't want to be late. I admit that I'd hoped for a bed in the abandoned house.

When I reached the dirt path that ran down the middle of the park, I saw her carriage parked beside the house. I hurriedly urged Tempest into a gallop.

Isabella was leaving a copse of trees as I came near the house. I dismounted and tied Tempest to the hitch rack by the front door but didn't rush to her. I suddenly experienced fear of rejection.

She joined me in the front of the hitch rack. She appeared oddly disconcerted. "You're early, Juan."

I shrugged. "It gives us more time together. Dios mío, Isabella, you have grown even more beautiful."

Her melodious laugh sent a tingle up my spine. "And you look more the renegade and bandido than ever."

"No, you said I was a lépero, remember?"

"That, too." She fluttered her fan in front of her face. "I will say this, you certainly are more manly. You always were a handsome rogue, but now you look like a man of steel. No wonder you frightened those caballeros at the paseo."

"Isabella . . . my love . . . I have never stopped thinking about you."

She slowly moved back toward her carriage where her driver was waiting. I didn't want her near the carriage where we would be in eye- and earshot of her driver. "Would you like to take a walk? Or peek inside the house?"

"No, I can't stay long."

As she neared the carriage door, I grabbed her arm and said, "Look," nodding toward my feet.

Her fan fluttered again. "Look at what?"

"At my boots."

"Your boots?" She shrugged. "You seem obsessed with them. Can't you afford a new pair? I hear you're quite wealthy. Perhaps you couldn't afford to bring me a gift, either?"

What an imbecile I was! I had not brought her a gift. I should be showering her with jewels.

"I'm sorry, forgive me. But look, don't you recognize the boots?"

"Why are you so interested in those worn boots?"

"They're the ones you gave me when I was in jail."

She laughed, but there was no music in it, only derision. "Why would I give you boots?"

"I—I thought—" My tongue stumbled. My meeting with her was not going well. I had dreamt of this moment for hundreds of nights, and now I felt like I was sinking into quicksand.

She climbed into the coach and pulled the door shut behind her. I stared at her dumbfounded.

"You can't go, we just—"

"I'm late for a social engagement." Her eyes were as flat as a Gila monster's, her voice was hard and distant.

The carriage lurched, and I noticed the driver had paused his whip crack to stare beyond me. Jumping to his feet in the box, he cracked his whip over the coach mules loud enough to wake the damned, and they hit their collars like battering rams.

Glancing over my shoulder to where the driver had been looking, I realized that a line of horsemen had crept up on me: five of them, masked, with swords drawn. I was unarmed except for a boot knife; my sword was on Tempest.

I ran for the horse as the riders charged. As the first one neared me, I suddenly turned and shouted, waving my knife and free hand. The caballo spooked, veering into other horses. Had a man done that to Tempest, the stallion would have pounded him into the ground, but these paseo ponies were not warhorses.

Just as I jerked Tempest's reins off the hitch rack, a rider attacked me, swinging his sword. I went under the stallion's belly. Tempest spooked and turned, kicking at the rider's horse when he brushed his rump. Now all five riders were joining in. Surrounded by five milling horses and sword-swinging men, Tempest was not in a good mood. A half-head taller than their un-blooded ponies, Tempest pounded them mercilessly with his iron-shod hooves. I hung onto the rein for dear life as Tempest kicked and bucked and shied bites at the other mounts with his teeth. I got my sword out of the scabbard, but the blade went flying as I tried to mount the stallion. Clutching his pommel, I finally swung on. Tempest and I galloped into a nearby copse.

A rider loped toward me. Leaning down from the saddle, he slashed at me with his sword. My boot knife was still miraculously in my fist, and at the last second I deflected the blow. Glancing off my thigh, the sword still drew blood. Meanwhile the horseman galloped past. Turning, he prepared to attack me from another angle.

Suddenly another horseman charged me out of nowhere, and I quickly reined Tempest in behind a tree. Charging past, his horse stumbled, and they both went down in a stand of trees thick with undergrowth, the horse's tack tangling in bushes. Holding on to the pommel, I swung down and grabbed a short, thick limb. When he saw me coming, he remounted his still-tangled mount, and, raising his sword, he braced for my attack. The limb went flying by him, but the second it took him to duck, however, gave me time to drag him from his saddle.

He hit the ground hard, and I dropped on him, my knee collapsing his gut. The air went out of him in a whoosh. I dispatched him with his own sword. Taking it in my teeth, I swung onto Tempest. It wasn't a good mili-tary sword—one made for truly lethal combat—but a fancy rapier, the kind the paseo dandies carried for show. In my skilled hand, however, it could decapitate a pig.

I would need that skill. Two of the horsemen were charging me. They were still handicapped by the thick brush and forest. One horseman pointed a pistol straight at me, so dead-on its muzzle looked as wide as my open grave. He fired, but his aim was off from the movement of his mount. Instead of hitting me in the chest, the ball hit my leg. Reversing his grip, he continued on, never breaking stride, swinging his pistol's barrel like a battleaxe. I countered with the rapier. He screamed as I lopped his arm off at the elbow.

The scream caused the other three attackers to stop and regroup. I didn't care. I spurred Tempest toward the closest rider. Turning to run, his horse panicked, reared, then bucked, throwing him. He was all alone now. His two companions were in full retreat, abandoning their comrade, gal-loping out of the wood as fast as they could.

I wheeled the pony and went back at the man who was on the ground. He ran, dodged around a tree, but I still ran him down. As I approached, he was afoot, trying to duck the downward sweep of my blade. Trying to behead him, I swung and missed. He looked back at me as he bolted, arms flailing, screaming in horror . . . and ran straight into a tree.

He lay at the tree's base, still as death, knocked unconscious. I left him there—horseless, weaponless, out cold.

Heading back into town, I found no sign of the riders or of Isabella's coach. The wounds in my leg were bleeding, the slash the more severe of the two. The pistol ball had been a graze. I tied a bandana over the slash wound. My wound was not as serious as that of the man whose arm I chopped off. He was dying, not only because his friends had abandoned him without stopping the bleeding but also because a cut or amputation at a joint was a death sentence.

I had no sympathy for the man. He was a cowardly dog. He and his worthless amigos had attacked me five to one. My death would have been murder, plain and simple. Attacking a lone man in a pack, like coyotes, is inherently dishonorable. I had not seen their faces, but I knew who they were or what they were: paseo dandies.

That I would be attacked by a gang of cowards angered me. But what made me sick to my marrow was not their treachery or the painful wound to my leg, it was Isabella's betrayal.

¡Ay de mí! The woman I loved had lured me to a meeting where I was to be murdered. How could she have committed this crime? The only motive I could see for Isabella cooperating with the cowardly swine was that her husband forced her. Her husband must have done terrible things to her to force her betrayal?

Even as I struggled to excuse her, however, the awful statements she had made still rang in my ears, breaking my heart. Ridiculing the boots she had given me. True, her husband's carriage driver was within earshot and would no doubt be reporting even now everything she'd said to me back to her husband. Still the cruelty of her words and the derision of her laughter tore at my soul.

But then I remembered the way she looked coming out of that copse, walking toward me in front of the cottage: the golden hair, that gorgeous smile, those utterly unforgettable eyes . . .

"Isabella!" I shouted at the night. "What did they do to you?"

I wisely did not return to my house nor did I try to run for it. I had lost too much blood. Instead I went to the one woman in this world who had the least reason to help me but who I knew also had a true heart.

Raquel hid Tempest in a friend's stable. "Andrés Quintana Roo, a member of a literary club I belong to, is hiding your horse," she said, when I awoke the next morning in her bed.

"I have ruined your blankets." The bleeding had stopped but not before soiling her bed.

"Blankets can be washed." She hesitated. "Your house has been burned. The official word is that you were crazy and attacked innocent, unarmed criollos."

"And then burned down my own house."

"Yes, that, too."

"Did I murder any widows and orphans?"

"The rumors teem like lemmings."

"You're being evasive. Tell me what's being said."

She sighed and refused to meet my eye.

"Say it. I can take it; I'm much man."

"For so much man, you have so few brains. The gachupines have spread a story that you tricked Isabella out into the country with a threat that you would murder her husband. That the caballeros came along and found her struggling with you—"

"As I tried to rape her."

"Sí, as you tried to rape her. They came to her aid, unarmed, and you attacked them. You killed two of them, seriously injured another, and then fled before they could catch you."

"Raquel, in your entire lifetime, have you ever seen a caballero go anywhere without a weapon?"

"I don't believe a word of the story nor do some others. But most people believe the worst. If you're caught . . ."

"I'll have no trial, no chance to defend myself." Nor would there be any money to purchase "justice" with. The viceroy would seize my bank credits.

I couldn't stay with Raquel. I'd bring only misery upon her if they caught me at her house. She was willing, but I wouldn't put her at risk.

"You can't ride your horse out of the city. Tempest is too recognizable, too conspicuous. I have discussed it with friends at my literary club—"

"With Lizardi?"

"No, we're all aware of his loose lips. Tomorrow my friends will disguise Tempest, and a group of them will ride out of the city with one of them mounted on the stallion. They'll leave him at a rancho of a friend of mine."

"Warn them to have the best rider on Tempest."

"They already know that. His bad temper is as notorious as yours. Getting you out of the city won't be difficult. Leona Vicario will pick us up in her carriage. You can lay down inside until we are across the causeway. She and her family are known and highly regarded throughout the city."

"Are they searching carriages and wagons?"

"No. Everyone believes you fled in one direction or the other, anywhere but back into the city. But we can't risk someone spotting you by accident."

"These friends of yours, the book readers, why would they help me?"

She hesitated again. "A new wind blows through the colony, one we hope will blow away the old and bring in the new."

"You mean revolution?"

"I don't know what I mean. But understand this: You have experienced personal injustice and have witnessed firsthand the social wrongs committed against other people. Still you have never taken any side but your own. I told my friends that someday you would take a stand and that when you did, all the power and anger of the toughest hombre in New Spain would be with us."

Leona Vicario reminded me a great deal of Raquel. Like Raquel, she was courageous, highly intellectual, and outspoken. They both pelted me with questions about conditions in Spain. Leona burst out crying at my descriptions of the atrocities committed against the Spanish people and the heroics of families defending their homes against the invaders.

We didn't discuss in the coach where I'd be heading, but Raquel had made a suggestion earlier. "Go to Dolores," she said. "The padre will be happy to see you."

"No, I'd bring trouble to the padre's door."

"Trouble is already at his door. I told you about the winds blowing in the colony; some of them are ill winds. He may soon need a strong sword at his side."

As usual, she spoke in riddles and mysteries. I knew something was brewing, but she'd tell me no more.

When we got to the rancho, I gave both Leona and Raquel great hugs for their rescue of me.

"Understand this, beautiful ladies: I have little left in this world of material value, but thanks to you, I still have a sword and a strong arm to use it. If you ever need me, send me a message. I will come to you. Your enemies will be my enemies. I will fight for you, and, if need be, I will die for you."

"You may find, Juan de Zavala, that someday your offer will be accepted," Leona said. "But hopefully not the dying part."

Raquel walked me to the corral and stood by as I saddled Tempest.

"I don't know how to thank you," I said.

"You already did. You said that you would fight and even die for me. Other than giving his love, a man can pay a woman no higher honor."

I looked away, embarrassed. She knew why I couldn't profess my love for her.

I mounted the stallion. He walked slowly out of the yard. When I turned to wave for the last time, she was rounding the corner where her coach was, a lovely figure in a black dress turning a corner.

It struck me like a thunderbolt from hell. I froze, breathless, then galloped Tempest up to her. She turned at the door of the coach.

"What is it, Juan?"

"Thank you for my boots."

Tears welled in her eyes. "You can thank my father. He would have wanted you to have them. Did you know he really admired you?"

"Raquel—"

"No, it's the truth. He had no respect for the caballeros, who did nothing but dress like fops and parade up and down the paseo. He said you were different, that you could ride better than a vaquero and shoot better than a soldier."

I left her with tears on her cheeks. Tears welled in my eyes too, but I assure you, only because the wind had blown dust into them. I am hombrón, and men like me don't cry.

SEVENTY-EIGHT

Dolores

TWO YEARS HAD passed since I had last ridden into the Bajío town of Dolores. Back then the church curate had still believed he could free the Aztecs from their bondage by teaching them Spanish crafts. In truth, I missed the old man.

As I approached the town, I realized that I also missed Marina. My head had been so fogged by thoughts of the beautiful but shallow Isabella for so long, I hadn't looked closely at the two strong, courageous women—Raquel and Marina—who had helped me at my lowest ebb and in my greatest peril.

I was over my infatuation with Isabella, yet every time I thought of her, a fist squeezed my heart. I couldn't accept that I had misjudged her so dreadfully . . . or that I'd been that great a fool. I still couldn't believe that she had willingly betrayed me. The more I thought about it, the more I was convinced her husband had coerced her. Why else would she do it? It wasn't possible that she hated me enough to want me dead. It was that gachupine bastardo husband of hers.

So while I had left the capital with my tail between my legs, I was not finished with the marqués. Someday I would return and settle the matter.

According to Lizardi, the viceroy's men not only had destroyed Padre Hidalgo's indio enterprises, they also had forbidden the padre to reopen them under pain of imprisonment. As I drew closer, I could see that the padre's vineyards and mulberry trees were gone; weeds thrived where grapes once grew. Nor were the stacks of pottery and raw materials in front of the building that once produced ceramics.

An indio taking his siesta jerked awake at Tempest's approach and hurried into the building that had once been the winery. His body language intrigued me. He had shot me a startled glance, like a watchman looking out for intruders.

Why would the padre need a watchman? Was he back in the business of indio industries? I shook my head. I didn't know what was going on, but I did know that the priest had all the cojones the gods ever made. He had defied the gachupines once, and he might be defying them again. Raquel had even hinted he was up to something unusual, something that could bring the padre into a conflict with the viceroy again.

As I came up to the abandoned winery, Padre Hidalgo came out of the building. At the sight of me, his anxious frown broke into a joyous grin.

"What did you think, padre, that the viceroy's constables had returned?"

He laughed and gave me a big hug. "I'm surprised that you didn't come back the same way you arrived, with constables hounding your trail."

"That may not be far from the truth."

As we walked slowly along the road that had once been lined with grape vines, I described how I had left Méjico City. He didn't appear surprised that I had fled the city with blood on my sword and warrants in my wake.

"I know about your adventures already," he said. "Raquel keeps me well informed. Of late, you've been the main subject. She sent me a communiqué two days ago telling me to expect you."

I threw my hands up in mock frustration. "Everybody knows what I'll do next except myself. Have no fear, padre, I won't burden you. I stop only to say hello to you and Marina and will move on before first light, unless of course, my miracle medical abilities are needed."

He laughed. "We shall see, we shall see." He walked with his hands clasped behind his back, his gaze to the ground. "Since your return from Spain—no, pardon, señor, since your birth—the gachupines have treated you abominably. When they abuse those they deem beneath them, the gachupines offend that great lady, Señora Justicia herself. One cannot fault the gachupines for the acts of the man who claimed to be your uncle, but the abuse they have heaped on you because you're not pure-blood Spanish is injustice in its purest form. And you stand in the same shoes as most people in the colony: our Aztecs, mestizos, mulattoes, africanos. And even criollos like myself must in their own way pay tribute to the gachupines."

My indifference to the plight of New Spain's masses must have registered on my face.

"Satisfy an old priest's curiosity," he asked, shaking his head. "Look into your heart and tell me what you believe."

"Unlike you, padre, I don't believe that men are intrinsically good. I don't believe in bringing justice and freedom to people who don't even know the meaning of the words. *Liberty, equality, fraternity*—these are words that the French gave the world but then guillotined people by the thousands. I saw with my own eyes how the French raped and plundered another country. And I see the valiant Spanish peasants—poor fools that they are—fight to return to the throne a notorious tyrant and a craven traitor. I won't fight for a cause because I don't believe the people I fight for deserve it or give a damn about me."

"Then you believe in nothing?"

"No, padre, I believe in Raquel, in Marina, and you. I believed in a young scholar named Carlos, who was willing to die for me. I believe in a guerrilla fighter in Barcelona named Casio and a whore in Cádiz who was braver and more patriotic than all the nobles in Spain. I believe in people, not causes or slogans, not flags or kings. I believe in a love for a love, a truth for a truth, a death for a death, an eye for an eye."

"My son, an eye for an eye leaves us dead and blind."

"Padre, I treat people as they would treat me. I know no other way, and if necessary—if I must fight—I will strike first."

"You say you won't fight for a cause. Will you fight for your *personal* right to be treated as an equal?"

"Padre, I'm a man. I expect to be treated with the respect and dignity that all men should be treated with. I'll kill any man who challenges that right."

"Excellent, señor. I am in need of experienced fighting men. Why you fight is less important than your willingness to fight. Come with me, I want to show you something."

He led me back to the winery. He pushed open the big wood door, and I followed him inside. It was a beehive of activity. Two dozen men and women, mostly Aztecs along with a few mestizos, were busy working. They sawed, planed, and shaped wood into long, slender poles.

"You're making lances?"

"Yes, my friend, lances with which to battle the savage beast, the beast that walks on two feet."

I followed the padre to the building that had been the pottery factory. Inside, more weapons were being produced: clubs, military slings, bows and arrows. I picked up a bow and tested its strength. I had hunted many times with a bow and arrow, one that was made by the Apache indios in a desert region far north of the Bajío. The Apache bows I used were far superior to the ones the padre's people produced.

So far the padre had not told me why he was assembling this arsenal and why he needed fighting men. I had come to a conclusion about the "why," but it was so bizarre that I kept my thought to myself and waited for the padre to tell me. But first, he had one more building to show me, the adobe warehouse where silk was once processed.

"*¡Dios mío!* Cannons!"

I stared incredulously at the work being done. The "cannons" were not cast from bronze or iron but made from stripped hardwood tree trunks throughout whose centers the workers had bored a hole. To reinforce these wood cannon barrels, the padre's people wrapped tight iron bands around them.

The padre took me by the arm. "Come, amigo, taste some nectar of the grape with me. I still have a few bottles of wine pressed from my own grapes."

Marina was waiting at the rectory house, her hands on her hips, a defiant look that said, "The bastardo has returned." We greeted each other formally, almost as adversaries. I could see in her eyes, however, she was glad to see me.

"You have grown more beautiful, transcending even that eternal loveliness you exhibited the last time I was here," I said.

"And you are an even bigger liar than I remember."

"Marina, where are your manners? Juan is our guest."

"You should tell your housekeeper to hide the silver, padre."

As I passed, she grabbed my hand and gave it a squeeze. She fought back tears. We were jesting in good humor, but the last time I saw her I was defending her against the attack of two-legged beasts. The memory of that brutality was not something she would forget. Nor would I.

The three of us sat at the table in the padre's kitchen. He poured wine for each of us and set the bottle in the middle of the table.

"First a toast. To our americano hero in the war against the French."

"I'm no hero." I did not protest strongly, but I wished people would make up their minds as to what I was. In Guanajuato I was lépero scum. In Cádiz, I was a colonial. In Veracruz, a mejicano. In Méjico City, a peon. In Dolores, I was an americano.

Both the padre and Marina had changed in my absence. They had become grimmer, less optimistic. I said, "When I was here before, you exuded high hopes and noble dreams."

"Those dreams are dead," the padre said, "and a more violent vision has taken its place."

The padre and Marina exchanged looks before he continued.

"You can trust him," Marina said.

"I fear not his loyalty but that he will challenge my sanity. Juan, you must have heard that the junta in Cádiz has given the colonies the right to political representation."

"I heard that the viceroy ignores the junta's proclamation."

"The junta is insincere as well. The proclamation is only meant to pacify us. After Spanish people drive the French from the peninsula and we once more have a king, he will repudiate the proclamation as well. Their promises of freedom are nothing more than bones thrown to a whipped dog."

I grinned. "I reached the same conclusion, but people in the capital place importance on Spain's lies."

"I've spent most of my life pondering the relationship between Spain and we americanos. The first time I appreciated the tight stranglehold the Europeans have on us, I was fourteen years old. I saw my Jesuit teachers ordered out of the colony because the king did not want them educating the indios. That was over four decades ago. Now I'm a man approaching the sixth decade of life. Since that time, the bulk of the population of the colony—the Aztecs, mestizos, and other mixed-bloods—has not improved their lot one iota." He spread his hands on the table. "Frankly, señor, in the almost three hundred years since the great conquest by Cortés, little has changed for americanos. The gachupines don't want things to change."

"The padre thought he could change the way the Spanish treated us by showing them that we were as capable they are." Marina shook her head. "You saw how they dealt with the padre."

"The gachupines will never free us without a fight." The padre stared at me intently. "To win our freedom, we must defeat them in the field."

"Padre, I have the greatest respect for your humanity and your intelligence. But wood cannons, lances, and slings are not the weapons of modern war. Are you aware of the killing range of a good Spanish artillery piece? Of a musket?"

"These things you speak of we will discuss at length, mi amigo. But what we have in our armory is what God provides."

"God won't fight this war."

"The padre's not a fool," Marina said. "He knows lances aren't better than muskets."

The padre patted her arm. "It is all right; he asks questions we must answer. We do have a plan, however, not one Napoleon would like, not one that even my criollo allies who are officers in the militia like, but this plan represents the only realistic chance we have. Americanos in the colony outnumber the gachupines a hundred to one, and most are peons. Criollos have the money and resources to drive out the gachupines. They won't do it, however, because they have too much to lose.

"That terrible task of bloody warfare falls on the people who have nothing to lose but their lives: the Aztecs and other peons. Unfortunately, they're also the ones without the weapons and training to fight a war, but they alone have the will to throw off this tyranny. Once the indios take up arms and prove that the gachupines can be defeated, the criollos will join and help us win the fight. Together, as brothers, all classes of people will join together to govern the new nation."

"When is this insurrection to begin?"

"We had planned it for three months from now, in December, but the plans have changed."

I listened quietly as the padre plotted his war against the gachupines. He had already confided his revolutionary intentions to Marina and to the loyal indios and mestizos who had worked in his wine, silk, and pottery workshops. Bringing workers into the fold was necessary to make weapons. The stockpiling had been going on for several months. He and a small group of criollo militia officers—none higher than a captain—would lead the revolt.

"We had wanted to begin our campaign at the fair at San Juan de los Lagos," the padre said.

I had been to the fair many times. An enormous event in the Bajío, it took place over the first half of December. Thirty to forty thousand people attended, the great majority, peons. The padre might well recruit thousands of them to his cause, not to mention that he could "requisition" enough horses and mules to outfit a cavalry.

"I'm sure," the padre said, "you've observed the ceremony of the Virgin de Candelaria."

"Miraculous" representations of the Virgin Mary, usually linked to a healing, cropped up throughout the colony. The Candelaria Virgin was originally a crude statuette, credited for miraculously saving the life of a little girl who had fallen and impaled herself on knives.

These miraculous representations of the Virgin awed the indios in particular. In times of great danger—famine, hurricanes, plague—the authorities hauled out their region's Virgin effigy and called upon it for deliverance.

"The fair would supply mounts, recruits, and a miracle worker," I said, not hiding my admiration for the cleverness of the padre's plan.

"I fear, however, the three-month delay would jeopardize our cause. We've made many weapons. If loose tongues betray us, months of work will be for naught. When word leaked out, the authorities crushed a similar conspiracy by Valladolid militia officers. Thus, we will begin in early October, just a few weeks from now. I'll do everything in my power to avoid shedding innocent blood, but there will be a time when blood must be spilled so liberty can take birth.

"And there will be a time when, like Caesar, we will have to cross the Rubicon and fight, or live out our lives under tyrants." He banged his fist on the table. "If history teaches us anything, it teaches us that people must fight to be free."

The enormity of the padre's intentions finally sank in. I was sitting in a parish house in a small town, listening to a parish priest and an india explain how they were going to drive the Spanish from the colony. They already had a cache of crude weapons, and the war would commence in weeks.

¡Dios mío! María Mother of God.

"You believe our plan is foolish, that a priest is not capable of raising and commanding an army, of winning battles against trained troops," he said.

"Padre," I said, shaking my head, "a year ago I would have howled with laughter at the notion of a priest driving out the gachupines with indios armed with lances and slings. But I was recently in Spain. Many guerrilla leaders were priests, and often the bands had weapons no better than what you are producing. And the armies they fought—and still fight—have been ranked as the finest in the world, not the ill-equipped, poorly trained conscripts that the viceroy commands."

His features brightened at my description of the war on the peninsula.

I lifted my goblet of wine. "I salute your courage and determination. I told you I wouldn't fight for a cause, but I will fight for you and Marina. You are my cause."

That night, Marina and I came together, eager but hesitant, lovers long apart. After our lust was spent, I lay back in the bed, Marina in my arms, her warm breasts pressed against my chest.

"Can a simple parish priest from Dolores," I asked, "truly drive out the gachupines and change the colony?"

"An insignificant young man from Corsica brought kings to their knees and seized the French throne. It's not the size of a person's shoulders or riches that shakes the world but the size of his ambitions. All our people need is a dream of freedom and the faith that they can win. The padre can give them the dream. He can bring them the faith."

 **SEVENTY-NINE**

DOÑA JOSEFA ORTÍZ de Domínguez, la Corregidora of Querétaro, was at home preparing for company: her young friend, Rachel, was expected from Méjico City. Entering her drawing room, her husband startled her with shocking news. As the corregidor, he was the most powerful administrative figure in Querétaro and the best informed.

"They know," Miguel Domíguez told her. "The plot has been betrayed to the gachupines."

"How?"

"A traitor. I have a suspicion, but it doesn't matter; too many people were involved."

"What will you do?" she asked.

"Arrest the plotters. Allende's name was the most prominent. He's in San Miguel. I'll send a messenger to the alcalde there with instructions to arrest him."

"You can't do that; we're among them!"

"I can't do otherwise. For their sake and ours, I have to go through the motions of making arrests. It's better I take them into custody rather than the gachupines. I'll stall the proceedings and help them work on their stories before . . . more drastic measures are taken."

Doña Josefa crossed herself. "We must warn our friends in San Miguel and Dolores, give them time to take action before they're arrested."

"It's too late. We can only hope that the authorities will blunder in their investigation."

"I—"

"No, you can't get involved. I'll see to that."

He locked her in upstairs. She was furious but helpless. Worried, she paced back and forth. The conspirators had to be warned. Allende had to be told that his arrest was imminent. He had to get to Dolores and protect the padre. If he didn't, the revolt was doomed.

"Ignacio," she said to herself. Because her husband Miguel was the chief judicial officer, Ignacio Pérez, the alcalde of the jail, lived beneath them. She took the broom handle and tapped on the floor a code she and Ignacio had selected in case she or her husband needed him. He came upstairs quickly and spoke to her through the keyhole.

Leading a spare mount by a long braided mecate, Pérez rode to San Miguel with the wind at his back and fear in his chest. His world was crashing down around him. He had talked treason with others, and now he feared his own jail would imprison him. Not only was his life at stake, he also had compromised the welfare of his family by attending meetings in which he, Doña Josefa, Allende, and others dreamed of a New Spain where people were free and equal. Now, he was an outlaw.

Ignacio Allende was not in San Miguel when Pérez arrived, but he located Allende's friend and coconspirator, Juan Aldama.

"Allende has gone to Dolores to speak to Padre Hidalgo," Aldama told Pérez.

"Then we must flee there."

 **EIGHTY**

I WAS IN a deep sleep when pounding on Marina's door awoke us. I jumped out of bed, grabbing my sword.

Someone shouted from outside, "Señorita, it's Gilberto."

"The padre's stableman," Marina said. "Something must have happened."

"The viceroy's men must have tracked me here."

"If so, you must leave. The padre will not tell them you were here, but others might have spotted you."

I quickly dressed as she went to the door, a blanket wrapped around her nakedness.

When she came back, she said, "He brought a message from the padre."

"In the middle of the night? What is it?"

"The padre says it's time to wet our feet in Caesar's river."

EL GRITO DE DOLORES
(THE CRY OF DOLORES)

EIGHTY-ONE

I REALIZED AFTER midnight that we'd crossed the Rubicon. That we crossed it in Dolores was fitting: In our poignantly poetic Spanish tongue, *dolores* can convey both pain and sorrow.

When Marina and I reached the padre's house, the war council was going full tilt. The padre huddled with two criollo militia officers, Ignacio Allende and Juan Aldama, and the alcalde of the jail in Querétaro, Ignacio Pérez. ¡Ay! The jail master didn't even give me a second glance when the padre introduced me. Raquel arrived on our heels. En route to visit a friend in Querétaro, she had come directly to Dolores when her amiga warned her away.

Rumors abounded as to the betrayal of the plan. One person said a foolish friend had confessed the plan to a priest. Another said that a militia officer, whom Allende had recruited, betrayed it to his superiors. Whatever the source, the conspirators had to flee or fight. Flight meant leaving their families, homes, and possessions and turning outlaw.

"It's time to fight," the padre said.

Captain Allende shook his head. "We're not ready. We lack sufficient soldiers, training, weapons, supplies—"

"They're not ready either. The Spanish regulars are all deployed in Spain fighting the French, not here in the colony. The viceroy has only the militia. When other militia officers hear that you and Captain Aldama are part of the revolt, many of them will join us."

"The viceroy has ten thousand militia he can field, perhaps even more," Pérez said.

"But not all at once. Isn't that true, Ignacio?" the padre asked Allende.

"Our units are scattered all over the colony," Allende said, "a few hundred here, a thousand there. The viceroy would need weeks to deploy a substantial force. One plan might work."

"And that is?" the padre asked.

"The one you have advocated: your Aztecs. They're not trained soldiers, but they have courage, and they will follow you. A company of musketeers would cut down a thousand, but ten or twenty thousand . . . ?"

"How do we know that many will respond?" Aldama asked.

"They've done it before," Padre Hidalgo said. "Hatred of the gachupines runs deep in the indio. Each time there's been a spark of resistance, they've flocked together by the tens of thousands. Their memories of the terrible punishment meted out to them for objecting to being starved by corn manipulations or other injustices run deep."

"My people have only their memories," Marina said. "Three hundred years of degradation seared into our souls."

"I regret that we must rely on untrained indios, but they'll follow the padre," Allende said. "I suspect that you already have a significant number waiting for your command."

The padre didn't respond, but I too assumed he did. He and his Aztecs wouldn't have created that weapons cache if they'd had no way to use them. Furthermore, the padre had needed a small battalion of Aztecs to make those weapons, and those indios would have friends. If a hundred Aztecs had produced the weapons, a hundred times that number could be ready and waiting.

It surprised me that men like Allende and Aldama, who served the viceroy and had so much to lose, would plot against the government. I didn't personally know either of them, but Allende's name was known to me. He had a reputation throughout the Bajío as a fearless hombre, a caballero who earned his spurs in the saddle, not at fancy balls. It surprised me that men who had spent most of their lives wearing the fancy military uniforms of the viceroy would have enough depth of character and social awareness to demand social change. The fact that Allende had well-thought-out suggestions, ideas that even the brilliant and courageous priest lent an ear to, was not something I expected from a career officer of a militia that was known to be lackadaisical and incompetent.

Other than occasional pirate attacks along the coast, which the militia defended against poorly, and occasional riots by the poor, which the militia put down brutally, in three centuries there had been little to defend against. Despite many threats, there had never been a serious invasion of the colony. The distances and terrain an invading army would have to cover, with the core of the wealth and population occupying the high plateau in the middle, made the colony an undesirable place for foreign powers to invade. Since much of the colony's wealth ended up being shipped to Spain, it was much easier to lie in wait for Spanish ships sailing from Veracruz.

"But what will happen when the viceroy fields eight to ten thousand trained troops?" Pérez asked. "Remember the great Cortés conquered millions of indios with a few hundred Spanish soldiers."

"Cortés had thousands of indio allies," the padre said, "and the Mejica were poorly led. If they had had a competent military leader instead of the confused and superstitious Montezuma, the war would have gone the other way."

"If we raise ten thousand indios—enough to overwhelm the few hundred troops the viceroy has in the Bajío—our fellow criollos will flock to our cause," said Allende. "I know militia officers and caballeros. They won't risk their lives and property until they smell victory. But when a militia officer joins us, he'll bring fifty or a hundred trained soldiers with him. Once we have two or three thousand trained troops, backed by our Aztec multitudes, the viceroy and his gachupines will have to give up the fight."

"And we will collect the gachupines and ship them back to Spain," Aldama said.

The padre stood up. "Then it's time."

"Time for what?" Aldama asked.

"To go forth and seize the gachupines."

I saw fear, wonderment, and even puzzlement on the faces of the men in the room. Only the padre and Allende appeared to be in total command of their emotions and resolve. They were the leaders, the two men of vision. The resolve of the others depended upon them.

Well before dawn, the bell of the Church of Our Lady of Sorrow rang. A church bell was not just an invitation to a religious service; it could also be a call to arms. From the time the church built the first missions, its priests relied on the mission walls and loyal indios for protection. In rural areas like Dolores, where an indio village had grown into a small town, the church bell was still a summons for help. When danger threatened, the priests rang the bell repeatedly, and those indios loyal to the mission, who often worked the nearby fields, gathered to defend it.

In a church whose name evoked sorrow and pain, the padre now tolled the bell as a call to arms. The date was September 16, 1810.

When light of the new day glowed in the east, we gathered in front of the church to wait for the padre to step out and announce why he had sounded the alarm. Besides those who had been at the council of war, at least a hundred peons had gathered.

The padre came out and spoke in a strong, firm voice: "My good friends, we have been owned by faraway Spain and treated as mindless children to obey and do the bidding of the gachupines sent to govern us, to pay taxes without representation, to be lashed when we question their actions. But in all families, the children grow up and must find a path in life that suits them.

"They force our indio americanos to pay a shameful tribute that arose as a tax on a conquered people by a merciless despot. For three centuries that tax has been a symbol of tyranny and shame. During that same time, africanos have been kidnapped and brought to the colony to work as slaves.

"No one born in the colony has been treated with the rights and dignity to which all men are entitled under God, not even those with Spanish blood. Instead, spur-wearers are sent to rule us, to collect unjust taxes, to stop us from developing crafts and trades that would bring us prosperity. We stay as bonded servants to feed their bottomless greed.

"Now that the French have usurped the throne of Spain it won't be long before the godless Napoleon sends a viceroy who speaks only French to rule us, to collect tribute from all of us. When the French seize us, they'll destroy our churches and trample our religion."

His voice rose in intensity, his features growing dark with the knowledge of injustice. My vaqueros would say that there was fire in his belly, the kind of fire that gives a champion bull the courage and determination to charge.

"The gachupines have failed in their duties. They rule and rob us and give nothing in return. The time has come when we must no longer be subjected to these bandidos who come over from Europe and whose only interest is to steal our wealth, tax us, and force us to serve them.

"The time has come for us to keep the French from seizing the colony, to force the gachupines to return to Spain, and to rule the land ourselves, in the name of Ferdinand VII, the rightful King of Spain."

He paused. Not one among us stirred, no one spoke. We were mesmerized by the power, the grand design of the man and his words.

"All people are equal! No one has the right to bloody us with spurs! No one has the right to steal the bread from our mouths, education from our children, to deny opportunities for all!"

He raised his fist and shouted, "Long live America for which we will fight! Long Live Ferdinand VII! Long live the Great Religion. Death to Bad Government!"

A shout went up, then a great roar from those assembled. I looked behind me. It seemed like only moments ago a hundred stood behind me. Now there were at least three times that many.

"It is time to seize the gachupines and take back our land!" he shouted.

Marina grabbed me, tears flowing down her cheeks. "Did you hear it, Juan! Did you hear it! The padre said we're free. We're equal to Spaniards. Our children will go to school; we'll have jobs, businesses, dignity. We'll determine who governs us, and thereby we will govern!"

I stared around at the people. All but the padre's few amigo conspirators were poor Aztecs and mestizos. Among that laboring class called peons, faces glowed with wonderment.

"But first we must fight."

I wasn't sure who spoke the words.

Perhaps they came from me.

 **EIGHTY-TWO**

WAR OF INDEPENDENCE," is how I heard the leaders refer to the rebellion they were starting. That's also what the Spanish called their war against Napoleon in Spain. And while Father Hidalgo and Allende had been born in the colony and called themselves americanos, both were Spaniards by blood and heritage. So as far as the leaders were concerned, it would be a war of brother against brother.

But as I thought about it, these men did not consider this rebellion as being against the Spanish *people* in general but against a small group of greedy men who wore the same spurs I once wore and bloodied everyone else in the colony with them. Allende had insisted that the insurrection be in the name of Ferdinand VII, who was presently a captive of Napoleon. It was wise to use Ferdinand's name because criollos had much to lose if peons suddenly were the ruling class. By stating that the Spanish king would still rule, it created a sense of stability for criollos.

My impression was that Allende was sincere about forming a government in the name of the king, but I was just as certain that a tyrannical king was not part of Hidalgo's concept of government by the people. To the padre, "the people" did not mean only the prescribed few but all people. He also had cleverly portrayed the rebellion as an act to protect the religion that dominated life in the colony.

In Spain, the great battle against the invaders was being fought by the common people who had taken matters into their own hands after their leaders failed them. Of those who immediately answered the padre's call to arms, almost all were poor peons—again, an army of the people—and the focus of their hostility was again "foreign" invaders, those who came to the colony for a few years to stuff their pockets and leave behind a wake of poverty and misery, not unlike what the French were doing in Spain.

Ay! Was there something wrong with me? Was it possible for a man to fight in *two* wars of independence in such a short space of time? A more important question was whether Señora Fortuna would permit me to survive a second war. Maybe that fickle bitch would decide I had used up too much of the luck she had doled out already.

The padre ordered our first assault the moment his speech had ended: We were to take Dolores.

I watched the preparations quietly, with dark forebodings. The padre ordered a predawn roundup of Dolores's gachupines and a search of their homes for weapons. We emptied the local jail of all prisoners sentenced for minor offenses, mostly political crimes—an indio who refused to pay tribute, a mestizo who insulted a gachupine—and filled it with gachupines, some still in bedclothes, all shocked and angry.

A small detachment of soldiers was deployed in the town, no more than a dozen men, a unit of the same San Miguel regiment to which Allende belonged. Used to obeying an officer, when Allende and Aldama entered their barracks and told them they were to grab their weapons and supplies and fall in, they did so without question. I wondered if any of them realized they had joined a rebel army and might one day face a firing squad.

Within a few hours we had seized the town without firing a shot—and achieved the first objective on the long road to independence. I was surprised at how quickly the conspirators moved. The indios, however, seemed surprised by nothing, including the hundreds of crudely manufactured weapons now being passed out. Word of revolution had obviously been sizzling among them.

I still was not impressed by the padre's cache of weapons. He had perhaps twenty muskets stored away, but they were old and inferior. As to his wooden cannons, I could only hope I wasn't near one when it was fired. The only serviceable weapons I saw were the personal weapons of Allende, his criollo amigos, a few local criollo volunteers, the barracks-soldier conscripts, and of course, my own. But a couple dozen well-armed men were not the essentials of a revolution.

Once the padre's small supply of lances, slings, and other crude weapons were distributed, most of his "army-of-the-poor" would still be pathetically ill-equipped. Many had no better weapon of war than a kitchen knife or an improvised wooden club.

When these poor devils charged into synchronized volleys from musketeer firing lines or into cannon shot, I shuddered to imagine their fright, their panic, the bloody casualties they would take.

True, the revolt leaders expected to seize the San Miguel armory, with which Allende was intimately familiar, and its large stock of arms and munitions, but I doubted the commanders there would simply abandon their weapons, especially when news came that a large force was marching on San Miguel.

Allende also expected the viceroy's colonial militia in San Miguel and ultimately those throughout the colony to desert and join the ranks of the rebels. Most of the viceroy's forces were units composed of gachupines as commanding officers, criollos as lower-ranking officers, and mestizos and other castes as foot soldiers. Indios were exempt from having to serve, but a few did so voluntarily.

Because criollos universally hated the gachupines, Allende believed that they would flock to the insurrection, bringing with them money, effective weapons, and their own mounts.

"I hope they get their wish," I told Marina and Raquel, as people around me excitedly jabbered about the birth of the revolution.

"You have a funereal face," Marina chided. "Start smiling or people will think you know some terrible secret."

Putting aside my own thoughts on what appeared to be an outbreak of insanity around me, I grinned at her. "I will smile for you."

I couldn't get out of my mind thoughts of the courageous sacrifices I saw all around me. The criollos taking up the fight were risking their lives and everything they owned, all that their families had accumulated over decades. The poor Aztec and other peons, if they lost, the viceroy's men would burn their fields, rape their women, and starve their children.

I rode away ahead of the main unit, but I had to keep turning and looking back at the people we called Aztecs and the castes called mestizos. Peons, their hats in their hands, had listened to the passions of a priest. Now they marched, men, women, babes in arms.

I remembered the war horrors I had seen and heard about, of what a bucket of nails blazing out of the barrel of *real* cannon did to a column of men, shredding flesh and splintering bone, of what volleys of musket balls did to ranks of men. I thought about war without quarter, to "the knife," and the bayoneting of wounded men as they lay on the ground and stared up at another human being who was about to stick a long blade in them, murder in cold blood.

The padre and Allende were not thinking about the horrors of war but of the freedoms that only fighting man to man with the viceroy's forces and winning could bring. They had hope, courage, and enthusiasm for a better world.

I thought about the sacrifices that Hidalgo, Allende, Aldama, Raquel, Marina, and others who possessed property and status were making. These brave people had comfortable lives but were willing to risk their lives and everything that their personal worlds had consisted of: homes, fortunes, and the very welfare of their families. That they were putting their own lives on the line to fight for millions of other people told of their supreme courage. The Spanish guerrillas fighting the French also had that kind of courage. I personally risked nothing but a life that only I found any value in possessing; I had no meaningful possessions, family, or even an honorable name.

I told the padre that I would fight for him, Marina, and Raquel. Now that I watched the faces of the leaders and the indios, their glowing pride and great expectations, I felt envious of them. They had a dream they were willing to fight and die for.

As we began the march out of the city, the padre and the criollo officers on horseback led the way. Behind them came the "cavalry" of the new army, a troop of men on horses and mules, mostly vaqueros from nearby haciendas who had abandoned their herding of cattle to join the padre's army, and the few criollos from Dolores who had decided to join. Many of the horsemen were mestizos, although there were a few indios among them. Next came the foot soldiers, almost all Aztecs, hundreds of them, with their machetes, cooking knives, and wooden cannons.

I don't think anyone made an accurate count of the "army," nor was it possible to do so because it was like a puddle of water that kept growing. One moment there were a hundred of us . . . then another hundred and another, as men, singly and in small groups, joined the parade. Soon it was a fluid mass of thousands.

No one took names, gave any instructions, did any training. There was no time and not enough qualified soldiers to train the horde. I suspect the only thing these indios knew was that at some point the padre would point at the enemy and they would go forth and do battle.

People carried food with them: already-rolled tortillas as well as sacks of maize and beans, and meat that was cooked and salted to keep it edible. I don't know how many had grabbed a store of provisions kept for emergencies or how much of the food the padre had been hording for this fateful day. Obviously he had been storing supplies because wagons loaded with supplies and pulled by teams of mules suddenly were part of the procession.

My admiration for this warrior-priest who read Molière, defied his government and church to create wine and silk industries by force of his will, and who had an incredible abundance of love for all, but especially for the downtrodden, soared. I would have thought the two experienced military men, Allende and Aldama, would have planned the logistics of an army, but the padre was a human whirlwind, capable of handling a dozen tasks at the same time and fearless in making decisions. Miguel Hidalgo, small-town parish priest, had taken up the sword as enthusiastically as he once took up the cross.

From the tone of conversations and body language, I sensed that the military-trained Allende did not want the priest to be in charge, nor did Allende's fellow officers, but the padre was able to attract large numbers of volunteers, something no one else had so far been capable of. I didn't know for certain whether or not Padre Hidalgo was aware of Allende's reluctance, of the officer's own ambition to be in charge, but if he was, he gave no sign of it. I had been around him enough to know that little escaped his awareness.

A warrior-priest, I thought. Not one of those "turn-the-other-cheek" conquer-with-love martyrs of the New Testament, but the "eye-for-an-eye" fire-and-brimstone prophet of the Old Testament. The ability to pick up a sword and wield it had been inside him all the time, waiting to be ignited when his frustrations with the injustices that the common people suffered finally burst. The wrongs to his people ate at him until he picked up a sword, just as Moses, Solomon, and David had taken up the sword to defend their people.

According to Raquel, humans had long engaged in war and religion as if they were two sides of the same coin. The conquest of the New World had been launched in the name of Christianity, or so the avaricious conquistadors shouted as they grabbed indio gold for their own purses. And didn't Michael take a sword and drive Satan and his fallen angels from Heaven?

As we marched toward San Miguel, I realized that the rebellion had begun with good omens: the maize was in full ear; there were hacienda pigs and cows aplenty along the way. We would not want for access to food, not at this time, at least.

I rode beside Raquel and Marina. Looking back at the many women and children accompanying the indios, I asked, "Why do they bring their families? To cook their meals?"

"What do you think the viceroy's men will do when they come to Dolores? What will they do to the women left behind in villages when all the able-bodied men have gone to fight?"

I realized the naiveté of my question. The answer did not take much imagination or even need to be expressed. And I noticed she said "when" they came. I don't think she realized her slip of the tongue. If the revolution was successful, the viceroy's men would not be coming to Dolores because there would no longer be a viceroy or a royal army.

Padre Hidalgo was suddenly beside me. He leaned a little toward me and spoke in a low voice. "So much is happening so fast I have not had a chance to discuss some matters with you. As soon as we are able, I need to talk to you."

He was gone as quickly as he had approached. Puzzled, I looked over at Marina.

"Has it occurred to you," she said, "that you are the only person in this army who has ever actually fought in a war? Not even the criollo officers have experienced warfare."

I almost groaned aloud.

How was I going to explain to these people that my experience in war was as a reluctant warrior and my main objective had been to stay alive? Did they think I was a leader of the guerrilla warfare against the French? Up to now, I had permitted others to overestimate my experiences and abilities, but I didn't want to get myself killed or put the padre's rebellion in jeopardy because of inflated notions of my military experience.

"Don't worry," Marina said, "I'm sure the padre thinks of you as more of a bandido than a soldier."

"Stop reading my mind," I snapped.

 **EIGHTY-THREE**

LATE THAT DAY we arrived at the small, unarmed village of Atotonilco near San Miguel. A large church complex dominated the settlement.

I was riding near the front of the line when the padre told Allende that they would stop and rest the men and the stock, that we shouldn't attempt to immediately enter San Miguel. "I wish to surprise them by entering at nightfall," he said.

The padre was clearly in charge. He had spoken quietly, but his manner brooked no disagreement. He had simply stated a fact.

Allende agreed with the strategy. How could he disagree? We had left Dolores with hundreds of men. Now our forces were an oceanic tide, our Aztecs alone numbering in the thousands. Before we had stopped, Allende rode down the line, estimating five thousand indios, but by the time he rode to the end and back the number had swelled.

At the church in Atotonilco, other priests greeted the padre. He went inside and soon reappeared with a banner blazoning the Virgin of Guadalupe.

"Give me your lance, cavalryman," he told a vaquero.

The padre attached the Virgin's banner to the tip of the lance and remounted his horse. He rode among the indios, holding the banner high.

"The Virgin is on our side!" he shouted. "Long Live the Virgin of Guadalupe! Death to evil government!"

Thousands of voices resounded. The shouts of the Aztecs shook the earth. Raquel and Marina roared with the multitude. Allende and his fellow criollos grinned with joy.

It had been a brilliant move by a master showman, a stroke of genius on the padre's part. The Virgin of Guadalupe was the patron saint of the indios in the area. Everyone in New Spain had heard the story in church hundreds of times.

Nearly three hundred years ago, in 1531, ten years after the Conquest, an Aztec convert named Juan Diego claimed to have seen the Virgin Mary as he plowed his field. He reported his sighting to the religious authorities, but nobody believed him. Diego claimed that on another occasion the Virgin ordered him to climb a hill. He obeyed and found flowers blooming on the summit in the midst of winter. He picked the flowers and carried them to the church in his serape. After he'd strewn flowers across the floor, a sweet fragrance filled the room. Imprinted on his serape was an image of the Virgin.

News of the miracle spread like a firestorm among New Spain's indios. Following the Conquest, the indios were in a spiritual vacuum. The priests who followed the conquistadors destroyed every remnant of their pagan religion. That the Spaniards had tread upon the Aztec gods and survived—and thrived—threw the indios into a spiritual abyss.

Most of the indios didn't fathom or even roundly reject the teachings of the priests. But Juan Diego's miracle changed all that: the indios suddenly had a spiritual figure to venerate. The conversions following the miracle numbered in the millions. A papal bull later made the Virgin of Guadalupe the patroness and protector of New Spain.

The image of the Virgin Mary painted on the cloth banner that Father Hidalgo displayed for the masses of indios was, of course, said to be identical to the one on Juan Diego's serape.

The padre had turned the war into a religious crusade. With one sacred banner, he allied his Aztecs with God.

Marina was so overwhelmed she burst into tears. I kept a tight smile on my lips. Was I the only one who had noticed? When the padre shouted "Death to evil government" thousands of voices had responded *Death to the gachupines.*

The padre passed the Virgin's banner to a young man who held it high as he walked ahead of the army: Diego Rayu, the novice priest had brought his own Aztec thunder to the revolution.

EIGHTY-FOUR

BEFORE WE LEFT Atotonilco, more cloth paintings of the Virgin of Guadalupe were mounted on lances. Now there were three warrior priests taking the lead, marching in the front of the huge horde, carrying high the banners of the Virgin.

What courage these men of God had! I knew how to fight with a sword and pistol, but these priests had nothing but their faith and courage.

The criollos evaporated before us: some vaqueros joined our cavalry from the haciendas we passed along the way, but the criollo owners and majordomos fled from what they regarded as an army of rabble. And it must have looked that way; our ranks swelled with Aztecs every foot of the way toward San Miguel de Grande. The pond that kept increasing was now a long river of humanity fed by streams and trickles of indios coming from every direction.

I found it amazing that the Aztecs didn't question the leaders or even ask where they were going. Abandoning their fields, they fell in line and marched, as did the mestizos, although in smaller numbers only because they were a smaller proportion of the colony's population. From the appearance of the mestizos' clothing, I could see they were poor peons, not small tradesmen or rancheros.

Many times I saw men on horseback between us and San Miguel pause and watch us, then wheel their horses and ride back toward the city as if the devil was breathing down their necks. And he was. I could only imagine their faces when they rushed through the city streets shouting that thousands of bloodthirsty Aztecs were advancing toward their homes.

I fell back to where Raquel and Marina were riding in line. They didn't discuss or care about the terrified looks of the gachupines and criollos but focused on the expressions of the Aztecs.

"Look at their faces," Marina said. "They're bright and full of hope. I can't remember a time when I've seen a man of our people laugh or even grin. They've been morose, full of sadness, humiliated and oppressed for so long, they've lost their sense of identity. Even their women were taken from them by the conquerors. As they march to redeem their honor, you can see the pride on their faces."

She was right. I had rarely seen a happy indio, except when he had a belly full of pulque.

"They're happy," I said, "because they're on a crusade. They're on their way to Méjico City, the Holy Land of New Spain."

They didn't understand that they might all be dead tomorrow.

"A children's crusade," Raquel said, "that's what we look like, not brutal knights in armor but innocents with hope and courage shining in our eyes because only children can be so ingenuous, so lacking in fear."

"A children's crusade?" Marina asked.

"Europe saw two such movements. Back in the Middle Ages, two boys each set out in Europe with other children following them, intent upon going to the Holy Land and reclaiming it for Christ. Both boys claimed to have had visions in which they were instructed to lead an army of children to reclaim the Holy Land from the infidel. Thousands of them marched across Europe."

"They marched to their doom," I added. "Tens of thousands with no place to go. Many were tricked onto boats and sold to the infidels as slaves by Christian ship captains." I grinned at Raquel, pleased at myself. I had heard the story from her many years before.

"Well, it won't happen here," Marina said. "We're not children, and our leader isn't on a crusade but simply wants recognition of the rights of all people. Someday you'll see indios dressed in the same clothes as everyone else, and you won't know the difference."

One of the criollo officers, a friend of Allende's, overheard Marina's remark as he trotted by on his horse. "A monkey dressed in silk is still a monkey," he sneered.

I pursed my lips as I watched the man's back. My nose itched for a fight. "It's too bad he's on our side . . . or I would teach him the meaning of social justice with my boot up his backside."

Raquel shook her head and muttered, "Once a bad hombre, always a bad one. We must all learn to get along together as brothers and sisters."

Marina and I exchanged looks. Raquel was an idealist. Neither Marina nor I were under any illusion that the criollos would give up their dominance of the lower classes until the peons won their freedom on the battlefield.

I rode to a higher point so I could view both the city of San Miguel and the horde descending upon it. Our puddle had swelled to an all-engulfing sea.

The priests led the way with their banner of the Virgin held high. Father Hidalgo and Allende followed next on horseback, with an honor guard of Allende's soldiers.

I'm not a man who has known God. Actually, I have spent most of my life avoiding Him in the hopes that He wouldn't notice me and hold me accountable for my sins. But as I watched the procession, for the first time in my life, I felt the power and passion of the Lord.

EIGHTY-FIVE

SAN MIGUEL DE Grande was Allende's place of birth. They knew him well as a young caballero, a man who romanced their daughters and braved bulls in the ring. He was admired, even emulated. Now he came home at the head of an invading army.

We quickly learned that most Spaniards had left the city. The ones who stayed behind had taken cover in the city's government building. Colonel Canal, in charge of the city's defenses, knew he could not win. Another officer, Major Camuñez, tried to mount a resistance, but the men and their officers all knew Allende and admired him. Almost the entire command, over a hundred men, joined us.

I listened quietly as the padre negotiated with Colonel Canal for the surrender of the gachupines barricaded in the municipal building.

The stalemate was broken when Allende said, "Inform the gachupines that if they surrender peacefully, I will place them under my personal protection. No harm will come to them."

As I bit off the end of my cigarro, I looked back at the mass of Aztecs, a tidal wave descending on the city. Eh, even if the indios listen to orders, how would they ever hear them? Or understand them?

I didn't think Allende had even thought it out; most of the indios spoke Spanish poorly or didn't speak it at all. Not to mention that they distrusted Allende, who, dressed in his flamboyant officer's uniform, was a symbol of tyranny in their eyes. The only thing Allende had going for him was approval of the padre, a man whom the Aztecs revered as a saint.

None of which would help the padre command an army of this size. How could his orders be heard? Who would enforce them without a chain of command enforced by lieutenants, sergeants, and corporals? How would soldiers with no training know how to obey the orders? Who in the lower ranks would pass on the orders?

It wasn't an army but a mob.

The pandemonium started after dark. At first, our indios broke into pulque taverns, which had closed their doors in expectation of a siege. One group of indios went to the jail, opened the cells, and indiscriminately released murderers and thieves along with political prisoners, anyone who pretended they wanted to join the insurrection. But the march to the city had been a long one for most of the indios, and soon they went to sleep.

All hell broke loose at sunrise.

Bands of Aztecs broke into the homes of both criollos and gachupines. They pillaged and destroyed, setting houses afire. Soon thousands of indios rampaged, smashing windows, breaking down doors of homes and merchant buildings. Loot was carried out by the armful.

Cries of "Death to the gachupines!" rang through the day. People of light-colored skin—criollos and gachupines who had not already fled the city, even light-colored mestizos—were dragged out of their houses and stores and beaten.

A throng of indios attempted to hang a criollo merchant. They had torn most of his clothes off when Allende and his officers on horseback charged into the crowd, with me behind them. The padre was not with us. I knew he spent most of the night checking seized foodstuffs and munitions. The army was in dire need of money; men had to be paid or how else would they support their families?

Allende tried to reason with the would-be hangmen, but they shouted insults back; he wasn't the priest they loved and trusted but just another Spaniard in a military uniform. He surged into them, knocking indios down with his horse, striking them with the flat of his sword, wielding it as a club rather than a lethal blade. The rest of us followed suit, finally breaking and scattering the indios. I hated to battle our own people, but the indios were out of control.

After routing the would-be hangmen, we rode down the finest, wealthiest street in the city. Mobs had attacked the luxurious homes and broken down doors. Allende's own house was on one side of the main square and his brother's on the other.

Joined by Allende's uniformed soldiers, we broke up the savagery and the looting with death threats and brute force, but dealing with the horde of Aztecs was like trying to grasp a fistful of water. No one was in charge.

When the padre finally arrived, he was a calming influence on their raging passions, but not even he could get them to settle down quickly.

Allende confronted him as soon as we had restored order. The criollo officer was red in the face from exertion and anger. "We cannot have this disorder, we'll lose the support of the criollos in the colony."

"What happened is a terrible thing," Padre Hidalgo concurred.

I could see from his face that he was conscience-stricken by the atrocities.

"But the Spaniard," the padre said, "has raped and robbed these indios for their entire lives. We can't expect the slaves to confront their brutal masters with equanimity."

"They're mindless savages!" Allende shouted.

"Savages?" Hidalgo's voice rose. "Do you forget the atrocities of Cortés and the conquistadors? Do you forget three hundred years of cruelty visited upon these people in the name of gold and God?" Hidalgo's voice became conciliatory but firm. "Ignacio, I share your concern. We both gave our word that no people would be attacked or their property plundered. But look around you. We are now in the third town since our announcement to drive the gachupines back to Spain. Our cry for soldiers has been answered . . . how many do we have? Ten thousand? Twenty thousand? How many of those comprise our criollo class? A couple hundred? Less than one out of a hundred who have answered the call?"

"They'll join us when they see we're victorious."

Hidalgo reached across and grabbed Allende's arm. "Amigo, we won't be victorious *unless* we have soldiers. The viceroy has eight, ten thousand trained troops at his disposal? In all likelihood, he's already ordered those regiments to march on us. Soon we'll be in the battle of our lives. And those indios whom you despise will do the fighting . . . and the dying."

The argument between the two leaders stayed with me as I found shelter for Marina, Raquel, and myself in a convent. The nuns welcomed us inside the gate as added protection. It had to be explained that Marina wasn't our servant.

I could see that the padre and the military officer were not brothers under the skin. Hidalgo was a true man of the people, a visionary who supported independence and a free society open to all races, religions, and classes. But Allende was a type I knew well: the caballero. Horses, fancy clothes—especially military uniforms—señoritas, big houses, all the trappings of an aristocrat. Like me, Allende had been educated more in the saddle than between the pages of books. He saw the insurrection as a military exercise—raise an army, beat the viceroy's army, declare a new nation—one in which he would drive the gachupines back to Spain, installing criollos in their place.

The padre burned with a vision of justice for all. Hidalgo saw the revolt not simply in terms of military tactics but as a personal promise to free exploited people from their bondage and forge a nation of equals.

I suspected that Allende bided his time until the day when he and other criollos could seize the fruits of the revolt. He had no other choice; the Aztecs, not his beloved criollos, would carry the insurrection on their backs and win or lose it with their blood, and they would neither flock to him nor obey him.

The criollo officers had lost control. Not even Napoleon himself could forge an army from this vast multitude of indios, not without time and money. What would happen when they encountered trained troops? Would they turn and run at the first volley of cannon fire and musket fire, as Allende feared? Or was the padre's estimation of the courageous, spirited Aztecs correct: they would fight and die for the cause?

On our march to Celaya from San Miguel, Padre Miguel Hidalgo was proclaimed captain-general of America. Ignacio Allende was made lieutenant-general. Juan de Aldama was third in command, with militia officers who had joined the rebellion assuming other field-grade commands. Warrior-priests walked at the head of the army carrying banners of the Virgin.

Drummers kept up a beat, though none but a few trained soldiers marched to its cadence.

Two days out of San Miguel the padre summoned me, and I met him at the head of the column. We rode together out of hearing range from the others.

"I understand you have declined a commission as an officer," Hidalgo said.

I shrugged. "That's for men who seek command and glory."

I didn't tell him that I knew Allende and the other criollo officers neither trusted me nor wanted me in their ranks. To them, I was still half-bandido, a peon who had humiliated and even killed their fellow criollo Spaniards.

"I didn't think you would take it. You aren't the type to enjoy barking orders . . . or taking them. I think of you more as a lobo, a lone wolf, than a peacock."

I laughed. He had read my thoughts: I'd thought of the criollo officers with their fancy uniforms as peacocks. I only considered a few of them good fighters. Even with his fancy uniform, Allende was mucho hombre and a tough soldier.

"You don't believe in this revolution, do you, Juan?"

I hesitated before answering him. "I don't know what I believe in."

"I know you said earlier that you would fight for your friends. But now that you have seen this army of Aztecs who dream of liberty, has your heart opened to accept them, too?"

"I've been through so much, heard so many stories even about myself, I don't know what is true and constant, but you've been my friend as have Raquel and Marina. When the time comes, I'll stand by you three, even at the risk of my life. But if you ask me whether I'd give my life for the criollo officers and the indios, the answer is no. As long as any of you three are with the revolution, I will be beside you. Otherwise, this fight has no meaning to me."

"I'm honored that you would fight at my side. But I want you to know that if your life must be given, I don't want it lost for me but for the people of New Spain."

He was right: I was a lone wolf. Maybe it was because I grew up unloved. For whatever reason, I traveled light . . . and alone.

"I've had many opportunities to observe you," Hidalgo continued. "In many ways, you're wiser than me." He waved away my protests. "No, no. I'm not talking about the books you've read but the life you've led. The rest of us have spent our lives in the Bajío, within shouting distance of towns like Guanajuato and San Miguel. You have seen more of the colony than any of us and have twice crossed a great ocean and fought against the finest troops in the world."

"I was in a couple of guerrilla actions, padre—"

"What do you think this is? Don't let the size of the army fool you. We have less training and are more poorly equipped than anything in Spain. No, you have one talent that Allende envies, and every man in the army would also if they knew you possessed it."

I frowned. "What's that, padre?"

"*Survival.* You escaped a death sentence from the viceroy's men half a dozen times, evaded the clutches of a crazed Mayan king, slipped the hangman's noose in Cádiz, and dodged French bullets in Barcelona only to return to New Spain, flee Méjico City, and now help lead a rebel army. You have prevailed in wars, not skirmishes."

"My ability to survive is directly related to my ability to duck and run," I said, laughing.

"Whatever it is, you have a singular ability to blend in here and there, then come back alive. That's why I want you to spy."

I shot him a sharp look. *A spy?* Spies got worse treatment than traitors when captured.

"I want you to organize and lead a small, select group who can provide us with critical intelligence. We're marching on Celaya and Guanajuato. I need to know their battle plans. Soon the viceroy's armies will attack us from several different directions. I must know the movements and the tactics of those armies, too. After Guanajuato we must take Méjico City." He gave me a sideways glance. "What do you say, Señor Lobo, will you be my eyes and ears among the enemy?"

"Señor Captain-General, I will serve you until they rip the tongue from my mouth or the eyes from my head."

"Let's hope it doesn't come to that."

I rode away from the army to have some solitude and ponder what I had gotten myself into. Another fine mess, no? I could already see Señora Fortuna grinning at my impertinence. But I was sincere when I said I would fight for my amigos. I wouldn't leave Marina and Raquel to the mercy of the viceroy's armies if and when the insurrection turned bad. Nor could I turn my back on the padre, whom I had begun not only to admire but revere.

When I returned to the two women, I gave them a haughty stare. "When I come into your presence, señoritas, I expect you to salute me as your commanding officer."

They exchanged looks.

"Ah, I see," Marina said, "you've been made a general, no? Well I have news for you, Señor General, the only man I ever saluted was my husband, and that was when I bid him good-bye after a jealous husband shot him."

"You two will have to learn respect if you want to work for me."

"What do you mean, work for you?" Marina asked.

"You want to be secret agents, don't you? I'm the padre's chief spy and spymaster."

Raquel gasped. "The two of us spies? You mean scouting the viceroy's armies?"

"Whatever it takes. Raquel, you will return to Méjico City, pretend to be loyal to the gachupines and keep your eyes and ears open. What you learn about troop movements and defenses of the city, you'll send the information to me by messenger. You must find friends you trust to carry the messages."

She squealed. "Has there ever been a female spy?"

I shrugged. "I don't know, but before you get too overjoyed, remember that if you get caught, you'll curse your mother for giving you birth."

"What of me?" Marina asked.

"The padre will need information about the defenses of Guanajuato and the road ahead."

"I'm to go to Celaya and Guanajuato and spy?"

"*We* will spy. I'm known in Guanajuato, but now a beard covers my face. Besides, who would suspect that Juan de Zavala, caballero and hacendado, is in town when all they see is a poor Aztec with his donkey and wife? He rides the donkey while his hardworking wife trudges behind, carrying his goods when she is not making his tortillas or finding a pulquería so he can quench his thirst."

 **EIGHTY-SIX**

Celaya

MARINA AND I arrived in Celaya midday on the following day, hours ahead of the army. I had expected to find barricades and armed troops challenging the entry of anyone who ventured toward the city, but the opposite was true: There were no defenses. We arrived in time to see the regimental commanders and most of their troops evacuating the city.

"The militia and the gachupines are abandoning the city."

"Some people are taking up arms," she pointed out.

Criollos and their servants were setting up a barricaded corridor near the town square.

Rumors covering every possible scenario raced through the city. Many believed the rebels would rape the city and murder everyone. Others claimed only the gachupines would be harmed. Some said the Virgin Herself led the army, and no one would be harmed.

The only accurate intelligence I had to report to the padre concerned the futility of resistance, and the wildfire resistance could ignite.

"There's a small force of brave criollos willing to fight for the city, a few dozen. If they fire a volley, I fear what our troops will do."

The question I left hanging in the air was whether the indios would run or rape the city.

The padre was relieved that the viceroy's troops had fled, but Allende was not. "I had hoped for the opportunity to address them and get them to join us," Allende said.

The padre woke me after midnight with a written message that I was to carry to the city's administrators, the ayuntamiento.

"Delivering terms of surrender," the padre said, "can be a lethal assignment. They sometimes shoot the messenger."

I shrugged off the danger. From what I had seen of the city's panic, I believed the town fathers would welcome a peaceful surrender.

I was shocked, however, at the language of the message to the city fathers:

> *We have approached this city with the object of securing the persons of all the European Spaniards. If they surrender with discretion, their persons will be treated humanely. But should they offer resistance, and give the order to fire upon us, we shall treat them with corresponding rigor. May God protect your honors for many years.*
>
> Field of Battle, September 19,
> 1810
> Miguel Hidalgo
> Ignacio Allende

> *P.S. The moment that you give the order to fire upon our troops, we will behead the seventy-eight Europeans we have in our custody.*
>
> Miguel Hidalgo
> Ignacio Allende

As the padre walked me to my horse, he said, "I'm saddened that I must behave barbarically while I wear the uniform of a soldier, but I am not the first man of God who had to take up the sword. Now that I have my own war to fight, I find myself more tolerant and understanding of a pope who sends an army to the Holy Land, knowing that thousands will die, many of them innocents."

He squeezed my arm. "Please tell them in the strongest terms that they must surrender the city without firing a shot. If fighting erupts, I may not be able to control the army."

In the predawn hours of September 20, I delivered the message to the alcalde.

"We need the response, pronto," I told him, after emphasizing the gravity of the situation.

"We must meet and confer," he responded.

I pointed at the steeple of a church. "Señor if there is any doubt in your mind, go to the top of that tower and open your eyes."

I left, wondering if a nervous trigger finger would fire a musket ball into my back.

My suggestion to study us from a high tower was a good one; the city officials would see campfires by the thousands, underscoring the scope of the danger they faced. Allende had ordered that the fires remain lit until an hour after the message was delivered.

Finally, a messenger emerged from the city around midday and announced they would permit entry without a struggle. They asked for time to "prepare" for the entry, and the padre gave them until the next day.

"What do they prepare for?" I asked the padre.

"They need time to hide their treasures," he said. "I don't blame them. And we need the day to organize a crude chain of command to prevent looting and to obtain supplies. With every passing hour, our ranks swell, increasing our need for food and weapons." He shook his head. "It's an almost insurmountable task."

We entered the city the next day. I was in the vanguard with Hidalgo, Allende, and Aldama. The lower classes cheered our arrival, but the criollos mostly stayed out of sight.

As we came into the main square, I looked up and saw a man on the top of a municipal building. Amid the cheers, I barely heard the shot but saw black-powder smoke billow from the gun. I don't know where the bullet hit, but the next moment all hell broke loose. Our people began returning fire for no discernible purpose since the person was already gone. Still the guns boomed, as did the passions of the Aztecs.

Surging in all directions, our indios looted as they had in San Miguel, but this time none of us, not even the padre, could stop them. They were too numerous and moved in too many directions. Allende tried to keep order. Galloping into the crowd, he slashed down with his sword at men breaking down the front gate of a house. His horse slipped on cobblestones and went down. I urged my own mount toward him. Clearing a path of indios away, I gave him a chance to remount, perhaps saving his life.

He drew his pistol, and I yelled at him, "No, it's no use. If you shoot, they'll tear you to pieces."

Frustrated, he galloped off, but not out of fear. He knew if the indios turned on him, the rebellion would be lost. A man of incontrovertible courage, he would have willingly gone down fighting had it served his purpose.

I averted my eyes from the savagery as I rode away. A single shot had ignited a riot in a small town. What would happen when we reached Guanajuato, the largest city in the region—and actual fighting erupted? ¡Ay! a beast had been unleashed, a wild thing that no one would be able to control.

EIGHTY-SEVEN

ALLENDE'S DREAM THAT criollos would flock to the revolution—an un-realistic goal from the outset—was shattered by the rioting at San Miguel and Celaya. Having been a Spaniard for most of my life—and a poor peon only recently—I understood the criollos and gachupines better than Al-lende, who was swayed by his hopes and dreams.

The criollos had had centuries to rip the spurs off the gachupines' boots and had not done so because it meant risking their own privileges and prerogatives. People with nothing to lose rose up, revolted, and died for a cause. Only a few idealists—the rare Hidalgo, Allende, and Raquel—would risk everything when winning meant nothing in their own pockets.

"The criollos will wait and see who wins," I told Raquel. "They won't fight for what most of them already have. They don't trust the peons and wouldn't abide a government in which the lower classes participated, much less dominated."

The truth hurt, but she agreed with me, saying that a few friends of hers in Méjico City—people like Andrés Quintana Roo and Leona Vicario—might risk their lives and fortunes for a free and equal society; the majority, however, would not.

"You're right, most will take a wait-and-see attitude. The criollos will make small gains if they force out the gachupines, but they could lose everything if the peons command the government."

She reported that prominent criollos who were asked to join the insur-rection had turned down the request.

"A militia officer in Valladolid, Agustín de Iturbide, is the latest. Al-lende didn't favor the man, but the padre was eager to have him join be-cause, like Allende, he is a well-known and admired young officer. He would have brought his regiment to the revolution."

I recognized the name. Iturbide's name had been linked romantically with Isabella.

Marina and I headed for Guanajuato to scout out the town's defenses while Raquel went to Méjico City to do the same. I sent two of the padre's trusted indio overseers with Raquel to protect her and to messenger her observations back to the padre. I had two more men follow behind me and Marina, so they could report back to the padre from Guanajuato.

One of the men I chose to follow us was Diego Rayu. He could read and write—an important skill in case we had to relay a written report—and he had been to Guanajuato before. For his companion, I chose an in-dio who was better with a knife than a pen. While Diego was a firebrand, he fought his battles with his intellect. He might need someone who wasn't as bright but could cut a throat when necessary.

When Marina and I set out, we had to ride past most of the army. A remarkable sight—tens of thousands strong, miles long, like some enormous primeval beast—our army stretched forever, its teeth bared all the way. There were fewer than a couple hundred military uniforms in the entire horde. Wives and children accompanied many soldiers in this war. A man carrying a crude club with one hand might cradle a child in his other arm. Some herded sheep, carried a quarter of beef over a shoulder, or led a cow on a rope, all acquired from the haciendas we passed. Almost everyone carried sacks of maize. Others shouldered plunder from the previous towns: men and women carried chairs, tables, even doors on their backs.

Had I seen this ragtag army when I was a young caballero, I would have had a hearty laugh later with my amigos in a tavern. But now, having seen firsthand what rage simmered beneath the calm exteriors of the expressionless Aztecs, knowing what hopes and dreams were in their hearts and minds, I suspected that the padre was right, that the barefooted horde possessed a power that would surprise the criollo officers.

It was smart of the padre to send a spy mission to Guanajuato. One of the great cities of the Americas, one of the richest in all the world, the government and mine owners would be prepared to defend their hoard of silver.

On our way to the mining city, we stopped briefly to buy tortillas and beans from a pulquería hut on the roadway. Pretending to be ignorant peons—a condition not far from the truth—I listened to the conversation of two criollo merchants while Marina pretended to scowl over a feigned disagreement. What I heard was not surprising but still unsettling. New to both his office and Méjico City, the viceroy had put huge rewards out on the leaders of the insurrection—dead or alive—along with a pardon for anyone who killed or arrested them. The church had reportedly excommunicated the leaders as well.

"Excommunication will trouble them most," Marina said. "Now they will not only risk their heads . . . but their souls."

 **EIGHTY-EIGHT**

WHEN WE WERE half a day from the city, I sold our mule and purchased a donkey. A mule was beyond the means of most poor people.

We arrived in Guanajuato on the Marfil road, the route I believed the padre would choose for his army. Soldiers had erected a checkpoint, questioning everyone who entered. I told them that my wife and I came from a village between Guanajuato and Zacatecas. I chose the village because I was familiar with it. The hacienda I once owned was in the region.

"Who's the alcalde of your village?" the sergeant who questioned me asked.

"Señor Alonso," I said.

"And your village priest?"

"Padre José."

"Why have you come to Guanajuato?"

"To see a curandero for my wife." A curandero was a healer who used magic to exorcise sickness.

Sitting on the donkey with her face down, Marina looked up and exposed red blotches on her face.

"¡Dios mí! Get along with you!"

Once we were out of the soldiers' sight, Marina got off the donkey and wiped berry juice off her face.

"It's a good thing you knew the alcalde and priest of that village," she said.

"I knew nothing. I made up the names, but he didn't know them either. He wanted to see my reaction, to judge whether I was lying."

"Fortunately, you are a seasoned liar."

Panic reigned in Guanajuato. Major streets were barricaded, stores closed, doors and windows boarded up. People hurried here and scurried there. A rider in a military uniform galloped by, carrying a message to an outpost or perhaps the capital, no doubt relaying pleas for help.

We roamed the city, talking to people, learning only that rumors were as numerous as the people retelling them. The lower classes were less fearful than the merchants and landowners. Many of the wealthier citizens believed Hidalgo to be a French sympathizer who would hand the colony over to Napoleon. I assumed Riano, the governor of the city and province, had intitiated those stories.

I considered tactics and terrain while we surveyed the city. Unlike Méjico City and Puebla, which had broad thoroughfares, Guanajuato featured short, narrow streets. While the defilade and cramped battle theaters seemed at first to favor the city's defenders, two conditions worked against them. Guanajuato sat in a canyon, whose surrounding heights favored an invader. Even the cathedral in the central plaza stood below a high, vertical cliff. Many houses were perched on slopes so steep that the ground floor of one was level with the roof on another. This unique topography gave the high ground to the invader, a tremendous advantage if the besieging forces had good cannons—something the army of liberation almost entirely lacked but a fact Riano might not know.

The second defect in the defense was the lack of defenders: It would take either thousands of regular troops to defend a city of this size, or the residents themselves would have to be behind the defenses.

Despite Riano's allegations that the padre's army was a Trojan horse for the French, most of the population was aware that Hidalgo and Allende planned to drive the gachupines from the country. Few of the common people would line up to die to defend Spaniards. The city had a significant criollo population that might remain loyal to the viceroy because it was to their advantage, but not a great number of those colonial Spaniards were willing to die for European Spaniards.

A visit to the pulquerías near the military barracks gave me information that I found hard to believe: Business was bad because there were so few soldiers. Most estimates were that there were fewer than five hundred soldiers in the city. The nearest significant detachment was a great distance away, under the command of Brigadier Feliz Calleja at San Luis Potosí.

"We don't know if Calleja is already on the march to relieve the city," I told Marina, "but it's a good possibility he's not. Riano has sent a request for his troops, but you can bet the general won't move without orders from the viceroy in the capital. Venegas, the new viceroy, has only been in the colony a short time. With all the confusion and the fact that Méjico City would obviously be the main target of the revolt, it's more likely the viceroy would have Calleja move to secure the capital rather than Guanajuato."

But that left Riano's tactics a puzzlement to me.

"It's not possible he has only hundreds of men. He can't defend the city with so few."

"Perhaps he doesn't plan to defend it," Marina said. "I understand he's a friend of the padre's. Perhaps he'll turn it over to Father Hidalgo."

I shook my head. "No, I know Riano. I've been at the balls that he and his son, Gilberto, have thrown. He's stubborn and resolute, he wouldn't surrender the city without a fight. To do so would not be honorable in his eyes. We must discover how he plans to fight with so few men."

"Why don't you ask him?" she teased.

I stroked my chin. "Maybe I will . . . or at least get him to show me without me asking."

Diego and his companion had followed us into the city. We made contact with them, and I gave Diego instructions to leave immediately and return the next morning, bearing a message.

Marina did not hear my conversation with Diego and asked me later, "What did you tell him?"

"Just a simple instruction. I told him to appear at the Marfil road barricade in the morning with the exciting news that he had spotted a vast army of Aztecs approaching the city."

"You're insane! Why did you do that?"

"When you're hunting, sometimes it's necessary to flush out the game before you can get a clear shot."

The next morning a guard from the Marfil barricade rode up to the governor's palace as if the devil dogged his tail. We watched the city from a hillside so we'd have a good view of the barracks and other strategic points. In less than an hour, I understood Riano's plan for defending the city. It came as a shock.

"He's not going to defend the city," I told Marina.

"What do you mean?"

"He's going to defend only the alhóndiga."

"What's that?"

"The alhóndiga de Granaditas—the granary."

I took her to the hillside above the building. The governor stored maize and other grains in the alhóndiga to ward off famines. Although the granary was situated on a rise, the Cuarta hillside—which looked down on it—was close by. Had we deployed real cannons on that high hill, the granary would have been indefensible. That meant Riano had spies, too; he knew we didn't have significant artillery.

This area was said to be named Cuarta, which meant "quarter," because a bad hombre had been drawn and quartered with one of his four body parts posted on the hill as a lesson for others. Not a very happy thought for one such as myself who had been accused of crimes far worse than those this unnamed bandido probably committed.

The alhóndiga was large, with two very high stories, perhaps a hundred paces in length and two-thirds that in width. Its walls were tall and strong, its windows small, appearing stark on the outside, almost without ornamentation.

"It looks like a fortress," Marina said.

"It is a fortress," I said.

The building had been under construction for nearly ten years and had only recently been finished, but I had been in it a number of times to select feed for my horses because parts of the building were in use before the whole structure was completed. It had only a partial roof, because half of the rectangular-shaped building's roof was open air. I had heard the open-roof design described as similar to that of a Roman atrium.

"Inside, it's divided into storerooms on two levels," I told Marina. "Two big stairways lead to storerooms in the upper level and an open-air patio in the middle of the building. The walls are massive. We'd need cannons to breach them, real cannons. For us, it might as well be a fortress, because we have nothing to breach the walls with."

The false alarm I raised had revealed the governor's plan. Riano had rushed to the alhóndiga, as had armed gachupines, some criollo supporters, and almost the entire uniformed military.

"He has only about six or seven hundred men," I said. "About half of them are infantry, maybe another hundred dragoons—the mounted soldiers you saw with short muskets—and fewer than three hundred armed civilians. That's why he won't defend the city. He'd need a force five to ten times that size to put up a viable defense. No doubt that he's supplied the granary with enough water and food to hold out for months, and he only needs to do so until the viceroy can send a relief force."

The only practical way we could attack the granary was from the front, at the main entrance facing a street. The front door was massive. The other entrance was sealed. Most windows were too high to reach and all were small, making them difficult and slow to crawl through.

Riano had done other work to defend the granary. He had approaches from nearby streets closed off with masonry, including his perimeter of defense, the premises and two buildings behind the granary: the house of Mendizabal and the main building of the hacienda de Dolores, a mining facility. He put up barricades at the bottom of a hill in an attempt to cut off an approach from the Río de la Cata.

"He should have destroyed the Mendizabal and Dolores buildings and knocked down the walls to prevent us from hiding behind them," I told Marina. "He has to split his forces to defend them."

The alhóndiga was already well guarded before my false alarm, more heavily than necessary to protect food and water. "He has the city treasure in the building," I said. "He didn't send it by mule train to the capital because he doesn't know which roads the padre controls."

"His honor only extends to the Spanish who will hold up in the granary. He's abandoning the city, only protecting Spanish treasures and Spanish lives. His duty was to protect the whole city. Now he will cost lives on both sides," Marina said.

"He obviously disdains our army," I said. "To him, we're a mob of indios led by a priest and a few renegade officers. We don't even have any officers from the regular army, just low-ranking colonial militia officers. He must have heard what happened in the towns along the way, know that there was no real fighting and that the indios are armed with the crudest of weapons."

Being a former Spaniard, I knew how he'd think: Riano believed that the indios would cut and run when they were hit with a barrage of musket fire that dropped men by the hundreds with each volley. I wondered about that myself. Untrained and without real weapons, once the indios saw the effects of musket fire, their enthusiasm for this revolt might quickly dissolve. But these were not things I could say to this firebrand Aztec without fear of getting my cojones cut off.

"We are many, tens of thousands," Marina said. "We will outnumber them fifty, a hundred to one."

I had wondered whether Riano's decision to stand and fight an overwhelming Aztec force—with about the same number of men Cortés had had—might have been deliberate. If successful, he could carve his own place in history, alongside Cortés and Pizzaro, the conqueror of the Incas.

When news arrived that Hidalgo's forces were two days away, Riano abandoned the city. Under cover of night, the granary became Castillo Guanajuato.

"The governor says the city must defend itself," an angry mestizo shoe-maker told me as we passed his hut. "They've taken all the muskets and most of the food in the city. They don't care about us." He spit. "Now we don't have to care about them."

EIGHTY-NINE

WHEN THE ARMY of liberation reached the outskirts of the city, I went out to meet them at the Burras hacienda. Father Hidalgo and Allende listened attentively as I described Riano's defensive strategy. I drew a map of the alhóndiga and the surrounding streets and showed them where barricades were set up and accesses sealed.

"You are certain that they have only about six hundred men? Nearly half of whom are civilians?" Allende asked. "And he's defending three different buildings?" The look he gave the padre questioned my sanity.

I laughed. "I've seen their preparations with my own eyes."

I understood their wonderment. One of the richest cities in the world, the third city of the Americas, a city with seventy thousand people, was being defended by a small force.

"But don't assume taking the granary will be easy. It's a fortress, and they're well armed. They have more muskets than our entire army, and real marksmen. And they're well provisioned. Without cannons for a breach, we can enter only by battering down the front door. Synchronized volleys from hundreds of muskets will cut the attackers down like scythes, especially when the defenders fire from the many small windows and from the roof."

I started to say it would be a slaughter but felt I owed the padre too much to impugn the wisdom of his actions.

Father Hidalgo asked me to accompany the two representatives who were conveying a surrender offer to Riano. If they surrendered, they would be treated humanely. If they resisted, they would be killed with no quarter given.

He handed me another note. "This is a personal note to Señor Riano. I know him and his family. I believe you do, too."

"I socialized with them at a few balls. We weren't friends."

"Nevertheless, you've met the governor and his son and know that they're honorable men. Give this note to Riano and show it to no one else."

The personal note to Riano read: "The esteem which I have ever expressed for you is sincere and I believe is due to the high qualities which adorn you. The difference in our ways of thinking ought not to diminish it. You will follow the course which may seem most right and prudent to you, but which will not occasion injury to your family. We shall fight as enemies, if so it shall be decided, but I herewith offer to the Señora Intendente an asylum and assured protection . . ."

I led the two emissaries to the alhóndiga. Me and one of the emissaries were allowed to enter blindfolded. They did not remove our blindfolds until we reached the roof of the building and faced Riano and his son, Gilberto. Riano gave no sign that he recognized me, though Gilberto squinted at me as if my appearance triggered a memory; but he didn't recognize me behind the heavy beard.

After reading the padre's demands, Riano had his comrades-in-arms assemble on the roof. He read them the note and paused, waiting for a reply. Prompted by an officer, the regular troops cried, *"Viva el rey!"*— Hurrah for the king. Then he consulted with the civilians, who responded unenthusiastically: "We will fight."

Riano's written reply stated that he was duty bound to fight as a soldier. He also gave me a private note for the padre, which I hesitated to read but did. Was I not a spy?

Riano's private note told the padre he was grateful for his offer to protect his family but that he would not need our protection, that he had already sent his wife and daughters out of the city.

Before long two couriers came out of the alhóndiga and whipped their horses frantically to race in different directions. One of the couriers was shot out of the saddle before he reached the outskirts of town. A message was retrieved from him, and I read that, too, on my way back to the army's encampment.

The message from Riano was to General Calleja at San Luis Potosí. He wrote: "I am about to fight, for I shall be attacked immediately. I shall resist to the uttermost, because I am honorable. Fly to my succor."

During our negotiations, I confirmed my estimate that Riano had no more than about six hundred men, of which at least two-thirds were soldiers. They were pitted against an army that now numbered in excess of fifty thousand. Only a few hundred of us were soldiers or were men like myself, armed civilians familiar with weapons.

Father Hidalgo had left Dolores with an army numbering in the hundreds, and in a twelve-day march to Guanajuato, the army had increased a hundredfold. But we'd had no time to train or discipline his turbulent sea of warriors.

"Riano will defend the barricades first," I told the padre and Allende on my return. "He has positioned his uniformed soldiers on the roof of the alhóndiga at the barricades outside on the street, and along the way down to the river. The civilians will man the two buildings in the rear and the lower floor of the granary."

"He'll keep a reserve," Allende said, "a small force, perhaps ten percent, rested and ready to be rushed to trouble spots. He has a small area in which to use his mounted dragoons. He'll let them dominate the street until they're forced inside." Allende jabbed the map of the area I had made. "Zavala is right. Our only way past their defenses is to drive them from the street and off the roof. Then we must attack the front entrance. The doors are massive, but we must breach them to win."

"How do you wish to proceed?" Father Hidalgo asked.

Allende met his eye. "We have a hundred times more untrained peons than regular soldiers. If we're going to attract soldiers to our cause, we can't lose them in this battle. The musket men in the fortress would cut our small force of professionals to ribbons in minutes. If we had cannons and the room to employ them, it would be different. We don't. All we have is manpower. My plan is to test the mettle of our Aztecs. Let's see if they're an army that can carry the day against militia."

Hidalgo didn't object, and I understood why. Allende, in his prideful way, was admitting that his professional soldiers could not win the battle. Our rudely armed, untrained "cannon-fodder" had to bear the brunt of the fighting.

Either the peons carried the day with their machetes and wooden lances, or the revolution would come to naught.

"We will pray," the padre said, "and then we will fight."

 **NINETY**

I TOOK A position on the heights north of the granary with a panoramic view that enabled me to see what was to be the battlefield and to watch in other directions for any surprises Riano might have up his sleeve.

An enormous number of people arrived, not as combatants but as spectators. Thousands of Guanajuato's citizens, mostly the lower classes along with some of the poorer criollos, had gathered to watch the battle.

Do these fools think it's a bullfight?

From what I heard all around me, they were definitely on the side of the rebels. They not only had been abandoned by the Spaniards but also had spent their entire lives under the Spaniards' heels. In their minds, the difference between a criollo and gachupine meant little; a Spaniard was a tyrant who oppressed them financially, politically, and spiritually, regardless of what they were called.

Shortly before noon, the vanguard of our army came into sight, pouring into the city along the Marfil road. Carrying high banners of the Virgin, six priests came first, followed by Allende's uniformed troops making a smart entrance to the military beat of drums. The crowds cheered at the display of military and religious strength.

Strictly for show, the priests and soldiers moved to the side almost immediately as along the causeway of Nuestra Señora de Guanajuato the Aztecs advanced. Naked to the waist—so they would not get blood on their only shirts—armed with machetes, lances, clubs, and bows and arrows, our Aztecs were a terrifying sight. Up to this point I had not thought of them as soldiers—or even as warriors—but as they moved to engage the enemy, they reminded me of the guerrilla bands I had fought with in Spain: men of the soil and mines who had the courage to face muskets in the hands of trained troops.

They crossed the bridge and came to the barricade at the cuesta de Mendizabal, where Gilberto de Riano commanded the troops.

"Halt in the name of the king!" he shouted.

He didn't wait for a reply, and none was necessary. Most of the indios couldn't have heard him, and few spoke Spanish. He shouted an order to fire. A volley of musket balls ripped into our advancing men. Many fell, but replacements kept coming. Another volley thundered, and more went down, but they kept advancing. A horn blew from Allende's command post, and the indios retreated.

The first shots had been fired; the battle had begun. The indios had faced musket shot and had advanced under fire. I felt a surge of pride at their courage.

Led by Allende's officers, the body of Aztecs formed into groups and approached the granary from different sides. In the meantime, the padre had taken possession of the city with more of our forces. I knew the plan was to throw open the jail and release prisoners if they agreed to join the cause. From my own days at the jail, I would say that there were few hombres who were incarcerated whom I would want on my side of a battle.

To my surprise, Father Hidalgo suddenly appeared, on horseback, pistol in hand, the true image of a warrior-priest. I leaped on Tempest and joined him as he rushed from point to point, giving orders for the assault and ignoring an occasional shot from a musketeer on the roof of the granary who thought he might get lucky.

Allende's militiamen positioned themselves at the windows and rooftops of those buildings facing the gachupine's positions, but they could have little effect on the granary defense. Marksmen with better weapons on the high roof of the alhóndiga picked off anyone who raised his head to take aim. I shook my head, knowing that the only way to take the building was to storm it.

Then an amazing process began. A host of indios at the riverbed down the hill from the granary began to gather rocks and break larger rocks into smaller sizes. Others carried the supply up the hill above the granary. I watched in admiration as the indios began raining the rocks down on the defenders on the rooftop of the granary. It wasn't possible to throw the rocks at the roof by hand; instead the ingenious devils used leather *slings* to propel the stones.

Marina rode up beside me, her face glowing with pride, as the men of her race armed only with slings took on Spanish musketeers. "It's David and Goliath!" she shouted.

Musket fire from the roof felled scores of indios, but it didn't deter the avalanche of rocks raining down. Soon the musketeers fled from the storm of stones, fleeing inside, abandoning the advantage of the high roof.

Dense masses of indios advanced on the barricades and buildings. Musket fire ripped through the ranks at point-blank range. It was impossible for the Spanish to miss; they had merely to point their weapons in the direction of the horde.

Marina's glow turned grim as we watched the slaughter grow. Aztecs were being killed by the hundreds, but they kept coming, stumbling over their dead compañeros, those without a machete gaining one from a lifeless hand.

I stared at the horrible carnage, unable to speak, unable to even gather a coherent thought in my head. I'd heard the stories of whole Spanish families armed with little more than cooking utensils fighting French invaders, but nothing I'd seen in Spain had prepared me for the slaughter of thousands of innocents before my own eyes.

They drove the defenders from the barricades and back into buildings. When the defenders of the barricades at Los Pozitos Street became hard pressed, Riano charged out of the granary with twenty men to support them. After calmly positioning the support troops, the governor made his way back to the granary and paused at the entrance to view how the battle was going. One of our own soldiers armed with a musket found his mark and put a bullet in his head.

I felt nothing as an ounce of lead ball blew off a corner of the governor's head. The plan to murder me once the Manila galleon got out of sight of land could not have been schemed without his permission. And Marina was right: He was honorable only to his own kind. He raised his sword to stop other men from enjoying just a few of the privileges he had been born with; now we killed him with that sword.

When I saw him fall, I realized something significant had happened. The governor of a large, rich province, Riano had been one of the most powerful men in New Spain. But he had been brought down by a peon with a rusty musket.

The war had truly been brought home to the gachupines.

The situation suddenly grew worse for the defenders as the Aztecs continued to press forward in the face of murderous musket fire. Riano's men at the barricades fell back, running for the doors of the alhóndiga.

All at once my heart raced.

Marina!

She had ridden into the midst of it, hacking at the defenders. Her horse went down from musket fire. I gave Tempest the spurs and slapped his rump. The stallion leaped forward. I grabbed the signal horn I had strapped to my pommel and let out long blasts as the stallion surged into the indios. They parted like the Red Sea for me, a few getting knocked aside by Tempest when they didn't move fast enough. I saw Marina look back at the sound of the horn. Her horse was down, but she was on her feet. She shot me a glare and turned around to join the melee.

Something smacked my hat. I had a vision of hot lead ripping off the top of my head, but my hat—and head—stayed on. I rode lower in the saddle, praying that the stallion wouldn't take a bullet. I came up behind Marina and grabbed her by the back of her hair. Wheeling Tempest, I headed out of the melee.

"*Akkkk!*" I let go; she'd smacked me with the flat of her machete. "Puta-bitch."

Musket shot smacked the ground around us. "Com'on." I pulled her up, and Tempest took us out of range.

Back on the hill with a bird's-eye view of the battle, I said, "I know you thirst to avenge every insult suffered by your people since Cortés, but you're being unfair to the padre."

"How?"

"He has tens of thousands of brave Aztecs willing to die for him. He needs a few good spies to stay alive long enough to help him win the war."

My argument seemed to have the desired effect of calming her rage. We watched the Spanish retreat into the granary. Most of them made their way inside, but others, including a detachment of dragoon cavalry under the command of Castillo, didn't make it before the massive doors closed. The soldiers left outside were caught in the open. Indios attacked and killed them without mercy. I saw one uniformed defender exploit the confusion. Removing his uniform, he joined the attackers as one of them.

With their leader down, the defenders were stunned, but we still hadn't bled the fight out of them.

Gilberto Riano appeared to have taken his father's place as leader. I saw him direct men who dropped explosives that detonated on the indios massed in front of the granary. I stared at the familiar-shaped objects for a moment before I realized what they were: mercury flasks, the type used to supply mines with quicksilver by my uncle. The defenders had filled them with black powder and shrapnel and attached short fuses. When they exploded, often igniting in midflight, the effect was devastating: razor-sharp, flesh-shearing metal flying like fire and brimstone blasted out of hell as the bombs exploded in the midst of the attackers.

But even as the bombs and musket volleys violently blew openings in the mass of indios, the breaches were closed as more took the place of their fallen comrades.

We left our position and joined the group surrounding Hidalgo and Allende. The two leaders were following the action and sending messages to officers on the front lines. The front door had to be breached.

Miners from the silver mines had joined our insurrection. The padre sent several miners, partially protected by large earthen vessels, up to the massive doors to attempt to breach them with iron bars. But they had little effect on the doors.

Suddenly a young miner, perhaps nineteen or twenty years old, stepped up to the padre. He removed his straw hat and shyly met the padre's questioning look.

"Señor Padre, I can set fire to the door."

"Set fire to the door?"

"Sí, if you give me fire, pitch, and rags that burn well."

The padre nodded. "I salute you, my brave son."

As the youth set off, Father Hidalgo called after him. "What is your name?"

"They call me Pípila," he said.

Watching the youth as he struggled toward the door, slumped under a large stone, which he held overhead, I was awed by his courage. He had rags and a container of pitch strapped to his chest, a lit miner's candle lamp attached to the bundle. A hail of lead rained down on him, ricocheting off the thick stone, but he continued on.

A mercury-flask bomb exploded overhead; the youth went down to his knees, the great stone that protected him from musket shot sliding away. He got back under the stone as the dirt around him kicked up from bullets. He crawled up to the door and paused for only a moment. *Catching his breath*, I thought. The next moment he was smearing the door with pitch and piling rags against it. He quickly set the door aflame.

I shook my head in amazement. Between the attackers and the defenders, for a certainty, more than a thousand men had died fighting over that door. And a guileless boy had breached it with a candle and some oily rags.

With fire consuming the door, indios surged forward, a group of them ramming the door with a tree trunk.

I could see the wild panic on the faces of the defenders who leaned out windows to drop bombs and fire their muskets at the indios at the door. Once the door went down, they would face the Aztecs man to man. Some leaned out windows begging for mercy. Another man poured a bag of silver coins down at the indios, the madness of the moment leading the fool to believe he could buy his life with a bag of silver.

At the last minute a white flag flapped from an upper window, and we all grinned with relief. The indios battering down the door stopped to cheer, when Gilberto Riano and two others suddenly leaned out from windows and dropped shrapnel-filled mercury-flask bombs down on the men.

The carnage was horrific, but so was the almost inhuman howl that went up from the Aztecs at the sight of their compadres treacherously murdered under a flag of truce. The indios renewed their assault on the door. When it burst open, they poured into the granary. Deadly fire at point-blank range mowed down the front ranks, but the indios were again a tidal wave with no beginning or end, a primal force that simply surged forward with more indios taking the place of their dead comrades.

The padre signaled me. "Take some of my trusted men and secure the treasures in the granary."

I gathered Diego, his fellow spy, and four more men. Marina came to join us. I snarled to get her to relent, but she just glared back. The woman was more stubborn than Tempest—and meaner.

The musket fire inside continued as I approached the granary doors with my men, but it was sporadic. A more terrible sound filled the air: the hellish screams of the defenders in the hacienda de Dolores. A mining facility adjacent to the granary, the hacienda had held out for some time, but our indios breached it just as I entered the granary.

I came through the opening, pistol in hand. A Spanish officer, wounded and bleeding from half a dozen cuts, stood on the steps of a stairway. He kept himself erect by leaning on a lance still flying his regimental colors, all the while cutting down indios with his sword. A lance took him in the stomach, then another and another until he was on the ground, impaled by a half dozen shafts.

The victorious indios rampaged through the granary, killing without mercy. They had paid in blood for this moment. Now it was blood for blood, life for life. A man begging for his life was beaten to death by a club. I had no pity for him; he had been one of those who, with Gilberto Riano, had thrown down the bombs under a flag of truce. Gilberto had fallen, too. His body was twisted at an obscene angle, his neck partially severed.

Where would the treasure be? The first time I entered the granary the soldiers had blindfolded me, then removed it on the roof. My lépero/bandido instincts, however, served me well. Through the open roof, I had observed a guard posted in front of a room on the second floor about halfway down the corridor. It was the only room where I had seen a guard posted. Riano would have scattered his munitions caches all over the building rather than in one place where they could be destroyed by a single explosion; so it was unlikely the guard was protecting arms. I quickly divined that the treasure was stored in the room.

Shoving past indios, I shot up the stairs, quickly outdistancing Diego and the others. The carnage all around me was stomach turning. Fighting went on in scattered parts of the second floor, but already clothes were torn from the dead, the wounded, even the living, as indios transformed themselves into gachupines with broad-brimmed leather hats, fancy pants, and silver-stitched jackets.

Anything that could be ripped or torn or found went to the victors. These were not just the spoils of war but trophies of conquest. Men who had never possessed anything but the ragged shirt and pants they wore, who lived in mud huts and didn't even own the dirt between their toes, now wore the costly jackets of men who had treated them as slaves.

Blood was everywhere: hemorrhaging from the wounded and the dead, pooled on the slippery floor, splattered on the walls, and smeared on the dying and the victors, on muskets and piles of maize. And, likewise, death was everywhere: in the cries of the victors and the screams of the defeated.

The door to the room in question was half-open, a dead Spaniard blocking its entranceway. As I stepped over the body and entered, I saw the chests with the coat of the arms of Guanajuato on them. Out of the corner of my eye I saw a movement. Stepping over the body had left me off guard, and I threw myself back as the blade of a sword came at me. I fell backward, my own blade coming up quickly, deflecting the other foil. I was still on my feet but off balance. Facing me was a Spaniard with blood on his face. He held a sword in his right hand and a pistol in his left. As he pointed the pistol at me, someone came up to the now fully opened door.

Diego Rayu suddenly leaped between me and the pistol, shouting "No!" The shot rang out in the small room. I avoided Diego as he was blown back toward me. Slipping around him, I came in low and then jabbed up, catching the Spaniard under the chin with my blade. He rocked back on his heels and collapsed.

I knelt beside the young fallen Aztec. He had deliberately taken a bullet meant for me, and blood enveloped his white shirt.

"Diego . . ."

He clutched my arm for a moment. "Amigo . . ." he whispered. Then his body convulsed, settled, and went limp.

I heard a noise from the downed Spaniard, who was gasping for air. I took my sword to him until he lay still.

When I turned around, Marina was there, sword in hand. Hers was bloody, too. She struggled to hold back tears as she stared down at the fallen Aztec. She said, "Too many . . . too many have died."

Late that afternoon the killing finally stopped, and the padre told us to take the survivors to jail. I had the trunks that were filled with silver and gold stacked outside on the street. I smoked a cigar as I waited for a wagon to pick them up. Watching the prisoners come out, I noticed a mestizo woman exit the granary. Riano had taken a couple dozen women to fix their tortillas and no doubt ease the urgings of their male parts during what he had conceived would be a long siege.

But this woman's features were familiar to me. As she was trying to slip into the crowd, I came up behind her and hit her in the back of the head, sending her crashing to the ground. Then I yanked off her hair.

"Ah, it's my old friend the notary," I said, grinning down at the bastardo who had tried to wring a confession from me when I had been in jail and was part of the plot to ship me off to my death.

He gaped up at me.

"Don't you know, Señor Notary, it is cowardly and shameful for a man to dress as a woman?"

I gave him a good kick.

"Take this swine to the jail," I told an indio working on the jail detail. "If he gives you any trouble, cut off his cojones so he won't have to pretend to be a woman anymore."

NINETY-ONE

FOR THE NEXT two days, the army of liberation ransacked the city, attacking and looting the homes and businesses of the Spanish. Allende had once again ridden into the crowds, slashing at his own troops with his sword, demanding that order be restored. Again, he failed, and this time I didn't join him. The padre ordered the troops to pass over the homes of married Spanish, but didn't curb the looting and celebrations. He understood the great passions that the Aztec victory had ignited. Allende and his officers, though brave and intelligent men for the most part, didn't understand the indio. They expected them to act like trained soldiers.

¡Ay! If they had acted like trained soldiers, they would never have charged the granary fortress almost bare-handed. Over five hundred Spaniards had died in the attack. They took with them two thousand indios. The carnage was so great, a long trench was dug in a dry riverbed to accommodate the bodies. The indios had achieved victory not through military stratagems but through cojones and blood.

I was not a spiritual person or even a sensitive one. As I walked through the streets of Guanajuato, I thought about how the battle had affected me. Even after I fell from grace with my Spanish ancestry and lived as a lowly peon, I disrespected the Aztec blood in my veins. I had been raised to believe that a drop of that blood polluted my system and gave me the dreaded blood taint, a social and racial disease as repugnant to "people of quality" as the pox.

Seeing the peons as people who were innately subservient to the wearers of spurs, I had believed implicitly in the myth of their inferiority. But as I watched the way the peons had fought, bled, and died for liberty, I realized that the padre was right: that three centuries of oppression had left the lower classes morose and defeated but that a true leader could reawaken their courage and resolve. That person was the padre, of course. They loved, admired, and revered them. He believed in them. They in turn showed extreme courage under fire, charging the lethal volleys with crude weapons and bare hands. Some, like Diego, had given his life not just for the cause but for a friend.

Did I have the courage to die for a cause? In my entire life, no cause had inspired me to risk my life. These peons didn't give up their lives for possessions or bedroom passions. They gave up their lives for a dream of freedom.

We'd all been baptized in blood and fire, and the images of what I witnessed haunted me.

Engrossed in my thoughts, I strolled past several of Allende's officers, who were standing in the street, watching the indios' rampage. One of them called the indios "filthy animals." It was the same man who said that a pig dressed in silk was still a pig. Without thinking, I drove my steel-toed boot into his groin. Clutching his crotch, he dropped to his knees in sobbing genuflection. His two comrades reached for their swords.

"Touch those swords," I told them, "and I will kill you all."

Marina joined me, shaking her head. "*You* are the animal, not the indios." She squeezed my arm. "But I know that was for Diego."

"For all the Aztec warriors who fell today. A piece of land, food for their children, freedom from slavery, not to die in some Spaniard's mine or under the hooves of a gachupine's horse or under his coach or whip—that is all they wanted. And they died for the dream."

She pretended to examine my skull. "Juan, a cannonball must have creased your head. This is not like you."

"Woman, you have always misunderstood me." I tapped my temple. "Don Juan de Zavala is not the mindless caballero you think him to be. Soon I will be reading books and writing poetry."

I shook my head at the anarchy around us. People who wore rags before were parading around in silks. Indios were ransacking inns and pulquerías, looting stores, setting fires.

"It's not good," I said. "We've won the battle, but we're losing the peace."

"What do you mean?"

"The people of the city are hiding, even the common people. They're terrified of the indios who were supposed to liberate them from the gachupines."

"The anger of our army will subside in a while," she said.

"Yes, but will the fears of the people of Guanajuato? Mark my words, Señorita Revolucionaria, we will see few volunteers from this great city. No regiments of trained soldiers, no criollos bringing muskets."

"Then we will win the way it was done today: with the courage of our men."

"They faced hundreds today. God protect us when they must face thousands of trained troops with cannons."

 **NINETY-TWO**

WE CAME TO Guanajuato on September 28 and left twelve days later for Valladolid, bequeathing Guanajuato a new and freer government. They also had a functioning mint and a factory to manufacture cannons.

Despite our casualties, our ranks continued to swell on the road to Valladolid to even more enormous and unwieldy proportions than before. Moreover, the men's spirits were high. We had captured a city that was second only to the capital itself in wealth and prestige.

I knew from the indios' speech and faces that they now believed that they were part of a larger cause: a struggle to redeem their people's dignity and freedom. Few of them could have expressed exactly what that meant, but you could see it in their eyes.

How much they understood about elected government was a mystery to me. I didn't understand it myself. Except for people like the padre and Raquel, I'd met few people who appreciated what it meant. Most feared elected government would lead to anarchy or even worse, tyranny.

More and more, I placed my faith in the humble priest who now led a mighty army with the fiery courage of biblical prophets.

With each passing hour, my admiration and awe for Padre Hidalgo grew. He was a man of both compassion and iron determination. He was not after reward, high office, or military power . . . he laughed at rumors that he was to be crowned king in Méjico City. He had had no military training, yet he led an army as if he were a trained general and veteran of the Napoleonic wars.

He wore a dazzling blue and scarlet uniform with gold and silver trim, one befitting a warlord and conqueror, but it was not to his liking. His coat was a lustrous indigo with red cuffs and collar, both trimmed in gold and silver galloon, and his shoulder belt was black velvet, similarly trimmed with gold and silver. From each of his shoulders hung a silver cord, and hanging from his neck was a large gold medal engraved with the image of the Virgin of Guadalupe. Allende's uniform was similar to the padre's, but he had only one silver shoulder cord hanging over his right shoulder.

I felt there was an even more obvious difference between the two uniforms. The padre wore his out of a sense of duty to his officers, understanding that it impressed the multitude and gave the soldiers confidence in him as a military man. Allende wore his with a sense of pride; he was a military man and had chosen the profession long before the insurrection.

Allende assured us the viceroy's total forces would only come to a tenth of the seventy to eighty thousand we believed composed the horde that flowed across the Bajío like a river at full flood. No one knew exactly or could even accurately estimate our army's size. With fighters joining and leaving at will, its composition was fluid, especially if one included women and children in its total force.

Leaving Guanajuato, Allende tried again to improvise a command structure. Dividing our hoard into eighty different battalions of about one thousand men apiece, he placed each under the command of an officer. Lacking trained officers to fill those positions, Allende commissioned almost anyone who was willing and literate—a prerequisite for sending and receiving written orders.

We hauled two bronze cannons and four wooden ones. So far, none had proved effective. Since neither Allende nor his professional soldiers were well trained in artillery, they had overestimated the value of cannons. The monster weapons were indeed crucial on a battlefield . . . when manned by experienced crews who knew how to maintain, load, aim, and fire them. They were almost worthless to us; we lacked the time and experience to teach even the most basic skills to our raw recruits, few of whom could load and fire a musket.

The padre sent forward on the road to Valladolid a detachment of three thousand soldiers under Colonel Mariano Jiménez. Marina and I went ahead of the detachment, in the company of a "guerrilla" leader named Luna and a gang he had assembled. Guerrilla units were popping up all over the region. As in Spain, many of the bands were idealistic freedom fighters; others were nothing more than bands of bandidos who robbed and murdered for personal gain. Stories of raids on haciendas, robberies of silver trains, and mule trains of merchants abounded. Luna, who previously had been a foreman on a hacienda, fell somewhere in between patriot and thief.

I discovered that Valladolid lacked an intelligent and courageous leader like Riano to organize a defense. Merino, the governor of the area, along with two high-ranking militia officers, had set out for the capital along the Acámbaro road. With Luna and his men, I rode to intercept him. We caught up with their slow-moving carriages, loaded with the town treasure, and took them and their dinero into custody.

Marina stayed behind in Valladolid to keep an eye on the situation as I took the prisoners to the padre. "When news of their capture came to Valladolid," Marina said later, "talk of resistance collapsed."

We marched into Valladolid as conquerors. We gained not just the city, but several hundred men from a regiment of dragoons and recently mobilized raw infantry recruits. But the recruits were little better trained or armed than our mob of indios.

The next day, all hell exploded. It began again with indios breaking into pulque bars, inns, and private homes. Allende led a unit of his dragoons up and down the streets, shouting warnings. When the warnings proved of no value, and the indios began to pillage, Allende ordered his men to open fire on looters. Several were killed, and many more were wounded. The fusillade was unfortunate, but it quelled the looting.

More trouble followed on the heels of the shooting. Dozens of indios became ill, and three died. A rumor raged that the townspeople had poisoned brandy the indios had stolen. Allende believed they had brought the sickness down on themselves by consuming foods that they had looted: Indios who had spent most of their lives on a diet of maize, beans, and peppers washed down with water or an occasional cup of pulque were suddenly gorging themselves on rich foods and potent spirits their systems were unused to.

Once again, Allende went into action to quell the disturbance, this time in an even more unusual manner than musket fire. On his prancing horse before the angry indios, he told them the brandy was muy bueno and that they had just drunk too much. To drive home his point, he drank a cupful and made his officers join him.

We left Valladolid on October 20. At Acámbaro, a great review of the vast army was held, the entire force marching before the leaders. Padre Hidalgo was proclaimed generalíssimo—or commander-in-chief—and Allende was promoted to captain-general. Aldama, Ballerga, Jiménez and Joaquín Arias were brevetted lieutenant-generals.

I still had my head on my shoulders and Marina on my heels to keep me aware of my faults.

 **NINETY-THREE**

THE ARMY CRAWLED toward Méjico City like a slow, endless, writhing beast. From Valladolid and Acámbaro, the padre directed the army on a route that would include Maravatio, Tepetongo, and Ixtlahuaca.

Marina and I spread out separately to check the route to the capital, she with her army of female spies, me with my gachupine stallion. Upon my return, Father Hidalgo called Allende, Aldama, and other senior commanders to hear my report on the large force blocking the way to the capital.

"The viceroy has sent an army commanded by Colonel Trujillo to stop us before we reach the capital," I told them. Trujillo occupied Toluca—the last significant town before the capital—with as many as three thousand soldiers.

"Colonel Trujillo has sent an advance detachment to defend the Don

Bernabé Bridge over the Río Lerma. I wasn't able to get close enough for an accurate count, but I'd say it was several hundred strong."

"He's secured the bridge in advance," Allende said, "because he intends to cross it with his entire force and engage us near Ixtlahuaca. We must take the bridge before he can reinforce it."

As we advanced on the bridge of the Lerma River, Trujillo's defenders fled rather than take a suicidal stand. Marina had returned with more information as our lumbering force finished crossing the bridge. She updated the padre, Allende, and the other generals.

"When the unit Trujillo sent to defend the bridge came running back, announcing that an army dozens of times larger than the viceroy's entire force was advancing, the colonel immediately wheeled his army around and retreated. He's planning to defend at the town of Lerma."

"There's a bridge there, too," I offered.

Allende nodded. "Yes, he'll defend the Lerma Bridge, hoping to keep us from crossing and gaining the pass known as Monte de las Cruces. After the pass, the road to the capital would be open to us."

A decision was made to split the forces. The padre would command the force heading east from Toluca toward Lerma, where they would engage Trujillo's forces. By forced march, Allende would take the rest of the contingent south from Toluca. He would cross the river on the bridge at Atengo, then proceed northeast to outflank Trujillo at Lerma.

"We will cut his retreat over the pass to the capital and squeeze him between our forces," he told the padre.

"This crony of the viceroy may be smart enough to defend the bridge at Atengo also," Aldama said.

"He's more likely to destroy it," the padre said. "He doesn't have enough troops to make a serious defense of both the Lerma and Atengo bridges. We'll have to get there before they destroy either bridge."

I operated between the two commands, watching for potential troop movements and surprises. On October 29, Allende's unit drove Colonel Trujillo's troops from the Atengo Bridge. Meanwhile, Padre Hidalgo marched on the Lerma Bridge.

Setting out alone, I went ahead of Allende's forces on the road toward Lerma, easily getting by Trujillo's rear guard by pretending to be a Spanish merchant fleeing a rabble army of murderers and thieves. It was easy for me: I had the arrogance and horseflesh of a gachupine.

When I arrived at Lerma, I learned that Hidalgo was approaching faster than Allende's forces. Though Allende's unit was smaller than the padre's, outflanking the viceroy's army via the Atengo Bridge swung him in a wide loop through the region. He had much more ground to cover.

No sooner had I arrived at Lerma than I witnessed Trujillo retreating with the bulk of his troops. The troops babbled endlessly about what happened. The viceroy's colonel had learned that the padre's forces were advancing east on Lerma from the Toluca road, while Allende's were moving to outflank him from the south.

Trujillo retreated back to the pass called Monte de las Cruces— Mountain of the Crosses. A popular site for bandido ambushes, its name came from the two types of wood crosses placed there: crosses in memory of the bandidos' victims and crosses posses used to crucify bandidos.

When Allende and the padre's forces joined up on the road to the las Cruces pass, I accompanied a patrol sent by Allende to reconnoiter what he estimated to be the strongest defensive position in the pass. By the time we reached the coveted ground, Trujillo's forces already occupied it.

By early the next morning, the thirtieth day of October, our advanced units were fighting Trujillo's troops. I swung wide around the potential battlefields, negotiated the heights on the north side of the Toluca road, and discovered that Trujillo was getting reinforcements. The royal forces were hauling up two cannon and close to four hundred men, most of whom looked to be mounted lancers who were, of late, vaqueros from the haciendas of Yermo and Manzano. By my estimate, Trujillo's royal forces were close to my original estimate of three thousand, more than two-thirds of which were trained troops.

Not a sufficient number compared to our force, but no one knew how our vast Aztec horde would fare against regular army units. I remembered the lessons that the Spanish—and French—learned on the Iberian Peninsula: a small number of trained French troops could put out murderous volleys of musket and cannon shot. By the same token, the Spanish usually achieved victory not with great lumbering masses like the padre's army but with small, tenacious bands employing mobility, ambush, and surprise.

Our main force arrived and engaged the royal forces shortly before midday. The vanguard of our attack consisted of soldiers, infantry, and dragoons from the provincial regiments who had come over to our side as the cities of Valladolid, Celaya, and Guanajuato fell.

These troops, mostly mestizos, now comprised a force almost the size of Trujillo's royal corps but with major differences: most of our "regulars" were untrained and poorly armed, and all were deserters from militia units. As a whole, they lacked the discipline and precise order of battle of the royal forces because few officers had come over to the rebel side. While we had a number of "generals," we lacked all the lesser ranks except the foot soldiers at the bottom of the heap.

Without good training, equipment, control, and the discipline of commanders, the uniformed troops were hardly better fighting units than the unmanageable Aztecs who made up for their deficiencies with overwhelming numbers. By the time I rejoined Allende and the padre's command center, hordes of indios on foot—great tidal waves of them on each side— and bands of mounted troops on horses and mules were flanking the advancing royalist troops.

I could see from the way orders were being rendered that the padre had left the plan of battle to Allende, the professional soldier. With our superior numbers, Allende encircled the royalist forces, sending units of better armed indios—men with at least machetes or steel-tipped spears—to positions on the heights, covering both flanks of the royal forces. Circumventing the opposing army, he had several thousand additional troops seize the road to Méjico City, cutting off Trujillo's eventual retreat. Allende commanded the trained cavalry, while, on the royalists' right flank, Aldama commanded the best-trained and -equipped troops he could find.

As the uniformed rebel troops advanced, Trujillo's cannons—masked behind bushes—cut them down with grapeshot. While the cannon volleys blazed alleys of death through the advancing columns, his musketeers also fired in timed volleys, pouring a lethal hail of one-ounce lead balls into the ranks.

The synchronized firepower wreaked havoc on our lines. Men fell, screaming from ghastly wounds, while others turned and ran. By some miracle Allende and his officers kept the retreat from turning into a blind rout. Our artillery—nowhere near as effectively handled or manufactured as the royal cannons—were quickly deployed and returned fire, along with musket fire.

Then I saw something that made me question my sanity. Courageous Aztecs, completely unaware of how cannons worked, were rushing up to the enemy's cannons and shoving their sombreros into the mouths of the pieces, believing that they could stop the murderous fire that way. Their raw courage was unimaginable.

Our main force pushed forward from the road to Toluca. With Allende on the right, Aldama on the left, and a fourth unit covering the road to Méjico City at Trujillo's rear, we had completely surrounded the royalists.

Had the insurgent forces been well-trained, armed, and disciplined, we would have finished Trujillo's army on the spot. Instead the battle continued on. Our rebel commanders could not direct enough troops at the royal forces at one time to deliver the coup de grâce.

We were now within shouting distance of Trujillo's troops, so close our insurgent troops were inviting the royalists to desert and come over to the rebel cause. Asking for a parley, Trujillo attempted discussions on two different occasions only to end them. When he invited a number of our troops to come forward and discuss a peaceful resolution a third time, he suddenly ordered his men to open fire. Sixty of our men were immediately massacred and dozens more wounded.

Infuriated, Allende ordered his troops to resume the battle with no quarter given. *War to the knife!*

With a third of his command slaughtered, Trujillo sounded retreat, abandoning his cannons. With more loss of men, he fought his way out of the encirclement and broke through our forces holding the road to Méjico

City. The retreat, which began as an organized maneuver, soon disintegrated into a chaotic rout. Many of Trujillo's forces were butchered as they fled, but that treacherous, cowardly bastardo himself escaped. I led a mounted force to search for him. I found out too late that Trujillo had escaped down the road to Méjico City, disguised in a monk's robe.

We had won the battle but as we looked upon the dead—and my guess was that over two thousand on each side had fallen—I wondered what we had gained. Besides two thousand dead, it was inevitable that we would lose thousands more to wounds and desertion.

We had faced a force twenty times smaller than our own. And we had defeated them by sheer weight of numbers alone. The indios had seen the effect of musket fire in Guanajuato and knew it could be lethal. But now, in a mountain pass leading to the capital, they had seen and felt grapeshot fired at close range and knew the horror.

"We won," Marina said, with pride.

"Sí señorita, we won," I said, without enthusiasm.

"Why are you looking like all is lost?"

"We soaked the ground with the blood of thousands. By tomorrow, ten thousand, perhaps twenty thousand, will have grown tired of this war and return home to harvest maize or milk their cows or whatever it is they do to feed their families. This was not a battle between two armies. We pitted Aztec passion for freedom against the reality of cannons and mass slaughter. Passion won. This time."

"You are a defeatist," she snapped.

"That and worse," I said, giving her my kindest smile. "In truth, I don't like me much myself."

The morning after the battle, the padre led his forces through the Las Cruces pass and descended the mountain on the road to the capital. The padre summoned me while the army set out.

"I need you to evaluate the situation in the capital. When we reach the Hacienda de Cuajimalpa, a day's march from the heart of the city, I'll call a halt and await your report. But you must move with all speed; I will not be able to control this tidal wave at my back. Sometimes I think it controls me."

Marina was not coming with me. She had been training a group of women who would observe troop movements and gather marketplace gossip. We agreed that she and her petticoat spies would go ahead of the army on the road to the capital, scouting for ambushes and gathering information.

Again, I went as a gachupine on my stallion because it was less risky than being a peon. Rich criollos and gachupines were on the run from the mob; the common people were in revolt. The viceroy's soldiers and constables would not give me a second look if I bumped into them. My main concern was not to fall afoul of guerrillas or bandidos who didn't recognize me as one of their own.

NINETY-FOUR

MÉJICO CITY—THE great prize of conquerors. It was the enchanting Tenochtitlán where Montezuma once ruled a pagan royal court that rivaled the absolute power and grandeur of Kublai Khan . . . the trophy sought by Cortés and his band of bandidos disguised as conquistadors . . . a city so dazzling that Cortés's men gaped in awe when from a distance they first glimpsed its great towers and soaring temples rising from the surrounding waters, wondering if they had not been charmed by demons in a dream. Now it was the first city of the Americas, the seat of the Viceroy of New Spain. Far removed from the mother country, the viceroy wielded the power of a king.

My first stop in the city was to see Raquel. Then I would find Lizardi, The Worm, and squeeze as much fact and rumor as I could from him.

Raquel was bursting with excitement. "Word of a new miracle arrives daily. Everywhere the padre goes, he reforms the government and gives rights to the common people."

I didn't want to spoil her euphoria, but I knew that words wouldn't win the war, and battles won didn't mean victory was clenched in our fists.

We sat on the edge of the fountain in the cool shade of her courtyard. I described the progress of the war since she left us in the Bajío. She listened with rapt attention. Then she updated me on Isabella.

"I know we can't have a meaningful conversation until you know what is happening with your love."

"I don't care about Isabella. I'm over that."

"You're a liar. Look me in the eye and tell me that."

Why is it women can see through my lies?

She said, "Things have not gone well for Isabella. I suppose one could say that she got what she deserved, but having been raised in luxury myself and finding out one day I was penniless, I feel some sympathy for Isabella."

"Her husband is without money?"

"That and worse. He had a series of financial reversals, all of them compounded by his attempts to cover his wife's excesses. But as his fortune became as flighty and unfaithful as his wife, he had to leave the capital, go to Zacatecas, and sell his interest in a silver mine."

"Tell me he ended up in Guanajuato and was killed during the granary attack," I said, hoping it was true.

"He isn't brave enough to have defended the granary. He left Zacatecas with saddlebags full of gold from the sale of his mine interest. On his way back to the capitol, a guerrilla band captured him. I understand he was smart enough to conceal his identity, giving them a false name. Had they found out he was a marqués, the viceroy wouldn't have enough money to ransom him."

"What band has him?"

"That I don't know."

"How did you know this story?"

She smiled. "It came from Isabella's mouth . . . in a manner of speaking."

"You've spoken with Isabella?"

"Of course not. The marquesa wouldn't discuss such matters with a mestiza who tutors the children of the rich."

"One of her friends is your confidante?"

"Not likely. I'm a confidant of her maid." She laughed at the look on my face. "Her maid's sister works for me, helping me around the house. When she can get away, Isabella's maid comes to visit her sister. Because Isabella once cost me a fiancée—"

I cringed with guilt, avoiding her eyes.

She grinned at my discomfort. "I was naturally curious—and jealous— of Isabella's luxurious life. As everyone knows, a woman has no secrets from her maid."

"What are you saying? Isabella's husband is a captive and she's penniless?"

"Yes and no. It appears Isabella's husband hid the gold before he was captured. While Isabella may not grieve long if her husband is killed, without the gold, she'll be destitute."

"How is she avoiding widowhood and poverty?"

"I don't know. Isabella has disappeared. No one knows where, not even her maid."

"Disappeared?"

"Charitable people say she's taken her jewels to ransom her husband. The less charitable . . ." she shrugged.

¡Ay! If I had my hands on the marqués's throat—one hand squeezing the life out of him while stealing his gold with the other—I could have . . .

"My God! You should see the murder and lust on your face. Does she mean so much to you, even after she tried to have to you killed?"

"You are imagining things. Tell me about the new viceroy."

"He is firmly in power and has the support of the Spanish population, criollos and gachupines alike."

"He must be spinning in circles trying to keep up with events, walking into a revolution."

"Don't underestimate him," Raquel said. "He's resolute about defeating us. You must judge the viceroy in the context of his time in the colony. He barely set his feet on dry land at Veracruz two months ago when the padre revolted. Since that time, he has seen insurrection spread like a firestorm."

"He was a military man in Spain?"

"From what I've heard," Raquel said, "Venegas is not a great military strategist, but another politician who gained his military accreditation through position and influence. He is, however, a desperate man, with thousands of similarly desperate gachupines backing him, not to mention that all the major criollo families support him."

"We didn't get significant support from the criollos even in the Bajío."

"They are frightened of the padre's revolution. With each new conquest news of the atrocities grow."

"We have experienced much looting," I admitted.

"In the end the criollos must risk their fortunes and back the revolution as an act of courage."

I burst into laughter.

"Exactly," Raquel said. "It won't happen. The only way the criollos will back the padre is if they know for certain he has won. Then they'll beat down his door to protect their interests. Until then," she shrugged, "the Aztecs and other peons must shed their blood alone in the name of liberty."

"What is the viceroy's plan for defense of the city?" I asked.

"He has armed the la Piedad causeway and the Paseo de Bucareli heavily and placed cannons on Chapultepec. But he has also kept a considerable number of troops in the heart of the city. A friend of mine, a criollo captain loyal to the viceroy, tells me that there is criticism of the viceroy's positioning troops so deep in the capital. They believe he should have the army go out and meet the padre on a field of battle, not on city streets."

"I need to get a look at the troop positions myself."

"We can do that mañana."

"How many can he count upon? Allende estimates about seven or eight thousand troops."

"More than that," Raquel said, "perhaps as many as ten or twelve thousand, because there's been efforts to recruit troops. His main problem was inherited from Iturrigaray. When Iturrigaray was viceroy, he dispersed troops all over the colony, scattering them in widely separated provincial towns. Now Venegas is congregating them into larger units, ordering some here to protect the capital and others to retake the Bajío. The viceroy has ordered the governor of Puebla to reinforce Querétaro. He is taking the la Corona infantry unit, a unit of dragoons, two battalions of grenadiers, and a battery of four cannons.

"To protect the capital, the viceroy has ordered the regiments in Puebla, Tres Villas, and Toluca here. He's also sent a communiqué to Captain Porlier, a naval commander in Veracruz. He's instructed the captain to seize all sailors from the harbor's Spanish vessels and deliver them to the capital by forced march."

She told me the Archbishop had stepped up the church's attack on the padre.

"Besides the excommunications, the church is having its priests denounce the rebels from their pulpits, fulminating that the rebels are not just seizing political power, that theirs is a godless attack on the church, to destroy the holy religion."

Excommunication was a powerful weapon of the church. In its more extreme form, *vitandus*, which certainly would be the decree rendered, the excommunication barred the person from the sacraments of the church as well as from a Christian burial, in other words barring you from heaven itself when you died.

I dismissed the church's actions. "The padre knows the Inquisition well, and he already knows about the excommunication."

"He can't ignore the allegations and charges. He has to publish his rebuttal. We're a Christian land, and regardless of how some of us feel, the people, even the indios, are bound to the church."

"What other bad news do you have for me?"

"The viceroy has offered rewards for the leaders of the revolt. He's placed a price of ten thousand pesos on the heads of the padre and Allende, also promise of a pardon for anyone who kills or captures them."

I shrugged it off. "A bounty on our heads was always expected."

"That's not the bad news. They're only offering a reward of one hundred pesos for the bandido Juan de Zavala."

NINETY-FIVE

THAT NIGHT, I scoured the various inns in the area of the main square for Lizardi. It didn't take me long to find him. He welcomed me like a long lost brother, not out of brotherly love but out of love for my dinero.

"You're safe in the city," he said. "The viceroy and gachupines are too busy trying to battle the revolt Hidalgo has incited to deal with a petty bandido like you. They've put a large reward on the head of its leaders."

Lizardi didn't know I was part of the revolt. I told him that I'd gone north to Zacatecas after I left the capital. I also didn't volunteer that there was only a hundred-peso reward on my own head. I was outraged when Raquel said that the viceroy considered me only a small-time bandido instead of a great revolutionary hombre. For some strange reason, she found my anger amusing. How do you explain to a mere woman that a token amount was an offense against my machismo?

I steered the subject to the revolution. Naturally, Lizardi was

contemptuous—or perhaps, more accurately, jealous—of the pamphlets
put out by sympathizers of the insurrections.

"The writers are almost always priests," he sneered. "What does a
priest know about life?"

I smothered a grin but couldn't help saying "Hidalgo is a priest, and so
are some of his generals leading the rebellion."

"They'll lose; they don't know how to fight a war. They're trying to win
the support of the criollos with their publications. They shout long live the
king, long live religion, death to the French. The dribble is put out by both
sides. The war will be won by guns not words."

I was able to obtain additional information from The Worm concerning the situation in the capital. Raquel, in her enthusiasm for social change,
had a tendency to see events in a light favorable to the padre's cause.
Lizardi, on the other hand, while he spoke of social change, really meant
an increase in rights only for criollos like him. But being fundamentally
against everything that everyone else was for, he gave me insights into the
current situation, insights I found disturbing.

"The padre will never take Méjico City, at least not without destroying
it. The battle here will be bloody."

"I'm sure the padre does not expect the city to fall to its knees and surrender when he's at the causeway."

"The padre is expecting a battle, but he is not expecting the destruction of the city, and that is what will happen. This city has the highest concentration of criollos and gachupines in the colony in ordinary times. Since
the rebellion began, thousands more have flocked here for protection.
They're terrified for their homes, their families, their lives and property.
When the padre's army tries to take the city, for certain, the gachupines
will fight; they have no other alternative. And most of the criollos will join
them."

I shrugged. "They'll lose. From what I have heard, the army of the
padre swells more every day. The rumors are that it'll be one hundred
thousand strong when it reaches here."

"Over a hundred thousand Aztecs: a mindless multitude, not soldiers.
What will happen when the fighting goes street by street?"

I already knew, but I had avoided confronting it. The same thing that
happened in Spain when the people fought invaders: violence and chaos,
the rape of the entire city.

Lizardi said, "In my opinion, when his rabble face thousands of regular troops and cannon fire, they'll show the feather and run, just as they did
at Monte de las Cruces. Everyone knows the padre mainly uses his indios
as cannon fodder."

I didn't correct Lizardi on how the battle in the mountain pass went. I
already knew that when Trujillo limped back to the capital with a fraction

of his command left, the viceroy had announced the battle as a great victory for the royals.

"Does the viceroy plan to send an army out to meet the padre's forces before they reach the city?"

"How would I know? Am I a moth at his ear?"

Lizardi was more of an ankle-biting flea, but I let that pass in lieu of some flattery that might open his lips.

"They say on the streets that you know what the viceroy will do before he does it, that he reads your pamphlets for instructions on his next move."

Shallow fellow that he was, he beamed at the outrageous lie and saluted me with his mug of wine. "True, I could run this war better than anyone. The viceroy sent Trujillo with only a couple thousand men to delay the padre's advance toward the city. Trujillo has proclaimed a great victory, but I have heard that the padre's rabble army routed him handily. In all modesty, I made a suggestion that buzzed around the city and has caught the viceroy's attention in a much more urgent way."

"Which was?"

"To kill the padre, of course."

"The ten-thousand peso reward—"

"No, no, no," he shook his head, "that reward's for fools. They offer it in the hope someone standing close to the padre will suddenly stab him or shoot him. The chances of his inner circle betraying him are about as likely as the pope canonizing me. The reward was just for show." Lizardi leaned close and spoke in a whisper. "The viceroy has hired an assassin to go in disguise and get close enough to the padre to kill him."

"Do you know what disguise?"

"Who knows? My source for all this is a cousin who works as a personal notary for the viceroy. The viceroy tells him things in order to have them recorded for the history of his viceroyalty. He doesn't tell him everything, but he believes the lethal blow against Hidalgo is to come from one of his own compañeros."

"Does the assassin have a name?"

"That's all I know; that it will be someone close to him."

I wanted more information about this heinous plot, but after two jugs of wine, I learned little else, which meant I had gotten everything he knew and most of what he could make up. The only other thing of significance I got out of The Worm was the assassin's motive: money. And the reward, Lizardi heard, was staggering: one hundred thousand pesos! A large fortune, an amount the viceroy didn't dare make public, for it showed how panicked he was about the insurrection.

Lizardi did have more information about the viceroy's other actions concerning the rebels. "He has issued a decree that anyone taking up arms against his authority be shot within an hour of capture."

"Doesn't give anyone a chance to prove innocence, does it?"

"Pleas of innocence or mercy are irrelevant. The peons hate all Spanish, and if they are not part of the revolt now, they might be in the future. But he has made an offer of a pardon to any rebel who shifts his loyalty to the government."

Sí, the viceroy would give me a pardon . . . and then hang me and others like me as soon as the padre was defeated.

He said, "You know what the padre's calling it, don't you? A reconquest. Do you know how that terrifies us? When Cortés conquered the Aztecs, he completely destroyed their government, religion, even their culture, leaving them without books and schools, taking away all their land and stealing and raping their women, before loosening diseases that killed ninety percent of them."

Lizardi stared at me with both disgust and horror on his face. *"What will happen to us if they win?"*

I had to leave the city, to warn the padre of the possible assassination plot and advise him of the viceroy's defenses and troop movements.

I hurried to rejoin the padre's army, leaving behind a city racked with confusion and fear.

 **NINETY-SIX**

I MET UP with the army midday at Cuajimalpa, having made good time on the road from the capital. Cuajimalpa was an "old" region in terms of human occupation in the New World; the name itself was of indio origin. During the centuries before the Spanish conquest, succeeding indio empires had ruled it. Marina believed the name had something to do with trees. She was no doubt right. It was a forest region of Las Cruces Mountains with an elevation higher than that of Méjico City. Here, wood was cut for the capital and water was sent down by aqueduct.

Hidalgo, Allende, and the other generals occupied an inn and buildings that ordinarily served diligences, the carriages that took passengers across the mountains via the Méjico City–Toluca road.

The sky was misty as I neared the first outpost of the padre's army. I found the clean, cool, wet air of the higher altitude refreshing after a couple days of smelling the capital's manure, open sewers, and dung-smoke fires. At the top of a rise, I turned in the saddle and looked back at the capital. A ray of sunlight broke through the clouds to give the city a flickering, shadowy glow, like the reflection of candles on a gilt altar. No one has ever called Juan de Zavala a man of God, but at times like this I have borne witness to the eerie beauty of my Master's touch.

Méjico City rested on the bone pile of a mighty pagan city, its great cathedral and viceroy palace on sacred grounds where Aztec temples and Montezuma's royal quarters had once stood. Like Cortés's men, I now stared at the distant city in fear and wonderment. I had marched with the army hundreds of miles, sat at countless campfires, plotted with my friends, and had spied on cities to ascertain their weakness. Against my will, I had come to care about our army and its fate.

Once, when Rachel and I discussed the hurricane of fire and blood that was descending upon the city, she told me about a great bird in ancient Egypt. Called the "phoenix," it had bright red and gold plumage and a melodious cry. During any age, only one of the magnificent birds lived, though it counted its lifetime in centuries. As the end of its existence approached, its nest burst into flames, consuming the bird. Then, miraculously, from the pyre sprang a new phoenix.

"From the ashes of old civilizations rise new ones," Rachel had said. "Most of the countries of Europe were once colonies of the Greek and Roman empires. From time immemorial, indios in the New World battled and destroyed each other, each new empire a little different than the one it displaced. The Spanish destroyed the indio nations and substituted their own laws and customs. Now it is time we americanos destroy Spanish dominance and launch a new epoch."

I shook off my fears and urged Tempest on. I realized that educated people like Rachel knew best, that they had learned things from books that were more worldly than what I had learned in the saddle. They knew that to make way for the americanos, the Spanish had to be driven out. And they knew that it was necessary to destroy the great city in the valley so that a brave new world could rise from the ashes.

Ay, what does it matter to me? I believe in nothing. The city treated me like dirt. It was no concern of mine if it was destroyed.

But I couldn't shake a feeling of anxiety when I thought about the city.

Word of my return had traveled faster than my stallion's hooves. Marina was standing in front of the house the padre used as his quarters. Her arms were folded and her expression one of mock scorn.

"So the viceroy didn't hang you," Marina said. "There are even officers in our own army who believe you should be swinging from a gibbet instead of in and out of the beds of women you seduce with lies."

I slipped off of Tempest and gave the reins to a vaquero whose duty it was to care for officers' horses. After I instructed him on how to care for the great stallion, I turned to Marina. I gave her a sweeping salute with my wet hat. "I have missed you, too, señorita. I will permit you to feed the emptiness in my stomach before you satisfy other urges that my absence has instilled."

"You can put a rein on your urges. The padre wants to see you immediately." She squeezed my arm as I stepped onto the porch. She whispered, "He wants to see you before his generals return from their artillery inspection."

"Did you miss me?"

"Only when my feet were cold at night."

The padre greeted me warmly. We sat at a table and shared a jug of wine as I told him of what I had learned in the city. Marina fed me salted beef, cheese, and bread to calm my growling stomach and joined us at the table.

He listened patiently as I reported everything I had seen and heard, except for the rumor that an assassin had been hired to strike him down. With so many other problems on the table, the padre would wave away a threat to his life. I wanted to get the other matters out of the way before I had a serious discussion about safeguards that must be taken to protect him.

"War to the knife," he said, after I had finished. "Isn't that what General Palafox told the French commander when he demanded the surrender of Zaragoza?"

"Yes, a fight without quarter, to the death."

"And the fighting went on from house to house, man to man—"

"Woman to woman, not to mention the bravery of the maiden María," Marina said.

I nodded. "Yes, and even children picked up rocks and cast them down on the invaders."

"War to the knife," he repeated. He stroked his chin and looked beyond me, out the window to where children were playing. "People defending their homes against invaders. The courage of my fellow Spaniards fills me with pride. Too bad the common people of Spain can't decide our fate. They would understand our need to escape the heel of the gachupines."

"You say that the viceroy is concentrating his forces inside the city," Marina asked, "and will force us to fight our way in? He won't come out and fight us as our army approaches?"

"I doubt he'll face us in the field," I said. "He hopes one of the royal forces he's ordered to his defense will attack us from the rear as we besiege the city. By keeping his troops inside the city, he will also force us to take it street by street—"

"House by house—"

"Yes, padre. As you know, the city teems with criollos and gachupines who view us as their foe. They have heard of those incidents in which the indios lost control—"

"Those incidents were trivial," Marina snapped. "How many times have the Spanish hanged a hundred Aztecs picked at random to frighten thousands?"

"I'm not justifying their beliefs, Señorita Sharp Tongue, I'm merely relating them. The battle for the capital will differ from that of other cities we've taken. The viceroy already has an army of thousands under his command, and every Spaniard with the courage to fight will swell the ranks. We'll have to take the castle and cannon mounts at Chapultepec and fight our way to the heart of the city, perhaps to the viceroy's palace itself."

"And what are our chances of success?" the padre asked.

"He's a defeatist," Marina warned.

"Everyone who doesn't agree with you is a defeatist. But, yes, padre, we can win. We must, however, go in with resolve. The battle could take many days. Our men must not leave the fight to harvest their maize."

"My people have taken the bloody blunt of every battle," Marina said.

I grinned at her rising ire. "As they must do so in this one. But they should be told the battle might last days. What is *your* opinion, padre? Do you doubt we can take the city?"

He splayed his fingers on the table and stared down at them as he spoke. "Never in the history of the New World, not even during the days of great Aztec empires, has an army the size of this one marched to battle. We lost twenty thousand to desertion after the last battle and already more than that have joined us. In two or three days, I am certain we will have far beyond a hundred thousand indios in our ranks. As we push our way into the city, more will join us from the surrounding areas in never-ending waves. In the region around the capital, live a million and a half people, and most of them are indios. By the time we storm the viceroy's palace, I suspect we will have over two hundred thousand in our ranks."

He paused and stared at us, his countenance calm but his eyes ablaze. He spoke in a hoarse whisper. "If so, nothing will stop them. Tens of thousands of indios will reconquer the city that once dominated their civilization, a tidal wave of rage and retribution avenging centuries of humiliation at watching their women being raped, at having their land stolen, their backs broken by the whip, and their souls shattered by bondage in the mines and haciendas. The viceroy has made a tragic error in garrisoning the city. He should march out and do battle. He forces us to fight our way into the city, demanding that we hurtle a hurricane of rage down every street of the capital. Once the battle begins and the indios see their comrades fall beside them . . ."

"It will be like the alhóndiga," I finished for him, "only instead of a few hundred angry indios taking revenge on the defenders, it will be hundreds of thousands."

The padre's features cracked with emotion. "Once their Aztec rage ignites," he whispered, "nothing will stop their bloody revenge."

"Santa María," Marina crossed herself.

I left them to check on Tempest and make sure the vaquero I gave the reins to earlier had rubbed him dry and fed him properly. I also needed fresh air. The discussion about the upcoming battle had increased my strange uneasiness about an attack on the capital.

The poor padre carried in his heart his love not only for the indios but for all people. And he couldn't escape his fate: his soul would be scarred by those who fell fighting for the revolution and by all those who fell fighting the insurgents.

I was approaching our makeshift stable when I saw a coach with a heraldic shield on its door.

The door to the coach opened and a man, laughing, stepped down. Behind him, joining him in their private joke, laughing gaily, was my darling Isabella. Had the earth opened beneath my feet and swallowed me, I would not have been more surprised. She saw me, too, and after a moment of stunned surprise, she smiled.

"Señor Zavala, so nice to see you again."

From her tone, we might have last seen each other at a social ball rather than at an ambush of murder and deceit. But right down to my toes I felt the bell-like chiming of her voice, stirred by her lush red lips, her white satin skin . . .

I kept my composure by removing my hat and holding it close to my chest and bowing like a peon before his master. "Señora Marquesa."

"This is Don Renato del Miro, my husband's nephew."

"Buenos días," I said.

He didn't reply but just took my measure. My hand instinctively went to my sword; he had insulted me. I was too far beneath him for a civil greeting. I knew him well, though this was the first time I had set eyes upon him. It was his type that I was so familiar with. He was tall and well proportioned, a rich, idle Spaniard but one who was physically fit. His clothes were of the finest cloth, his boots as soft as a fawn's ass. I knew from the way he carried himself that he would ride well, handle a sword and pistol expertly, and no doubt was doused with expensive perfume that gave him a sweet smell.

I knew him because he was so much like me . . . when I was a gachupine. He was a caballero, no doubt about it, but not an alameda dandy. He was not hard from life in the saddle as I was, but he moved as one who was quick on his feet and just as quick with a knife, especially when your back was turned. I had instantly sensed something slippery about him . . . I knew an hombre malo when I saw one. I had had much practice at it.

Isabella said, "You must pardon us, but we have a meeting with the padre."

I gave the nephew a dark look as he swept by me. It was unworthy of me to think of such a thing about Isabella, but I had to wonder whether something other than a family bond had brought them together. Her sparkling eyes and the lightness in her step belied concern for her hostage husband. Was it jealousy on my part? Did my heart still ache for this woman who had lured me into an ambush?

Ay, you wonder why I didn't throw myself on the ground and grovel at the sight of her? You think me that weak? That spineless? Eh, I'm a tough hombre and tough hombres don't grovel.

Besides, the ground was muddy.

When I finished rubbing down Tempest, I lay in the horse shed on fresh hay near the corral and smoked a cigarro. I was sucking on a wine jug when Marina found me there.

"The gachupine puta you desire is talking to the padre."

"I lust only for you, and don't call her names. She's a lady."

"And what am I? An india slave you sate your lust on but don't consider a woman of refinement?"

"You're an Azteca princess, the embodiment of Doña Marina herself. I love you from afar only because I'm a lowly lépero."

"You're a liar . . . about everything except being a lépero. Aren't you interested in knowing why she's meeting with the padre?"

I blew smoke rings. "Isn't it obvious? Bandidos who swear fealty to our cause hold her husband ransom. She wants the padre to intercede."

"They were discussing the matter when I found myself in need of fresh air. But I'm glad I saw her. I always wondered what kind of woman you would desire. She's perfect for a man who only thinks with his garrancha: pretty on the outside but shallow and witless within."

I blew more smoke rings; she wasn't through with me.

"But that nephew, Renato," she said, "what a man! Handsome, dashing, a real swordsman—"

She kicked my leg.

"What was that for?"

"Your look of jealous rage when I mentioned the nephew. You haven't gotten over that gachupine slut." She put her hands on her hips and glared down at me. "Well, listen to this, Señor Lépero. Your woman was falling all over the man when she was speaking to the padre. As a woman, I can tell she's spreading her legs for him."

She ran from the shed. As I watched her retreating back, I suddenly realized that I had drawn my dagger.

NINETY-SEVEN

THE GENERALÍSSIMO REQUIRES your presence."

I was playing cards with indios when the order came. I tossed in my hand and followed the padre's aide.

Two hours had passed since Isabella and her husband's nephew had gone in to see the padre. I had watched them come out of his quarters nearly an hour ago and climb into her coach. The coach stayed where it was, curtains drawn . . . and I was certain that I had observed it sway and bounce a little from the movements of the two inside. The movement was enough to send my imagination and temper soaring.

I was halfway to the padre's inn when Marina intercepted me. "Strap on your sword and have a pistol under your coat," she whispered.

"Why?"

"The padre sent a surrender demand to the viceroy. The criollo officers don't know it yet, but the messenger has returned with word the viceroy has refused the demand."

"That's no surprise."

"The officers have objected to the delay caused by waiting for a reply. They're angry that we haven't already marched on the capital. They want Allende to assume command."

"The Aztecs won't follow Allende. Despite anything heard from the other officers, Allende himself is an honorable man. If he made a move against the padre, he would do it to his face and explain his reasons."

"Allende isn't the only criollo officer in this army. Stop thinking like a gachupine dandy and arm yourself."

Is this my curse in life, to love strong women? I sometimes wonder what it would be like to have a woman who polished my boots instead of using hers on my backside.

We assembled in the main room of the inn. Besides Marina, the padre, and myself, Allende, Aldama, and six other high-ranking officers were present. I noticed a small dog had attached itself to the padre. His aide carried it outside so it wouldn't disturb the meeting.

"As you know, amigos," the padre began, "Viceroy Venegas has rejected our terms for a peaceful surrender of the capital. Instead, he's rallying the city against us. He has had the sacred image of the Los Remedios Virgin removed from its shrine and brought to the cathedral. A witness tells me that Venegas went to the cathedral, knelt before the Sacred Virgin, placed in its hands his vice-regal staff of office, and appointed the Virgin captain-general of his army."

Religious fervor had risen to a fever pitch as the revolutionary army closed in on the capital. The viceroy's conscription of the Virgin de los Remedios was a masterstroke, mirroring the padre's recruitment of the Virgin of Guadalupe.

"My emissary says that the viceroy has created los Remedios banners in imitation of our own Guadalupe ones. Thus, when our armies meet in the field, each side will be asking the Mother of God to speed victory to them."

Allende stood and said, "Each day we delay gives the viceroy more opportunity to prepare. We must follow through with the victory in the pass. We know the viceroy has sent desperate pleas for military commanders all over the colony to march to his aid. When the people of the city see the dust raised by tens of thousands of indios en route to their city, they'll panic. Thousands will flee. If we attack now, we carry with us the momentum we've gathered. If we hesitate, the Spanish armies in the field will attack our rear while we are bogged down fighting to take the city street by street."

General murmuring among the military men supported Allende's opinion that they must attack the capital immediately.

Father Hidalgo spoke slowly, his eyes going from one general to another. "I have given this matter great thought, because we have so many complications to consider. We overcame the viceroy's forces in the mountains but now face a much greater force in the city. And, as we all know, other royal forces are moving to relieve the city. In addition to the many casualties our army suffered in the battle for Las Cruces, we now suffer thousands of desertions. Our men are tired and poorly equipped. I do not believe that the fighting level of our army is as high as we can make it. We need to replenish our supplies of powder, musket balls, cannons."

"What are you saying, Miguel?" Allende asked. "You want to spend more time preparing here at Cuajimalpa? We don't believe—"

He stopped, because the padre was already shaking his head. "No, not here, we would be exposed to the viceroy's forces. I have decided we will move our forces back to the Bajío to regroup."

The padre's statement exploded in the room. Officers gasped in disbelief and jumped to their feet. My hand went to the hilt of my sword. Allende muttered a curse. He was as shocked as the others. The priest didn't flinch. "We have come a great distance in a short time. Starting with a few hundred, now we lead scores of thousands. We must shine in God's eyes; otherwise we would not have achieved so much. And the victory of the revolution is not just along the path we march. In the north at Zacatecas and San Luis Potosí, to the west at Acapulco and in a dozen other places, the people rise against the gachupines."

"True," Allende said, "but we must secure the final victory by taking the capital now."

"We're not ready to fight an army in the capital that's both large and entrenched."

"We have to fight," Allende emphasized. "That's why we are here, why you made the shout for freedom in Dolores."

"We must fight when we're better prepared. The Bajío is open to us; we'll go there and regroup, resupply, then set out again."

"That would be a great mistake—"

The padre shook his head vigorously. "I have made my decision. In the morning, we turn the army north."

"Insanity!" Allende struggled with his emotions. For a moment I thought he was going to leap at the padre. I eased my sword a third of the way out of its scabbard. Across from me, I saw Marina tense, her hand buried in her coat. If Allende moved toward the padre, she would attack him with her dagger.

I couldn't depend on Marina stopping Allende if he went for the padre; the general was too strong and swift. My left hand went to my gun, and I kept my right hand on my sword. I would first shoot Allende, because he was the most dangerous and at almost the same time strike at Aldama with my sword.

Allende suddenly spun on his heel and rushed from the room, his face a mask of rage. Silence followed his exit. Two of the other officers stared at me, and I stared back. I suddenly realized that indio vaqueros with machetes were assembled just outside the door. I caught Marina's eye and nodded. She was one smart woman. She should have been a general.

Aldama broke the silence. He spoke slowly to keep control of the emotion in his voice. "Padre, you are our leader. We all look to you for counsel and wisdom, but this matter is purely a military one. We must respectfully insist that you permit our military training to override your opinion. We're in striking distance of the capital; we're moving with enormous momentum. By the time we reach the outskirts of the city, our army will double—"

"I'm sorry. I've made my decision. Notify your officers to pass the word, we march north in the morning."

The officers filed out, anger, frustration, even shock written on their faces. With the others gone, the padre appeared ready to collapse. As Marina went to him, I stepped outside to make sure that the officers who left would not be coming back in a hurry with their swords drawn. I nodded at the vaqueros who had assembled outside the door. "Stay alert," I told them.

Marina came out behind me. She spoke rapidly to one of the vaqueros in an indio tongue. I followed her words enough to realize that she was instructing him to have a hundred men at the ready—she suspected a murder plot.

Spaniards might conceivably return with a company of men and place the padre under arrest, but I sensed that Allende or Aldama would not lead them; both were men of honor. I mentioned that to Marina. "If there is to be trouble from either of them, they'll confront the padre to his face, not stab him in the back."

"I protect the padre, from whatever source. You said there was an assassination plot. Now I'm sure trouble is brewing."

"I don't doubt that. I saw the faces of the officers when they left. They've risked everything for this moment: their fortunes, families, reputations, their lives. The only thing that can save them from the wrath of the gachupines is to win the war and destroy the citadel of Spanish power. They wanted a quick fight, an overwhelming force of indios and a certain victory. With the capital only hours away, we are now making a long, hard journey to the Bajío, prolonging the war and its outcome."

"The criollos see this revolution," Marina said, "as a way to defeat the gachupines through the spilling of Aztec—not criollo—blood. They see the revolution in military terms; they don't understand that the padre sees it in human terms. He doesn't want to destroy everything the revolution stands for just for the sake of winning battles."

"You knew?" I asked her. "You knew he had decided not to attack the city?"

"I guessed, but he'd told no one."

"It makes sense: regroup, come back stronger."

She locked eyes with me and lowered her voice as she spoke. "He prayed that the viceroy would surrender the city. You know why he's not attacking the city. You just don't want to acknowledge it."

I knew the padre shared a common bond with the criollo officers who joined the revolution: courage. But he was worlds apart from them in how he exercised it. For the military men, a man stood tall only when he fought. But the padre knew that it often took more courage to back away from a fight, even one you knew you could win. No, it was not a lack of military skill or courage on the padre's part that kept him from attacking the city. It was not even an abhorrence of bloodshed; much blood had been spilled at the battle for the granary.

"War against the people of the city," I said.

She nodded. "To attack the city is not to do battle with an army; it is to do war to the knife against the *people*."

"He took to heart my descriptions of the bravery of the Spanish people battling the French invaders—"

"Hearing it from you only confirmed what he had already concluded, that's why we stopped here rather than continuing to the capital. He hoped that the viceroy would spare the city, that he would either surrender or have the courage to march out and meet on a field of battle. When the viceroy established his defenses in the heart of the city, the padre realized that he couldn't win without house-to-house fighting. That's why he sent you into the city, to confirm what he already knew."

"He wouldn't be able to control the rage of the Aztecs."

"God Almighty Himself couldn't control one hundred thousand of my people who suddenly had the opportunity to strike back at the bastardos who have kept them enslaved for centuries." She shook her head. "Those criollos don't understand. The padre knows blood will have to be spilled to bring the revolution about, but he launched a revolt to fight *Spanish* armies, not people. His plan is to draw away from the capital, regroup and resupply in the Bajío, and wait for the viceroy's armies to seek him out. He will meet them on the field of battle."

I was humbled by the padre's intelligence, foresight, and humanity. I wasn't sure what caused me to care only for women and horses . . . and for a simple priest who was capable of holding the whole world in his hands. Whether he had been a good priest or a bad one, I didn't know; certainly from the church's standpoint, he was often a problem, asking questions that they didn't want to answer, questions like why churches had become storehouses of wealth while children starved. Now he saw beyond the battle to all the people who would suffer and die if he allowed himself to think only as a military man.

"Don't think he's just a priest while you're a real man. The padre was not born a priest; he was born on a hacienda and raised as a caballero with a horse between his legs and a pistol in his hand. But unlike you and Allende and the other criollo officers, he doesn't think with what he has in his pants. And he has more heart than a saint. He'll fight gachupines who have no reason to be in the colony other than to steal and enslave our people, but he won't war on people defending their homes.

"He's in charge," I said. "The officers can't change that. The criollos they expected would join the revolt have not done so. The ones who joined are brave and reckless, but they must understand that they don't command the Aztecs. That will keep them from attempting to remove the padre."

"That will keep some of them from trying it, but not the ones who see themselves as king if the old king is dead. Nor will it keep your mystery assassin from the capital from attempting it." She tapped me on the chest. "Keep your eyes and ears open, señor. Without the padre, the revolution will be lost."

I was about to retire to the company of my horse, a jug of brandy, and a cigarro, when the padre's servant came out and called my name. "He wishes your attendance. You and the lady."

"Marina—"

"No, señor, the Spanish woman."

Only then did I realize that Doña Isabella and Renato were approaching.

NINETY-EIGHT

ISABELLA FLASHED ME a radiant smile. The nephew gave me an indifferent glance, the empty expression of a gachupine wiping his muddy boots on the back of a prone servant. The purpose of such expressions was to let peons know they were beasts of burden, nothing more. If he hadn't been a guest of the padre, he would have gotten one of my boots up his backside, the other in his cojones.

The padre faced a window, his back to us, when we entered the room. He turned to greet us, poker-faced. His features revealed nothing of the man who had just backed down career military officers in a furious test of wills.

"Señora, señores, I have called you here to discuss that matter of common interest. Juan is my right arm in these situations. He was away on a mission of great urgency and has not been informed of your request." He spoke to me. "The marquesa has suffered a great tragedy. Her husband, Don Humberto del Miro, one of the most noble and distinguished Spaniards in the colony, was recently arrested by followers of our revolution who demand repayment from him for monies that the marqués took in the form of profits. Unless repayment is made, the revolucionarios holding him will be forced to implement sanctions."

The padre was using polite terms to say that Isabella's husband was a thieving gachupine pig and that the bandidos holding him would skin him out with hooked knives and hot pincers, then pack his bleeding carcass in rock salt if he didn't come up with ransom money.

"I am also informed that prior to his capture, Don Humberto hid a considerable amount of gold, the proceeds from a mine sale. And, as best we know, the revolucionarios holding him don't know his true identity, nor do they know he possesses hidden gold. Is that correct, señora?"

"Yes, we need to recover the gold before the bandidos do."

"To buy your husband's freedom," I added.

Isabella's hand flew to her mouth. "Of course, that's what I meant . . . to buy his freedom."

"How do we get the gold?" I asked.

The padre chuckled. "That's why the señora is here. She doesn't have the funds to buy her husband's freedom and can't retrieve the gold until her husband is free. She's asked that I intercede. As you know, Juan, many of our revolucionarios operate independently."

I nodded and had the good manners not to mention that some of them were more bandits than revolucionarios.

"In this case, the leader of the group—a man who calls himself General López—is not willing simply to turn over the marqués to us. He wants to be paid. After all, he has to feed his troops."

"But of course," I muttered.

How can they maintain themselves in pulque and putas if they don't steal?

"Due to the panic gripping the colony, the señora cannot raise the ransom."

"How much is he asking?"

"Five thousand pesos."

I shrugged. "Not a king's ransom."

"He doesn't know the man is a marqués. Even if she raised the ransom, she probably couldn't get to López, who is headquartered far north in León. The entire Bajío is in the hands of the revolutionary movement. There is also the matter of insuring that General Lopez keeps his promise once he is paid."

He nodded at Isabella. "What I have arranged with the señora is very simple: We will provide safe conduct to León. We will also pay the ransom demand to Lopez. In return, we will get half of the gold that the marqués has hidden. She believes his gold hoard to be in excess of two hundred thousand pesos."

"Yes, that's how much he got from the sale," she said.

The padre raised his hands and smiled at me. "You see how simple it is, Juan? You escort the señora and her husband's nephew to León, pay the ransom, collect the gold, and bring half of it back to me."

I kept a straight face. "Sí, simple beyond words."

The padre told them he needed to speak to me alone about military matters, and they left. Isabella gave me a warm smile as she exited.

As soon as they were out the door, I said, "No problem, padre. I escort these people across hundreds of miles of territory patrolled by roving bands of highwaymen and royal army patrols. If I don't get caught and murdered by bandidos or the viceroy's men, I pay off this López, who calls himself a general, and hope he doesn't get suspicious and fry my feet over an open fire to find out where the rest of the money is. Assuming I fool him and obtain the marqués's freedom, I still have to learn the location of the hidden gold and seize half of it before Don Humberto and his nephew can murder me. Then, after dodging the roving bands of bandidos and royal soldiers for hundreds of more miles, I return with the gold."

I was immediately embarrassed. "The mission is insignificant compared to what you have to deal with every day."

"We all have our duty to perform. Yours is as dangerous as those soldiers who receive the first volley from the enemy's muskets. I'm asking if you will do this mission, Juan, not commanding you to do so. I'm sure you can understand the importance of the marqués's gold to our cause."

I shrugged. "A hundred thousand pesos is a lot of money. By coincidence, it's the same amount the viceroy is offering for your life."

"If I could give my life and spare our people the horrors of war, I would cheerfully deliver myself to his assassin."

"When do you want us to leave for León?"

"In the morning, but not directly to León. The most direct route to the north would take you into the arms of royal forces. I need to get a personal message to José Torres, who is operating somewhere near Guadalajara. This amazing man was nothing more than an uneducated laborer who asked me to permit him and a few followers to seize Guadalajara. At first I was taken aback, but something about him caused me to have faith. I've heard that he has had some success against royal forces in the area. I will give you a message to deliver to him. Hopefully, you will be able to locate him."

"This General López—"

"A bandit and murderer with no alliance to our cause but not a stupid man. A diamondback rattles before it strikes; López doesn't. And watch your back with the marqués's nephew. He needs us now, but under his breeches he's a gachupine. Once the gold is recovered, your death would profit him greatly."

The padre didn't mention Isabella. I didn't know if Marina had told him of our history but decided not to bring up the subject. I was confused as to what my own feelings were.

Father Hidalgo gripped my shoulder. "Juan, when I said you were my right hand, I didn't express all that you have meant to me. You have been my eyes and ears, and I'll sorely miss you. But your mission is important. The marqués's gold can buy us cannons and muskets."

I paused at the door while he made one more observation.

"The capital is a transcendently beautiful city. Such beauty is singularly rare and eternally precious. It would be a great sin to destroy God's gift."

 **NINETY-NINE**

ISABELLA AND RENATO waited for me outside.

"I will need a good horse," Renato said, "and a spare. Bring me the best mounts in the camp, and I will select the ones I want. My saddle and—"

I wasn't certain if it was the look on my face or the look of alarm on Isabella's face as she reached out and grabbed his arm. "Renato—"

I stepped closer to him, causing him to take a step back. "Listen, Señor Nephew, your life's blood is not hemorrhaging from your throat, and cojones still tremble between your legs only because the padre asked me to help Isabella. But you're irrelevant to this mission. If you continue to annoy me, I'll cut out your liver and feed it to a cur."

Isabella stepped close enough for me to smell her sweetness. "Juan, you must forgive him. He's from Spain and is not aware that you were . . . are . . . a caballero. Please do not take offense. I need your assistance. Will you give it to me?"

"The last time I answered your call I was nearly murdered." I grinned. "But I am under the padre's command. I'll assist in getting your loving husband back into your arms and his gold for our cause."

"Gracias, Juan, that's all I wish."

"We leave at dawn," I told them. I jerked my head toward the corralled horses. "Find mounts for yourself and be prepared to pay for them. We'll use the six mules attached to your carriage."

"Use for what?" Renato said. "They're needed to pull the marquesa's coach."

"She won't be traveling by coach."

"She can't ride a—"

"Do I appear dense to you? Or are you simply so stupid you have no understanding of how we must travel?"

He stiffened, and his hand went to his dagger. Isabella grabbed his arm again. I prayed he would draw his blade.

"Renato, you must apologize to Juan," she said.

She couldn't have humiliated him more had she smacked his face.

"It is all right, Señora Marquesa." I laughed. "When I require an apology, I'll beat it out of him."

"*Renato!*" She grabbed his dagger hand. "Stop it!"

He took a deep breath, and then underwent a complete metamorphosis: his eyes glazed over as if he had been sniffing loco weed, and he smiled.

"My apologies, . . . *señor*."

His words sickened my stomach. I'd never sung with the angels, but I hadn't slithered like a snake, either. A man of honor would have pulled his weapon. To swallow my insult while harboring murderous rage was deception, not honor.

"We can't take your coach," I told her. "It's too slow and would attract bandidos. You'll ride in a litter so we can leave the main road. If we stay on the road, a royal patrol or band of bandidos will quickly waylay us. Two of your carriage mules will be used to straddle the litter; the others will carry supplies." I nodded toward the inn. "The landlord has a litter out back. Buy it from him."

I left the two of them and found Marina, standing by the stable.

"I need four vaqueros," I told her, "good riders who have proven themselves in battle and who can use a machete for something more than chopping maguey. I need—"

"Your needs have already been answered, Señor Lépero. The padre told me to look to your supplies and honor guard this morning. I have twelve men for you, all skilled with horses and weapons and blessed with courage. They all have muskets, the oldest and rustiest that we have, but only one ball each." She grinned. "You see, the padre learned much about guerrilla warfare from you."

"How is it, señorita, that I seem to always be the last to know what course my life will take?"

She smiled, sweet and sour. "Perhaps it is because you do not know how to deal with life yourself. You approach life much like an enraged bull bleeding from the banderillas impaling its shoulders. You stomp wildly around, blindly; no one knows what man you will gore or what woman you will mount."

I left her after agreeing I would ride out to a lake and take a bath before I crawled into bed with her later. When I returned from my bath, I gave Tempest extra feed and explained to him that we would be heading north in the morning.

"Talking to your horse?"

Isabella had entered the shed behind me. She shook her head. "That always annoyed me when you courted me in Guanajuato. I never knew whom you loved the most, the horse or me."

Tempest answered for me with a whinny. I stroked the side of his neck. "Horses are much more loyal than women."

"Yes, I know. You can starve them, beat them, ride them until they drop, and all they require is a few handfuls of grain. Women require much more."

"Some women require even more than other women," I murmured.

"And what do you have to offer a woman, Juan Zavala? One day you were the grandest caballero in Guanajuato and the next you were a murderous bandido. Word comes that you died in the Yucatán, and then you return from the dead as a hero of the war in Spain. Rather than leading a peaceful life, on your return you approach a married woman, embarrassing me and humiliating my husband, who would suffer sure death if he called you out."

"You lured me into a trap."

"They said they would beat you to restore my husband's honor. What did you expect me to do? How many women are entitled to conduct their own affairs? Make their own decisions? I did what my husband told me to do because I'm a good wife."

I threw the feed bucket against the wall. "They disgraced me in Guanajuato and nearly murdered me in Méjico City, and I was at fault? Maybe I'm responsible for your husband's capture, too?"

She frowned at me. "Of course you're responsible. The humiliation you dealt caused business problems for him. Men who had done business with him for years suddenly called in his loans, so he went to Zacatecas to sell his mining interest."

¡Ay! The woman was saying that I was the source of her problems, the loss of her husband and fortune? The accusation was so unexpected, I didn't know what to say.

She came closer. "Whatever happened in the past must be forgotten. We must start over again. Back in the capital they say that this revolution the padre has started will change the face of the colony, no matter who wins. Things will change for us, too, Juan. Help me free my husband, recover my fortune, and we shall be together forever."

Later that evening, I took Marina with a pent-up passion that had raged in me for years. Spent, I rolled off her and lay gasping for breath. I saw the flash of the knife blade in the light of the single candle burning in the room. I jerked back, and the blade barely missed my throat but caught my ear. I rolled away from Marina and onto my feet, clutching my cut ear.

"I'm bleeding."

"I'm sorry I missed your jugular."

"Have you gone loco?"

She threw the knife aside and slipped back under the blankets.

"If you call me Isabella again, I will cut off your cojones and shove them down your throat."

¡Ay de mí!

 **ONE HUNDRED**

W<small>E AWOKE TO</small> shouting outside.

"We're under attack!" Marina cried.

Only after pulling on my pants, did I grab my pistol and sword. After all, to die without pants on would be a great indignity.

I ran outside to find Marina. She had armed herself with a machete before pulling a blanket over her nakedness.

As we stood there in the hut's doorway, half-naked and well armed, the padre's aide-de-camp, Rodrigo, ran to us. "Come, there's trouble."

When we hurried to the padre's quarters, we discovered that neither were we under attack by the viceroy's army nor were the criollo officers revolting.

"Poison," the padre said. He spoke the word softy, as if it were hard for him to pronounce. "Someone has attempted to poison me."

He pointed at a plate on the table. "It was in the beef."

We followed his gaze. The dog that had adopted him lay on the floor, dead.

"I gave him a piece of beef," the padre said.

"I fed the padre late," his aide explained. "He wasn't hungry, but finally I convinced him he must take food or ruin his health."

"Who prepares his food?" I asked.

"His cook."

The cook was in his tent. He lay face down behind maize sacks. I knelt beside the body and turned it so I could see his face. His throat had been slit.

"Dagger," I said. "Someone slit his jugular."

No one had seen the attack on the cook. The padre's aide had found the tray on a table already there. He thought the cook had gone to relieve himself.

No one had seen anything suspicious. Whoever killed the cook and poisoned the padre's food had disappeared into the night.

When I returned with Marina to her tent, I saw Isabella and Renato standing outside the carriage. Something bothered me, but I couldn't put my finger on it.

Awakening in the middle of the night, I realized what it was. When I had insulted Renato, he hadn't reached for his sword or pistol; he had grabbed for his dagger.

The cook had been killed by an expert knife man.

At first light I saddled Tempest and told Isabella, Renato, and the vaqueros that our route to Guadalajara would take us back over the mountain pass. "We will be less likely to face the viceroy's troops in the high rocks."

After checking our stock and supplies, I made sure that Isabella's litter was properly hitched to the two mules. When we were ready to move out, I paused beside Renato, who was preparing to mount his horse.

"We must have peace between us, señor," I said.

"Of course."

"But be aware that I know you're a swine and that I'll no doubt kill you before this mission is over." The devil must have put these words on my tongue.

As we left, the great, unwieldy multitude that was the padre's army was awakening like a big, sleepy, undulating beast. I waved to Marina and the padre. They stood on the front step of the padre's quarters and watched us leave.

I suspect the great Aztec horde was puzzled at turning away from the capital. The criollo officers were unhappy to abandon it. Having rubbed shoulders with those of greater book learning than myself, I had, in my own opinion, sharpened my mind against theirs in the way a whetstone hones a blade. Even so, I didn't know if the padre's retreat was wise.

I knew in my bones that what had occurred in those few moments yesterday in which the padre had by force of personality saved a great city from being sacked, would be discussed and debated by scribes and historians for many lifetimes. It was as critical a moment as that when Caesar pondered crossing the Rubicon, when Anthony and Cleopatra lay in bed and discussed stealing an empire, when Alexander the Great pondered what he should do when he was informed that his father had been assassinated and the throne was contested. Jesus Christ experienced such a moment when he made the fateful decision to go to Jerusalem during Passover. Cortés had cast the dye when he ordered his own ships burned at Veracruz to strand his army on dangerous ground and force them to conquer or die.

Eh, I was beginning to surprise myself by my command of politics and history.

Turning in the saddle, I saw that Isabella and the bastardo nephew were staring at the horde of half-naked indios preparing for their march.

"Look at that multitude, you gachupines," I shouted at the two of them over my shoulder. "Look at the peons you have spat upon because you thought God stood at your side. But they have God on their side now, and theirs is a terrible god of rage. They frighten you, don't they? They should, amigos, because they want what you have. Remember them well, because the next time you see them, they'll be burning your houses and rustling your haciendas . . . They'll take your silver and gold and the land you stole from them . . . They'll whip your backs and bed your women!"

I spurred Tempest and shot on ahead.

 ONE HUNDRED AND ONE

THE GUADALAJARA REGION was a long, hard ride from the encampment at Cuajimalpa. I drove our band on at a fast pace, trading our tired horses and mules along the way for fresh mounts, replacing the ones that went lame or simply wore out. I had mortified Isabella when I told her she couldn't bring her carriage or maid, but she endured the trip's hardship and boredom without complaint.

My problems with Renato subsided. We were both too occupied with the demanding pace to bump heads. Still I hadn't forgotten the way he caressed his dagger. And the more I was around him, the more suspicious I became of him. Besides his love of daggers, something else bothered me. He was a good rider, as good as I. While riding was second nature to a caballero, I found some of his mannerisms alien, such as the way he used a knife when he ate, how he was able to sit on his haunches and eat a plate of food as if he'd spent his life on the trail. I finally decided that what bothered me was his uncharacteristic hardness; wealthy young caballeros were notorious for their physical softness, not their survival skills.

I wondered whether he was really a young man of great wealth or a seasoned soldier of fortune hired to protect Isabella, kill her husband, defraud Hidalgo . . . and murder me.

I kept one man riding point a mile ahead of us and another scouting the rear, watching out for royal patrols and bandidos. Each time they spotted a large group of men in our area, we left the road. Besides my worthless life, I carried nearly twenty pounds of gold as ransom money—more than enough to tempt most men.

When we were a day's ride from Guadalajara, we heard that Torres had taken the city. I was amazed that a man unschooled in the military arts—and in his case also illiterate—could capture an important city.

Upon arrival, I permitted Isabella to check into an inn for the night. Instructing Renato to purchase fresh mounts for our trip to León, I immediately went to the government buildings at the city center to find José Torres, the rebel leader who had made himself master of the city.

I had been to Guadalajara only once, when I was fifteen and accompanied Bruto on a business trip. While silver-rich Guanajuato dominated the Bajío, Guadalajara was the largest city in the western region. Its wealth and prominence came not from mining but from its position as the region's marketplace for agriculture and its commercial center.

Torres had captured a real prize. Although the city of Guadalajara had a population of only about thirty-five thousand—about half of the number in Puebla and Guanajuato—the intendancy of the province was composed of over half a million souls, making it the third largest province in the colony. The administrative region of the intendancy extended to the Pacific Ocean and all the way along the coast north to the two Californias.

In many ways, Guadalajara and much of the Bajío had developed differently from the Valley of Méjico in the heart of the colony. Lacking the teeming indio population of the tradition-bound central plateau, the Guadalajara region developed a farming and ranching culture. Much to the displeasure of the gachupines, these small landowners were more independent in both attitude and deed than the peons of the central valley.

The city was founded by another of the breed of Spanish plunderers, Nuño de Guzmán, an enemy of Cortés in the snake pit of Spanish politics. In 1529, eight years after the fall of the Aztecs, Guzmán set out from the capital with an army to explore and subjugate the western region. Two years later he founded Guadalajara, although the city changed locales three times before settling at its present location. He called the region New Galicia, naming it after his native province in Spain, and anointed himself Marqués de Tonala, aping Cortés's noble title of Marqués del Valle.

In bringing the region under his authority, he brutally pillaged the land, burned villages, and enslaved indios. The indios called him *Señor de la Borca y Cuchillo*, implying that he used both noose and knife to kill. There's a story that he hanged six indio headmen—known as caciques—

because they didn't sweep the path he walked on. The viceroy ultimately tried him for his excesses and shipped him back to Spain.

After the great silver strikes in Zacatecas and Guanajuato, Guadalajara became a major provider of food and other needs of the mines.

As I walked through its main square at siesta time, I passed a couple performing a dance reminiscent of the courtship of doves, the jarabe. A dance of flirtation, the man vigorously pressed himself on his coy woman partner. I saw one version of the dance in which the woman pranced around a hat that her mate had tossed on the ground. The scene reminded me of the time I watched a sardana performed in Barcelona and of the machinations of the beautiful women I met there. And the one I was now dealing with.

Isabella and I had hardly spoken during the hurried journey. She gave me a smile whenever our eyes met, but I would keep my features blank, pretending that I wasn't affected.

I found the rebel leader at the governor's palace. A courier from the padre had already arrived, bearing a message that no attack was to be made on the capital yet. The message I bore was verbal: I told Torres that the destination of the padre's army was the Bajío but that the padre needed to know what support Torres could provide.

"As you can see, I captured the city for the padre and the revolution. I await the generalíssimo's arrival," Torres told me. "The whole city will turn out to welcome the conquering hero when the padre honors us with his presence."

Torres offered me more men to supplement the twelve I already had, but I declined. A dozen men I could pass off as vaqueros from a hacienda; if I arrived with a small army, I would arouse suspicion and start a war with the bandit leader.

I informed him that the word on the streets was that he governed well. He accepted my compliment with modesty.

"I've learned that running a city is impossibly complicated. Teaching a herd of jackasses to dance would be easier than administering to a city's needs and reforming its political system."

I shook my head in wonderment as I stepped out of the government building. Miguel Hidalgo, a small-town priest, had raised an army that was shaking all of New Spain. Just weeks ago Torres had been a laborer on a hacienda, and now he had conquered and ruled the Guadalajara region: over half a million people.

I had been present with Marina when the padre told a short, stocky priest that he should raise an army and fight from the jungles in the Acapulco area. "Who's this priest that is supposed to raise this army?" I had asked her at the time.

She said his name was José María Morelos, a forty-five-year-old priest who had been born into poverty. He'd been a muleteer and vaquero until the age of twenty-five, when he began his studies for the priesthood. Since becoming a priest, he had held curacies in small, unimportant places, administering to peons.

"How does the padre know that this man can raise an army and fight a war?" I had asked. I was a caballero—the best shot and best horseman in the whole colony—and I couldn't raise and lead an army.

"He has fire in his belly," Marina said, "and Christ's love in his eyes."

From a mine supplier, I bought black powder, fuses, and empty mercury flasks. I didn't know what to expect from the bandit who called himself General López, but I suspected that he would react better to a kick than a loving caress.

After dispatching a porter laden with my purchases to our camp, I strolled through the marketplace, where I spotted an ornate comb designed to secure women's hairdos. Shaped like a silver rose, it featured a pearl at its center and closely resembled a silver comb Isabella had favored when I courted her on the Guanajuato paseo. On impulse, I bought the haircomb and found my feet taking me to a barber. After a shave, haircut, and bath, I splashed a perfume of rose petals on my clothes to hide the trail smell and went to the inn where Isabella was staying.

She was almost a widow, wasn't she? I felt it was my duty to console her . . . and perhaps water her garden. That pudgy little marqués probably needed to tie a thong to his manhood and the other end to his wrist in order to find it.

I whistled as I took the stairs up to the second floor two at a time. I was at the top of the stairs when the door to Isabella's room opened. Renato came out. Isabella came out the door and grabbed him to pull him back in. She saw me and stepped back, slamming the door.

Renato stood perfectly still, his hand on his dagger.

I nodded at this hand. "Someday you will lose that hand."

 ONE HUNDRED AND TWO

WE SET OUT the following morning for León, fifteen strong: the twelve vaqueros, Isabella, Renato, and their generalíssimo, namely me. The trip would be another hard ride but was less than half the distance we had covered to reach Guadalajara.

At our encampment on the first night, Isabella whispered to me, "You're a fool, Renato is family. It is not what you think. He had been telling me a story about my husband in his youth."

"You're right. I am a fool." I gave her my back and went into the woods to relieve myself. I didn't know what to think of her and Renato, so I tried to not to think about them and focus on the mission.

I was familiar with León, the city we would stop at before going on to the village where the general named López ruled. I had stopped there many times on hunting trips. As with so many cities in the colony, León's namesake was a great and famous city in Spain. The colony's city was in a fertile river valley, a day's ride from Guanajuato.

This was dangerous territory for us because a major royal force under the command of General Calleja of San Luis Potosí was known to be on the march.

When León was visible in the distance, I ordered our men to make camp and went into town in the company of just one vaquero. From the frightened townspeople I learned that López was the terror of the region. He had established himself in a small village on the road that led north and was collecting a "toll" from all who passed. Though he professed alliance to the padre's cry for liberty, his only interest in "governing" was in how much booty he could plunder . . . before he was caught and hanged.

I told Renato that only three of us—he, a vaquero, and I—would go into the village and negotiate for the marqués's release. We'd take an extra horse for the marqués to ride and a vaquero to watch our horses if we had to go inside to negotiate with López. Isabella and the other vaqueros were to wait outside the village for us.

"Shouldn't I come?" Isabella asked. "If my husband is too weak to travel, he may want to whisper to me the location of the gold."

I laughed. "Before you put a knife in his gut?"

Both of them flushed.

"That's not—"

Renato held out his hand to stop her. "No, you'll hold us back if we have to run for it."

"We won't run for it," I said.

"How do you know? You think this bandido—"

"We'll be outnumbered a hundred to one. If we can't bluff or negotiate our way out, they'll kill us."

They took a moment to appreciate our plight. Isabella clutched her neck. "What will they do to me before they kill me?"

I ignored the question. The answer was obvious.

"We should bring the men into the village with us, make a show of strength," Renato said.

"Twelve against hundreds are a show of strength? Our strength is an unknown factor to López if we leave the men out of the village. If we take them in, he'll murder the bunch of us and keep the ransom and the marqués."

"Why don't we have the bandido bring my husband out of the village, meet us in the open?" Isabella asked.

Renato shook his head. "He is right. We can't let him see how few we are. If he came out, he'd have his whole army with him and see that we're little threat. We have to go in. Have courage, my darling, we will not fail."

I had to give Renato credit; he questioned my decisions, but he wasn't stupid. He acquiesced when he saw I was right. But he did have a loose tongue, calling his "aunt" darling. It was pretty obvious he had been poaching on his uncle's woman. I would have to kill the dishonorable bastard.

I was after the same woman, but it wasn't dishonorable; I wasn't family.

When the village came into sight, I posted ten men in the high rocks above the road. I gave them instructions on how to use the mercury-flask bombs. They were to light them on my signal and throw them down onto the road.

Renato nodded at the flasks. "How many men will they kill when they explode?"

"None. They're to raise a commotion, simulate cannon fire, and make the bandidos think we're a large force with artillery."

"You don't think this López will simply take the ransom money and turn over the marqués?"

"What would you do if you were López?"

He shrugged. "As you suggested, kill the emissaries, rape the woman, keep the gold. I'd then hold both her and the marqués for another ransom."

"So we'd better let him think we're an army."

I left Isabella and her mule litter with a vaquero who would tend the horses for the ten other men. The twelfth man went with Renato and me.

"*¡Ay!*" I whispered between clenched teeth as we approached the village. Two naked bodies hung from a tree. Both the men had been flayed and burned alive, their eyes and tongues pulled out . . . before they were strung up. A crudely lettered sign on a piece of wood hung from their necks. Each sign read: NO RANSOM

It wasn't much of a village: a few dozen shacks, a humble church, and a pulqueria. The only people I saw were bandidos. The villagers had either fled or had been murdered.

About fifty of López's cutthroats were waiting for us.

Under my black frock coat, I wore three oiled-silk money belts with four long pouches to each belt. Two of them I strapped across my shoulders, crisscrossing my chest. The third I'd buckled around my waist. They averaged seven pounds of gold each. Not that these curs needed gold to kill someone. They would have cheerfully killed us for the boots on our feet. Hell, they'd have killed us *por nada*.

I sucked on a cigarro and grinned at the welcoming committee. I knew exactly where the so-called "General" López had found them. They were charter members of the same scummy brotherhood I'd jailed with in Guanajuato. López had emptied the prisons and scraped the gutters to recruit them.

One of the bandidos staggered drunkenly toward me, waving a pistol, his other hand out as if he expected me to fill it. I kicked him in the face, catching him under the jaw with my heel. The kick lifted him off his feet, snapping his neck with an ugly-sounding *crack*! He flew back onto the ground.

His compañeros laughed at the show. When I glanced back, two of his amigos were already fighting over the man's heel-less, floppy-soled boots.

Another fifty or more of the creatures waited in front of the village church. They looked like cannibals waiting for dinner guests. Canek the Bloodthirsty was a cultured hombre compared to these slimy, two-legged centipedes.

A fat, drunken beast bursting out of an undersized Spanish officer's uniform staggered out of the church and hailed us.

"Welcome, amigos. You bring me dinero? No dinero—?" He made a hanging gesture with his hand and a strangling sound.

The gaggle of human nightmares laughed uproariously.

I left the horses with the vaquero and went inside with Renato behind me. We followed General López to his "office," a thronelike chair on a platform in front of the altar. The men outside followed us in. He flopped onto his throne, took a big swig from a mescal jug, belched, and wiped his mouth with his uniform sleeve. I didn't hurt his feelings by pointing out that his uniform was that of a lieutenant.

I gave him the written authority from the padre, commanding him to turn over the marqués to me. From the way he looked at the message, I realized he couldn't read. He stared at the message for a moment, wadded it into a ball, and bounced it off my chest.

I said, "As you can see, Miguel Hidalgo, Generalíssimo of the Army of America, sends his greetings. He commands you to turn over the prisoner Humberto to me. Naturally, you will receive an accommodation in the amount of three thousand pesos."

The price was five thousand, but it was better to let him negotiate me up.

He drank and belched again. "Your generalíssimo has had some difficulties lately."

I raised my eyebrows. "What do you mean?"

"We captured a royal messenger today. He died under, uh, questioning, but he told us that an army under General Calleja had routed the padre's army at Aculco."

I suddenly felt ice cold. "Is the padre—"

"He wasn't captured. The messenger said he escaped with some of his army."

He was telling me we had just lost a negotiating point.

"The Bajío has reinforcements that will swell the padre's army till it envelops all of New Spain. No royal force will stand before it," I told him, "and the padre will remember your kindness."

"*My* army will drive the Spanish from the land and place the padre on a throne as king." López waved at the scum in the church.

I could see war and politics were not his strong suit. I cut short the haggling. "I have your gold."

"I want ten thousand."

"Five is all I have, there is a large force waiting for me, they'll get restless if I don't hurry back. We need to move on and meet up with the padre. Bring in the prisoner. We must confirm his good health."

They brought him in through a side door. In the capital, I had only seen Don Humberto from a distance. Now he was no longer the fat, arrogant aristocrat who wiped his boots on the lower classes. He was pale, emaciated, his eyes hollow and haggard, with no flicker of recognition. The bandits had replaced his fine clothing with filthy rags. I could not avert my gaze from his hideously haunted eyes: They were like the broken, empty windows in an abandoned building.

López stared at me with half-closed eyes. "What is so important about this merchant that the generalíssimo himself is ransoming him?"

I grabbed the marqués by the back of his shirt and propelled him toward the door. "The ransom money is outside."

Rabble went out the door in front of me, thinking they would grab the gold off Tempest. The gold wasn't there, and the stallion's ill temper turned explosive when dirty hands and smelly bodies got too close. He kicked a lépero in the head, another in the pelvis, and I sent the rest scattering with my flashing blade as I broke through.

Lopez had followed me out with a bloody machete in hand. The vaqueros' first flask bomb boomed in the distance. The blast stopped everyone cold.

"My army's firing its cannons," I said. "Next they'll shoot nail canisters in." I shrugged. "They're restless. They haven't killed anyone today."

Another blast thundered, its echo replicating over and over again against the rocky hills outside the village.

I unbuttoned my loose-fitting black frock coat, exposing the two money belts crisscrossing my chest like bandoleers and the third strapped around my waist. I unhooked all three and threw the twenty pounds of gold bullion at the bandido leader's feet, one belt at a time. They each landed with a thump.

"You can keep the belts," I said.

Throwing the marqués up onto a big deep-chested roan, I lashed his hips to the cantle and pommel, then cross-tied his wrists to the saddle horn. I knotted the reins across his mount's neck. Grabbing the twin ends of the mecate, which I'd attached earlier to his roan's headstall, I vaulted Tempest. The mecate would serve as a lead rope.

Behind me López was busy keeping his "soldiers" from the gold. A man bent down to grab at the gold, and Lopez's machete sang through the air and into his nape. Blood detonated, and the severed head hit the dirt with a *thunk* as I mounted Tempest. Another echo rang and replicated through the camp.

Renato cut out of the village at a high hard lope. I followed, leading the marqués by the mecate, slashing out at rabble with my saber when they got too close, while the vaquero took up the rear.

Lopez was shouting and pointing at us. I didn't need a gypsy to tell me that he hadn't bought my story about having an army. The flasks had made a loud noise but no cannon balls had exploded nearby.

Tempest caught up with Renato. Glancing over my shoulder, I saw the older man was trying to clutch the pommel but was barely hanging on.

"They'll be riding up our back trail!" I shouted. "We need to get off a musket volley!"

"I'll take Don Humberto to Isabella and join you afterward."

I handed him the mecate, and he continued past our men up in the rocks. The vaquero and I dismounted, tied our horses, and joined the other men.

"Load both your muskets."

I put five men on my left and told them to fire the first volley on my command, the men to the right to fire the second.

"This rabble is untrained. If we knock a few from the saddle, they'll turn tail and run."

And if they didn't, we were finished because each man had only a single musket ball. I'd been able to pick up black powder in Guadalajara because it's produced for the mines, but, with a war raging, musket balls were as rare as gold.

A horde of bandidos rode out of the village. Their mounts ranged from good hacienda workhorses and mules to donkeys. They came down the road five abreast with López front and center.

"Everyone, aim for Lopez." With him out front, it was a good bet that we'd hit something, men or horses.

I ordered the men to hold fire until the bandidos were two hundred feet away. I gave the command for the first volley. Four of the muskets went off. Another sent a ramming rod flying; in his haste, the man had forgotten to remove it. López was knocked off his horse, and two other horses in the front rank went down.

The second volley went off, and another man and horse went down. I grabbed a flask bomb, lit the fuse, and tossed it. It exploded harmlessly in the air a hundred feet from the nearest man, but it made a terrific noise.

It wasn't necessary; the whole pack had about-faced and headed in three directions of panic, all away from us.

"To the horses!"

I mounted Tempest and led the way to where the horses were waiting. The horses and mules were gone. So were Renato, Isabella, and Don Humberto. The vaquero whom I left with the horses lay spread-eagled on the ground, his throat slit.

"Up there!" one of the men shouted.

He pointed at riders cresting the hilltop, heading north around the village. Renato led the way, Isabella behind him on the horse with her arms around his waist. Renato led the marqués's roan by a mecate. Behind the marqués, two other horses were rope-led. The mounts they didn't take with them, they'd run off.

The rabble army would soon find the courage to make another attack. I had eleven men and one horse among them, the horse of the vaquero who accompanied me into the village. Some horses that had been run off were still in sight, grazing.

"We need to round up at least six horses," I told the men. "You can ride double into León." I held out my hand and helped a man mount behind me and the horsed vaquero did the same. I rode the man out to a horse, and he mounted it. When we had six horses for the eleven men, I gave them money to see them back to the padre.

"Where are you going, señor?" one asked.

"To avenge the murder of our amigo and the betrayal of the padre."

"Then God speed to you and your sword."

 ONE HUNDRED AND THREE

MANY TIMES I have traveled great distances from Guanajuato to hunt, losing myself in the wilderness. I preferred to hunt game with the same horn-backed bow that the Chihuahua Desert Apaches used with such murderous skill. But one didn't shoot game from a great distance with an arrow. Instead, you had to sneak up slowly and take it by surprise. With a desert-mountain mule deer, you often had to track it for hours, or even days, following its hoofprints. This was how I now tracked Renato, Isabella, and Don Humberto.

I followed the prints of their horses as they circled around the bandido village and continued north. The marqués was captured about twenty miles north of the village and had hidden his gold before he was taken. That meant by early tomorrow morning, they would arrive in the area where Don Humberto had buried the gold.

I followed the tracks in no hurry. My objective was not to catch them. If I did, there would be a fight and the possibility that Don Humberto would be killed before I could learn his treasure's location.

So I just followed at a safe distance, keeping an hour behind them. As I did when I hunted deer, I would—when the time was right—go for the kill.

The next morning I ate my hard biscuits and resisted the urge to chew on salted beef because it would increase my thirst. The region was arid but with some river valleys that produced stunted scrub trees and some sparse graze for Tempest. But I couldn't count on finding water ahead.

As the day wore on, I followed their tracks higher and higher. After crossing the timberline, thick groves of trees covered the ascending hills. My recollection was that I'd be able to quench my thirst on the other side of the hills, where a river forked into two smaller streams.

A couple of hours before midday I heard a sound. I pulled Tempest to a halt and listened. It came again, a man's voice, a cry of pain. No, not just pain but agony. *The marqués.* I hadn't heard Don Humberto speak, but I was sure it was him. Renato's voice I recognized.

I slipped off Tempest. Rather than tying his reigns tightly to a branch, I tied them loosely so they would slip off if he gave them a good jerk. "If I whistle, come to me," I told him. I never knew if he understood these things, but I did know he was smarter than most men I've known.

The sounds had stopped. They appeared to have come from the rim of a sheer cliff, rising a hundred feet above me. It was too steep to climb. I backtracked, going down the same way I had come until I found a slope I could climb. When I reached the level I thought the sound had come from, I crept slowly through thick brush. I found him in a small clearing. He was on his back, lying by a campfire that had burned down to gray embers. Above the embers stood a tripod fashioned from crossed poles lashed crudely together with a rope dangling from its apex.

He was alive: that much I understood from the slow rise of his chest. Not by much, however. I smelled burnt flesh. His feet and scalp were badly charred: they'd broiled his feet black in the fire, then hung him by his ankles from the tripod head down over the slow-burning fire.

I also smelled an ambush.

I saw only two possibilities: they had charred his feet in the fire to get the location of the treasure. When they couldn't find it, they returned and hung him by his hocks over the fire. When he gave them a new location, they left him to search for it. The other possibility? They left him as bait for me.

I relaxed my body and cleared my mind and lay completely still. This was how I hunted in areas I knew the game had passed; it permitted me to stay for long periods without fidgeting.

Don Humberto's respiration was raspy, a grating preamble to a death rattle. I sensed an ambush, but I had to enter the opening.

I pulled out my sword and pistol. Taking a deep breath, I rose to a crouch and slowly dogtrotted toward Don Humberto, expecting a lead ball in my heart at any moment.

The rasp was fading, weakening as I knelt beside him. "It's me, Don Humberto, the man who ransomed you."

His eyelids slowly fluttered open. He didn't make eye contact with me. I don't know if he even saw me.

"Why did they do this to you?"

"I told him," he whispered hoarsely.

"You told Renato where the gold is?"

"I told him."

"They went for the gold?"

Something like a laugh burst from his throat. "He hurt me . . ."

"Just relax, amigo; the pain will be gone in a moment."

His scrawny hand grabbed the front of my shirt and pulled me closer. "I lied," he whispered. "I spoke falsely."

"Where is it?"

"Where the river forks . . . in a cave . . . indios hid it in the cave with rocks, where the rivers fork," he said, barely loud enough for me to hear. "I . . . killed them."

I made the sign of the cross.

"Will God . . . forgive me?"

He didn't wait for my answer. His life escaped with a last breath.

I knew the spot the marqués spoke of. I'd camped at the fork of the river three years before. I didn't remember a cave, but high water wore and gouged out many holes along the route carved by the river.

Don Humberto had more cojones than I had credited him for, but I suspected he cared more about money than anything else. I wondered how much torture he would have taken before he gave up his wife.

A scream came from the bushes behind me.

Isabella!

I ran toward the sound, again expecting an ambush and ready to face it head-on. I had reached my limit. It was time to make good on my promise and kill Renato.

I caught a flash of him as I crashed into the brush like a bull, the mindless El Toro with the bleeding wounds Marina accused me of being. I fired the pistol. The shot hit exactly where I aimed, right in the chest. Except that I instantly realized that there was no flesh behind the coat I had fired at. It was a ruse.

I spun around, swinging my sword. He went under it, coming up as soon as the sword passed over his head. I leaned back as his dagger flashed. It sliced across my chest, cutting through my coat and shirt. I felt the sting of the blade as I fell backward, brush jabbing at my back. I knew what was coming, and I twisted and rolled before I hit the ground. The thrown dagger stuck in the ground next to me.

I tried to roll away as he aimed his pistol. The explosion sounded and I couldn't get out of the way. The ball hit me in the groin. I felt the burn and my mind exploded. I jerked to my feet and rushed him in a mindless rage. I had two things no man trespassed on—my horse and my manly pride.

I hit him with my shoulder, sending a shock wave through my body from the pain in my chest. He staggered back, and I hit him in the face. He fell back, and, exacting eye-for-an-eye, I kicked him in *his manhood*. He dropped the sword and fell to his knees, clutching his painful parts with both hands. I grabbed the sword he had dropped. I had promised to chop off his dagger hand, but his neck looked too inviting.

Before I could raise the sword I saw something out of the corner of my eye. A heavy tree limb, thick and solid as a musket butt, was being swung like an axe. Hammering my temple, it sent me flying to my left. As I went over a cliff, I caught a flash of Isabella with the crudely fashioned club in her hands, her eyes bright with excitation, a hint of a leer curling her upper lip.

I dropped a dozen feet and hit a hard surface, excruciating pain exploding through both body and brain. I heard a scream and knew it was my own as I rolled off another ledge and continued to fall. I tumbled head over heels down the side of the incline.

When I came to a rest, I lay still, a loud humming in my ears, my eyes seeing double. It took a moment before I realized I was a hundred feet down, not far from where I had tethered Tempest. I felt paralyzed. I groaned, unwound my arms and legs, and the pain came alive. I tried to whistle, and it came out as a whisper.

"Tempest," I yelled, but it was not much of a shout.

Ready to scream, I got onto my knees and got another yell out for my horse. No reply. With the power of Hercules, I managed to get to my feet.

I found Tempest near where I had tied him. He had gotten loose and was grazing. I staggered to him, ready to pass out. "Bastardo," I told him. I pulled myself onto the beast with sheer will.

I couldn't manage finding and transporting the gold. It would weigh about eight hundred pounds. I needed men to load it, mules to carry it . . . and an army to protect it. I had to patch my wounds and get to León. Then back to the padre and his army.

I was weak from pain and shock as Tempest carried me away. The image of Isabella came to my mind.

Bitch. She was a slut who helped to fry her husband's feet, then hung him by the hocks over a fire. May she herself burn in hell.

I DON'T KNOW how long or how far Tempest carried me. I knew my life's blood was running out of me. The only way I knew to stop the bleeding was to burn the wound with a hot iron or a blaze of black powder, and I didn't have the strength to do either. I didn't even have the strength to guide Tempest. Dark shadows slipped into my mind, threatening to drop my mind into a deep void.

Thoughts and visions ran through my head as if I had journeyed from this world to the underworld my Aztec ancestors traveled in after they passed from the sorrows of this life: Carlos dying in my arms, a glass of brandy from Bruto, the screams and cries, the dead and dying at the granary . . .

I came back to the present with words in my ears. My eyes and ears slowly made a connection with a voice and body. Tempest had stopped. I realized people stood around the stallion and were staring up to me.

"You are seriously injured, señor."

It wasn't a question.

The world began to swirl around me, and I fell into a black, boiling, bottomless pit.

Not one fine house in all of New Spain would have taken in an injured stranger. However, I didn't heal in a house but in a peon's hut in a small Aztec village. These simple, unpretentious people had taken in a stranger.

When I was well enough, I checked my clothes and gear. Nothing was missing, and they had washed my clothes.

I had no knowledge of how much time I had spent in that hut while the specter of death hung over me. It could have been days or weeks. I had a hard time communicating with the woman and her husband who cared for me. They didn't speak Spanish.

I was on my feet, a little unsteady, but determined to round up Tempest who was hanging around the village somewhere, when I heard horses galloping into the village. Thoughts of escape slipped away as the hut was surrounded, and I was told to come out of the hut.

I stepped out and blinked under the power of the midday sun. A dozen men on horseback surrounded me.

"Identify yourself!"

I recognized the uniforms: royal militia. The speaker was a lieutenant. I knew his type: like Allende and the Aldama brothers, he was a criollo caballero. But he was fighting for the viceroy.

I had been captured by the enemy. Next I would be dancing for the hangman.

The lieutenant pointed his pistol at me. "State your name!"

"My name?" I lifted my chin and straightened my shoulders. "Señor, you are addressing Don Renato de Miro, nephew of the Marqués de Miro."

That afternoon, I retold my story to Captain Guerrero, the commander of the unit, as we chewed on meat and bread washed down with wine. I went over what had happened to me, telling the same story I had given his lieutenant. Guerrero was another criollo officer. As the marqués's nephew, I was a gachupine of noble blood, making him my social inferior.

"The infamous bandido, Juan Zavala, ambushed my uncle and me. After murdering my beloved uncle, the blessed Don Humberto, he stole his gold."

"The beautiful Isabella?" Captain Guerrero asked, pouring us both another cup of wine.

I crossed myself. "Murdered by the bandido."

"No! Not Isabella. Did he first—"

"You know his evil reputation."

He shuddered. "That mestizo devil will pay for violating a Spanish woman. When we capture Zavala, I will personally squash his cojones with thumbscrews and gouge out his eyeballs with my dagger."

I prayed that bandidos had captured and killed Renato and Isabella. I gave the officer a blow-by-blow account of my heroic battle against the bandido Zavala and his murderous band of killers, making sure I gave him the same story that I gave his subordinate.

He listened, commiserating as one caballero to another, and brought me up to date on the padre's war of independence.

"We have retaken Guanajuato and driven out the turncoat Allende and the other traitorous officers."

I pretended elation at the news, but each new defeat of our forces was a kick to my stomach. Things had not gone well since the padre refused to turn the horde loose on the capital.

The consensus among Calleja's officers was that the padre had gone to Guadalajara and that Allende would rejoin him there to regroup.

I listened, ate, drank, and was about to tell the captain I needed to move on when an orderly entered and whispered in his ear.

The captain raised his eyebrows. "As you know, General Calleja was your uncle's close friend. The general has spoken fondly of Don Humberto. He would never forgive me if I didn't notify him that we'd found you. He's instructed me to send you to him, so you can tell the story of his amigo's murder at the hands of the cutthroat Zavala. A full military escort will ride with you, assuring you a safe journey for your meeting with the general."

¡Ay! He might as well have sentenced me to the scaffold. But I smiled bravely. "Where is the general?"

"Guanajuato."

I smothered a groan. Life is a circle, no? How long would I last in that fair city before someone pointed out that I was the brigand Zavala? On the good side, I had my beard back and long hair, had lost much weight, and my clothes looked like they had been slept in and befouled, all of which was true. Even Tempest had trimmed down because of sparse graze. We looked like we had gone through a war in a pig sty and lost. But I should not have been frightened of someone recognizing me, because things soon got worse.

"General Calleja will want to know all the details of the terrible crimes, so leave nothing out." He gave me a glance. "And since your family is one of the noblest in New Spain, no doubt he'll want to discuss the marqués's estate in his report to the viceroy. Did the marqués have children? Or are you his heir?"

I shrugged and tried to look as if I wasn't ready to foul my pants. I didn't have the faintest idea of the composition of the marqués's family. I still wondered whether Renato was the man's nephew or a paid assassin, hired to kill the padre and help Isabella recover the gold. But whatever Renato was, as the marqués's close friend, the general would know I was an imposter.

Why is it that when my feet are in the fire, someone throws lamp oil on the flames?

The captain refused to let me ride Tempest, which sent my suspicions soaring. They didn't want me on a horse that could leave their own eating its dust. Furthermore, he accompanied me and the escort for the entire journey to Guanajuato.

The last time I saw the city, I was part of a triumphant army that had killed hundreds of Spaniards in the granary. Now as I entered Guanajuato there were grim reminders that the gachupines had retaken the city. Bodies hung from makeshift gallows along the busiest street.

The captain said, "This is just the beginning. By the time we finish, the only rebels in Guanajuato will be dead ones."

We paused near the alhóndiga. The air was thick with blood and revenge. Panicked prisoners were hurried out of the granary, which was now a jail, a priest beside them mumbling forgiveness in Latin as the men were shoved against a wall. As soon as the priest stepped aside, the prisoners were shot. Their bodies were hurriedly dragged aside to make room for the next stampede. The dead left behind brains and bone, guts and blood, on the cobblestones. Bodies were stacked like logs off to the side.

"They'll be carted off to a mass grave," the officer said.

"Their trials must be quick," I said.

Very quick, I thought. Calleja had not been in the town long enough to have conducted legal proceedings.

He laughed. "God conducts our trials. We don't have the time, men, or inclination to spend months weeding out the miscreants. Instead, the general has ordered a lottery. If his men draw your name, they arrest and execute you out of hand."

With a straight face I said, "In the early days of the Inquisition, when inquisitors believed there were heretics in a town but couldn't discover the guilty ones, they would order everyone killed. Torquemada, the Grand Inquisitor, told the troops, 'Kill them all. God knows His own; he'll sort out the souls of the innocent from the wicked.'"

He howled and slapped his thigh. "That's very good, Don Renato. I'll repeat your words to the general. He'll be pleased to know his methods are sanctioned by the church."

People watched the executions from the rooftops of houses on the hillside, whole families gathering together as if watching a play. They had watched the battle for the alhóndiga, too. And again the jeers were for the defeated.

Calleja was in the office of Riano, the governor who had died defending the alhóndiga granary.

I was brought into a waiting room adjoining the office, and for an hour I watched a steady stream of officers and civilians go in and out. No one did a double take at me or shouted my name. Fortunately, most of the people who would have recognized me were gachupines and wealthy criollos who were now dead or had fled to the capital.

I knew a bit about the general, whom some people called a chino— behind his back. Calleja wasn't Chinese, but people called him that because his skin had a yellowish tone from jaundice. Félix María Calleja del Rey's reputation as a soldier was discussed many times by Bruto and his friends around the dinner table during my youth. Calleja was reputed to be an ill-tempered little man, much given to punctilious military airs. They said his two great loves were flattery and cruelty. But despite his hard edge and demanding nature, he was considered a good soldier and was popular with his troops.

He was born into a distinguished family in Medina del Campo in old Castile. As a young man, he had seen action as an ensign in a failed campaign against the dey of Algiers. He had come to New Spain about twenty years ago and served in frontier units until Madrid ordered that the colonial militia be divided into ten brigades. Calleja was given command of the brigade at San Luis Potosí, where he married a wealthy woman in the city and became the most notable gachupine in the region.

The padre, in his eternal wisdom, had foreseen that the general would become his chief nemesis. Almost as soon as the cry of independence was made from Dolores, the padre sent a troop of horsemen to Calleja's hacienda at de Bledos to arrest him. Calleja narrowly escaped and made it to San Luis Potosí. However, because so few ready troops were available, he needed a couple months to gather together enough men, arms, and supplies to field a sizable army.

At the moment, the ill-tempered military man didn't look pleased to see me.

I gave a humble bow. "Don Félix, it is such a pleasure—"

"You are a thief and a liar."

He knew who I was. I was doomed!

"You are a disgrace, a man with no honor, no honesty, no integrity, no decency."

What could I say? Did he not know me well? Was one of the gallows I saw in the town square waiting for me?

"Your uncle, bless his soul, told me all about you."

Bruto discussed me with Calleja?

"His death has only magnified your sins."

"Don Calleja—"

"Silence! You're no better than a maggot." Trembling, his hand shook next to a pistol on his desk. He stared at the pistol, his face convulsing. The man was going to shoot me dead!

He struggled to control himself. "You disgust me, you cowardly dog. I'd hoped our paths would never cross. Now we finally meet because of your sainted uncle's death. That you should be alive when your esteemed uncle and august aunt are dead is an affront to God Himself."

Sainted uncle and . . . august aunt? Bruto never married. I had no aunt.

"What have you to say for yourself?"

"I . . . I don't like me much myself—"

"Silence! You have no excuse for letting that lépero dog Zavala kill your family."

I opened my mouth, and the little dictator told me to shut it.

"And letting him defile your beautiful aunt. A peon ravishing a woman of Spain. A real man would have died fighting to protect her honor."

I tried to agree but nothing came out.

"I'm sending you to the capital under armed guard. You're fortunate it won't be in chains. You came to the colony with a wicked reputation from Spain, a disgrace to your honorable family. Your uncle told me many times of your bad deeds. If our beloved nation was not struggling against the French, I have no doubt you would be rotting in the king's jail. *Get out of my sight!*"

I was almost out the door when he said, "I'll recommend to the viceroy that you be placed in the front line of the defense of the capital. Having lived without honor, you will at least die honorably."

• • •

Life was good. Don Humberto did have a nephew after all, freshly arrived from Spain, and as wicked as hell. I still wasn't sure Isabella's thug-friend was the real nephew, but at the moment I didn't care. Whoever Renato was, wherever he was, his name had kept me alive . . . at least for the moment.

That night I had a sumptuous meal at an inn, bedded a puta, then another, and another. I felt beloved of God. Perhaps He had forgiven my many transgressions. A sneaky suspicion entered my mind that He might be saving me for a more terrible fate, one befitting my many sins, but for the moment life was good.

The next morning I joined a company of dragoons escorting a messenger with a communiqué for the viceroy. If I stayed with them until Méjico City, I would truly end my days on the scaffold. I had Tempest between my legs and waited for my chance to escape.

We were two days out of Guanajuato when I got permission from the lieutenant commanding the dragoons to bring back a cow we saw in the distance for dinner. He sent two dragoons with me. I left the dragoons convulsing in their own blood and took their horses with me as I rode off to rejoin the padre.

 **ONE HUNDRED AND FIVE**

Guadalajara

YOU SHOULD BE *dead!"*

Ay, women are never satisfied. I come back with my wounds still raw, my pains still sharp, returning from death's other river on behalf of the revolution, and Marina still wasn't satisfied. Was she saying that it was too bad I wasn't dead because I returned without the gold . . . or that my wounds were so bad, it's a wonder I didn't die from them?

Isabella, the woman I had loved for so long, had tried to murder me. She had ripped another piece from my soul. If I found out that Marina felt that the gold for the insurrection was more important to her than my life, she would have crushed me, too.

I had explained to a sympathetic padre and an unsympathetic Marina why I returned empty handed. I told them that I knew where the gold was hidden but that I hadn't been able to recover it because of my wounds. The padre had understood, but Marina had eyed me with unalloyed suspicion.

"I left the gold in order to retrieve it later, not for myself but for the padre and his army," I told the cynical señorita. "I've told the padre where it is. He can get it if I'm killed."

The padre acknowledged that he knew where the gold was, but right now that was irrelevant. His army's fate was even more precarious than when I'd left. He listened with greater concern about my description of Calleja's forces and was grateful for the work I'd done.

His gratitude did not stem Marina's ire.

"If that gold doesn't go for the reconquista, I will personally cut out your lying tongue," she said.

The padre patted her hand. "Juan did his best. He was betrayed."

"Had he done his best, he'd have the gold."

"I can return immediately for the gold," I said. She had stung my pride. I would retrieve that treasure if I had to crawl with it strapped to my back.

"The treasure will have to wait," the padre said. "We have a battle to fight and no use for gold at this late moment unless we were to make cannon balls out of it."

Marina and I left so he could continue the preparations for the battle to come, and it was approaching quickly. The armies had already maneuvered near Calderón Bridge east of the city.

I would be at the battle but only with a loaded pistol in hand in case a royal soldier got close enough for me to shoot. On my way back to Guadalajara, I took a fall from Tempest after running from a royal patrol I had encountered near Atotonilco. The fall ripped open my wound, and it turned raw and ugly. By the time I made it to Guadalajara, the wound was red and swollen. My whole body felt hot.

We retired to Marina's room at an inn where she was staying near the battlefield. I learned she'd taken the room for my comfort.

We drank wine and made love . . . ¡Ay de mí! I confess, I wasn't up to my usual mucho hombre standard in bed. To my shame, my garrancha rose, only to lose its power almost immediately. Marina had no sympathy. In fact, she had contempt.

She examined my groin. "It didn't matter where you were hit. You lost your manhood to that bitch years ago."

I groaned silently. I had to keep my mouth shut. I was still weak and in pain, in no condition to take on Marina, mentally or physically. The fact that Isabella had tried to and nearly did murder me, didn't soften Marina's rage. Marina would have been more pleased if Isabella had succeeded in taking my life. She acted like a woman scorned. And she was right; she was an Aztec witch who saw through my black lies and dirty deeds.

"What happened at Aculco? Why did we lose the battle?" I asked to get her off my back. Aculco was the battle in which the bandido leader said the padre's army had suffered a defeat.

"There was no battle. Meeting up with Calleja's army was as big a surprise to the royals as it was to us. He was proceeding south to relieve the capital when we were on our way north. We were in no condition to do battle. After breaking camp at Cuajimalpa, perhaps half of our force melted away. They had about five or six thousand royal troops, while we had perhaps four to five times that many, almost all Aztecs, of course.

"Suddenly the two armies were facing each other. We didn't have time to even organize into battle formations. The padre ordered a retreat, which turned into a rout when we couldn't maintain order. We lost most of our artillery, some supply wagons—"

"The putas?"

"Yes, we lost our whores, too. Is that all that matters to you?"

I groaned, aloud this time. "Since I can't say anything to please you, cut off my tongue."

"That's not the only thing I will cut off if I find out you lied about the marqués's treasure." She gave my cojones a squeeze that made me sit upright. She pushed me down. "I like you this way, too sick to fight back."

"Tell me about the battle."

"I told you, it wasn't a battle. We pretended to prepare to fight, but retreated instead. We fought skirmishes, and our retreat was disorderly. Still, Calleja didn't pursue us with his main force because he couldn't maintain ranks, either. The man is Satan incarnate. You witnessed his atrocities in Guanajuato, but every place he marches, he leaves behind people hanging from trees. His intent is to terrorize our supporters into abandoning the revolt."

"Has he?"

"He puts fear into people, but we're stronger than ever. Our soldiers make gachupine prisoners suffer the same fate as Calleja's victims. The padre wanted to stop their revenge, but he couldn't control them. Spanish prisoners were executed, but it hasn't stopped Calleja's slaughter."

"The chino is a beast," I agreed. I told her how he held a lottery of death, hanging innocent people because it was more expedient than trials.

She said that when the padre ordered the army to turn away from the capital, he led them back to the Bajío. They had traveled only a few days when they nearly collided with Calleja's army at Aculco.

"Calleja was so close, we saw the padre was right when he refused to proceed to the capital. Calleja's army would have attacked us in the rear while we were besieging the city."

But that possibility had not stilled the criollo officers' displeasure at the padre's refusal to attack the capital.

"Allende, the Aldama brothers, all of them are angry at the padre. They once again claim that a priest isn't fit to command the army."

"But they have no army; the only army is the padre's indios."

"True, but the criollos keep thinking like jackasses. They've never been able to come up with a way of maneuvering tens of thousands of untrained indios. They only know how to lead trained troops. It always falls back on the padre because only he knows how to command their passions."

After the debacle at Aculco, they marched to the Bajío, moving in the direction of Celaya and Querétaro. To allay the animosity between the padre and the criollo officers, Allende split off and took a large force to Guanajuato.

"He believed he could manufacture cannons and other munitions there," Marina said, "and fortify the city to withstand a royal siege."

In turn, the padre went to Valladolid to recruit fresh troops and supplies.

"We had no sooner arrived in Valladolid when we got word that Torres had taken Guadalajara." Marina then said the padre's expectations changed after he had turned away from the capital. "He had always hoped that thousands of criollos would join us and that large units of the militia would defect to our side. He knew now for certain that that was not going to happen, that he would have to rely solely upon indios who had courage and heart but lacked training and weapons."

He saw the capture of Guadalajara as an opportunity to once again raise an enormous army of indios. Torres pleaded with him to come to the city, to use it as his base.

"We arrived there with less than eight thousand troops, but our ranks began to swell again from the first day." Marina's eyes glowed with pride. "The city greeted the padre as a conquering hero with marching bands, troops of dragoons, cannon fire, church bells, even a 'Te Deum' sung with full orchestra."

Good news about the reconquista came from other parts of the colony. Much of the north—Zacatecas, San Luis Potosí, and the sparsely populated arid region beyond—strongly favored the revolution. All over the Bajío, royal authority had broken down, and royal messengers were being waylaid by revolutionaries and land pirates. The priest Morelos in the tropical Acapulco region had made spectacular achievements.

"The padre sent him with just twenty-five men and no guns to raise an army. He already had several thousand fighters, but he refused to meet the royal forces on battlefields. Like your peninsular amigos, he fights as a guerrilla." Marina laughed. "Morelos had been an even poorer priest than the padre. He nearly starved to death attending the seminary before he was accepted by the church. Now he leads an army."

The eve of the great battle that was to take place tomorrow with Calleja's army was four months to the day that the padre proclaimed the independence of the colony.

A few days earlier, we had learned that Calleja was advancing with the largest Spanish force ever assembled in the colony. Marina had spied on Calleja's progress, and she estimated his strength at about seven thousand troops. We would have ten times that many, but ours would be an unwieldy mass pitted against seasoned, well-armed troops.

Knowing that the battle was at hand only increased the conflict between the padre and the criollo officers. Allende said they couldn't control and direct such a massive multitude effectively. He advocated dividing our forces and throwing seven or eight units of ten thousand each at the royals in successive waves, rather than risking all with one massive attack.

Padre Hidalgo disagreed.

"He said it would just make control many times harder, that we'd suffer mass desertions if the horde was divided up," Marina told me. "The padre believes that our best chance is to overwhelm the royals with our vastly superior numbers. If we keep pushing at them, he believes they will be the first to break and run."

I agreed with the padre's plan. If the army was split into a number of parts, it would be even harder to control. If the lead unit broke and ran under fire, the troops behind it wouldn't stand their ground either. The great human mass didn't respond to commands but to the flow of the mass as a whole: if the head turned, the rest of the body went with it.

Allende had even suggested abandoning Guadalajara and retreating again to continue to arm and train soldiers. But that would mean the loss of tens of thousands of indios from our ranks. Besides, Padre Hidalgo was a warrior priest. Unlike the criollo officers, he believed that right would triumph over might.

Once again—as it had when the padre refused to rape the capital—rumors about an officer-led coup d'état raced through the camp, and stories of another poison plot against the padre raged. Marina was in command of the indios assigned to protect the padre amid the chaos. I told her which officers to keep an eye on. I still didn't believe that Allende or the Aldama brothers would harm the padre, but not all the officers were as honorable or as intelligent. If they killed the padre, the Aztecs would wreak vengeance on every criollo they saw, and the army would evaporate.

No one knew exactly how many poor, landless peons had flocked to the padre's banner. I estimated eighty thousand, but most of them were armed only with knives, clubs, or wood pikes. We had gathered nearly a hundred cannon and a huge quantity of black powder and balls, but the cannons were all of inferior quality: some iron, a few bronze, and many nothing but wood bound with iron straps. We were still plagued by the lack of trained cannoneers to fire them.

Our cavalry was still composed of vaqueros armed mostly with wood lances, though a number had machetes and a few rusty pistols. We didn't have warhorses for our dragoons; their mounts were an odd assortment of undernourished hacienda nags, stolen silver-train mules, and indio donkeys, many of which bolted at the roar of guns, the crash of cannons, the sight and smell of blood.

We marched out of Guadalajara, an endless parade of citizen-soldiers, only a handful with uniforms, few with real weapons, but all with heart and courage, the most courageous of all leading us. Dressed in a dazzling blue, red, and white uniform adorned with glittering gold braid, the padre was the conquering hero, raised to apotheosis.

"We're carrying enough supplies with us for a march on the capital," he told his assembled officers before the parade. "As soon as we have routed Calleja, we shall claim all of New Spain for americanos."

I choked up from the passion of his words, the elegance of his manner and speech, the way he rode tall on a spirited white stallion that pranced down the street as the people of Guadalajara cheered.

The armies faced each other near a bridge spanning the Calderón River. We were eleven leagues east of Guadalajara, a long day's ride for a man on a horse. It was an area of arid fields and hillsides, sparse vegetation, dry grass, and stunted trees.

The padre had our troops occupy the bridge and, on the approach to Guadalajara, take command of the high ground. He positioned the army cleverly: Calleja would find an assault from our front or our rear, which was protected by a barranca—a deep ravine—equally difficult.

That night we sat in the darkness, tens of thousands of us, with more campfires dotting the hills than stars igniting the sky.

Early the next day we learned that Calleja would move quickly against us.

I said, "Calleja's coming into this battle with two things in his favor: He has no respect for our army as a military unit, and he saw it turn tail and run once before."

Marina glared at me and scowled.

I still bridled at her dismissal of me as a "defeatist." In truth, I believed we would beat the Spaniard. We were superior to him in size, position, and we possessed the *spirit* to win. But I also knew Señorita Fortuna is one fickle puta.

I wasn't fit for real fighting, so the padre used me to reconnoiter. From a tree on a high hill, armed with a spyglass, I watched Calleja divide his army into two parts. Even at a distance, I recognized his uniform and saw that General Flon commanded the second unit. Flon, unlike the meticulous Calleja, was notoriously impulsive.

From the way the formations lined up, I surmised that Calleja would strike our left flank while Flon hit us on the right. I sent a messenger to the padre with that information.

Calleja attacked with fierce determination, slowly and methodically, pushing his troops against our front lines. We couldn't stop the heavily armed, inexorably advancing troops who moved forward behind a blaze of musket fire and grapeshot. Still our army's front lines did not retreat; *they stood their ground and were slaughtered*.

Calleja made slow progress, but then the impetuous Flon did something that surprised me and no doubt Calleja, too. His unit suddenly charged our superior position with Flon himself leading the assault.

I shook my head in amazement. Allende and the padre had expected the army would divide and attack in concert, but Flon lunged precipitously, hammering us with everything he had, while Calleja's forces advanced doggedly, meticulously.

"The bastardo wants the victory all to himself!" I shouted down to Marina.

Flon, however, was attacking our strongest position. We repulsed his troops once, then again. When his artillery stopped firing, I shouted down, "His artillery is out of ammunition. His troops are pulling back."

I couldn't keep the excitement out of my voice. Calleja still pushed painfully ahead, his artillery firing up at our higher positions, but I was certain victory would be ours!

An explosion erupted, nearly knocking me from the tree, and then another and another, enormous blasts, as if the earth itself had opened up in volcanic fury. I held on to the tree, stunned, my ears ringing, the acrid smell of black-powder smoke searing my eyes and nose.

I looked down to see if Marina and the other runners were okay, certain that a close cannon shot had struck. She had been knocked off her feet but was already rising.

"What happened?" she shouted.

"Mother of God!"

I stared in horror at the top of the hill. Raging fire and great clouds of smoke were rising from where our munitions wagons were gathered. A lucky round from Calleja's artillery must have struck a munitions wagon, igniting its black-powder cargo. When it went up, it ignited another nearby wagon and then another and . . .

"No!"

The shout burst from me as I gaped at the chaos rapidly spreading through our ranks. How many of our men had been killed in the initial explosions, I don't know. Hundreds for certain. Even worse, great clouds of thick, black smoke now engulfed our ranks as fire broke out in the tall brush and dry forest where our troops had dug in. Our ranks began to disintegrate, melting not from the steady advance of the Spanish troops, but from an inferno of fire and smoke.

I scrambled down the tree, dropping the last ten feet, my wounds screaming. Smoke already engulfed us.

With Marina and others beside me, we moved away from the advancing forces, joining the terrible retreat, confusion all around us. Even the wind was against us, blowing smoke and fire at us instead of the enemy, raining down cinders onto the dry grass and brush, starting fires everywhere.

The tidal wave of Aztec warriors that we had hurled against other forces was now a maelstrom of humanity battering itself to pieces in the dense smoke.

I held onto Marina, pulling her with me, choking and coughing, our eyes burning, as we fled the hail of lead put out by the advancing troops.

What the Spanish forces could not do by force of arms—after six hours of combat and with half of the Spanish forces in full flight—Señora Fortuna had done. That unpredictable bitch had made Calleja master of the battlefield with a single lucky shot.

 **ONE HUNDRED AND SIX**

WE RAN FROM the battlefield, routed not by force of arms but by smoke and fire, Nature's army of conquest. We left behind paeans to victory and lost dreams of glory. We carried with us the bitter taste of defeat.

Once again the leaders separated, this time escaping in different directions. Marina and I went with the padre. The only riders we took with us were four of the padre's bodyguards. Handpicked by Marina, they never left his side. Many more would have come, but the padre didn't want a troop of dragoons accompanying us. He hoped to be anonymous, inconspicuous.

"He thinks God is punishing him," Marina said, "and because of him, all those who follow him."

"Punishing him for what?" I asked. "For caring about people? Giving up everything and risking his life so poor people can own a piece of land and be free? God didn't direct that cannon shot, it was El Diablo."

Near Zacatecas, Allende and other criollo officers, along with mounted troops, joined us at the hacienda del Pabellón . . . and brought trouble with them. Allende and the Aldama brothers demanded to speak to the padre alone. Marina drew her dagger, and I pulled my sword. The padre stepped between us. "No," he said, "put away your weapons. I know what they want."

They wanted the padre to turn both the command and the revolution over to them. What command? I wondered mordantly. What revolution? Were we not on the run from the royal army?

Still much of the north was in the hands of our compadres, and when they returned, the padre and Allende awed me with the audacity of their plan. We would go north, through Monclova, into and across the colony's Texas region to the city called New Orleans in the Louisiana territory, newly acquired from France by the United States. Once in New Orleans, with the gold and silver we had "requisitioned" from the treasuries of Guanajuato and other cities, we could acquire fine artillery pieces and high-quality muskets. With money and arms, we could raise and train another army.

"When we return to the colony to challenge the gachupines, we won't lead a horde of tens of thousands of untrained, poorly armed indios but a well-equipped, trained army, marching to drums and firing on command. All is not lost!" I told Marina.

She laughed and clapped her hands. "They won't be able to stop us; behind our trained army will be an endless ocean of my people. This time we americanos will take the capital, and the whole colony with it."

Still the criollos resented the padre. They increasingly believed they no longer needed him. In a moment of anger one of them implied that if he died en route, they would take control of the revolution's treasure trove. With that much gold and silver in their hands, they could train a professional army for the cause of independence . . . or retire to great houses and live in luxury in New Orleans, no?

But again Allende and the Aldama brothers refused to harm the padre. They were angry at him, blamed him for undermining the revolution by refusing to attack the capital and for not following their advice at Calderón Bridge, but they were men of honor; defeat would not drive them to murder the man they had earlier chosen as their leader. Moreover, Allende was now in command. The padre had retreated into his own thoughts. He no longer communicated with us except in gentle tones when we brought his food or when one of us made a comment about the terrain or the weather.

We had stopped at the grand casa of the hacienda when a messenger arrived with a dispatch from General Luis de la Cruz, a high-ranking royalist officer. I later found out from Marina that the general had sent a copy of a general pardon offered by the Spanish cortes to everyone participating in the revolution. Cruz urged the padre to accept the pardon and order those under him to take it.

Marina showed me the padre's reply.

> In the performance of our duty we will not lay aside our arms until we have wrestled the priceless gem of liberty from the hands of the oppressor . . . A pardon, Your Excellency, is for criminals, not for defenders of their country.
>
> Let not Your Excellency be deluded by the fleeting glories of Brigadier Calleja; they are only lightning-flashes which blind rather than enlighten . . .

The way north was hot under the noon-day sun but bitter-cold at night. On we rode into the forbidden zone, the vast Chihuahua desert that extended hundreds upon hundreds of miles across the Río Bravo to Santa Fe and the

Texas province, a parched world of dust devils and cactus, savage Apaches and scorching heat. Our journey was further exacerbated by the interminable distances between the precariously arid waterholes.

The Bajío ranged from fertile fields to the rocky, hilly terrain of Dolores and the Guanajuato mountains. But the journey north was rugged desert in which water could be obtained only at long intervals and in meager quantities. We continually feared that the next hole or well would be dry.

A large group with a big thirst, our expedition now included sixty other leaders: priests and criollos who had thrown their lot in with us, most of them riding in fourteen carriages pulled by teams of mules. We had a couple hundred cavalry, still mostly vaqueros armed with lances and a few militia dragoons who had defected to the revolt when our banners flew high. Behind the elite and the horsemen came nearly two thousand foot soldiers, indios and mestizos, few armed with more than machetes and knives.

We bore little resemblance to a military unit: we didn't close ranks, marched to no cadence, maintained no particular order. Generalíssimo Allende did not believe any of this was necessary. No forces in the area were large enough to threaten us. The royal forces were at least a week behind us, if they had bothered to follow at all. And no indio groups, not even the savage Apaches, could threaten an army the size of ours.

We expected no opposition from any military units in our path north. Because the north was sparsely populated, only small, scattered militia units were available to the viceroy, And even those could not be depended upon to support the royal cause. Because of their distance from the capital, the viceroys of New Spain did not maintain as firm a grip on the northern provinces as they did the rest of the colony. Northerners were hardy and had to work harder to survive than the people to the south. They were quick to join the independence movement after news of the grito reached them. The word coming from Lt. Colonel Elizondo, a northern officer recruited to the cause, was that the padre would be welcomed at Monclova as a hero.

Despair continued to hover over us as we made our way. The panic of defeat was gone, and so was the initial jubilation over the fact that we would retreat all the way to New Orleans and buy fine weapons.

We were a day from water at the Bajan wells when the woman who had dominated so much of my life came storming back into it like a swirling poisonous black wind from the Aztec underworld.

I stared at the words written on a message carried to me by a peon on a donkey.

Come to my aid, Don Juan. Renato holds me prisoner.

"How did you come by this message?" I demanded of the messenger.
"A priest gave it to me."
"Which priest?"

"At Bajan wells, señor. He's the priest I carry supplies to from Mon-clova."

The wells were to be our next watering hole. Monclova, a larger settle-ment, was further north.

"How did the priest come by the message?"

He shrugged. "I don't know, señor."

"Where's the señora held?"

He looked confused. "Señora?"

He knew nothing about Isabella. He had been handed the note, given my name, and instructed to find me among the insurrection's army. It hadn't been hard to find me; Marina and I had been riding point to avoid the dust kicked up by thousands of feet and hooves.

Marina read my mind as I stared at Isabella's handwriting.

"You're a fool! It's a trap."

"Silence, woman. I'm not fooled. I'm not going for Isabella; I'm going to kill Renato."

"And if he kills you instead?"

I grinned at her. "Then you will have to find someone else to slice with your sharp tongue."

I blocked a blow from her whip with my elbow. She was one tough woman.

I followed the muleteer north toward the Bajan wells, leaving behind an angry woman and a lumbering army that was strung out for miles.

Many thoughts flowed through my mind. I had lied when I told Marina that my only motive was to kill Renato. Perhaps I would kill Isabella, too. But before I did, I would make her get down on her knees and beg me for forgiveness. I would make her confess to all the crimes she had perpetrated against me. Then, if I was convinced of her sincerity, I would stare down at her, sneering, contemptuous, my sword ready to chop off her head, and in-stead of killing her, like a priest, I would absolve her of sin but not forgive her. "I no longer love you," I would say. "You're lower than a dog."

Of course, to be fair, if she was to convince me of her innocence, that Renato had forced her . . . Well, she would be a helpless victim, no?

 **ONE HUNDRED AND SEVEN**

AT BAJAN WELLS, a settlement had grown up around the watering hole, supplying travelers and mule trains that plied the trail to the northern ter-ritories. A small church was the centerpiece of the settlement. I followed the muleteer to the church. As we came into what passed for a town square, the gate to a courtyard next to the church opened, and Renato stepped out. He was on the other side of the square. I gave Tempest a slap on his flank and surged forward, drawing my sword.

I hadn't covered half the distance to the bastardo when soldiers armed with muskets poured into the square from every direction.

I jerked Tempest's reins to change direction and break through a line of soldiers to my right.

"Shoot the horse!" Renato yelled.

A volley of musket fire erupted. A ball hit my left thigh, and I felt Tempest shudder beneath me as he went down. I slipped loose from him, hitting the ground with a force that knocked me breathless. I groped for my sword, which had fallen several feet from me, and got to my feet, swaying dizzily, sword in hand. My eyes were blurred, but I heard Renato shouting commands not to shoot me as he ran toward me with a dagger in hand. He didn't want me dead because he wanted to torture the location of the treasure from me.

As I staggered toward him to meet his charge, a horse and rider broke through the circle of soldiers, and I heard a familiar yell.

Marina! The warrior-woman had followed me.

She sped past me and drove her horse at Renato. More musket fire erupted. Her horse stumbled and went down. Like a circus trick-rider, Marina hit the ground feet first with her machete in hand. Her momentum sent her stumbling toward Renato as she tried to gain her balance. She almost ran into his arms. As she came up to him, still off-balance, she raised her machete to strike him. He stepped in, blocking her machete arm and plunged his knife into her gut.

"No!" I screamed. "No!"

He grinned at me as he put his free arm around her and pulled her against him, twisting the knife in her gut. She slipped to the ground at his feet as I limped and staggered toward him, blood flowing from the wound to my thigh. I was a dozen feet from him when I heard steps behind me. In the corner of my eye I caught a glimpse of the musket butt, and the back of my head exploded. I crashed onto the ground again, dazed.

"Don't kill him!" Renato screamed. "Take him to the well inside the courtyard."

Two men grabbed me by the arms and dragged me through the open gate and across the churchyard to a water well surrounded by a round, adobe brick wall about three feet high. A wood frame built over the well held an iron pulley with a rope draped over it.

"You two stay," he told the men who had dragged me. "The rest of you out, get out of here."

I knew why he wanted privacy. He had not spared my life out of friendship.

Renato grabbed the rope that held the bucket used to retrieve water from the well. He cut the bucket off and handed the rope to one of the men who had dragged me. "Tie it to his legs. Roll him over so I can tie his hands."

As I lay face down in the dirt, Renato knelt down beside me and tied my hands behind my back with a leather thong.

"Eh, Señor Lépero, son of a whore, I knew you would come back to me."

"I'll die before I tell you anything."

"Yes, you will die soon but not until I am finished with you. Before I am done, you will beg me to send your soul to hell."

He stood up and kicked my thigh wound. I gasped involuntarily from the pain.

"Pull him up," he told his two aides, "and lower him into the well head-first."

Headfirst?

The bastardo was going to drown me. He was a smart hombre. Drowning was particularly nasty. I was told by my guerrilla friends in Spain that it was better to be chopped up or beaten to death than to be tortured by water. When you are cut or hit, you pass out or your body goes into shock, and the pain dulls. Not so with drowning because your body has a constant need to breathe, death being the only escape, and Renato would keep me from giving up the ghost until he was ready.

My feet went up first as the men pulled the rope. When they had me in the air above the ground, they released the rope, and I fell headfirst into the dark pit. On the way down I scraped my shoulder against the sharp edge of a rock that protruded from the well's inner wall. I didn't have time to yelp with pain as my shoulder ripped open before I hit the water.

For a moment the water was cool, a welcome relief from my wounds. I hadn't had the presence of mind to suck in and hold a breath of air before I was submerged, but it wouldn't have mattered. Water got into my nose immediately, and I gasped out whatever air I had. When air went out, water came in. I sucked it in, and my brain exploded in a flash of sparks. I jerked violently, compulsively, like a great fish that had just been hooked through the tail.

I suddenly realized I was being pulled up. When I was back at the top, Renato leaned over the edge and spoke to me.

"Where is my treasure? If you tell me, I'll let you live."

I spat water and vomit at him.

They dropped me again, and I flew back down, ripping my back and snagging my wrists so hard on a protruding rock I thought I'd broken my arms before I hit the water. This time I went all the way, and my head hit the bottom. The blow gave me a brief flash of comfort as my body went dead, but a second later my lungs—against my will—sucked in water and burst into flames.

Through the fog enshrouding my brain, I realized that I had been hauled up and Renato had ordered the men to permit me to catch my breath. Like any good dungeon master, he knew that torture only worked on the living.

"Tell me where the treasure is, and I'll let you lead me to it," the devil whispered in my ear.

"I will lead you to your grave."

He ordered another plunge into the dark pit.

Wrestling with death, I fiercely pulled at the wet leather thong around my wrists and felt it yield. During the last drop, the wrist thong had briefly caught on one of the sharp stone protrusions jutting out from the inner well wall, and, yanking my arms up, I'd feared the caught thong would dislocate my shoulders, even as blinding agony seared through my joints. But then I'd felt the thong give as I broke from the sharp outcrop and continued my fall. I yanked again at the thong, and suddenly my hands were free.

When I was hauled back up, Renato leaned over the edge to taunt me. "This is your last chance, son-of-a-whore, if you don't—"

I reached out. Getting a hold on his jacket, I pulled him to me. He came over the short wall, grabbing onto me. As he fell toward me, I pushed him down, but he grabbed my waist. The weight was too much for the two men pulling the line. I heard a yell, and then Renato and I flew down the shaft. He struck the rock extending from the side of the wall with a *thunk*.

When we hit the water, we both went under, but I was jerked above the water line by the men with the rope. I got an arm around Renato's neck and held on. The men above couldn't pull us both up. He didn't struggle like a man with all his strength, and I realized he must have been stunned by the protruding rock. With my arm around his neck, I kicked off from the side with my feet and bashed his face into the stone wall again and again all the while it took them to haul us up.

The haulers had hooked a mule to the rope to haul us up, but I was the only one that made it. When we'd reached the top, I let go.

I lay on the ground, my wrists tied again, as they lowered a man to get Renato. They brought him up, dead . . . just the way I wanted the bastardo to be.

From the conversations around me, I picked up that they awaited orders from Lt. Colonel Elizondo. My brain was waterlogged but was working well enough for me to recognize the name of the officer in charge of the region for the revolution. He was to greet the padre and Allende when they arrived at the wells.

That a revolutionary leader would team up with Renato to steal money designated for the revolt wasn't implausible; men are universally greedy. To do it so blatantly, however, was strange. That I had been lured away from the army, captured, and tortured, would circulate through the camps tonight. How would Elizondo explain his actions?

A feminine voice from my past asked when the colonel would arrive. I twisted on the ground. She sat on a chair, shaded by an umbrella. On a table beside her were a bottle of brandy and a full glass. She fanned herself and smoked a cigarillo.

She had watched her lover torture and murder her husband, watched him torture me, watched her lover dragged dead from the well . . .

Her eyes lowered and met mine. They stared blankly at me. I could have been one of the peons she used as a doormat.

A troop of men entered the courtyard, and the man guarding me uttered Elizondo's name.

The crunch of boots, expensive boots, stopped next to my head. I twisted and looked up at the officer standing over me. He wore the insignia of a lieutenant colonel.

I had overheard from Allende's criollo officers that Elizondo had been a captain before the revolt and had asked Allende to make him a general. Allende had refused and promoted him merely to lieutenant colonel, saying he needed more soldiers, not more generals. Allende had made a bad decision, no?

"You are either very brave or very stubborn, señor," he said.

"I am neither. The treasure belongs to the revolution and is in the hands of the padre. Renato never understood I could not give it to him. I didn't threaten the man with retribution from the padre. That would just have hastened my death.

"The revolution is over. In a short time the treasures stolen from the king will be in the proper hands."

"Traitor!"

"No, a realist. The royals have won. Long live the king." He smirked at me.

"The padre has a large army approaching—"

"The padre is not in command, Allende is. And the army is strung out for miles. I have instructed the leaders to come forward with their mounts and carriages to drink first so the wells can refill before the main army arrives. They'll find a surprise at the wells."

It was a good plan. The leaders would fall into the trap. Once they had the heads, the army would be useless.

I grinned up at him. "You'll get your reward in hell for betraying your compañeros."

"Actually, my reward from the viceroy will be quite handsome." He turned to Isabella. "As you have heard, señora, your husband's treasure is gone. But perhaps I will be able to make your stay in the north . . . more pleasant than it has been."

Without looking in my direction, she pointed at me with her foot. "Is there a reward for him?"

Mountains Where the Cougars Lurk, 1541

MY SOUL FLEW with the night wind, carried along as the breeze moaned and whistled through the mountains. My people believe the wind's eerie song was the wail of spirits as they are swept to the Underworld. Their weeping was an evil omen to those who heard it because it attracted Xipe, the Night Drinker who drinks the blood of sinners during the hours of slumber.

Ayya! I had no fear of the vampire's thirst—my life's blood had been left on the battlefield when I brought down the Red Giant and the great warhorse he had ridden. Don Alvarado had broken his neck when he hit the ground, but taking his life had also cost my own. My journey now was to Mictlan, the Dark Place, where the skull-faced Mictlantecuhtli reigned. But the Dark Place was not where souls came to rest—it was a vast, gloomy Underworld divided into nine hellish regions that had to be traversed during a four-year journey fraught with violent trials.

In the golden days when the gods of the Aztecs ruled the heavens, a warrior who fell in battle did not suffer the torment of the nine hells. Instead, the afterlife was a pleasant one. He ascended to the House of the Sun, one of the thirteen heavens, and traveled across the sky with the Sun God from dawn to dusk, as an honor guard for the fiery spirit. During the hours of darkness, they engaged in mock battles for enjoyment. There was feasting and the companionship of comrades and women. Women who died in childbirth, people who drowned or were struck by lightening, and those who went willingly to the sacrifice slab also found a place in the thirteen heavens, though not one so grand and privileged as that of the warrior.

After four years in the heavens, they were transformed into birds with rich plumage and descended back to earth, flitting from flower to flower, partaking of the nectars.

But Aztec gods no longer ruled the heavens. The Christian deity called the Almighty was King of Heaven. Aztec souls—and Aztec people—were now consigned to hell.

The daunting trials in Mictlan I must endure in the afterlife that awaits me dominated my thoughts as I flew into a crack in the mountain. The first eight hells in the Underworld are physical challenges—I must make my way between two mountains clashing together, swim a raging river, crawl among deadly snakes and hungry crocodiles, climb a cliff with jagged edges as sharp as an obsidian blade, survive a frozen wind that cuts like knives, battle raging beasts and eaters of hearts. After four years, if I survive and find my way to the ninth hell, there I will prostrate myself before Mictlantecuhtli, the King of Terrors.

If he finds me worthy, he will give me the Peace of Nothingness by turning my soul into dust and scattering it on the sand and dirt in the parched land that lies to the north . . . that place called Chihuahua.

Chihuahua, 1811

ELIZONDO'S AMBUSH WENT off as planned. As the main army slowly brought up the rear, one after another, the revolutionary leaders were ambushed and captured as they approached the wells.

Two of the leaders displayed great courage. Father Hidalgo, warrior-priest that he was, tried to fight. He drew his pistol to engage the enemy, but the horsemen with him, seeing they were outnumbered and out-gunned, pleaded with him to put down the weapon.

Allende also showed rock-hard courage. Refusing to surrender, Allende fired off a shot at Elizondo before he was overpowered. But his recklessness cost the life of his son, Indalecio. The twenty-year-old was killed when bullets struck the carriage he rode in.

The leaders of the revolution were herded across the desert, like shackled cattle led to slaughter, to the governor at Chihuahua. The purpose was to keep the padre far away from the heart of the colony for fear its indios would rise up in his support.

As for me, I was an inconsequential criminal of no importance, except for the hope that I would reveal where the marqués's treasure was located. *Sí*, it didn't take long for my captors to find out that I had not delivered the treasure to the padre. So rather than executing me immediately, the fate of so many lesser revolutionaries, I was taken in shackles with the padre, Allende, and the others as an animal is led to its abattoir.

For six hundred miles we slogged across a barren, parched wasteland to Chihuahua. Chained hand and foot, we marched, day after day, week after week, our bodies aching, our mouths and muscles burning.

It broke my heart to see the padre tormented as a common criminal. He was older than the rest of us—twice as old as most of us—and the trek was hardest on him. Allende and I had a determination and machismo that kept us from complaining, but we couldn't match the padre for sheer courage. He had a moral strength and an iron will that none of us possessed.

Someone with an unofficial interest in my welfare accompanied the military expedition to Chihuahua. Isabella rode in the coach with Elizondo as his "special guest." My former love had obviously recruited a new inamorato to assist her quest for the gold. How long would this bitch flog my soul with sharp spurs and a barbed whip?

Chihuahua: home of a breed of small dogs with a big bark and snapping jaws. A provincial town of about six thousand cradled in a valley nearly a mile high, it was in the middle of nowhere and surrounded by desert. It was a mining center but on a smaller scale than Guanajuato. Its northern location made it a natural place to sympathize with the revolution, but that movement was now in chains.

We were marched in shackles down the main street, paraded in dust and rags, worn and beaten bloody for all to observe. The governor issued a warning to the populace: watch the prisoners being paraded but show no support.

I was not angry at my humiliation; whatever disgrace I suffered, it was less than I deserved. But my heart burned for the padre.

They watched silently, these common people whose hearts and dreams the padre had fired by his vision of freedom for all but who were now disillusioned. Despite the prohibition against emotional displays, sobs and tears poured out as the padre staggered down the street—like the rest of us—in wrist shackles and leg irons, weak with pain from the deprivation of our desert crossing. But like Christ shouldering his cross, the padre did not falter. Squaring his shoulders, he kept moving forward, refusing to show any weakness, still inspiring us all.

I silently mourned Marina's death, the brave sacrifice she had made for me. I was grateful that she had not lived to see the padre in chains.

REQUIEM

I'M TOLD THIS prison cell is my last stop before hell's inferno. Nothing would please the guards more than to see me burning in a lake of fire. For five months the inquisitors have visited on me, day and night, their own version of hellfire everlasting as they tried to pry from my lips the location of the marqués's treasure. Theirs has been a thankless job, for I have cursed their fathers, questioned their manhood, and spat in their faces.

Yesterday a priest came, offering me "a final opportunity" to cleanse my soul and purge my heart . . . by disclosing the treasure's whereabouts. I told him that when he brought me physical proof that God commanded me to tell him, that God had granted him a license to remit sins, I'd cheerfully tell him where the treasure was.

¡Ay! Instead of taking me up on my generous offer, he fled, shouting that I was a heretic who would burn forever in balefire. He wouldn't have long to wait to get his wish. Tomorrow my execution would be celebrated.

Was I ready give up the ghost? Ready for the goddess of justice to drag me to judgment? To punish me for my innumerable transgressions? No, not until I transgressed one last time on this planet we call home.

Before I started this long confession, did I not say I would avenge myself on the one who had betrayed me?

It's said the devil taunts those who leave unfinished business on earth, that his mocking words are daggers in your heart. El Diablo is one clever bastardo, no? He knows that it is not our triumphs we carry beyond the grave but our regrets.

I heard voices outside my cell and the rattle of a key in my cell door. The door swung open, and a priest in a hooded robe entered. Seeing another one of his ilk did not please me.

"*Hijo de la chingada!*" I growled. "*Chingo tu puta madre!*" Calling him the son of a wanton woman, I then told him what he could do with his mother.

"Such language, señor, to a man of the cloth." A delicate hand pushed back the hood, revealing a lovely face.

"Raquel!"

A key to the cell door, a sharp sword, and a fast horse might have been more welcome . . . but not by much. After we hugged each other for what seemed to be an eternity, she pulled bread, meat, and wine from under her robe. We sat down so the condemned man could enjoy his final repast.

"Tell me about the padre and the others," I said.

The criollo officers had been shot in the back because they were considered traitors. They had met their maker over a month ago.

"Allende, of course, was defiant to the end. He became so angry at the judge that he broke the manacles holding him and struck the judge with a piece of chain before the soldiers could subdue him."

Only one of their officers had disgraced himself. The criollo officer Mariano Abasolo, to save his hide, testified that Allende forced him to participate in the revolt. The supplications of his beautiful wife, Doña María—and no doubt a payment in gold—obtained for him a prison sentence in Cádiz.

Unlike the spineless Abasolo, the padre had faced the military court with dignity and grace. Brought in chains before the judges, he stood tall and assumed responsibility for the revolution. He freely admitted he had raised armies, manufactured weapons and ordered gachupines executed in retaliation for the murder of civilians by the Spanish commanders.

"He regretted that thousands had died for the cause of liberty," Raquel said, "but he believed that God would have mercy on him because the cause was just."

Because the padre had to be defrocked by a church process before he was executed, the officers had been executed first. The court ordered the officer's heads pickled and preserved in brine until the head of the padre joined them.

At daybreak on July 31, 1811, the guards led the padre from his tower cell to the prison courtyard. When the commandant asked if he had anything to say, the padre requested that candy he brought be given to the firing squad when they finished.

Raquel's voice trembled as she described the death of a man whose ideals and courage had fired the passions of millions.

"The padre went to his death with the same courage he showed at all times in life. He faced the twelve-man firing squad without flinching. Because he had been a priest, he was allowed to die facing the firing squad. To help them with their aim, he placed his hand over his heart.

"The marksmen however were less resolute than the good father. Eleven of them missed, and only one ball struck his hand. The commandant ordered them to fire again, but the shots again missed the mark. Finally, an officer ordered several soldiers to administer the coup de grâce with muskets held inches from his heart."

Tears welled in Raquel's eyes.

"And with him died any hope of independence," I said.

"Don't say that. When the padre shouted the grito, he started a fire that burns eternal in the hearts of all those who love freedom, and it's not a flame the viceroy can extinguish. It continues to spread and will consume the greedy gachupines who plunder not just our money but our hopes and dreams, our freedom and our lives."

"Do you really believe that or are you just—"

"Yes, Juan, it's true. What we have fought for—and so many have died for—is not forgotten. Each day the flame grows brighter. Father Morelos and others are keepers of that flame and carry on the fight. Each time one of them falls, another picks up the torch. The Spanish have more trained soldiers than we do, they have muskets and cannons while we have clubs and knives, but we are fighting for our homes and families."

"As the common people of Spain themselves have done against the French."

"Yes, and we have our own Geronas and maids of Zaragoza. The viceroy and his minions don't understand. They think they can stamp out the fire, but it's spreading everywhere. In Guadalajara and Acapulco, in the capital, the jungles of the Yucatán and even here in the deserts of the north, its flames blaze. The cry will resound again and again, until we're free."

Her tears were gone. Her eyes, clear as God's own heaven, burned with the dream of freedom.

She was right. I knew it in my heart. The padre had unleashed a spirit that had awakened the people of New Spain. That spirit now burned in the hearts of peons, men and women savaged and scourged by the whips of mine and hacienda owners. No longer whipped dogs, they now had the courage the padre had given them to stand and fight, and the gachupines would not recognize it until it was too late for them.

Raquel spoke of Marina. "I saw to it that she received a proper burial. Someday, when it can be done, the women of the revolution will salute this Doña Marina as the First Lady of Liberty."

She hugged me and said with genuine concern, "Juan, I've tried—"

"I know. Don't worry; I'm not afraid. I won't show fear. I won't dishonor the padre and Allende. I wouldn't give the gachupines satisfaction."

She cried softly against my shoulder, and I smoothed her soft hair. I don't know what is in me, the devil must make me do such things, but one moment she was crying on my shoulder, and the next I had her on my cot, both of us gasping with passion. I made love to her as if we were the last two people on earth, the last two people in the universe, now, forever, till the end of time.

For the first time in my sordid life I made love *with love*, with all my heart and soul and mind. I like to think Raquel knew at last how much I loved her. Now. Then. Always. No regrets.

¡Ay! It was better than a Havana cigarro and bottle of brandy, better than hunting jaguars on horseback and closing in for a final shot from the saddle, better than a bright spring morn with the sun coming up like thunder, the grass lush and green beneath your toes, your hated foe dead at your feet on the field of honor.

Before she left, I held her close and whispered a secret in her ear.

Alone with my thoughts, I knew what I had to do. When the guard opened the judas window and shoved in a bowl of beans, I said, "Tell the commander of the guard I want to see him."

"Of course, I'll tell the captain that the Prince of Léperos commands his presence," he howled with derision.

"Do it now, cabrón. Tell him I wish to cleanse a secret from my soul."

When the commander arrived, I said, "Have Doña Isabella come to me."

"You're insane. Why would she want to see you?"

I grinned and blew smoke at his face through the judas window.

"Tell the señora that there is something she needs to know about her husband's treasure."

As a child, when I was sick or bedridden with broken bones, I would try to think about what it felt like to be perfectly well. As I waited for Isabella, my mind played that same sort of game. I lay back and thought about the good times in Guanajuato when I was a young caballero driven by the power of horseflesh beneath me and a woman's touch.

Had Bruto's deathbed confession not shattered my world, what would life have been like? ¡Ay! I would have fought—and died—as a rich gachupine at the alhóndiga alongside Riano and his son, Gilberto. I shuddered at the image. To have died clutching my gold, slain by men who fought for the right to walk the same street as me, would have been to die without honor. To fight for *things* or the privilege of *spurring* others confers not honor, only opprobrium.

For the first and only time in my life, I had done something right. I had real honor, not the unearned respect that a caballero demands but the realization that I had stood up and fought for something that was right.

Stretched out on my bed, my back against the wall and my feet on the floor, I mulled over my many sordid achievements as well as the petty injustices I had suffered over the years when the door opened and Elizondo stepped in. Isabella was behind him. She stopped before entering.

"You have something to say?" the turncoat officer asked.

"I have nothing to say to you. My words are for Isabella alone. Wait outside."

"She will not speak to you alone."

I shrugged. "Then leave, both of you; and call the executioner. I'm ready to ascend to my heavenly throne and accept my crown."

Elizondo laughed. "The only crown you will get will be the hood placed over your head before you're shot in the back."

"The memory of your madre's moans as I gave her pleasure will comfort me in the grave."

"I wish to speak to him alone," Isabella said.

Elizondo hesitated. I knew what both of them were thinking: Isabella didn't want me to speak in front of Elizondo. If I revealed the bullion's location and he heard me, he'd grab the gold for himself. And if I told no one, it would be lost to them both forever.

The officer shrugged and waved her in. "I'll be right outside. The door will be open. Yell if he bothers you."

"Juan wouldn't harm me." She gave me a smile as radiant as the rainbow's end.

Ah, how that smile scintillated! No woman had lips as luscious, eyes as exquisite. She was truly a woman to launch a thousand ships . . . burn the topless towers of Ilium.

I closed my eyes and took a deep whiff of her perfume as she sat on a stool beside my bed. It was intoxicating. The indios call pulque "400 rabbits" because too much of the drink can make a man's mind race in many different directions. Isabella's scent was infinitely more intoxicating than the finest brandies in the world. I was living proof. It stripped me of my good sense and robbed me of my resolve.

I opened my eyes. She sat still as a statue, as if posing for a painting. I shook my head. "Isabella, I want to hate you. I want to crush you under my heel, but you bewitched me the first time I saw you."

She sighed. "Poor Juan. Life has not been fair to you. They took me away from you and made it impossible for us to be together. It was the blood, of course. I truly cared for you, wanted to marry you, but when they revealed that your blood was not Spanish, it became impossible."

"Tell me, Isabella, have you ever seen my blood?"

"Your blood? Of course not."

I reached over to the wall and sliced open the palm of my hand on a rough edge of stone. I showed her my hand.

"I've never understood this thing about blood. You see the color of mine? I have killed many men, gachupines and Frenchmen among them, and their blood was always the same color as mine. Even the blood of your husband—a man with a centuries-old title of nobility—was no redder than mine."

I reached across, took her hand, and forced her fingers into my blood. "Look at it, Señora Marquesa. Is the color any different than what you bleed each month? Is it any different than the blood Marina bled when your lover shoved his dagger into her gut?"

I pulled her close to me. She stiffened and pulled back.

"You promised to tell me where the gold is," she said.

"Sí, I will keep my promise."

I pulled her to me and whispered in her ear. I told her exactly where her husband had hidden the treasure. Ay! Her perfume was even more intoxicating when I held her against me.

After I finished whispering, she looked into my eyes. Her lips were only inches from mine. Her warm sweet breath fanned my face as she spoke.

"You have spoken the truth?" she asked.

"The truth, exactly as your husband told it to me."

She sighed again. Her lips brushed mine, and I felt a wave of desire that curled my toes.

"I'm sorry, Juan. I know you've always loved me." She leaned back a little and stared into my eyes again. "Is there anything I can do for you?"

Smiling, I said, "You can die soon."

I grabbed her throat with my right hand and squeezed her windpipe with all my strength, lifting her from the stool. She tried to scream, but it came out as little more than a whispered gasp.

"For Marina," I whispered.

I pulled her to me, face to my face, lips to my lips. Tears ran down my cheeks. I still loved this woman. I would have died for her.

I would die because of her.

My grip crushed her larynx and the bones in her throat. By the time Elizondo and the commander of the guard beat me to my knees and ripped my hands from her throat, Isabella lay still on the floor.

Even dead, she was beautiful.

 **ONE HUNDRED AND TEN**

THEY CAME FOR me while it was still dark. The men who took me out of the jail were not the regular guards. They gave no greeting, and I offered them no resistance. I was finished with my work on earth. I didn't fool myself with the delusion that the gates of heaven would be thrown open for me. But perhaps the devil could use another swordsman and crack marksman, no?

Outside, still chained, I was placed in a wooden cage atop a cart. It was a cage for wild animals, and I suppose that was how they thought of me. As the cart rolled out of the prison courtyard, I noticed something odd for the first time: none of the men were in uniform. From their clothes and horses, I took four to be criollos, the other four peons.

When they took me from the prison, away from the courtyard where the firing squad did its business, I knew I would meet my end on the gallows. It was to be expected. In the eyes of the gachupines, hanging was the least honorable way to die, so that was to be my fate. But I didn't deem hanging dishonorable. I knew who and what I was. I didn't know who my father and mother were, but I knew that in my veins ran the blood of the Aztec.

I had traveled with a scholar to the forgotten cities of ancient empires and had seen the wonders of Spain. I had witnessed great bravery on the battlefields of two continents from unarmed criollo priests who led charges carrying banners to simple peons who tried to stop the carnage of cannons by stuffing their straw hats into the barrels.

I thought of myself not as a disgraced gachupine or as the son of an india whore, but as something entirely different. I realized that it was not the gachupine in me that made me the finest caballero in Guanajuato; a man wasn't judged by his bloodline but by his deeds. By fire and blood, I had achieved a rebirth: my own *reconquista*.

The gachupines were wrong when they said the colony's atmosphere made us inferior to those born in Europe. To the contrary, the air we breathed and the dirt we trod made us as strong and diverse as any people under the sun. The padre had proven that to the chagrin of the gachupines when he instituted Aztec crafts that were as good as anything made in Spain, and he had proved it again on the battlefield when untrained, crudely armed revolutionaries flung themselves at cannons and muskets in the cause of freedom.

The night was dark, but the moon took the edge off the darkness when it poked through the clouds. During one of those brief illuminations I realized the criollos now had covered their faces. They were not wearing masks but had their hats pulled down and bandanas pulled up.

I stared at the scaffold as the cart rumbled by it. A shudder crept up my spine. I was on my way to be executed, but we had passed the gallows. And why were the men now hiding their faces? But I could see that the men who had taken me from my cell were on a mission of death; it was obvious in their grim silence.

In a moment of moonlight, I saw the embroidered insignia on an armband of a criollo: a cross with a horizontal sword, adorned by a smaller cross and a crown. *Hermanos del sangre*. Brotherhood of the Blood. Spaniards who banded together in unauthorized "posses" to track down and punish wrongdoers, particularly highwaymen. A brotherhood of death, they specialized in swift, roadside "justice." Bandits plagued New Spain's roads, so to most the Brotherhood was a necessary evil created by the viceroy's failure to safeguard the roads. And the punishments they rendered would have made the viceroy himself cringe.

When we came up to the hillock at a fork in the road leading to Chihuahua, I knew why they had taken me out of the prison: I was not to be hanged or shot.

The realization hit me like a thunderbolt from hell. Hanging and shooting were honorable deaths for revolutionaries and common criminals, but I was no common criminal. I was an Aztec bandit who murdered a gachupine woman. If a caballero prided himself on anything, it was the protection of women, those of his same blood and class, of course. And I had violated the most important taboo: I had loved and murdered a woman of their class.

They were issuing no ordinary punishment but one that would send a message to every Aztec and mestizo in the land: Do not touch our women, or you will pay the ultimate price.

They were going to crucify me!

I laughed aloud, startling the men as the cart pulled to a stop at the bottom of the hill. I was still roaring with laughter as they pulled me from the cage. None of them understood.

I had lost again to Isabella. My downfall had begun in Guanajuato with me arguing with Bruto over my wish to marry her. I had been driven out of Méjico City and turned back into a bandido because of my love for her. Now, even from the grave, Isabella had reached out to claw my soul.

"She's a bitch from hell, the devil herself," I shouted. "I executed her for the murder of my amiga. She murdered her own husband!"

They didn't know what I was talking about and didn't care. The criollos didn't touch me. Instead, their underlings dragged me up the hill, where they ripped off my clothes and boots.

The workers nailed a hefty wood beam crossways onto a tree. Spread-eagling my arms to the crossbeam, they lashed my wrists to it. One of the peons stood by with hammer and spikes.

A criollo stepped forward and began reading a list of my crimes. Some of the charges I recognized; others were new to me. Only one fact made a deep impression upon me: They were unsure whether I was a full-blooded Aztec or a mestizo, words they had created to deride those of us born in the New World. That stuck in my head as the man with the spikes stepped forward to do his duty.

I locked eyes with the man who was to nail me to the cross.

"Did you hear that slander? These Spaniards don't know what to call me."

I grinned at him.

"I am *mejicano*, señor, just like you."

RAQUEL

Guanajuato

RAQUEL STOOD NEAR the outside corner of the alhóndiga de granaditas, the fortresslike granary where the first great triumph of the revolution had taken place. Doña Josefa, la Corregidora, came up beside her. They stared up at a steel cage hanging above them. The head of Miguel Hidalgo was in the cage.

"The padre has returned to the alhóndiga," Raquel said. She wiped tears from her cheeks.

A gruesome display was at each of the other three corners of the granary: the rotting heads of Allende, Aldama, and Jiménez occupied the other places of honor.

"What of the gallant Juan de Zavala, the man you loved. Where is he resting?" Dona Josefa asked.

"I buried him with Doña Marina. She loved him, too. And in his own way, I know he loved both of us."

The women read the sign nearby:

THE HEADS OF HIDALGO, ALLENDE, ALDAMA, AND JIMÉNEZ, NOTORIOUS DECEIVERS AND LEADERS OF INSURRECTION, THEY WHO SACKED AND ROBBED THE PROPERTY OF GOD AND THE CROWN, WHO LET RUN WITH GREAT ATROCITY THE INNOCENT BLOOD OF LOYAL OFFICIALS AND JUST MAGISTRATES, AND WHO WERE THE CAUSE OF ALL THE DISASTERS, DISGRACES, AND CALAMITIES THAT WERE AFFLICTED UPON AND EXPERIENCED BY THE INHABITANTS OF ALL PARTS OF THE SPANISH NATION.

NAILED HERE BY THE ORDER OF SR. BRIGADIER D. FÉLIX MARÍA CALLEJO, ILLUSTRIOUS VINDICATOR OF ACULCO, GUANAJUATO, AND CALDERÓN, AND RESTORER OF PEACE IN AMÉRICA.

"You have heard the stories that the padre recanted his dream of freedom and revolution? That he wrote his renunciation freely and without coercion in his own hand?"

"Of course I've read the lie. The viceroy's publishing it throughout the colony. When the document speaks of the padre's regret that people died, it speaks the truth. He had great love for all people. But the words that repudiate our right to govern ourselves are lies. They were not written by his hand."

Doña Josefa spoke in a whisper. "My husband, the corregidor, stormed around our casa for an hour denouncing the recantation as a lie. He cannot understand why the viceroy would attempt such a transparent fraud. When the viceroy published the recantation, people asked to see the original that is supposed to bear the padre's handwriting and signature. Do you know what he said? That he doesn't have the original, that Salcedo, the governor who took possession of the document, lost it to bandidos."

"The fraud won't help them," Raquel said. "The force of ideas the padre unleashed have spread to all of New Spain. We are at war with the gachupines, and nothing will stop us until we have driven them from our shores."

"Where will you go now? Back to the capital?"

"Not yet. Juan set a last task for me to complete. When I visited him in his cell, he whispered the location of the marqués's bullion. It's strange, Josefa, that the revolution will be financed by a gachupine's gold, stolen by a notorious bandido."

Doña Josefa nodded at the bulge in Raquel's abdomen. "Let us hope the child you carry will grow up in a nation that respects the rights of people."

"Juan never knew who his father and mother were. Our child will know that his mother and father fought to create a nation in which all people were free and equal and that his father gave his life in the struggle. If we fail, he will carry on the fight."